KEY

KEY

THE DYNASTY OF EARTH AND STARS

BOOK ONE

KYLIE LEANE

PUBLISHER
Kylie Margaret Leane

COVER ARTIST
Jorge Jacinto

COVER DESIGN
Kylie Leane

ILLUSTRATIONS
Kylie Leane

KEY
The Dynasty of Earth and Stars: Book One
Paperback Edition
ISBN: 978-0-6451032-6-7

Orginally published as KEY: Age of the Dragon's Conquest
/ Chronclies of the Children: Book One 2013

For information:
authorkylieleane@gmail.com

Kylie Leane can be found online at
kylieleane.com

Other Works By Kylie Leane
The Northland Rebellion
Orphans & Outcasts: Book One
The Mirrors of Tikal: Book Two

For Mum and Dad

Thank you for being the Towers that
hold together my crumbling world.

not all Destinies have Roads
some must be carved with Sweat and Blood

THE BLESSING

We all start out on a road thinking we
know the path sure and true
But I tell you, now,
we cannot possibly fathom the twists and
turns in which our story shall go.
Instead, The Great Inker of the skies beyond writes our
ever-flowing saga with celestial dust to spin us
always onward through life.
Though we may lose, and we may gain,
There is never a thread left unwoven or a reason left
unknown in any tale that is told.
I say unto you, fellow wayfarers of well-worn paths,
take up your pack, your blade, your cloak, and your lantern,
for there is darkness ahead.
You will need your light to guide you,
your pack to feed you,
your blade to protect you,
and your cloak to warm you along this tale.

*It is customary in Pennadot when a traveller leaves a
way-side inn to speak blessings to the Sun by the resident
altar and wash hands in the liquid gold by the door.*

SO HERE I GIVE YOU A BLESSING
TO SEND YOU ON YOUR WAY, DEAR FRIEND:

May the blazing sun always shine behind you,
May the wind blow westward for you,
And may the stars dance your road
to light the way homeward,
So shall the fair and bliss favour you,
O traveller of myths, legends, and tales.
Fear not the blood, the tears of sorrow,
For a narrow road that is lonely and fraught with despair,
Will bring you to a City laden with Gold.

Sun-Saint Abl'ayn – Sundate 0298DC

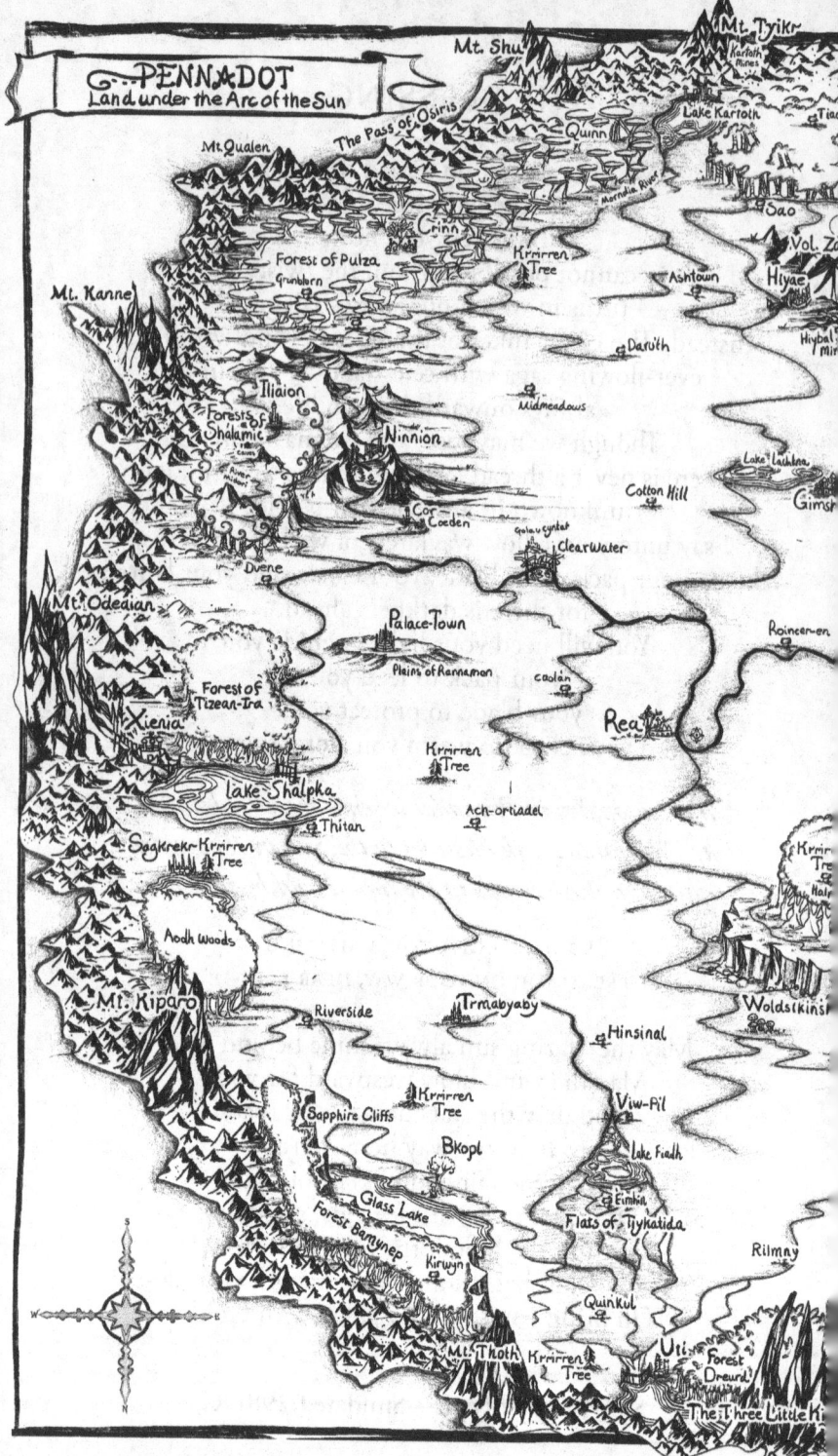

PROLOGUE

Uprising of the Provinces

There is nothing that is greater in valour than to die in the place of another.

Pennadotian Human Proverb

Land: Pennadot
Black Day – Sundate 8600DC

David drove his small dagger beneath the cuirass of the Palace guard, watching as the man slowly stopped struggling against the hold of Citla's birth elemental. His frantic, chaotic breaths seemed to sink along with his chest. David reached up, closing the man's glassy eyes that stared beyond the ceiling to the Almighty Sun that beckoned all in death. Carefully, he removed his blade. Blood pooled onto the marble floor. He climbed off the man who had been Sun-cursed to spot them in the inky shadows.

"You should have just kept walking…" David whispered. The blood that coated his hands was tacky, difficult to rub off on his royal clothes. He had already killed several guards. Guards who had no quarrel with them, who were simply performing their duty to the Emerald Crown. His stomach clenched. Radiant light emanated from his burning skin. He clamped down on the growing frustration boiling his star-blood. He could not risk an episode, not now, not on this day that had become night.

Citla emerged from the russet gloom cast by distant flames from the smouldering metropolis below the Palace. Her painted white face did little to hide the overuse of her birth elemental gift. Metal toxins were building up in her blood, showing through her paper-thin skin in wiry, twisting lines travelling up from beneath her black dress.

"Thanks for holding him down," David murmured.

Citla inclined her head.

"David? David is it safe now?" His brother's soft voice broke through the distant sound of war that every so often rattled the glass of colossal windows. Luminescent green eyes peered out from beneath a hood, brighter than the starlight shine of Daniel's luminous skin and hair which they had struggled to hide.

David reached for Daniel's wrist, dragging him deeper into the thick shadows cast by the towering pillars. "No! It is not safe." He pointed his blade at his twin. "I told you to stay hidden. If someone sees you, everything Father and Mother have worked for will be ruined! Everything I have planned is ruined—"

A flare of pain caught him in the chest; the potency of it caused him to stagger forward and he rasped out a startled, gurgling cough. David clamped a hand to his lips as the familiar taste of blood dampened his mouth and, against his will, it leaked through his fingers. He could not, he would not, have an episode.

With a cry, Daniel was at his side. "You are pushing your body too hard, David."

His body. His tiny little body, sickly, crumbling, falling to pieces from the inside. He had not ever known strength, and, yet, he needed strength for his twin. Daniel's trembling hand reached for his face, trying to brush away the shimmering blood. David pushed it aside. He could not falter, not this day that had become night, when the sky-sea had turned grey with ash, and flames burned the skirts of Palace-Town in a violent, terrifying dance of betrayal.

He wiped at the tainted starblood and hauled himself upright. "We must hurry."

"Can we not just find Mother?" Daniel whimpered.

"That is what we are doing!" David snapped. "Come on!"

They ran deeper into the Palace's twisting corridors. Each breath he took was fire to his rotting lungs. Was it sweat that was cooling his cheeks, or tears? No matter the steps he took, the idyllic childhood his brother had lived was burning away in a turning wheel of war. He needed to reach his father, the Sovereign King, before the province lords and his once-trusted uncle, Steward Zilon, found him. David glanced back at Daniel, his starborn glow hidden under layers of clothing so thick that it hampered his running. Not even Zilon knew the greatest secret of the King and Queen: that there was not one prince, but twins. It was a façade they had managed to maintain, even with David's failing health.

They dashed down a set of stairs, deeper into the maze of passages. It was growing ever darker as the daylight outside was choked by the increasing haze of smoke and ash. Palace-Town was burning. The people were suffering, all for the fancy of fools who had listened to the silver tongue of deceit.

"Your highness!" Citla's warning stalled him. David shoved his twin roughly into her arms as the three of them almost barrelled straight into a lone guard.

The crest on the guard's cuirass caught his eye. It was not the Sun Crest, the emblem of the Palace Guards; it was the spiked tower of Shalamic, one of the usurping provinces.

David drew his dagger and thrust. His first blow was knocked back by the halberd the guard swung with alarming skill and speed. He dodged, twisting around the man's legs, and lashed him hard in the crook of his knees, trying to pierce the hide of his armour. The guard staggered and artfully winged his weapon across the curve of his shoulders. David ducked, rolling, and sprang upright to fend off another blow, only for the guard's halberd to suddenly drop with a clatter. The man's face twisted in agony and his hands grappled for his neck.

"Citla?" David twisted around. "You cannot use your birth elemental anymore!"

Citla held out her hands. "It is not me."

From behind dancing, scorched lengths of a half-fallen tapestry a figure emerged on elongated legs. Large foot-claws, with an equine curvature, tapped softly on the marble floor. David's tense trembling eased as the filtering, eerie light of the non-day played off dirtied black fur and ash-covered feathers. Chans was always graceful, though he seemed to walk with the burden of his blood-clan's weight draped over his shoulders. Some would have said it was an air of superiority, of aloof detachment, but, to a true seer of the heart, it was a crumbling wall of protection against terrible pain. Black, leathery wings unfurled from the Batitic's hips; they had yet to lose their childhood feathers, but the great wingspan was already enough for the young Batitic to cocoon himself within.

Thin, slanted eyes shone cinder red and focused away from the choking province guard. "Are you harmed, Milord?"

"No. Thank you, Chans."

The hands of the guard dropped away from his throat, and his body slumped against the floor. Chans raised an eyebrow. "I expected him to live a little longer, given his physique. How disappointing."

"You slowly removed the air from around his head, did you not?"

"I did. Time delayed deconstruction conduction, otherwise the body would be useless to me. The head would blow off. Learnt that from experience." Chans walked past him, and David glanced down at his protector's shredded robe, tainted with the filth of battle. Chans had been outside, fighting; the sickly-sweet scent of conduction energy circled around him like a thick haze. David licked his lips. It was difficult not to think of the odour of blood conduction as a poisonous sweat.

Chans flicked his conductor several times at the lifeless guard. The heavy smell David had long equated with the catacombs where the ancients were buried filled the air with hints of burial herbs and spices, and the aromatic oils the Sun Monks dipped linen in. The guard stood, turning to face Chans. David shivered. He had never seen Chans perform Soul-Weaving upon a human before. It bore no semblance to the animals his protector had often revived for his tender-hearted twin. He was facing a puppet, and nothing more.

"Scout the area ahead for me," Chans ordered.

The guard left. Daniel whimpered against his neck and David squeezed his hand.

"He…didn't do anything to us, why…did we…why did he have to die?"

"He saw us." David looked up at his protector. "No one can see us. No one can know."

"I understand, Milord Prince." Chans bowed his head.

Citla inched forward. "Please tell me you found Skyeola?" She clutched both her hands together.

Chans smiled, showing his fangs. He extended one wing to reveal a basket tied to his waist. Within, a tiny kitten was curled up, his sleep more than likely magically-induced. David resisted the urge to reach out and stroke the soft, feathery little cheeks of the babe. He was safe. Zilon had not hurt their little fosterling. Each one of them, in their own, strange way, had committed to raising the kitten away from his cruel, psychotic parents.

"I am pleased to tell you one good thing has come from this affair. My mother is dead." Chans carefully closed his wings, hiding away the precious bundle.

David looked up in alarm. "You killed her?"

Chans sighed. "If only I had." He tossed a bag to David. "I did as you requested."

David caught the bag, peering into it, nodding at the contents. It was all there, just as he had asked. Chans had never let him down. Now the second phase of his plan could begin.

"Thank you, Chans. I need you to take Daniel and Citla—" He dropped to one knee as a coughing fit erupted, and he vomited blood across the floor. He glared at it, how it shimmered like starlight on a pond, mocking him. He was the firstborn son of King Delwyn and the Fairy Queen, and he would not live past his tenth sol-cycle. Daniel anxiously wiped at his mouth for him. David looked wearily at his brother and reached up a hand, clasping his twin's neck, resting their foreheads together.

"Oh, *Deiniol*, I am so sorry…"

"*Dafydd*," Daniel whispered.

David kissed his forehead. "Be strong."

He turned to Chans, ignoring the fear in his protector's gaze. Chans would have followed him, but his orders came first. He was being cruel, forcing his protector to guard his brother but it was finally his turn to protect, his turn to burn brightly for a moment before fading with the dawn.

"A group of Papa's faithful paladins will meet you in the catacomb passages. Get Daniel out of the Palace," David commanded.

"And after that?"

David raised an eyebrow. "Do what you wish."

"Even if it means coming to find you?"

David stared into the stark red eyes. Chans had always called him a Blood Rose Prince, but, truly, the name should have been reversed. Chans was the one with Blood Rose eyes.

"Do as you wish."

Chans nodded. "As you command, Milord."

He could not order Chans away; it was too cruel, unjust. Even if it meant Chans would—

David shook his head, trying to rid himself of the encroaching doubt and fear building up as he stripped out of his bloodied, ruined clothing, changing into a fresh outfit from the sack. It was a simple trick, really, one he and Daniel had pulled countless times over the sol-cycles. Less and less as his illness had begun to alter his appearance too much, but in this shadowy, murky light, and in the fray of war, no one would fathom that there were two Princes.

He ignored his twin. It seemed now, with the change of clothes, that Daniel was finally realising the intent behind his actions and his breathing had grown erratic again.

"You had best hurry." Chans shifted on his foot-claws. "My father is in the Ljoruaithne. The province lords will likely break through the Palace doors soon. If they find you, they will kill you."

"That is the plan." David buckled the royal jewels around his neck, their weight eerily familiar.

"Wait…" Daniel grabbed his hands, stalling him from placing the golden, leafy circlet of the crown prince atop his head. "Stop this, David."

"*Tsk vala*, Daniel." David wrenched his hands away. "They want our line dead! You are the heir to the Emerald Throne. You are our hope, our star, our sun, our future. The province lords cannot kill you this day that is night."

Daniel's chest swelled and he thrust a finger towards David's face. "You are just as much those things as I am!"

"Someone must die today, and since I am already dying it matters not if it is me." His voice broke for a moment as his twin's green eyes flooded with tears.

"It matters to me!" The pitch of Daniel's voice cracked a nearby window, causing Chans to snap around in panic. Citla grabbed the young prince, trying to smother his words.

"Your highness, please calm down…"

"David. I am ordering you to stop this! Stop it and come with us!"

David reached out, clasping Daniel's trembling hands. "This is why we were born identical, in every little detail." He smiled. "Even those little moles on our backs." He stroked their shimmering hands together, watching as their radiant skin flared like two mirrors. "This is why Papa and Mama made sure I was never revealed. So, I could protect you." He reached up, gripping his brother's tear-stained cheeks. He wanted so dearly to remain here, with the twin who had been his warm sun when the cold medicine had filled his veins.

"I was born," he choked back blood, "so that you could live…and I…was given this illness…so that I…could die for you. Pennadot must have an heir. Zilon and the province lords will lose if I do this. Let me go."

Daniel pulled away. "I forbid it."

"It is too late." David smiled weakly, adjusting the crown. "This is so much bigger than us. It always has been." He pushed Daniel into Chans' strong claws. Chans clamped down on his twin's shoulders. Daniel's piercing eyes glared at him from beneath the hood he wore. He was not going to receive a blessing from his twin, he was unsure why he had ever thought he would.

David glanced at Citla. In her frilly black dress, she was the perfect little toy of the court. Always they had been paraded like miniature adults, and, today, they had to be those adults. Reaching out he pressed a finger to her lips, brushing aside a tear that trickled down her white, powdered cheek.

"Look after him always, Citla," he whispered. "I entrust him to your care. Be with him. Never let him out of your sight, promise me this."

Citla nibbled her lip. "I promise, Your Highness." She followed Chans and Daniel into the yellow-stained darkness.

Chans glanced back momentarily. "Goodbye, Blood Rose."

David breathed in deeply through lungs riddled with holes and filling with cursed starblood. He tilted his head towards the sky-sea encased in pillows of smoke. This day of blackness and never-ending night was the day he had been born for, and this was the night he would finally die.

Zilon, a man he had once looked up to as a beloved uncle, had become a warped, foul monster. Like roots twisting up from the soil, something had wrapped itself around his uncle and begun to rot the once-great Steward.

It was not his place to know why, nor to find out what—it was his place to die in his brother's stead.

And he was not afraid.

No.

He was not afraid.

"Let's go," he motioned to the nearby shadow.

Chans gritted his fangs, causing his jaw to ache. He had to deal with this order quickly, so he could hurry and return to Prince David's side, but the catacombs were a maze of long-forgotten roads that had been buried under eons of dirt and decay. Like a network of spider-webs, the tunnels contorted their way beneath the colossal, ancient city, built upon layers of cities that had come before it. Each tier told a story, each held the history and the foundational building blocks of the nation, along with countless entombed mysteries. Very few maps had ever been drawn of the seemingly endless system. He needed no map, not when he had been given access to the original blueprints. A Batitic's natural skill of memory recall was a true gift when the catacombs would become his new home.

The stifling humidity, the rocks beneath his foot-claws, and the murky scents that clogged his tender tongue, would smother him like they had smothered the forgotten past. If he managed to survive this day that had become night, there would be no returning to face the wrath of his father, for by choosing to save the royal heir of the Emerald Throne, he had betrayed the Dragon to whom his blood-clan had pledged all allegiance.

Little Prince Daniel's cries were muffled by the mouldy, dank walls. Every so often, the hood that cloaked his starlit shine bounced aside in their frantic pace, emitting a shimmer throughout the darkness. Citla would so swiftly cover his dazzling glow as though snuffing out a fire. Even down here, in these labyrinthine depths, it was not yet safe. Would it ever be safe? Citla would stay by his side. She would never let him go, not now, not with an order from David as his last will to her.

"How much further?" Citla's soft voice carried through the darkness.

The murk seemed to drag at his limbs, wrapping tightly

around his neck, trying to pull him back to Prince David and he had to force himself forward. Chans glanced up at the ceiling. The old, worn limestone rocks were beginning to thin out into a sheen of purple-tinted metal fused together in hexagon patterns.

He forced a smile. "Not long now."

He slowed his pace, foot-claws scraping the wet stones. Anxiously he checked under his wing. Skyeola was still safely cocooned in his little basket. What was he going to do with the tiny kitten? Return the babe to the surface and back into the arms of their father, a man willing to sacrifice everything for a monster? Was that even an option?

What was he supposed to do—

He halted, holding out a claw and Citla jerked Daniel to a stop. The prince bundled himself up against her back as if expecting something terrible. Chans flicked out his conductor from its wrist-holster; the elegantly crafted piece of wood and melded iron hummed. He peered around a corner, his long ears twitching as he listened for the muted sound of distant voices and the padding of boots. His forked tongue tasted the whiff of fresher air, and on that breath was a scent of roses. Relief spiked his neck feathers. He knew the scent, and he knew the voices approaching them.

A boy suddenly burst around the corner, almost colliding with him and he stepped back as the child flung up his arms in alarm.

"Master Jarid, watch yourself." Chans caught the boy before he toppled over. Jarid's freckled face lit up with a smile.

"Chans! Father, Father! It is Chans!" Jarid dashed back to Lord Davis Telvon of the Icali-pi Province. Chans' knees almost went out from under him. He grappled for the wall, holding himself upright. There were still province lords loyal to the Emerald Throne. They were not alone. A small part of him had feared they would have no allies to meet.

"Little Lord Chans, you made it." Lord Davis approached. "And you as well, Maiden Citla."

Citla gave a quick curtsy.

Chans surveyed the gathering of exhausted paladins and several city guards. They watched him warily. Undoubtedly his appearance and relation to Zilon was putting them at ill-ease. He turned to the tall, red-haired Lord Davis. "Is she here? The Fairy Queen?"

"I'm here, Chance. Don't…don't let Daniel…don't let him see me yet…"

Lord Davis' eyes closed, bowing his head as Chans pushed past in a panic at the broken, slurred, high-pitched speech. He pulled to a halt, staring at the ancient wielder of time, slumped against the wall. Hazanin was the only Zaprex he had ever laid eyes on, and the depictions of the fairy-race did them no justice, for the reality of seeing one was so much more incredible than a worn scroll could ever suggest. They had once ruled the air beyond the sky-seas, and masterfully healed the lands below with arts that a Batitic such as he craved and hungered for.

Softly-shining blue blood leaked from an open wound that had split metal plates beneath glossy green skin. Lady Linda Telvon, Lord Davis' wife, was trying to reseal the gash with iron from a guard's armour. The mechanical interior of the graceful creature buzzed and crackled in protest.

"What happened?" Chans burst out. It was not like Hazanin to be so careless, to allow such harm to come to itself.

"Got a little caught off guard."

"But you cannot be hurt—"

"I was wearing my golem." Hazanin's weary red eyes focused on him, shining beneath round spectacles. There was an unexplainable age reflecting in the black scleras that Chans drowned in every time the Zaprex looked at him.

"I believe that's all I can do." Lady Linda sat back, setting aside her blacksmithing tools. "I apologise for the rough job."

Long ears tweaked backwards and Hazanin shook its head, smiling in gratitude. "It's enough for now. Thank you, Linda." Hazanin weakly motioned Chans forward and he approached. "This is where our journey begins, you and I…" The delicate, small hand seized his claw. "Are you ready?"

"Hazanin-*sama*, I would follow you anywhere, you know that."

"I know." The ancient being sighed, giving his claws a firm squeeze. "And I am cruel for using you so."

With great effort, the little creature slowly stood. The action caused a ripple of attention to shift through the gathering of paladins and guards. It was as though the fairy pulled all light from the nearby lanterns in tiny blocks, layering them over its ethereal appearance until a woman stood in its place. Ebony hair was tightly bound into a thick braid, away from still stark and sharp features, but the humanness seemed to soften them. Her eyes remained just as red and shone with a mechanical glint as she walked forward.

"*Domo arigato dozaimasu*, Chance. You've done well."

Chans bowed his head. His order was complete. He had brought the prince to those who would keep him safe. He settled a claw against the basket that held Skyeola. If only the kitten had such a future.

"Do not worry, Your Highness." Jarid peered rudely into Daniel's hood. Jarid had always been discourteous of personal space. Daniel never understood why David liked Jarid; the boy was obtuse.

"My Father is going to take us to our castle, and you'll be safe there! I promise!"

"I do not want to go to your castle." Daniel turned away.

His stomach was churning. Up and down, up, and down. It was as though he was still running. David. David. Where was David? Why had he left him? How could David do this?

"Daniel…"

Daniel jerked. "Mama."

She was kneeling beside him where Citla had once stood.

She was wearing her golem, making her look human, but he could tell something was wrong, the illusion was not as perfect as it usually was. The natural red glow of her machine eyes showed through, and her sunstone skin had a lacklustre tint.

"Mama…" He flung himself into her arms none-the-less. She still cuddled him, even if it was against a hard metal breastplate.

"You've been very brave, my little star prince."

"Mama, you have to stop David. Please! He said he's going to die instead of me. You must stop him. Mama. Please!"

She whispered, "You know I'll do what I can."

Daniel's shoulders slumped. Something was very, very wrong. Mother never admitted defeat. Even when David begged and screamed to end his pain, Mother kept trying, seeking every possible technology remaining of her people to fix him.

"Mother…" He backed up.

She held his arm. "Hush now, my little one." She brushed back his hood, releasing his radiant shine and the murky passage they were within lit up in swirls of painted colours. Daniel cringed at his own starborn glow. His mother gently stroked his forehead, softly whispering his favourite lullaby. He blinked rapidly. Why was she crying?

"Mama…"

He sought Citla. She stood beside Chans, who was firmly gripping her shoulder as if holding her back. Lord Davis was hugging a sobbing Jarid. This was wrong. He reached up a hand, rubbing his own cheeks. Why was he crying? Something inside was being stripped away as though paper was torn from a book in his mind. His mother's long finger settled upon his forehead; her glinting red eyes were heavily set with lines of sorrow, making the sudden realisation of the betrayal slightly less agonising.

"Do not do it, Mama. Please."

"*Gomen*, my sweet one," his mother whispered, "but tomorrow, when you wake up, all this will be a vague dream. You will not remember David, nor this terrible day that is night. It is best all be forgotten to you. David is dead to us now. *Gomen*, Daniel…*gomen*, my little star prince."

A sharp pain caught his temples and he flinched as he fell backwards into nothingness. It was worse than sleep; it was a deep pit that enveloped him, shrouding his body in darkness, choking out the burning gift of the starblood that flowed in his veins. His limbs grew heavy and he slumped forward, murmuring, painfully aware of the tears cascading down his cheeks, and that they no longer glittered as they once had.

"But…I do not want…to forget…my brother…"

CHAPTER ONE

A Messenger does not deliver a message,
Without bearing a sword with which to strike,
A shield to hide behind,
And a friend to lean against…
When both sword and shield have failed.

Messenger Proverb

Land: Pennadot
Province: Pulza
High Moons – Sundate 8711DC

A soft breath of dawn fiddled droplets of dew upon the enormous leaves of the colossal forest. Snaking roots and branches formed a weave of roads through dense layers of waterfalling moss, that rolled down the mountainous trunks of great evergreens and climbing ferns netting the canopy. Barely a glimmer of the harsh Pennadotian summer Sun burrowed its way through the knitted foliage. The still, chilled air that lingered from the deathly cold night rested over Zinkx as he watched the nearby slave caravan trundle down a root-road, still paved with golden limestone. His grip tightened on his bow as he leant out further, holding a vine, trusting that the olive-toned paint he had smudged over his sunstone skin would be sufficient to allow him to blend into the forest's shifting shadows. The caravan turned in the direction of the small local town in the distance, situated up high in the trees. It would stop there for a few days, and continue to the cesspit that was Crinn, the major city of Pulza. It was not an abyss one desired to fall into, the slave markets of Crinn, and the mere thought churned his stomach.

The pve'pt he had been pursuing since the break of dawn suddenly darted past, several branches below. Zinkx gave chase in an instant, weaving through the sharpened spikes of the ferns, leaping across the canyons formed by the branches and roots, releasing and yanking on his gravity bubble to propel himself skilfully through the forest.

Not all Humans could master the skill of gravity-control, but it was almost as though he had the golden wings of legend returned to him when he could keep pace with Pennadot's fauna.

Their chase stopped as abruptly as it had begun.

The high-hoofed mammal paused atop a large, flattened root.

It flicked its long ears, large black eyes observing the shrouded undergrowth.

Zinkx sank into the murk, watching as the pve'pt waited. He eased himself forward, his heavy boots leaving imprints in the dampness of the moss. Carefully he shifted his gravity bubble, making no sound as he slipped an arrow from his hip-bag. He raised his bow, focusing on the pulsing song of the animal's long, graceful neck. The chilled air nipped at his fingers as he drew back the string, breathing steadily in the rhythm of the forest. The pve'pt's white, unblinking eyes settled unnervingly on him. The creature blurred in his vision. No longer was it a pve'pt but a ghostly child, hand stretched towards him, tongues of flames blistering pale flesh. A wretched scent of sulphur swirled around him.

The arrow buried itself in the flesh of a tree.

With a startled leap, the pve'pt skittered away into the darkness.

A deep voice disturbed the silence. "It is unlike you to miss a shot."

Zinkx sighed as he walked to the arrow, tugging it free. He shoved it back into the quiver at his waist. His Khwaja emerged, pushing aside a glittering fern leaf. The towering Kattamont blended well with the forest, as though this had once been his homeland, and not the desert-seas of Utillia beyond the Southern borders. His Khwaja acted too Human for one of the beastial races, even wore Human clothes over his magnificent golden fur, though his shaggy mane had to be tamed by countless braids. It was all in an effort to assimilate, to aid a crumbling society of children who had needed a father-figure.

"Apologies, Khwaja, I will try again." Zinkx inclined his head.

"Never you mind, Zinkx, lad. Something tells me it is not your day for hunting pve'pt."

A warm gaze settled on him like a hug. Zinkx shrugged, trying to dispel the sensation. Receiving comfort felt unnervingly wrong and twisted. He had wrapped reassuring embraces around so many of his brethren, only for them to be torn away mere minutes later.

"I shall hunt for us. My stomach is feeling extremely dissatisfied by your lacklustre attempts to fetch us brunch." His Khwaja clapped a large paw across a barrelled stomach.

"Khwaja, it takes an army to keep you fed."

He was playfully shoved. "Good thing you do the work of an army, heh, lad."

Zinkx stared ahead, unfazed by the jovial jesting. If only it were true; if only he could be effectively an army of one, then lives—so many lives—could have been saved. He was running out of time, and this meandering morning did little to still his irritation. His Khwaja sighed heavily and unlatched several hip-bags from his waist, laying them by his feet.

"Take the skins we have been collecting to the nearby village and trade them for food."

Zinkx reached for the bags. "And the slave caravan?"

The Kattamont tugged on his shaggy air-gills. "Saw that, heh? Hm. I am loath to upset the balance here."

Zinkx flinched, pausing momentarily from strapping the packs around his waist. He hesitantly glanced up, noticing his Khwaja's arched brow. Green eyes studied him. In the faint glints of sunlight, greying hairs could be seen throughout his Khwaja's fur, his tangled beard glistening with threaded-in jewels.

His Khwaja was old—the esteemed title of Khwaja was given only to those who had survived long enough to earn it—but it seemed a mockery to have bestowed it upon one so very timeless. Yet it was the only title their little society had for someone who should have been revered for his sheer lived wisdom.

The old lion breathed in deeply and shook his head. His rounded ears twitched as he chuckled wearily.

"If you see an opportunity arise, you may deal with the slavers as you see fit."

Tight muscles, bunched up around Zinkx's neck, loosened a little and a pain in his jaw eased.

"Yes, sir."

His Khwaja folded broad arms over a heavy-set chest, and bent slowly forward, staring down at him with deep green eyes.

"But do not do anything stupid."

Zinkx held out his hands innocently. "When have I ever done anything stupid, Khwaja?"

He was given a deadpanned glare. "Shall I start from—"

"I'll be careful." He grabbed a vine, swinging away.

His Khwaja's gruff, playful voice carried to him as he descended to the road below. "The mere thought of you trying to be careful is what terrifies me, my *aiv'a*."

The small village of Grunblurn was situated high in the canopy of the vast, rolling forest of Pulza, where its crops could grow across the enormous cupped leaves of the evergreens. As high up as he was, Zinkx could make out the smudges of grey mountains of the magnificent Ovin-tu, the silver beast-shaped pinnacles that crowned Pennadot's vast circular landmass.

CHAPTER ONE

The Pennadotian Sun was fierce in Summer, and great parasols had been constructed throughout the areas of the town that protruded above the canopy. Zinkx knocked back his straw hat, breathing in the spicy scents of the thrumming market. Brightly coloured prayer flags danced between market stalls and thatch-roofed houses balancing on branches. The air of his birthland was sweet; he did not need to breathe it through the filter of a visor. It was a drastic change to the toxic fumes that hung over the Trenches he had been raised in.

Eight months he and his Khwaja had already journeyed, searching the ruins of long-forgotten technologies for the Key. Some places only his Khwaja knew of, lost to the very filaments of time. For centuries, Messengers had known the Key only as a legend, an illusive object that would aid in turning the tide of their war and, perhaps more so, save the lands of Livila.

Such lofty goals seemed beyond him; though he knew their world was dying, the Key simply meant freedom. His choice to leave the House of Flames had not been a willing one. His gut still twisted with a festering bitterness of the High Elder's ultimatum. Return with the Key within a sol-cycle or those under his command would face the consequences of insurrection.

Their petty, childish squabbles seemed so small on the scale of the war they fought, and, yet, the desperation to save his Squad—the people they protected—drove him forward.

He was running out of time.

Even someone as scarcely dreamathic as Zinkx was haunted by the rumbles of distant thunder, the cries of the earth as the borders of the lands were gradually torn asunder.

He arched his head back, studying the cloudless sky-sea. Messenger scholars could only speculate as to what was causing the borders of the lands to shatter and pull apart. Beautiful little towns like Grunblurn would someday be swallowed up by the encroaching horrors of a dying world—like his people.

Zinkx shifted aside as a wagon trundled past, the noise momentarily causing his muscles to tense up. It was a near-constant force bearing down upon him, the reminder that he was not in the Trenches, but the strain never wavered. Every movement of the bustling market crowd caught his attention; the wagon wheels against the golden road churned his stomach as he expected the noise as a precursor to an eruption.

He dragged a hand through his hair, sweeping the sweaty locks aside. The once-addictive adrenalin of battle had become a weary new type of internal war. He turned, dodging several Kelib men carrying heavy sacks of rice. Their voices were cheerful, their brightly painted faces full of laughter and life. Zinkx watched the young men vanish down a street. He missed his Squadron, and the families they had built in secret. War-forged bonds were not easily broken, and the Trenches had provided the fire for such iron connections. Beyond the Ovin-tu Mountains, he had left his Messenger siblings in the midst of battle, and he felt unbearably exposed without their moral support.

Pennadot had been safe, its people left to grow ignorant of the suffering others had endured for their contented living.

It was changing.

Perhaps not suddenly, like a crashing storm, but slowly like a disease creeping through a plant. An influx of captives from Pennadot were being sent over the Ovin-tu to be processed into the Dragon's Army, and there were only so many caravans Messengers could save. They had managed, for now, to keep the Dragon's forces mostly contained to Coltarian but the filth was spreading.

Zinkx sighed. Amongst it all, he had his task. Even if no one knew what it was, or whether it was a tangible object, he had to find the Key—the lives of those he had left behind depended on it.

He shook his head. He had to find the Key. He was running out of time. He also had to get some jewels for his skins, or he would forever be subject to his Khwaja's complaints about him being a useless travelling companion.

"I pull my weight…" Zinkx muttered. "Can't help it if I weigh less than he does."

Grunblurn was a town full of lively colour, there seemed almost a festive vibe that hid the muted grey undertones that lingered deep beneath the surface. Large fungi sprouted between lavishly decorated stalls. Several naked Kelib children, their green-skinned bodies painted in tribal oils of reds and yellow, pointed ears twitching in excitement, darted after glittering sky-dragon kites. Zinkx drank in the sound of their laughter. In the Trenches they were far too deeply engaged in a war to laugh often and so freely, but here the children had such pleasure. There was no fear of death doomed upon them, unlike the children born within the Cultivation Guild, who grew up knowing that their conscription into the Blood Armada would lead to them dying young. Yet, just as the House of Flames had a sinister flavour to its culture, so was there a smoky haze that could not be chased away from the air of Grunblurn. It more than likely infected the entirety of Pennadot.

While Humans stood out like weeds, the native Kelibs blended in naturally with Pennadot's rich, vibrant colours, their emerald skin and macramé clothing mimicking the hues of their vast homeland. They were built for the weak gravity of Pennadot, with chunky, shortened bodies and near-unbreak-able skeletons. Kelib bones were used often in clan weapons. They did not need to fear walking with a spring in their step like Humans, nor bother with weighted shoes as a reminder that Livila was not their home.

Unlike the unity of the Humans though, the Nine Clans remained in a near constant state of war. Not since the Dawn Age, when the Krrirrens had ruled, had there been harmony amongst their people.

Zinkx squinted. It was completely an illusion of his own mind, the smoke. That was all he could call it, despite there being no true haze in the air. The festivity created a smoke screen. The lingering distaste that he could never wash out of his mouth when he entered Pennadotian towns, no matter how joyful they were, the smoke permeated and, in that haze, the Kelib women wandered like ghosts. Prized for their beauty, yet herded like cattle, he could not comprehend how the proud Kelibs had subjugated, in a slow, twisting grip, their once-mighty Krrirrens.

Perhaps there was something he could not see through the smoke. Was he biased from his sol-cycles of only knowing Kelibs who had grown up entirely swaddled with distain for their Pennadotian cousins? Whatever the case was, something unnerved him.

He navigated easily through the markets, selling several of his skins to the local hunter's guild. With a pouch full of jewels, he quickly set about buying a bag of provisions, enough for at least several people, before he ducked down a side street. The slavers' compound was set a little away from the town itself, deeper into the trunk of the colossal evergreen that Grunblurn was built into. He swung the pack of provisions over his shoulder and took the nearest road. His Khwaja may have preferred that they leave Pennadot as it was, that they be nothing more than passing glimmers of light flittering through the leaves, there a moment, gone the next, but Zinkx had always followed Messenger code: Do that which was right before him. And, right now, what was right before him was a slaver caravan to sabotage.

He slipped into the compound through a damaged section of the wooden wall, hacking at it with a blade, making it larger before marking it with a red arrow from chalk in his kit. The bag of provisions, he left beside it. He had to quell his urge to get higher and gain a better vantage point; instead, he stuck to the shadows and followed the heavy imprints of cartwheels in the slick mud. The wagon itself had been secured in a court-yard near the stables, the diabond that had been pulling it led away. Zinkx sighed, scrubbing at his scalp. "Focus on the first task…"

This all would have been considerably easier if he still had his squadron with him, and the absence of them was jarring. Even eight months into his journey, he still expected their presence. They had moved as a single entity. Without them he was a head without a body. He needed a commotion, something that would distract the slavers long enough for him to sneak around. A spark of energy scattered down his arm, but he quickly quelled the urge to use his birth elemental gift.

Starting a fire in a town made almost entirely of wood, in the middle of the forests of Pulza, at the height of the Pennadotian Summer, was the epitome of stupidity. One wayward spark of his birth elemental gift would be all it took for the tinder-dry world above the canopy of the great forest to ignite.

"Tsk," Zinkx peered around the compound yard. A water reserve was suspended high on the trunk of the vast evergreen the town was built around. Numerous pipes dropped from its base, with one trailing down to the compound.

"That'll do." Zinkx unhooked his bow, nocking an arrow. He aimed to fire, halting only when shouts erupted from the wagon. The slavers were dragging on a chain, hauling out a Kelib woman. His grip on his bow clenched. She landed roughly in the mud amongst the jeering fray, but her forward motion carried her with purpose and force towards the Kelib leader. Her fist struck the Kelib man's face and Zinkx flinched as the man was sent barrelling backwards into a water trough. An eruption of cheers sounded from the gathered slavers as the Kelib woman swung her chained fists, missing several of them by inches.

Her bare, bloodied feet pounded the pavement, splitting the rocks with her movements. Only the Kelib men in the group dared approach. Zinkx sighed, stowing his bow and arrow. He had wanted a distraction; this would do for now. Quickly he ducked around the stables, emerging from the other side behind the wagon. A single slaver guarded the rear, though his attention was drawn to the ensuing fight. Altering his gravity bubble, Zinkx ran, grabbed the man roughly, and smothered his mouth with a glove. He drove his blade into the slaver's throat. Blood seeped out and the body grew heavy. Zinkx slowly lowered it, pulling out his blade, cleaning it quickly on his sleeve. He searched for the keys attached to the slaver's belt and tugged them free.

"May Osiris still walk you to the Sun," he whispered.

Zinkx peered into the wagon. Two young Human men, a Human boy of barely ten, and a Human woman. Slipping into the darkness he quickly set about unlocking the shackles. He offered them blades, only for the woman to shake her head and gather the Human boy into her arms. Zinkx glanced at the boy's broken ankle.

"The Kelib woman is causing a bit of a commotion. You can easily escape through a hole in the compound wall directly parallel with this wagon that I marked with a red arrow. I left some provisions there for you. Descend as quickly as you can into the forest. In the town of Hulbrath, about a week southeast of here, there is a Messenger-run inn called Dry Wood. Tell the landlord that Commander Zinkx Maz sent you. They'll look after you."

"You're really a Messenger?" one of the young men asked, staring at the blade he had been given in new wonder.

"I am." Zinkx poked his head out through the wagon flap and held it open for them. "Go. Sun's Blessings to you. Don't look back."

"Thank you," the boy whispered.

Zinkx ruffled his hair. "Be brave."

"That Kelib woman—" The eldest of the young men turned back.

Zinkx waved at him from the wagon.

"Worry about yourself, lad. Go."

He climbed through the wagon, picking in disgust at the bloodied chains. It made an inner part of him itch in horror, the thought of involuntary confinement—imprisonment—and a choking sensation of never being free.

Yet freedom—true freedom—was a construct of his mind. No matter the walls that surrounded him, the chains that might bind him, the orders that ruled him, if he considered himself free by choice, was he free? He had thought so, until the noose around his neck had tightened and the High Elder's hammer had come crashing down to shatter the illusion of freedom.

He flipped back the curtain of the wagon entrance and sat lazily on the driver's bench. It took several blows, but eventually the Kelib woman was brought down by a fierce strike to the head. She staggered, landing on her knees. He winced in sympathy as she was dragged away. The lead slaver wiped mud and blood from his clothes.

He could walk away now. This had absolutely nothing to do with his search for the Key, and, yet, the desire to slam fist to flesh was near palpable. Zinkx called out, "Guess you didn't expect that, heh?"

"She's hardly been worth what I paid."

Several of the men were staring, trying to gauge if he was, indeed, one of them. Zinkx smiled, playfully twirling the shackle keys as the leader searched his own belt. Zinkx smirked. The Kelib woman had far more of a plan than simply causing a commotion for the sake of it.

Zinkx flung his keys in front of the Kelib man. "Looking for those?"

He stretched his legs out playfully as he lent back, watching the confusion in the faces of the slavers turn to indignation. Several rushed at him simultaneously. One he took out with a kick, the other he sent hurling backwards with an outward thrust of gravity. The urge to draw his blades at so many opponents twinged in his stomach as he dropped, rolled, and bounced up to land amongst the fray. He had already caused enough of a commotion that Khwaja Denvy would be extremely disappointed in him.

"Fine…" he growled, knocking out one last nearby slaver before accepting the bag that was flung over his head. He was slammed into the mud. A volley of kicks showered him until a large hand dragged him up by a fistful of his hair through the bag. Zinkx winced at the foul breath of the face pressed against his own.

"Yeh're mine, Human."

Spitting in the man's face was futile through the cloth

bag, and head-butting a Kelib was a very stupid thing to do considering their bone density, but he was sorely tempted. Zinkx sighed, dropping his shoulders back in defeat. "Guess so," he muttered.

He was dragged down several long flights of stairs, and through winding corridors. He kept count, listening for the change in the footfall of the slavers as their boots impacted denser wood. Eventually, they paused and he heard the unbolting and opening of a heavy door. He was thrust inside hard enough to stagger and fall.

Zinkx lashed out a foot, kicking at the solid iron door as it slammed shut. "Absolute rots, the lot of you."

He lay in damp, putrid hay, the smell not at all appealing, even through the hood he still wore. "Hm, that hurt." He stretched out a leg. The slavers had not been gentle. But he had freed their merchandise, so they had a considerable gripe with him. "Hope they made it out…"

"You are a fool." The voice came from the furthest corner of the cell. Zinkx rolled slowly, testing his aches, tasting the blood in his mouth. Nothing seemed broken from the rough beating, but he was going to feel the bruising for weeks. A festering part of him could not help but think that he deserved the pain.

"What, from my performance, indicated to you that I was a fool?" Zinkx picked himself up and sat in the sloppy straw. Wearily, he raised his bound hands and dragged the hood from his head. It made little difference removing it; the cell was dark, the air stagnant and pungent with rot. He blinked, wiping the sweat and sticky blood from his eyes as they gradually adjusted. Small phosphorescent fungi began to flicker into his vision, forming spiderweb patterns across the walls. He focused on them, grateful for the meagre light. It was the eerie silence, though, that made him realise how dense the mighty trunk of the great evergreen they were within truly was.

"No free man would willingly confront the slavers."

"Freedom is a construct of the mind." Zinkx turned in the

stillness, searching for the source of the voice. A tiny, flying pin-lizard fluttered past his nose and he watched as it darted swiftly towards its flock. The little creatures that usually infested the forests at night clustered around a figure in the corner. Their brightly-coloured wings haloed around the woman, nibbling at the salt of her sweat and blood. Her ribs were cracked, he realised, hearing the wheeze in her sharp, shallow breathing.

The pin-lizards' glow brightened, giving him more than a shadow. It was the Kelib woman who had struck so fiercely at the head slaver—who would have been in danger had he not been a Kelib also; the blow would have crushed any Human's skull. She sat with her arms bound firmly by iron spikes. Her long black hair, with blue strands coruscating in the light from the pin-lizards, was a tangled, unwashed mat, almost obscuring her pointed ears.

Zinkx crawled towards her on his knees. She reacted instantly, raising a single, chained foot in defence.

"Get back, Human scum."

Her defiant glare broke through her obvious fear.

Zinkx clicked his tongue as he raised his bound hands. He stumbled over the Kelib language. It was rough and barky on his lips instead of smooth and slick like the laziness of Common Basic.

"I won't hurt you."

"Liar," she grunted. "And you dirty your tongue with my foul language."

"Your language is not foul." Zinkx managed the sentence with slow ease. "Only difficult to manage. I haven't spoken it in a while, that's all."

He bowed his head in the customary greeting of the region. "I am Zuksk."

She arched an eyebrow at the oddity of his name. In Kelib it sounded muddled, but it was ruder to offer the Human translation.

After a long pause, she answered. "Shan'ta'lee Shir-Hara of

the Eighth Clan."

"Shanty…" Zinkx translated softly. "Shanty…Eighth Clan," he repeated. He frowned down at his bound arms. There were Nine major Kelib Clans spread across Pennadot. The Eighth was the largest, situated within the Province of Pulza, and it ruled the slave trade with a fierce and terrifying force from the city of Crinn. Yet he had never heard that they sold off their own highly prized, extremely productive women in such a manner.

Had that changed?

"You are the aid the forest gods have given me for my prayers? A Human man?"

Zinkx leant on a knee, smiling wearily. "That ugly, am I?"

Her own grin showed her bloodied teeth. He noted the still oozing gash across her forehead. The Kelib slaver had been fierce to take her down. "You are a twig without leaves."

"Not sure what that means, but it doesn't sound good." Zinkx shuffled nearer. The closer he drew, the worse her wounds appeared in the muted light. The beating today had not been the first. His throat dried at the signs of torture. Heavy boned limbs and silken skin had long been ripped into. Someone had taken a hot knife and slashed through several of the intricate tattoos engraved into her flesh, and the poisonous ink shone faintly in the darkness. Kelibs within the House were proud of their tattoos, wearing them as a form of their cultural heritage, but he knew that in Pennadot they had the same effect as chains on a Kelib woman.

"Want to get out of here?"

She laughed bitterly. "Aye, but why would you bother? You are Human, and Humans have no care for Kelibs."

"Doesn't appear that Kelibs have much care for Kelibs either," he offered back.

She frowned.

He made a gesture with his bound hands. "This is Pulza. It's the cesspool of Pennadot, so I hear."

Her teeth snapped together. "I was born in these forests."

"And they are lovely. The slavers, not so much."

The hint of a smile ghosted her lips. "The same could be said about my sisters and my husbands."

"Was that a joke?" Zinkx raised his brow.

"Perhaps."

Zinkx laughed. "Come on. I think we've sat in this rot long enough, don't you?"

"You have a plan?"

Zinkx dropped his head back. "Hm, it's more of a vague idea." He thudded the bottom of his boot several times, knocking free a hidden blade. Bending over, he cut loose his hands from their bonds, rubbing at the raw skin on his wrists. "All right." He hopped up. "Let's take a look at your chains."

Shanty shook her head. "These are reinforced Kelib bone chains. You will not be able to break them."

He crouched beside her, cupping his chin. "Oh, come on. Where are the keys you took from the leader?"

"You figured that out?"

"I figured out that you had more of a plan than getting yourself beaten up."

She sighed. "I swallowed them."

"Ah. Long term plan, then."

She indicated her sparse attire. "They search me often."

"Not sure if search is the word for it," he muttered.

Shanty snorted and raised her chin. "So, now what, Human? With those weak arms of yours, I doubt you could do anything worth a ballad."

Zinkx pointed to himself. "Me, hardly. But have you ever heard of the Zaprexes?"

Shanty shook her head.

"The Fairies, maybe? Or the sky-gods?" Zinkx felt around beneath his pants. The slavers had taken his hip-bags, along with his kit and twin blades, but their search had stopped at those. Set slick against his skin a thin, almost invisible belt lay flush across his waist. He tugged at one of the small pouches attached to it.

"You mean the little green ones. The fay? The Mor-Mors tell stories of them. It is said they helped nurture the great Krrirren Trees." Shanty frowned. "They're but a tale from long past."

Zinkx reached for one of her shackles. "Where I come from, some of their things still lie around for my people to use. We call this a matchstick."

He held the thin laser against the metal of her shackle and a hiss sounded as an oily, tarry smell filled the cell. Shanty clenched her fist in his hand, and he tightened his hold. "Almost there."

With a soft clatter, the shackle came away and Shanty's arm dropped as though weighted. Zinkx shifted to her left arm, repeating the process, and then her feet until both were free. The skin beneath and around the shackles had been rubbed raw, infection already beginning to set in. He reached for his hip-bags and the medical kit he kept there. Zinkx clicked his tongue at their absence.

"Tsk," he hissed. "Sorry. My med-kits were with my gear that they took."

"It's fine." She held her wrists to her chest. "I have endured worse."

He squeezed her hands. "But you shouldn't have to. Get up when you feel like you can. I'll work on the door. You might need to open it for me. I have a feeling its built for Kelib strength."

He left her side to inspect the door. It was indeed built entirely for the use of a Kelib. More than likely it took several Human men to open it. Zinkx twisted the matchstick in his fingers, increasing the strength. He was going to burn through the few remaining ones he had, but it could not be helped. With a sigh he aimed the thin laser at the first hinge. The metal melted away faster than Shanty's shackles had.

"Who are you?" she suddenly enquired from the darkness.

Zinkx crouched to work on the second hinge. "Just a passer-by."

"Do not think me an idiot, Human."

"Was I implying that? I am, very simply, a passer-by."

"No mere passer-by would put themselves into a such a situation."

"Hm, perhaps I am not a simple passer-by, but a complicated one." He threw a grin over his shoulder.

"You are not as amusing as you think yourself to be."

The second hinge snapped apart. Zinkx threw away the dead matchstick. His fingers twitched at the action. Slowly he was throwing away pieces of his home, of his squadron, of life within the Trenches and, yet, the haunting memories never felt all that far away.

"I'm a *Messenger*." Zinkx turned to Shanty.

"The harbingers of death?" she whispered.

"Is that what they're calling us these days? Hm. The bards get ever more creative."

"I don't believe you."

Zinkx shrugged. "It matters not."

No doubt even a Kelib from the forests of Pulza had heard the barbaric tales, told by travelling bards, of Messengers and their bloodthirst in battle, fabricated ballads about murderous warriors with no emotion, who stole away children if they wandered out at night. Did they tell such tales because the reality was so much more terrifying?

He glared at the door.

Even if he forced his gravity-bubble outwards to open it, the noise of the action would draw too much attention. He glanced back at Shanty as she staggered onto her tortured feet. The pin-lizards swirled around her in a dance, following her and the scent of her blood. She approached him, arching an eyebrow up at him. She barely reached the middle of his chest, even with her shoulders drawn back taut and her head lifted. He almost pulled away as her hand reached up to run curiously over his face.

"It's paint..." she murmured, pulling her fingers away.

"Oh." Zinkx nervously laughed. "Sorry. Yes. I've got body

paint on. It's helpful for blending into the forest and masking my scent when hunting."

Her brow furrowed. "How interesting."

Shanty put her shoulder to the door and shoved. Zinkx cringed in sympathy as her raw, bare feet slipped on the floor. The door ground open. Zinkx grabbed her before she fell and he yanked on his gravity, realising too late that her mass far exceeded his own and he had forgotten to account for it. He landed roughly on his knees, breaking skin at the landing. "Ouch…" he groaned.

Her laughter was muffled in his leather vest. He wondered how long it had been since she had laughed without inhibition. Zinkx rolled off her, bouncing up with a spring to offer his hand.

She stared at his hand before accepting it curiously and he heaved her up with a full extension of gravity control. Shanty curled her fingers several times. "How did you…?"

"There is a bit of a knack to it. It's called gravity control, but a Human has to be very attuned to Livila to manage it."

"You could lift me?"

"I wouldn't so much as call it lifting, as nullifying the…you know what: never mind. Not the time."

He peered into the corridor. No guards. They might be chasing the Humans he had set free. Zinkx sighed, hoping they were safe. "We're clear." He looked back into the cell, to the waiting Kelib woman in the darkness. Slowly she took his hand in a trembling grasp. There was a dam of courage behind her grip, waiting to be broken, to be flooded out. He tightened his hold and they slipped through the gap into the murky light of the corridor.

The damage done to her was tenfold in the light. Blood had caked itself over her green skin, gluing together older wounds that were beginning to heal skewed. Even if he managed to get her to his Khwaja, neither of them could heal the scarring. Zinkx removed his vest, offering it to her and she held it momentarily before slipping it on.

"Thank you." She whispered.

"If my Khwaja was here he'd offer you something nicer, but, alas, it is only me." Zinkx sighed, tapping out the count of steps the slavers had taken to bring him to the cell. He looked back at Shanty. She had begun to deftly braid her waterfall of inky hair, preventing it from trailing across the floor by wrapping it loosely around her neck.

"I've got to fetch my gear."

"Can we not just go?"

He shook his head. "My twin blades alone are worth more than what a slaver would earn in a sol-cycle. I can't leave them here."

"If you insist."

"Follow me."

"Do you know where we are going?"

"I have a vague idea."

"Is your head full of only vague things?"

He chuckled. "You know, I think it might just be."

Keeping close to the walls, walking by the light of the tree-sap lanterns, they crept slowly through the corridors of the slaver compound.

Every so often the sound of voices caused Zinkx to abruptly stall. Beside him, Shanty would grow rigid like a dry stick.

The voices never grew closer than a muted muffle in the dense wooden environment.

Zinkx gently urged Shanty further, taking their climb up through the web of interlinking corridors.

"How long have you been with the slavers?" he enquired.

"Several months, I believe."

"And before that?"

"My husbands."

"Your husbands sold you?"

She shrugged. "I suppose I was not being dutiful enough. They were promised something, they did not receive it, thus they sold me back to the Crinn Markets."

"Ah, so you already came from the Crinn Markets?"

Shanty nodded. "All my Sisters did."

He paused, looking back at her. "I was under the impression that women of the Eighth Clan were not treated in this manner."

Shanty raised an eyebrow. "In what era do you live?"

Zinkx sighed. "Sometimes I wonder that myself."

"We are bred as a commodity. To get out by any means is our greatest goal."

Dropping his head back, Zinkx muttered, "Pennadot is a festering wound."

His arm was hit. The slap was probably intended to be light, but Shanty had not tempered her force. He doubted she had any interaction with Humans to gauge her strength by. He could not contain the wince as his skin smarted.

"Sorry!"

He rubbed at the spot. "Bit patriotic, heh?"

"The soil upon which we grow is important. Do not disrespect it."

Zinkx smiled. "I'll remember that." He glanced down the corridor to a door ajar. No one had entered or exited over the course of their conversation, and the loud murmur of drunken voices inside the room caught his ears. He had to make his move now. He brushed Shanty's arm lightly.

"This is going to go fast. Stay behind me."

Gathering his gravity bubble into a tight coil, Zinkx burst through the door. In a single glance he assessed the armoury and grabbed the nearest spear resting by the wall. Three men, two Human and one Kelib, barely had time to register his movement and stand as he vaulted into the room and swung the spear, releasing the weapon along with a burst of gravity. It slammed into them.

The Kelib took the full brunt of the force and crumbled unconscious, while the two humans were hauled back against a wall. Zinkx landed between them, smacking them both in their spinal nerves. Their bodies collapsed. A swell of nausea beset him. He went down on one knee, clasping a hand to his mouth, holding in the urge to vomit as his mouth dampened. The dizziness faded. Zinkx breathed out his unease as he slowly stood on weakened legs. He had put a little too much power into the swing the moment he had noticed the Kelib man.

Shanty anxiously approached. Zinkx sent her a reassuring glance.

"I'm fine. Need to recalibrate my own gravity to Livila's."

She frowned. "This sounds troublesome."

"Well, I suppose Humans are." He stepped over the first unconscious slaver, beginning to search the armoury for his gear. If they had dared touch any of his stuff—

He caught Shanty's movement in the corner of his vision. The swing of a dagger in her grip. He barely made it to her side before the blade struck the chest of the nearest unconscious Human man. It took all his focus to force his gravity bubble into his hold around her wrist to halt the momentum of her strike. The backlash burned the muscles of his arm and shoulder.

She struggled against him, trying to drive the blade down against his hold.

"Whoa, whoa!" He tightened his grip around her wrist and wrapped another arm around her shoulder, pulling her gently back against his chest. "This will not make you feel any better."

"It will."

"Perhaps right now, yes, but, later, you will look at yourself very differently. Their freedom has been stolen, like yours, simply by life choices and not by force."

She slowly lowered the blade as his hand fell away.

"Killing them will simply take away their choice to choose again."

Her head dropped and her shoulders sagged. Zinkx stepped away.

"And if they keep choosing this foul road they are on?" she muttered.

"Eventually our choices catch up with us." Zinkx gathered

up his hip-bags, slinging them around his waist. Their familiar weight was reassuring. He strapped his twin blades across his back before hunting for his bow and arrows, finding them discarded nearby. Zinkx hissed in irritation at the treatment of his weapons.

Shanty flung the dagger away.

He gestured to it. "You should keep it. There is a difference between hatred and self-defence."

Her face twisted in disgust. "Swords and blades are only for men."

He smiled. It sounded like the anger that had been in her had burnt away like a quick flame, and she had returned to herself, alarmed at her actions.

"I know a few women who will argue with you on that." He picked up the dagger she had discarded and stowed it away. "But considering your fists can probably do more damage than any blade, I won't press the point."

She had regressed into a shell, her shoulders curling. It seemed the thought that she had almost taken a life frightened her. There was something fragile behind the roughness that she projected as a shield. He took her hand once more. "Let's not linger here. We have a way to go before we're free of this place."

The carved-out interior of the evergreen reminded Zinkx of the manic insides of an ant-nest. Had a Kelib, or a Human, even made the chaotic twists and turns inside the great towering tree? Or was there a creature that burrowed deep into the wood, hollowing out the passages? That seemed far more likely.

"I would not want to meet whatever it is…" he muttered.

"Whatever what is?" Shanty asked.

"The creature that made these tunnels."

"The *Hajkn*. You speak of the *Hajkn*. They are harmless unless attacked. Kelib boys will hunt them together, to forge their root bonds."

"Not sure what that means, but it sounds very—" He urged her back with a sudden arm against her chest. Shanty tensed against him. Heavy bootsteps were thudding down a set of stairs. Stairs he knew were their one and only exit into the upper level.

Two—no—maybe three men. Humans if the thudding of their iron-weighted shoes was anything to go by. He glanced back at Shanty. She was anxiously tugging at the frayed edges of his shirt. "It'll be fine," he assured her. "Stay behind me."

He burst up the stairs, meeting the three men head on. They entered his gravity bubble, losing their footing enough to disrupt their concentration. Zinkx smashed his elbow into the nearest man, knocking him against the wall. He dropped.

The second managed to draw a blade. Zinkx ducked, cracking the palm of his hand into the slaver's knee before snatching his wrist and throwing him into the third man.

Shanty stepped uneasily over the first man as Zinkx urged her up the stairs. "We're almost there."

He could only blame the rush of adrenalin as to why he did not check the entrance. The moment they broke into the larger room, he knew there was no way he could reach the main doors of the compound when at least fifteen slavers were gathered around a fire-pit and the cookery pot bubbling over it.

"Ah, *jarki*," Zinkx swore. He dragged Shanty behind him, turning in the opposite direction to the exit as the group by the fire-pit scrambled to attention, shouting and howling in alarm. He took another set of stairs, around and around. It seemed impossibly endless.

"Zinkx!" Shanty cried.

He leapt over her, gaining momentum by parkouring from wall to wall. His kick slammed the encroaching slaver down the stairs, knocking several more over. He smashed the nearest window open with his elbow, leaning out.

He balanced on one foot, aiming an arrow at the nearby water pipe from the reserve above.

He fired.

A torrent of water exploded free, shattering the windows and bursting into the tight confines of the stairwell. The stairs shook. Shouts erupted from below as the water tore down the side of the evergreen.

Urging Shanty along another corridor, Zinkx tested each door. Most were locked; others did not contain a room with a large enough window.

The floor beat with the thunder of pounding steps. A battle cry sent a rush of panic through him. The Kelib head slaver charged down the hallway, eyes a tinted yellow of rage. Zinkx caught the force of the immense strike in the centre of his bow, with barely a moment to spare, feeling the aftershock vibrate through his muscles. He twisted, allowing his flexible, thinner Human body to somersault over the Kelib. He twisted his legs around the slaver's neck and sent them both slamming to the floor.

"Shanty! Break the window in the next room. Now! Do it."

She vanished through the door. The head slaver's grip tore into the flesh of his thighs even as he struggled against the lack of air. Zinkx drew a blade, aiming for the man's side. The Kelib grabbed Zinkx's arm, drawing blood with his nails. Forcing back the onslaught of nausea, Zinkx released his birth elemental gift down his arm. Lightning sparked off the dagger, dancing across the floor in violent lashes. The Kelib's grip loosened. Zinkx slammed the blade through the man's chest.

"What are you?" the slaver slurred.

"A Messenger," he whispered into the Kelib's ear. "May you return to the soil you grew from."

He rolled out from beneath the heavy body. His Khwaja was going to grouch at the state of his already-threadbare clothing. Zinkx flexed his trembling, bleeding hand several times. Lightning had scorched the skin, drawing new scars over old ones. The tingling sensation would eventually fade, but it was always an irritating backlash. He kicked at the blackened dagger and hissed in disgust.

"Bone blade. Explains the backlash. Should have noticed that." With a stagger he entered the room Shanty had rushed into. The window had not been shattered. Zinkx kicked the door shut and dragged a chair across it.

"Shanty?"

She was hiding behind a set of shelves.

"Shanty, it's fine. He's dead."

She peered through strands of hair, tears staining her cheeks. "You're alive."

Zinkx crouched in front of her. He wiped blood off his hands and offered them to her. "It'll take a lot more than a Kelib man to kill me. I told you, I'm a Messenger. Come on. Let's go."

"Go? Go where?" She looked around. "We're stuck in a room."

"Hardly stuck." Zinkx plucked a paperweight from a nearby table.

"Do you trust me?" He turned towards her, grinning.

She frowned. "No."

"Hah, that's okay. Sometimes I don't trust myself either."

He flung the paperweight at the window. The glass shattered, the shards that reached them halting in mid-air as though captured in a net. Shanty blinked in surprise at the shimmering burst of light refracting across the walls. Zinkx batted the floating shards aside and heaved himself onto the window ledge. He held out a hand to her.

"Let's go."

The moment she accepted the hand, she lifted lightly off the floor.

Her eyes widened and a gasp of surprised joy escaped her lips as she floated weightlessly.

The door slammed open. A throwing knife struck the nearby window shelf.

"Time to go." Zinkx swept her up. Shanty shrieked as he leapt out, sailing past the remains of the water gushing out into the courtyard.

He landed roughly on the roof of the stable, barely managing to maintain his balance as an arrow pierced his shoulder. Zinkx dropped Shanty. She yelped as she floated, bobbing in the air. Another shower of arrows rained down. Zinkx expanded his gravity bubble, catching several of the scatter. The wooden roof buckled and they both fell through. Zinkx stopped them, and the surrounding debris, in midfall. They floated for a moment several feet above the ground before landing in straw and dust.

Zinkx groaned, clutching at his chest. Shanty scrambled towards him, ripping shreds off her torn gown. She strapped up his bleeding shoulder. "You're pushing yourself too hard—"

He grabbed at her hands. "I'm fine."

Shanty pulled away in alarm. "Your eyes…"

Zinkx quickly turned away, rubbing at his eyes. He clambered onto his feet. "It's frustrating being unable to properly use my birth elemental. I don't want to cause a forest fire."

Several of the horses were panicked at their rude entrance. "Can you open the stable doors?" Zinkx asked.

Shanty headed to the large double doors. Zinkx opened each of the separate stalls, shouting at the horses, stirring them into a greater frenzy as they rushed from their shelter. Shanty cowered against the wall as the steeds cantered out into the courtyard, the stampeding of hooves amplifying the commotion outside.

"Wait!" Shanty cried as the last horse made for the stable doors. "Take that horse!"

Zinkx called back, "No, a horse will get tangled in the forest. We need a diabond." He rushed deeper into the stable. He knew the slavers had at least one diabond; he had seen it pulling the wagon.

He shoved the last stall open, revealing a caged enclosure. The beast within startled awake, its silky coat of melded grey and white gleaming with a shimmer of flames as it surged up.

Eyes as red as the lava pits of Coltarian studied him, and Zinkx breathed in deeply at the fierce rage behind the gaze. The tongues of animals was not something he had studied well, but he was mildly dreamathic, enough that perhaps an understanding could be broached.

"Let us ride you." He held out a hand. "Let me set you free. Please."

Her growls continued. Zinkx reached into her cage. "Darling, let me get you away from this place."

The diabond's long wolf-like ears twitched and she crouched, lowering herself in permission. Zinkx stepped forward and hoisted himself onto the curve of her back. He felt muscles loosen as the powerful beast rose and bounded out of the stall. Shanty gave a cry at their sudden emergence. Zinkx grabbed her hand, pulling her up onto the diabond's back in front of him. He wrapped one arm firmly around her, gripping the diabond's mane with the other.

"And away!" He laughed as the diabond charged free of the stables and they scattered the gathering of slavers like a wave. In several great leaps the diabond carried them through the compound and out into the dense forest. Looking back up at the town of Grunblurn, Zinkx gently urged the diabond on. He had caused a considerable commotion. More than likely it was going to have repercussions.

"You really are a Messenger."

Zinkx looked down at Shanty. She was staring at him, staring beyond the humid fuzz of his ebony hair, the peeling green paint, and his Humanness. Her Kelib gaze was looking deeper, making him feel unnaturally exposed and stripped naked.

"No…" She turned away abruptly. "You're more than that."

"I really am just a passer-by," he murmured.

CHAPTER TWO

The cycle is for Eternity;
Eternity is the cycle.
The cycle was broken,
And we wept for Eternity.

Extract from the Song of Sorrows

Borukoshu darted swiftly through the clogged metal boulevards of the city's lower-ground levels. A near constant hiss of steam seemed to follow its light steps. Despite its crippling age, it delicately manoeuvred around the large, thunderous carts that transported the sludgy overflow of Black Fuel from the city's ancient turbines.

Momentarily, Borukoshu paused, drawn by the glints of the polychromatic shine of the Great Shields against its visual circuits, like a moth hypnotised by light. For as long as this incarnation could recall, for as long as its visual circuits had functioned, all it had been able to gaze upon were the Great Shields.

Hidden—once forbidden—fragments of Borukoshu's frayed lifetimes filtered through its neurons, blurring up memories of blue skies. Rich and deep, so deep Borukoshu would need a ship to escape the horizons and burst forth into the glittering ocean of stars beyond.

Its thin, rust-encrusted chest shuddered out a sigh. The Great Shields had held back the vast, toxic ocean since the time of the Sinking of the Cities. Though it doubted any Zaprexes still functioning recalled the songs of application that dated so far back. Living in blissful ignorance had become the escapism of Borukoshu's people, or perhaps even their self-imposed punishment for their failure to save a dying world.

It drew back into the eerie, artificial light that smothered the corridors in a sickly emerald as the hot glow blended with gathering yellow clouds of smog swirling between the crystal spires of Cal'pash'coo. The incandescent skyscrapers mocked Borukoshu. Its lifetime lived in the dazzling high world above the smog seemed so long ago and yet, compared to the eternity of its scattered existence, it was as though a mere week, or even a day, had passed. But it was raw and savage for it had been this run, and a part of it—the rusting part that ached and burned with each step it took towards its destination—wished to end the pain.

Those who dwelt above, lived without rust, without the decay of slow ionisation. Their philepcon liquid did not dry and eat their own bodies from the inside out. They remained eternally youthful, stuck without a cycle, believing they had been forever—that this world of smog, steam, and lightning storms had been forever and would continue forever.

Their world had become an endless line.

It was no longer a circle, growing ever bigger with each repeat.

They had forgotten it all—

The gods they had once been.

The songs they had once sung.

Songs that had once bridged entire universes.

Songs that had held the power to save worlds.

Yet Livila had defeated them. They had not been prepared for the awakening of an old foe, and the fracturing of not only a world they had tirelessly pieced together, but the very foundation and fabric that had originally held it in place.

Now they were only a shadow of the strength they had formerly commanded. An empire of crystal and iron, brought to ruin in a single remaining city of rust. It looked back through the gaps in the boulevards, to the smoky smog, glimpsing the flickering lights of the gleaming skyscrapers. They had forgotten, in their grief, the cycle that was fundamental to their very existence.

Sparks scattered through its limbs, making the recollection painful. It had never forgotten. Its thin, arthritic hands grasped its bag of supplies tightly to its chest.

It was impossible to forget when it had been given the most precious of gifts.

A Hatchling.

Of all the things that could have brought their empire to an end, it had been the inability to reproduce that had caused their extinction. Their power had always been in their number, like a swarm of insects. They could only build that which their numbers sustained.

Would one—

Would one be enough?

Borukoshu skipped as the heels of its spectator boots threatened to dip into the gaps of the wire meshing over the walkway. Its long ears provided balance, and Borukoshu twisted, its old gravity-drive whining in protest as it kicked into gear. A robotic cart narrowly avoided it, and it tipped its bowler hat to the driver, despite its automated nature. A single large lens turned towards Borukoshu and a charred claw was raised in response. Centuries of being left to their own pre-programmed existence had exposed the machines of the lower levels to a slow degeneration. The few Zaprexes, like itself, who had chosen exile, had long given up trying to manage the failing systems.

It would all fail and come crumbling down someday.

Borukoshu turned down a side alley, pausing only when a soft vibration jiggled from the hand-device buried in its heavy coat. In the gentle fall of the toxic rain, it shuffled about, finding the slim hologram pad.

The lenses of its cybernetic eyes flickered, focusing on the alert symbol glittering red as a sequence of numbers counted down.

"Never enough time," it whispered as it approached the

porch of a small apartment, squeezed between the giant foundations of two colossal skyscrapers. Several maintenance bots scampered around on the metal walls, repairing new damage from the acidic rainfall. It placed its free hand against the doorframe. An azure glow scanned its cybertronic retina. The old door's mechanisms whirred as they unlocked and slowly the iron slab ground open. A rush of freezing air slapped into Borukoshu. It sighed in relief at the tantalising chill, before scurrying indoors, giving the heavy door a boot. It shuddered closed, groaning all the way, locking the hot, toxic world outside, and confining within what needed to be kept safe.

From the upper room of its poky little home, a harmonious, sweet voice lifted in a tantalising song. Borukoshu could feel the melody wrapping itself through its old systems as it tried to rewire broken connectors. Its Matrix Crystal pulsed against its ribcage. The song was as familiar as the home it had built. Wearily it dropped its bag of supplies and slung its hat onto a rack. With a spark its antennae sprang free of their confinement, and the sensation of being off-balance eased.

Its home was a rather stagnated dwelling, clean and neat as all Zaprexes characteristically desired a residence to be, but it had tried hard to give it a comfortable, homey atmosphere. Several of its lifetime runs had been Human, and Humans had an odd particularity to rugs and macramé to brighten a house. It had needed to make these from found objects, but it considered the rug that covered the acid damaged floor to be one of its best works, despite it being nearly entirely made of plastics sourced from the dump.

The upper-floor was created wholly from a husk of a rusted out ancient star-glider engine, which had been wedged into the high domed ceiling to make an additional room.

"Semyueru! *Tadaima*[1]!" Borukoshu called out. Its voice scratched through its worn voice-box.

The singing stopped abruptly. A loud thump from upstairs caused Borukoshu's ears to twitch rearward as it opened a slot

---

1 *I'm back (home).*

in the wall to shelve away its soaked overcoat. The humming of a primed anti-gravity drive filled the small home. Borukoshu turned as the tiny Hatchling appeared over the balcony of the sleeping quarters, leaning over the rickety iron railing. A brilliant smile lit up like a gasoline bulb between cheeks still rosy with unprocessed red blood that had yet to fully assimilate through the child's Matrix Crystal. It would take at least another several sol-cycles for the full cybernetic conversion.

"Biri!" Semyueru's voice chimed out like a bell.

It was an affectionate abbreviation of its name that eased the pain of its rusted joints. Borukoshu was the Hatchling's negative parent, but it had not seemed natural in this lifetime run to be named thus by an offspring. The uncomfortable sensation created by even thinking of the designation was, no doubt, trauma lingering from some echoing run-through—

Osiris—

A flicker of static distorted its optical lenses. Borukoshu grabbed for the table edge, keeping itself upright.

"No. Not now. Just…a bit longer…Hazanin, please, just a bit longer…"

The distortion faded, returning it to the cool cosiness of its little rusty home.

Its time was running out.

"*Okaerinasai*[2]! Biri!" Semyueru squealed.

Borukoshu felt its liquid lungs swell as the bubbly, raven haired Hatchling tore down the spiral stairs with arms thrust high in exuberance. There was nothing particularly different, nor overly striking about the child compared to any other Hatchling who might have been born centuries prior. It was thin, though with sweetly rounded cheeks that held a mischievous smile. Liquid green skin, richer emerald than its own silver, floated over the child's still-forming soft metal hull that would someday protect its interior workings.

"Careful down those stairs, Semyueru. You know very well your hull is still growing," Borukoshu chided, dusting off its

---

2   *Welcome home!*

brown robe. "Your gown will get hooked in your anti-gravity drive and you'll roll all the way down here, sure to bruise something in the process."

It bent. Its hip replacement popped, but it ignored the sharp pain and gathered its bag of supplies from the floor.

Semyueru's little form whizzed past, its home-spun gown a blur of blue, voice a raw mechanical squeal as it skipped, looped, and pirouetted through the air. The dear little Hatchling was completely unaware the movements it was enacting had once been a dance that had led their people across universes.

Borukoshu hauled its bag to the main-room table, punching the cooling unit with the toe of its shoe as it passed. With a heave, it dumped the contents of its trip onto the iron table, built from an old wheel of a cart. It quickly caught a stray bottle of cold glucose liquid before it rolled from the table.

Its weakened form tipped as it was hit roughly by the speeding Semyueru buzzing about in the air. That was perhaps the only difference that set Semyueru apart from any other Hatchling: the energy that it, alone, could produce as a singularity. Zaprexes always came in pairs—Negative and Positive—unless a Zaprex was a fusion.

Born into a Dynasty when that Dynasty faced annihilation, perhaps they could have been called harbingers of death. No, truly, they were the beginning of a new cycle, of rebirth, of beginnings.

Borukoshu laughed as Semyueru twirled around it. It was always the same; Semyueru's smile never seemed to fade. Though it was a joyful sight, its heart broke as the emotions it evoked fizzled through damaged pathways.

It was exhausted. This body had suffered enough. Emotion had burned through its hull, leaving it raw, twisted, and bent. Even closing its eyes meant seeing lifetimes filled with more suffering.

Osiris, I am here—

Time was running out.

"Guess...guess what I...I...learnt...t'day!" Semyueru

clutched at Borukoshu's robe, fingers playing with the beads that weighted the fabric.

It was a fascinating little programming issue, Semyueru's phonological processing. It hoped that with time the child would grow out of its stuttering. Semyueru had time—time for many things—

Time was not Semyueru's enemy.

Picking out two cups from the bench, Borukoshu flicked its visual lenses downward at the child. Semyueru's eyes were enlarged by giant holographic spectacles perched upon the tip of its little button nose. The glasses glittered with moving cryptograms, still scanning data.

"What did you learn today, *ne*?"

"The Land of Pennadot…you…you know…the one… with the…the land with the Star-Kings! It…it…once had really dense gravity…but…but the Zaprexes came and used machines to change it. We…we…helped the trees grow really…big!"

Borukoshu raised its eyebrows, scooping the child up with one arm. It hooked it onto its bony hip.

"I'm guessing you finished that data-pad on gravity-wells then, *ne*."

"*Hai*! *Hai*! Is that dinner?"

"Correct assumption. This is indeed dinner. So, what else did you learn today?"

It was one of its main purposes in life, to keep Semyueru's mind filled with data from the long-forgotten archives that it collected on its scavenger hunts. Someday the Hatchling would need the information to develop a solution, for there would be many problems to solve, and perhaps some Zaprex's knowledge from long ago would aid the child's understanding of the alien world beyond the Great Shields.

Semyueru blinked, the soft click of its eyelids breaking the sudden silence. "In our database there is only information on ten lands. Why are there so few?"

Borukoshu pondered the question as it settled Semyueru

into a high-chair and passed it its glass of glucose liquid. "Have you considered that our database is incomplete. Perhaps it could even have been corrupted."

"Who...who...would do that?" Semyueru burst out in indignation.

"Perhaps history was written by those who lost," Borukoshu murmured.

Semyueru tilted its head to one side. "I don't understand."

"Never mind, dear one." Borukoshu brushed back Semyueru's hair. "For now, ten is a nice, logical number." With crippled fingers it drew lines upon the table, creating a holographic map. "Each land is connected by a Border—"

"The tectonic plates. I know that...and they...are...falling apart...because Livila...lacks a gravitational pull of her own. We do not know...why...but...she is collapsing into space."

Borukoshu glanced down at its boots. No—it knew why. Far more terrifying forces were at work than a collapsing planet. "*Hai*, this world is being eaten..."

Semyueru's attention snapped around like a switch being flicked. It jerked up, antennae and ears going rigid as it stared at the ceiling. The house's blue lights flickered. Through the air, a shattering crack echoed as thunder vibrated the iron walls.

"Smog, smog, smog storm! Yay!" With a spark of energy, Semyueru flew from its chair, around the spiral staircase and up into the second floor with a squeal.

Borukoshu laughed. It scrubbed a hand through its silvering hair.

"I suppose dinner can wait." It sighed, taking its own glass, carrying it carefully up the stairs. As it reached the upper level, it noted Semyueru typing in a code on the holographic screen over a crystal console. Shelves of data-pads lined the walls of the bedroom and library. Semyueru darted away from the hologram, back to its side, giving a whirl of delight before clutching at its arm in glee.

The metal-encased ceiling folded back slowly, the steel blinds rolling away to reveal clear shield-glass. Little maintenance bots scurried across the hexagon panes, trying to find a suitable hiding spot. As the final blind clanked back, the expansive network of the glowing skyline simultaneously underwent the dimming of lights at nightfall and the beginnings of a smog storm.

"I love smog storms!" Semyueru let out a giggled shriek as thunder jolted the foundations of their small home once more.

Borukoshu snuggled into the cherished embrace as lightning danced in the pollution far above and acidic rain clawed at the shielding. A sharp, blinding crack of energy lit up the dimness and a rumble vibrated the walls, making their world sing. Semyueru bared its fangs, grinning back at the results of the destroyed environmental system of their city.

"Biri? Why…why…do each of the lands…have a… unique song?" Semyueru whispered.

Borukoshu settled itself into a swinging anti-gravity chair, with Semyueru on its lap. It brushed the Hatchling's mop of hair aside from its holographic glasses. "The songs of each land speak of their individual splendour, but, just like this lightning, they allow a path to be conducted from…" it poked Semyueru's nose, "here to here." It touched its own. "It will be up to you to find a way to open these paths."

Semyueru pouted. "I don't understand."

"Someday you will." Borukoshu sighed heavily. "I've had a long day. Now, how about you sing me my favourite song, *ne*?"

Semyueru nodded, its antennae bobbing back and forth. With an energetic spring it leapt into the air and spun through the emerald glow emanating from the sickly, drab world outside. Borukoshu sank back in aching exhaustion, loosening each tight meta limb into the weightlessness of the anti-gravity chair.

In the pocket of its robe its hand-device vibrated again.

A little, sharp stab twisted like a cold needle into its chest.

Time was running out.

Or, perhaps—

Time was catching up with it.

Borukoshu took a deep gulp from its mug.

In the background, the song Semyueru sang as it moved in the air, dancing an ancient pathway back to the Little Blue Planet, soothed the staggering loneliness that had crept up upon it. It studied the lines of the lightning, striking in vectors through the yellow smog. They reminded it of the Data-Ways its people had once networked across the lands.

"We'd fixed it," Borukoshu whispered. "We had fixed this world. We didn't deserve this."

Time was running out.

Tomorrow's dawn would be its last.

It sipped its drink in contentment and smiled.

"I'm ready, Hazanin."

CHAPTER THREE

A Kelib's fist is strong but his vengeance is far stronger still.
Tangle with a Kelib and you risk the fury of not just one
man, but several generations of men.
Their women, however...
Well...
I assure you...
Their women have but one agenda...
To take back what was stolen from them:
Their freedom.

J. Dustin, Sundate 1223, Between Kelibs and Humans,
First Edition, Alya – Pennadot, Scrolls For Sale

The fear of pursuit had long faded with the density of the vegetation growing into an entwined mess that only a diabond could navigate swiftly. In the gloom of the forest's dark undergrowth, the diabond shimmered, her fur rippling like a constant gleam of fire. Zinkx held onto her mane with one hand, the other tightly gripped around Shanty. She clutched his thighs in a vice, fiercely enough that his skin would bruise, but she was stiff, unable to move with the flow of the animal beneath them.

A part of her was clearly terrified of the darkness they plunged through. Perhaps afraid of the unknown she was heading into.

Zinkx gently eased the diabond into a slower pace, and the beast began to pant heavily. It had been as anxious as they were to escape Grunblurn, it seemed.

Zinkx glanced up. It was impossible to see the sky-sea from their depths amongst the foliage and branches, but night had fallen before he had the chance to notice. A whole day had vanished. Solar-fungi danced in the misty world, lighting their surroundings with ghostings of day.

The diabond's paws made large mats of the surface growth atop the roots it padded across. Strings of moss swelled back to life, covering their tracks.

Zinkx shivered at the swift resilience of the surrounding vegetation. The balance was off. Nature was thriving, out of control even, when he knew the Ancient Ones had sway over such systems. Was their influence waning?

People were dying—not only dying; they were being carted off to be processed into the Dragon's armies—and yet the earth did not seem to be mourning. If anything, it was rejoicing.

"Well, can't complain…" he muttered. "At least it means we've reached camp quicker."

Shanty stirred at his words. Her chest expanded with a deep breath. "Where are we?"

"About three hours out from Grunblurn."

"Three hours?" Shanty looked up at him in disbelief.

"You've been a little out of it."

Zinkx eased the diabond to a halt and slid off, gesturing to Shanty to remain mounted. He peered through the dense, twisting roots, all linked together in oddly mangled shapes as they reached to the sky-sea. They were covered in a dazzling array of tiny pinpricks of bio-luminescent flowers. The scent was sweet, scarce enough not to be over-powering. He thought them reminiscent of the night sky-sea, a swirling vision of the dancing stars. Poetic, considering where their camp lay therein.

"Khwaja and I, we camped out in an old Zaprex ruin just through here. It's exceptionally beautiful." He urged the diabond to follow him through a tight gap in the roots. "There is a spring; you can wash up, if you don't mind the water being ice cold. Khwaja will have a fire going, though, so that will help." Hopefully talking would ease the anxiety he could sense from her. She had leapt out a window, entrusting her life, her freedom, to a stranger—to a Messenger.

Gradually the thick roots gave way to reveal the old ruins, though he, himself, would hardly call Zaprex monuments 'ruins', for they always seemed just as hauntingly beautiful to him as if they were completely intact. The forest had grown around the hexagon plates and crystal spires, creating a mystical merging of metal, crystal, and wood. If there had once been a ceiling of some kind, it had long ago vanished along with the cybernetic fairies that had manned the station. What was left was a lonely, empty hollowness that made his chest ache.

"It's waiting…" Shanty's voice startled him.

Zinkx looked back. She was wiping tears from her cheeks. He nodded at her words. "Yes. It is."

He led the diabond up several flights of crystal stairs, emerging onto what his Khwaja called the observation deck. A thick mat of moss coated the floor. Fallen trunks and branches crushed several of the crystal terminals. His Khwaja had dragged the logs to the fire pit to gradually burn through them. The old Kattamont was currently crouched by the warmth of the flames, adding herbs to a pot. Zinkx touched his stomach as it clenched tightly at the aroma of a meal.

"Ah, so, my wayward son finally returns. I thought perhaps you had been shipped off to Crinn, and I would need to come and rescue you."

"Haha. Funny." Zinkx reached up, aiding Shanty to dismount.

Turning towards him, arching a brushy eyebrow, his Khwaja shook his head with a wry smirk of amusement. "So, you decided to cause a ruckus."

Zinkx glanced away. "I had to."

His Khwaja sighed. "No, you did not have to. You chose to. I thought by now that you would understand your actions have consequences."

"I wasn't going to leave slaves—"

"We both know you are more than capable of dealing with a situation without the ruckus."

Zinkx shouldered the disproval.

"But…never mind that now. What is done is done. You'll be happy to know I made sure the four Humans were well on their way to Hulbrath. This must be the Kelib woman they mentioned."

Despite Shanty's obvious fatigue, she had pulled herself upright in awe as his Khwaja stood to his full towering height by the fire. Zinkx was momentarily thrown by the difference. He had forgotten how short Kelibs were, but it was most noticeable when one stood beside the overwhelming and majestic frame of a Kattamont as grand as Khwaja Denvy.

"Hello, dear one." Denvy stepped forward. He extended a paw, slipping it under her chin to tilt her head upward.

Shanty flushed, clasping her hands together as she repressed a tremble. "You're a forest god."

"And here we go." Zinkx rolled his eyes.

His Khwaja batted him gently over the back of his head. "Behave."

Zinkx tugged the diabond away, urging her in the direction of the fire. Denvy chuckled, lowering his paw from Shanty's chin. "I suppose, dear one, your people would call me thus. Over the centuries I have been named many things. Truthfully, I am just a very old, very tired gentleman."

Shanty bowed low. "Please forgive my appearance, lord."

"There is nothing to forgive. And, please, call me Denvy. None of this lord business."

"But you are a forest god."

"Hm. I'm nothing fancy."

"I wouldn't say that, Khwaja." Zinkx called out from beside the fire. "You make wonderful meals."

Denvy offered his paw to Shanty. "He thinks only with his stomach, honestly."

"My Mor-Mor said men are useless unless fed."

"Hm, wise woman, your Mother-Mother."

Leading Shanty to the fire-pit, Denvy crouched beside their assortment of packs. "Well, neither of you are getting a meal until you are washed, and your wounds are cleaned. You both stink of all manner of foul things."

Denvy removed the wooden ladle from Zinkx's hand and

shoved a bag of medical and cleaning supplies into his arms to replace it. Zinkx pouted.

"Take the lady down to the spring. Treat your wounds. You'll get your meal when that's done."

Zinkx nodded.

"Shanty, can you walk?"

She raised her chin. "Yes."

The air around the spring tasted different. It tasted like honey. As he finished patching the arrow wound on his shoulder with the last remnants of liquid sealant, Zinkx sighed. It felt like pieces of his home were flaking away as he used up his supplies.

"You still alive over there, Shanty?" he called out.

"I'm fine."

"Just checking." Zinkx sat at the edge of the spring, dipping his feet into the cold water. He scrubbed off the dirt between his toes. "Making sure a river-god hadn't enchanted you."

He felt around in his hip-bags, finding a small jewel to toss into the spring. A long association with his Khwaja had taught him to be well aware of the entities that walked between the Realms.

"Do not be ridiculous, Human."

"Hm. You'd be surprised. Happens more often than you think, according to Khwaja Denvy."

He dried his feet, and pulled his boots back on.

"I'm leaving a fresh set of clothes on the rocks," Zinkx called out. "They belong to Khwaja. He apologises for that, but it is all he can provide for now."

"Can you leave your vest with them?"

Zinkx paused, glancing down at the leather armour. "Ah. Sure." He added it to the pile. "I'll be up the steps a bit. Call me when you are finished. I'll help bind your feet."

"Thank you." Her reply was soft. He heard water slosh about. Zinkx leant on a nearby wall, picking at moss as he waited. Shanty's stamina was impressive, though the allure of being clean was extremely enticing. He scratched at his neck, grateful to be free of the body-paint he had smeared over himself.

She tugged the hem of his shirt. Zinkx glanced over his shoulder. Shanty stood in the loose-fitting, enormous, and somewhat-frayed spare shirt of his Khwaja. It dropped to her knees, revealing how she had haphazardly wrapped her raw, damaged feet with linen. His leather vest she had added over the shirt and tightly buckled it.

"I told you to call me."

"I am fine." She headed up the stairs.

Zinkx ran a hand through his damp hair. "You really should not be walking on those feet."

Shanty's shoulder's hunched. "Very well…" she murmured. "But only the stairs."

"Only the stairs." Zinkx carefully collected her in his arms. Several rocks and sticks floated around them. Shanty reached for them, pulling them into her lap as he climbed the stairs. She began platting them like beads into her damp hair.

Making it back to the observatory, Zinkx settled her onto the mossy surface. She almost buckled and grabbed for his shoulder. He winced. "I can carry you by cheating. Your grip can still crush my bones."

"Sorry. Sorry."

His Khwaja approached. "Ah, yes, yes. Learning how to temper your strength around delicate Humans is a process." He offered his paw to her. "No need to do so with me."

"Delicate?" Zinkx pointed to himself. "Excuse me?"

"Yes. Delicate. Like a piece of pottery." Denvy waggled his eyebrows as he settled Shanty on a log by the fire, offering her a bowl. Zinkx thumped down beside the lounging diabond. She raised her head slightly, and puffed out a snort of smoke, before settling once more, her tail flicking playfully. Zinkx accepted his own bowl and the flat bread Denvy handed him.

"Thank the Sun…"

Denvy smiled. "You're welcome."

Seating himself, Denvy spooned out his own portion. He looked across the fire-pit at Shanty.

"I never got your name, dear one?"

"I apologise. I am Shan'ta'lee…" she paused. "Formerly of the Eighth Clan."

"Ah, Eighth Clan, heh." Denvy rubbed his bread. "That does explain your injuries and tattoos."

Shanty looked up in surprise.

Warily, she touched her exposed shoulders. The faintly glowing markings embedded into her green skin were clearly visible, despite the slashes marring several of them.

Denvy bent forward, resting his chin on his paws.

"You're a breeder."

Shanty opened her mouth, only to squeeze her eyes firmly shut and turn away. Denvy nodded, placing his dish aside. He picked up a blanket from the nearby bedroll and wrapped it around her shoulders. "Not to worry, dear one. You are safe from such things while you are here. Rest peacefully again, at least for this night."

"Thank you."

Zinkx stared at his empty bowl, his mind wandering back to the meagre war rations he had been so grateful for after weeks of near starvation out on the Front Lines. Meals always tasted better whenever he had gone a long stretch of time without eating. There had been something incredibly appetising about the wooden, dry bars, that tears always dampened his cheeks at the mere hint of them. What were the children eating now? Had Ellyllon improved the flavour of the ration bars like they had talked about doing?

His stomach clenched suddenly. The bowl he held dropped as he covered his mouth, forcing the nausea down. Denvy's paw rested on his shoulder. "Come back to the present, lad."

He licked his teeth. "I'm fine."

"Hm." Denvy picked up the bowl. "I'm sure you are."

Flopping back, Zinkx snuggled into the furry side of the diabond, the warmth the beast radiated tickling his skin. It was eerily similar to the sensation of lava gliding over the surface of a battle-suit. Denvy shook his head at them. "A fire diabond, Zinkx? Really?"

"You'll thank me when the Twin Winters fall. You're simply jealous I'm not a child and don't cuddle you anymore." Zinkx threw his blanket over himself, closing his eyes as the deep breathing of the diabond lulled his racing heart.

Denvy snorted in amusement. "Zinkx. We'll need to pack camp tomorrow and head out of this region."

Zinkx managed to open a single eye to wearily follow the movements of his Khwaja as he shifted around the camp in his usual nocturnal routine.

"We haven't even begun to search for the Key in all the places we could," Zinkx said.

Denvy added a new log to the fire, causing the coals to spark embers into the darkness.

"We have stayed long enough."

"But, we haven't looked—"

"Zinkx, the Key is not in this region." Denvy shook his head. His weary gaze glanced around the Zaprex ruin they were camped in. "I can feel them, the songs within these ruins; they have long passed into slumber."

Zinkx rubbed at his eyes. "Then where do we go?"

"Shalamic," Denvy offered. "If my memory serves me well, Shalamic was once a shipyard. There will be something there. Stay hopeful."

Hopeful. The thought turned his mouth bitter. He was chasing legends, trusting in intangibility—hope seemed so slippery in his hands.

"And what of you, dear one? You're more than welcome to journey with us. Or, if you have a place to go, we'd be happy to help get you there."

Zinkx glanced up as his Khwaja addressed the Kelib

woman. He expected distrust, considering Denvy was offering their assistance when they were undeniably strangers in a
strange land. But it was confusion that furrowed her brow.

"Why would you aid me?" she murmured.

"It's Messenger code." Zinkx shrugged.

"What he means is that you need our aid, and Messengers
do not often have the luxury of thinking beyond tomorrow,
so we keep life simple: we do that which is directly before us,"
Denvy explained.

Shanty hesitated to speak, and even when she did, her
voice was a low whisper.

"My...sisters...were sold separately. I don't know where
they all went...but... I do know that our Eldest was bought
by a rich Spider-Road merchant. A good man, my Mor-Mor
said."

"Hm. A rich Spider-Road merchant. That's not much to
go on." Denvy tugged an ear. "Did your Mor-Mor say anything
else? Perhaps a name for this merchant?"

Shanty frowned. "It was many sol-cycles ago. I was very
young when our Eldest was sold, but I do recall his name being
rather strange." She looked over at Zinkx and the faintest hint
of a smile touched her lips. "Bkyri-kirk."

Denvy blinked in surprise. "Oh, well, I suppose that is a
little different."

"Why? What does it mean?" Zinkx asked.

"Ugly-child," Denvy translated. "With a name that
distinct, I am sure we'll find out something about him if we
ask around."

"You would do that?" Shanty clasped her hands tightly.

Denvy smiled. "Of course, my dear. Now, get some sleep,
you need to allow your mind to rest as well as your body to
heal."

Shanty's first deep sleep in many long months had been one of peace, safe in the warmth of the fire, burning throughout the crisp night. With the moss beneath her, she had sensed the gentle drum of the forest, the song of her ancestors mixed with another melody that seemed to echo with a metallic ring. Whenever she stirred from the pain growing in her wounds, she was aware of the forest-god's presence wandering the camp like a prowling guard. His green eyes would glint in the darkness and sleep would once more swell over her in a wave.

Shanty woke. She scented smoke from the low burning coals nearby. Zinkx was crouched beside her, his wavy, ebony hair pulled back from his face in a high ponytail. His hand quickly withdrew from her shoulder. Without the green bodypaint, his skin reminded her of clay, made rosy by crushed topaz. His lips were pink, his blue eyes flat, and his ears like cups coming out from his round skull. He was attempting to keep his distance while maintaining familiarity and kindness. He had been nothing but gentle with her—yet a small, lingering part of her, tugging at her chest, knew he was still a man. He did not look like her husbands, with all the odd Humanness twisting his features. Was that why the fear eased somewhat? Was he sensing the nervousness and moving with her?

"We've got to leave. Hurry." Zinkx's deep voice was hoarse with strained weariness. It made her wonder if he had slept as well as she had.

"The slavers?" Shanty worried as she crawled out from the covers.

Zinkx sent her a smile over his shoulder. "I almost wish it was…"

She frowned at his strange words and aided in packing the bedroll she had used. Zinkx scurried around, so quickly deconstructing the camp into packs on the back of the diabond that she wondered how often they had needed to leave in a rush.

She blurted out, "Where did the saddle come from?"

Zinkx finished strapping his hip-bags around his waist. "Khwaja Denvy dreamed it up last night."

Dreamed it up? Shanty looked towards the stairs as the old forest-god emerged from the lower levels, appearing far more worn than he had the night prior. The weariness had deepened the age lines across his brow and shadows hollowed out the pits of his eyes. Denvy held out a thick, woollen dress to her with a smile that melted her rising fear.

"A gift, dear one. So, you won't need to wear my old things. I know you Kelib ladies are very particular about your attire."

She took the offering. It was heavy, the fabric weighted around the ankles, like she would have designed it. The cloth was a deep red, with veins of black rimming the hems. "How…"

"Dreamed it up." Denvy shrugged.

Zinkx took it from her, stuffing it without much care into a bag on the diabond's back. "Khwaja is a Dreamathic. He can dream things into existence. Unfortunately, he can't dream us out of here."

Denvy sighed. "Yes, well—"

"Come on. We need to go," Zinkx cut him off.

Shanty gasped as she was lifted off her feet. Zinkx settled her into the diabond's new saddle, and climbed up in front of her. He looked back at Denvy.

"I'm sorry, sir. This is my fault."

Denvy gave Zinkx's thigh a solid pat. "Never mind it now, *aiv'a*. We've known it was only a matter of time before they would catch our scent." He urged them on with a wave. "Go, I'll be right behind you."

Shanty grappled for a grip on the saddle as the diabond burst forth. Leaves and sticks snapped and ripped against her face. She blinked back tears from the stinging pain. Amongst the blurred sea of emerald, Shanty caught glimpses of Denvy's golden fur. He kept pace with the diabond, moving like a wild animal being hunted. Only glints of sunshine streamed through the canopy, betraying any passing of time. They had been fleeing long enough for the Sun to find pathways through the thick undergrowth. Yet whatever was pursuing them was faster than they were. It seemed to move with the very shadows, making the darkness feel alive with a sickening breath she had never thought it had.

Zinkx suddenly pulled the reins. The diabond swerved. Shanty curled up, crying out as Zinkx ducked them under several tree roots.

Overhead, a pulsing, vomiting mass of shadows swelled. It shifted into a beam of sunlight and morphed into the corpse of a province guard, with the effect of being strung along on fibres. It swept back into the shade once more and the image of the decapitated Human dissolved, revealing a snarling beast of twisted-together dead flesh and bones.

The diabond backed slowly away. The monster curved open its head; a wide cavity of teeth and foaming acidic liquid emerged.

"Stay on the diabond," Zinkx commanded.

"Wait! No!" Shanty choked out.

It was happening again. His eyes, which she was sure were naturally the purest of blue, like fine gems, had turned a burning green, with a fire she could only compare to the boiling heat of the Sun. Shanty felt the release of his gravity from around her, causing her to sink solidly into the saddle. Zinkx was flying, drawing his twin blades that he had not touched the day prior in their escape.

An electric charge surrounded him, building in magnitude, until it frazzled her hair. He swung a bolt of lightning like a whip, and it lashed through the shadow.

Shanty covered her ears as a high-pitched screech of pain echoed through the forest. The monster entered the light again, reverting to the Human corpse. She wanted to retch in revulsion from the foul stench it released. The surrounding flora was already beginning to decompose.

It roared, centring enflamed red eyes upon Zinkx. He twirled his blades. They hummed with energy. It was almost too fast for Shanty to see—the moment the vile fiend struck Zinkx, sending him into a tree. She cried out at the eruption of lighting as he dropped to the ground with a heavy thud. The monster twisted towards her.

"No..."

Shanty cowered in the saddle of the diabond as it backed away, snarling, muscles coiling in anticipation. She clung on. Zinkx had praised her fists, the strength she had. But this creature was no slaver. It was emptiness and sorrow; even the cry it made seemed lonely. Its claws reached out for her longed-for touch. Her eyes refused to look away from the opening mouth. It was not going to eat her—was it?

Her world went slowly black.

It was going to take her back to a world of iron and walls, to pain and solitude. She would never see her Sisters again.

The diabond suddenly began to bark.

Shanty wrenched herself away. In the darkness, light flared. Flames erupted from the diabond's mouth as molten saliva dribbled out of the enraged beast beneath her. The monster reared back with a hiss. Shanty screamed. The blow that struck the monster down came fast and hard, with a swirl of water that drenched her and the diabond. An enormous blade crafted entirely of water, hewed the fiend apart in a single sweep. As it arced back through the wound it had created, it froze solid, and the monster shattered into pieces.

Denvy landed beside the diabond. The water that soaked them both drew back to the flowing sword he wielded. It was easily three times her height, and the liquid that formed it coiled around the forest-god in a snake-like motion. He flicked icy droplets aside as he approached her.

"Sorry, dear one." He tweaked her chin with a paw. "I had to deal with another before I got here. Zinkx! Stop lying about."

Shanty gasped as Zinkx landed on a nearby branch.

Denvy looked up, frowning at the young man.

"I'm not your Hunter," Zinkx snapped.

"Did I say anything?" Denvy touched his chest, affronted.

"You had a look. I'm used to fighting with a Squad, not on

my own." Zinkx leapt into the saddle. "There are four more on approach. Perhaps if we divide them up—"

"They know I'm here. They would never willingly take me on, one on one." Denvy massaged his temples with a claw. "Frankly, I'm surprised it took them this long to come after me. This is what I get for leaving the House…"

Shanty could feel the tension building in Zinkx's grip on the diabond's saddle. He was trembling. She could not bring herself to reach out and soothe a hand over his back to offer any ease.

The forest-god finally shifted, bringing his weapon to rest in front of him. "You will keep running and continue your mission. I will get the Twizels[3] off your back. If I manage to come out on top, I will meet you in two weeks at Hulbrath."

"Khwaja. I cannot let you fight four Twizels alone. You know that is not how it is done." Zinkx fingered the reins of the diabond as it began to grow restless.

"Have some faith in your old man."

"Khwaja, please…don't send me away…" Zinkx whispered.

"Zinkx. Go," Denvy urged.

Zinkx turned the diabond and flicked the reins. Shanty looked back. They were already too far to see Denvy, but the screeching of the foul monsters rose through the forest. She cringed against Zinkx's back. His breathing had grown erratic and uncontrolled. Shanty pressed her forehead against the heat emanating from his back. The kindly forest-god had been ripped out of her life so quickly—

Her head snapped back around.

An image, like inky paw prints making smear marks over her eyelids, played over her mind, imprinting into her thoughts.

The words formed one by one.

Look after him, please.

The touch was gone, leaving her devoid of all emotion and a splitting pain in her skull. Her arms tightened around

---

3   *The Dragon's minions – they must take a host body to exist within the Primary Realm.*

the Human man she held, but she tempered her grip, for the weight of the task that had been bestowed upon her would require a tender touch.

"I will. I promise," she whispered.

CHAPTER FOUR

Oh je-oh, je-oh, je-oh, do I want to go, go, go, to the city
on the hill, hill, hill.
There it crowns, atop the mound, like a rounded coin,
It shines so bright!
A Sun in the day! A star in the night!
Oh je-oh, je-oh, je-ooooh, do I want to go, go, go to the city
on the hill, hill, hill.
Jewels in the sky, the towers to spear, so high, so far.
Swimming in green, it is a pool of gold, drawing you in,
until you are unseen.
Oh, je-oh, je-oh, je-oh, take me to the city on the hill, hill,
hill.

Spider-Road Travelling Tune often sun by Human
children in a rhythm of stamping feet and clapping hands

Land: Pennadot
City: Palace-Town

Skyeola's bag, mostly containing an assortment of books,
bounced along behind him as he ran down the long corridor
towards the wide-open doors leading to the Palace Gardens.
A warm morning breeze tantalised him, carrying the scents of
the Summer flowers in full bloom. Sunlight glistened through
the glass ceiling, creating dancing waves of sparkling colours as
precious gems reflected glints of the glorified light. He twirled
on his foot-claws, caught up in the exuberance that made his
thin chest swell until it was tight against his clothes. As much
as he adored the Palace, the only home he had ever known,
with its never-ending corridors of light and colours, its lush

gardens of great evergreens and countless galaxies of flowers, knowing he was leaving was the greatest thrill of his young life. Finally, he was to adventure beyond the walls that had sheltered him, to see more than the hazy view from the High Tower of the Palace.

He burst out of the open doors, catching the fluttering of the grand wall hanging draped down from high above, bearing the emblem of the royal ten-armed Sun. With a whoop he stretched out his wings and bounced around, embracing the full shine of the glorious, clear blue sky-sea. It was going to be wonderful day. Grabbing his bag, he jumped onto a low wall, balancing playfully to make his way through the snaking rows of flower beds. Every so often he caught glimpses of Palace-Town below. The Palace was already up high, frequently lost amongst the clouds, but, even so, the spires of Palace-Town itself were nearly as tall and wrapped in gold and silver. The great city, the heart of Pennadot, sat like a jewel in a sea of green known as the Plains of Rannamon. Three rings forged Palace-Town, four if the Palace was counted as a ring, but it never was referred to as such on the plans he had uncovered. A network of silvery spiderweb-spiralling aqueducts carried water throughout the interlinking rings, waterfalling into reservoirs.

He loved how everything in Palace-Town, even the Palace itself, reflected the glory of the Sun. The architecture was rounded, everything sparkled, and light seemed to emanate from every corner so that even shadows never seemed entirely dark.

Pennadotian Summer was a season of polar temperatures, though. The days would grow hot from the Sun's glare, but the heat would then escape into the cloudless night sky-sea, turning the land frozen. Rain seldom fell in Summer; if it did, it was likely in the South somewhere. Instead, the mighty Cor River, the river-system of Pennadot, called the Silver Snake by the Kelibs, kept the land alive throughout the long, long dry spell.

He clutched at his small jewel pouch. He hoped he was

taking enough for offerings along their journey. This was to be his first Summer away from the Palace—what if he had all the customs wrong? What if his books were old and outdated?

His father, Lord Steward Zilon Mazaki, had always been so starchy about his education when it had come to the world outside. Skyeola sucked in a deep breath, his forked tongue hissing as he released it. All his begging over the sol-cycles had paid off. His father had promised that on his two and tenth sol-cycle he would be permitted to journey from his home when the Court of the Emerald Throne recessed.

So, this was it. That promise was today. His father had to fulfil it.

He puffed out his chest once more and swept past several guards stationed by the marble columns that ringed a courtyard.

"Oh, *tah*, it's li'l Lord Sky'ola." The guard's accent was twangy, the heavily abbreviated slang distinctively different to the speech of the nobles he had lived amongst all his life. Skyeola's furred ears twitched at the loose words. Silently, he translated them.

He spun about on his foot-claws. "Morning! Sun's Blessings."

"Yeh fine'ly be off on a li'l 'venture, lad?"

"That I am. I will see you come the Fall of the Leaves." Skyeola gave a delighted laugh as he rushed across the smooth stones. He ducked and weaved between several servants, keeping his back muscles strained to tuck his wings away. Then, with a bounce, he popped out beside the royal entourage. Despite the significant age difference between himself and those in the small gathering, they were the closest people he had to friends. They never treated him differently for being a Batitic. They encouraged him to continue his studies and praised him for his input on problems and daily palace life. Though he doubted the comparison would have been a welcome one, deep inside he considered them something like siblings.

But it was just one—one in particular—to whom he had always felt the tightest of connections, even though the young

Human man was regarded as the highest of royals in the decaying civilisation. He could never explain it, but something akin to a little silver thread seemed to be braided between them to always tug him back to the side of the glistening, dazzling, Sun-filled man.

He heard his name called out by the familiar, rich voice and his fur puffed out in happiness. "Finally, Skyeola, I thought you might have gotten crushed under a pile of books again."

Skyeola yanked hard on his book bag. His foot-claws caught in a crack in the stonework and he tripped, landing face first. Laughter sounded as someone rushed to his side. He was picked up like a feather. He was not noticeably big—he should have weighed more, but food never did taste right in his mouth somehow.

"Your highness!" Skyeola blinked through the strands of his now frizzled black hair. Small silver beads strung throughout the braids tinkled. "Um. Sorry. Sorry." He covered his sore, moist nose as he was set back on his foot-claws and gently brushed off.

"Every time I see you, Skyeola, you end up flat on your face or under some books. You really do have to be more careful. Here, let me take…is this…full of more books? Did you pack any clothes?"

Skyeola grinned sheepishly. "I will just wear yours."

"Did you hear what the little sprite said, Maiden Citla? He said he will wear my clothes. Please tell me you thought ahead and packed something for him."

"I believe Butler Malik has it organised, Your Highness."

"Thank the Sun."

Skyeola's back was being continuously brushed as he was fussed over by the exceedingly tall young man. The prince was a Kimwyn—a cousin to the Wynnila breed of Humans—in that they were technically Wynnila but for the lack of pigmentation in both their skin and hair, leaving them sheer white in the Pennadotian Sun. Kimwyns were also generally taller than any Wynnila Skyeola had ever seen in the Palace. But it was not his breed that set the prince apart from other Humans. A Kimwyn, after all, was simply another face amongst a people of many faces.

No—what caused the prince to turn heads was the way his skin refracted like diamonds in any light, casting a shimmering halo around his body. Even his long, pale hair, woven down his back, glistened with stardust.

Skyeola smiled wistfully.

The prince was a Starborn.

The only Starborn.

Though, for all the beauty of the young royal encapsulating the very essence of the Sun, it was his eyes that Skyeola adored. Like sharp, bright green pools of grass, they were unique only to Starborn Humans according to all readings he had done on the subject. The prince's starblood lay dormant, his eyes, as beautiful as they were, did not burn with an inner flame. Someday, Skyeola felt certain, someday they would.

He had only ever known the prince by that title—Prince.

It was a manner of address that created the illusion of distance between them, that stretched the braid of silver connecting them. Often, he wondered if even his father knew the prince's name. Surely, as Steward and head of state affairs, his father would be required to know something as important as the true name of their Sovereign?

But, behind the green eyes that looked down upon him, and the well-practised smile, Skyeola saw through the mask crafted from sol-cycles of careful layering. The cracks were easy to see once one knew where to look. The prince did not seem to know himself, and he was drowning in a sea of wretched loneliness.

Was he the only one who saw it, the way the prince's smile screamed at the world for someone to save him?

The prince gave Skyeola's cheek a fond rub. "I see. Butler Malik has dared enter the lair that is your chamber. A brave man, Butler Malik."

It was not so much a case of bravery, but that Butler Malik

could get past the protective runes he had carved into the walls late one night, in a fit of manic paranoia against prying palace maids and—his father. He was quite certain there was no place in the whole palace where Butler Malik could not find him and carry him back to the Harem for a bath and a meal if he forgot either for several days.

He frowned. Now that he thought about it, it seemed rather peculiar that Butler Malik would allow them to go. The protection of the prince fell to Butler Malik, and beyond the domain of Palace-Town the Butler's arm could not reach. Neither could the Butler leave Palace-Town—not even to protect the Prince. Would they even be safe without him?

Skyeola rubbed his arms.

"Um…Your Highness…are you sure this is…are you sure we are permitted to go?"

"I am the Prince of Pennadot, Skyeola, not the Prince of Palace-Town. I would like to see some of my kingdom."

Skyeola rolled his eyes.

The non-answer was an answer in and of itself. The prince was forcefully using his authority to step beyond the boundaries of his protection. Skyeola twisted his claws together. To be included in the escapade was exciting, and comforting. They were not going to leave him behind—

A firm hand settled on his shoulder and he momentarily tensed his wings before his tongue scented rich perfume on the air. Skyeola looked up into the painted face of Butler Malik. Short white Kimwyn hair framed sharp features that were toned with the mineral makeup the Harem Family wore, like masks hiding away their identities, so they merged into a uniformed unit. Butler Malik's mask always reminded him of the peacocks that roamed the gardens. He often wondered why a man so quick on his feet had chosen such a slow, useless bird as his emblem.

"What are you wearing, Lord Skyeola?"

"Clothing." Skyeola looked down at himself and his hastily dressed state.

"You did not see what I put out for you this morning?"

"It looked uncomfortable."

"Thus you decided to wear exactly what you've been wearing for the past three days?"

"It is just going to get more dirty."

Butler Malik pinched the bridge of his nose. "Northern Moon, give me Strength." He handed a bag to Maiden Citla and Skyeola pouted at the contents, knowing that a seamstress had worked overtime to make him several new outfits. He was again fussed over, this time with more deliberate effort as his hair was combed and braided. Butler Malik always seemed to have everything he ever needed in his large coat pockets.

A small ball of warmth collected in his chest as it always did whenever he was nestled between the adults, and, though they spoke over him, and around him, he was at least being noticed as his hair was tugged back and forth into some fashionable form.

"Your Highness, I once more want to express my grave displeasure about this trip."

"You have made it very clear how you feel, but it is worth the risk."

"Your life is not worth any risk. I cannot protect you beyond the borders of Palace-Town."

The prince sighed. "I know. Which is precisely the reason why we must go. If Lord Galvon's missive about having uncovered a Zaprex relic is true, it could change the dynamics of the Court. Malik, I want to ease your burden."

"It is not your burden to ease, Your Highness."

"It is. I will never be taken seriously in this court if I cannot gain the respect of the province lords and ladies."

"Lord Galvon is not a man to be trusted," Butler Malik insisted.

Another voice spoke. "I do concur with the Butler in his assessment of Lord Galvon."

Skyeola shrank back against Butler Malik, attempting to become invisible, at the sound of this voice. To anyone else the comment might seem warm and kindly, with a hint of jovial jesting to the hissing accent, but for Skyeola the tone was jarring, and it twisted into his gut with all the fierceness of a dagger.

"Lord Mazaki," the prince addressed the approaching Steward. The majestic Batitic loomed even taller than the prince. It was difficult not to fear the elegant creature, a fear Skyeola could only drive inward until it ate at him with self-loathing, knowing he was a near mirror of his father in appearance. Though his father insisted he looked every bit like his mother, he could not comprehend where the elder Batitic saw such a reflection.

Zilon's robe of cascading red, deep purple, and ebony pooled around his foot-claws, creating an illusion that he glided. His massive wings acted as part of the attire, draping along behind him like a regal train. The scent he carried was one of conduction, a sickly sweet power of a sorcerer steeped in rotting blood. Skyeola shuffled under the controlling gaze that settled upon him, and, once more, his robe tightened as his chest expanded in little, frantic breaths. He clenched his wings tight, forcing himself to control his panic lest his father see it.

It was impossible to escape it—that he was of the Mazaki blood-clan—blood-kin to such an incredible conductor. He could not even compare, not with his meagre attempts to prove his worth.

Red eyes, with red irises to match, stared into his own. Zilon smiled winsomely, revealing fangs. His father was masterful at setting those around him at ease, and watching him work always left Skyeola's fur feeling oily and grimy.

"Your Highness, this little escapade of yours is a dangerous idea."

"I think the sky is falling; you are agreeing with Butler Malik." The prince sighed.

"Your protection is paramount to Pennadot." Butler Malik's fierce pink eyes focused on Zilon.

"I feel confident in Lord Telvon and Maiden Citla's

abilities." The prince gestured behind him to the waiting horses. "And I would greatly appreciate it if we could leave. I made
a bet with Lord Telvon about how long it would take to make
our way through Palace-Town."

Zilon inclined his head as he strode forward. "Of course,
Your Highness. But if I could have a moment with my kitten—"

The forcefield formed instantly, with Zilon striking it as
it rose from several hexagons that flashed to life across the
garden path beneath them. It had the wavery appearance of
shimmering water; sometimes, Skyeola had seen it form icicles.
The prince always looked shocked when it appeared, as if he
forgot every time that it existed, before his expression shifted to
frustration and then his mask slipped back into place and that
tight smile returned.

It was a forcefield reserved only for the prince, but if one
stood close enough to him, to his warmth and the glow, they
could be included. Skyeola stared down at the hexagon pattern
beneath his foot-claws. It was so beautiful. If only it was always
there—

His father was speaking, affronted and annoyed—a fake
voice...or maybe not—

"Your Highness, this continued notion that I am a threat
grows wearisome."

"Wonderful, then perhaps upon my return we can discuss
my coronation to the Emerald Throne," the prince retorted
testily.

"Indeed, Your Highness. Perhaps we can." Zilon ignored
the red warnings blinking across the shield. Skyeola froze as a
claw reached for him, passing through the forcefield unheed-
ed, though the hexagon flakes crafting the illusion of water
crackled red in protest. His father's skin hissed. Skyeola scented
burning flesh on his forked tongue.

He was urged away from the radiance of the Sun that was
the prince, away from Butler Malik's protection, and into the
cloud of oppressive, smothering smoke that was his father.

Just as Butler Malik was the only one who could bypass

the protective runes he hacked into his chambers walls, so was Skyeola the only one who could be dragged out through Butler Malik's protective shield—and the knowledge stung him. Why him? Why was he left, abandoned, on the other side?

He had to bite the inside of his mouth fiercely to keep back the heat of tears as his father knelt, clicking his forked tongue as he straightened his robe. "My treasure, were you not going to say goodbye? I expected a visit this morning."

He forced the words out. "I apologise, Papa. I was very excited."

"Yes. So I can see by your dishevelled appearance. I expect you not to appear like this again."

"I will not, Papa."

His father's strong claws took his cheeks, holding him in place.

"Be safe, my kitten. You are my last earthly treasure. It is not lightly that I am allowing you to leave my side."

"Do not worry, Papa."

"I do worry. You are still far too young—"

"Papa! You promised!" Skyeola fought back tears. He was so close to being free—even for just a Summer.

"Yes. I know. I know." Zilon sighed. "Goodness. You do look like your mother when you get upset."

It was not possible for sadness to linger in his father's eyes, but sometimes he thought he saw wisps of it remaining.

Zilon stood and stepped back several paces. The forcefield surrounding the prince faded and Skyeola hesitantly turned and stepped towards the warmth.

"Be safe," his father called out, and Skyeola winced.

The prince offered a hand to him. "Come on, let us leave this golden birdcage, you and me; together, we shall get some freedom for a while."

Skyeola nodded. He tried to sound happy as he forced more words from his ashy mouth. "Are we taking the sky-carts?"

The prince laughed. "Ah, that is my bet with Jarid. I have declared we shall not take the sky-carts and, therefore, I think we shall take longer to get out of Palace-Town than the allotted three days."

"Oh, Jarid must be thrilled about that." Skyeola managed a weak laugh. Lord Jarid Telvon was a constant grouch, never much fun to be around at all with his stark, judging glare.

"Thrilled, indeed." The prince smirked down at him. "So, are you ready to see the outside world?"

"I am." Skyeola allowed the prince to lead him away. He dared not look back. He could feel them, the scorching eyes of his father, watching him. He had never actually seen the expression that he imagined on his father's face when he experienced the painful glare that made his fur crawl, but, somehow, deep within the recesses of his psyche, the image of an enraged monster floated like a memory from infancy.

Could the texture of a name feel wrong to a person, like the silken sheets he lay upon? He knew the bedding was not his own, just like the name that was supposed to be his did not feel like it belonged to him. Rarely had he spoken his name aloud, for the very taste of it on his tongue was bitter, like evoking a death curse. It echoed in the cavern of his mind, one single, haunting word. No one addressed him by it; he was left to carry the burden of knowing it alone. To those around him he was simply a prince, he had no identity outside of his position. It was almost as if he never would. They were disappointed in him, it seemed—as if he had done something terrible that he had no memory of. Each morning he woke to the same sensation, a pit in his stomach and a hollowness that made him ill. He was missing a piece of himself, but he had no idea where to even begin looking for that lost fragment.

A warm tear rolled its way down his cheek. His hand rose from the loose Summer bedding to brush it aside in a daily ritual. Gradually his eyes opened as sleep fell away. He was welcomed into a Sun-kissed chamber, filled with dazzling, reflective crystals beaded up high in the lofty, domed ceiling. He rolled, pulling the sheets as he stretched in the wide bed.

The open window overlooked the Second Ring of Palace-Town. Warm morning air drifted into the room situated in one of the sky-cart ports. Jarid's nagging wish to take the sky-carts would now be fulfilled after all, since travelling through the lower levels had been deemed too unsafe. Skyeola's disappointment had been very clearly visible, and he was sure his feelings were equally apparent. Experiencing the grungy city life of Palace-Town had been something they had both hoped for. Palace-Town was a city of circle upon circle; even the aqueducts that carried water throughout the interlinking streets ran loops around each other in beautiful patterns that could only be appreciated from a height. The ancient architects had built the city with some purpose beyond his comprehension. It made navigating her inner workings a challenge, so he could respect the concern for their safety amongst the mayhem.

Travelling by sky-cart was a luxury for the high-born and those who could afford it. It halved travel time within such an enormous, chaotic city. He held out a hand towards the sheathing skyline of golden towers that reflected the morning sunlight into the room, through the hanging crystals and jewels across the ceiling, and onto his face. The blue horizon and the haze of the Ovin-tu Mountains was such a vast distance from them.

His eyes focused on the glitter of his skin. According to those around him, it was a curse that every royal had been born with, haunted by the myth that their bloodline was descended from the heavenly stars who partook of earthly pleasures. He snorted in amusement. Somehow the truth—whatever it was—had to be something far more farfetched if that was the legend.

Even so, the shine set him apart. It made him unique.

The word 'unique' made him want to vomit.

His name, his uniqueness, was supposed to represent his

Sovereignty over Pennadot. But the power granted to him by the Sun in centuries past was but a fickle fable now. He had become naught but an idol to be looked upon, whispered about, and thought of as beautiful.

He may as well have been a statue.

"Blessed Sunrise, Your Highness." He listened to the soft footsteps as his Maiden padded her way across the room, loud enough to make herself heard. Usually, she was too quiet to penetrate his awareness as she drifted about like a cloud. Citla had been a constant in his life; as far back as his blurry haze of memories reached, Citla's presence had never left his side.

The Maiden was already flitting about, gathering his attire for the day. Her thin lips tried to smile in greeting but the simple expression had never come easily to her. She had yet to powder her face in white, in the tradition of the Harem Family, and it was rare to see her without the thick layers of caked-on mineral makeup and black-coated lips.

The prince hooked a knee under his chin.

In a manner, their Summer vacation was also one for his Maiden as well. The prying eyes of the Palace that always followed her were surely a burden. As petite and slender as Citla was, almost doll-like if she did not don her walls of black armour and flowery dresses of grey, he was well aware that if he desired someone dead, he need only ask her.

She would kill anyone for him.

More than likely she already had.

He looked away, sighing.

"Such forlorn thoughts on such a beautiful morning— what ails you?" Her hand brushed back strands of his hair, long black nails massaging his scalp. The prince threw back the bed covers, slipping out to accept the garments she offered.

"An invisible prison."

Even his clothing was a prison. He could not escape it before crossing out of Palace-Town; until then he was a doll to be dressed up and admired. The corsets burned his back and crushed his chest. After all these sol-cycles, he thought he would be used to the heavy garments, but still his body ached. He could not wait to be far enough away to be rid of the loathsome costumes.

Citla pulled a white shirt over his head, rolling its tight, lacy sleeves down his arms to end as gloves over his fingers. Each tiny pearl had to be buttoned, but her hands were deft and practiced. As she finished with the travel attire, twisting his mass of hair tightly into a bun that she fixed in place with several golden clips, her hands fell to his shoulders.

"Perhaps, Your Highness, you should see your position not as a prison, but as your heritage."

He looked out the window, across Palace-Town and the dull, bustling noise of the lower levels. "Heritage of what...?" he muttered.

Citla left his side. Her shadow stretched across the chamber as she walked past the length of the large window. The prince tracked her footsteps. They passed through a scattering of tiny paper cranes and origami stars, amongst loose books and scrolls, to reach the endearing sight of Skyeola curled up in his little nest of blankets.

His thick wings encased most of his body like a cocoon. Juvenile feathers were fluffed up around his neck, hiding his head away in a protective little bundle. The prince knelt and reached out to stroke the soft down.

"Perhaps we should stop hiring him a room if he keeps nesting in here with us."

"That is entirely up to you, Your Highness." Citla picked up Skyeola's discarded clothes, giving them a sniff. She clicked her tongue in mild disgust, deciding against them and tucking them away.

Something moved under the sheets. The prince's hand shifted to his concealed blade, pausing only as glinting, colourful feathers, like those of Lord Zilon Mazaki, snaked out to reveal a fluttering tail.

"Citla..." The prince looked at her. "Since when has Skyeola had a tail?"

She pulled out a clean outfit from Skyeola's chaotic travel bag.

"I believe he has been hiding it from his father. It is a sign of young Batitics maturing to choose their pathway in the family bloodline. If Skyeola has a tail, then he must have chosen the male pathway."

The prince rubbed his chin. "He could choose? I did not know this about Batitics."

She approached and knelt beside him. "I do not know much of it. Just what Brother Malik has told us in passing. It has a lot to do with the inheritance of their ancestral memories and, therefore, the direction of their skills as conductors. It has been my concern for some time that Zilon has been grooming Skyeola in the direction of his late mother."

There were times when his Maiden expressed pure vitriol in her voice, a hatred of people the prince had no recollection of even knowing, such as Skyeola's mother.

"It would seem Skyeola was a step ahead of your worries."

Citla shook her head. "Which makes me only more worried." She reached out and gently began to shake a thin shoulder. The tail curled away under the bedsheets and a wing gradually unrolled as Skyeola unfurled limb by limb.

Citla set out Skyeola's clothes and stood. "I will leave him to you. Please get him up."

The prince rested both elbows on his thighs, and chin on his hands. "Ruthless of you."

"As I am aware," she quipped back over her shoulder.

Skyeola had rolled over completely and curled up again. The prince shook his head. It had been like this every morning; trying to get Skyeola out of bed had become a chore. Reaching between the Batitic's thick wings, the prince lifted Skyeola clean off the bed. "Come on, time to greet the Sun."

"I don' wanna."

"Speak properly." The prince carried the bundle towards the window and settled him down on wobbly foot-claws, turning him to face the warm glow.

"Open your eyes." The prince scrubbed his fingers through Skyeola's tousled mop of hair. "Face the Sun. Time to wake up."

Skyeola yawned and rubbed at his face. The prince gently braided the long hair away from his large, faintly illumed, red eyes.

"You have missed your morning prayers to the Twilight twice now." The prince chided.

"I do not care about my father's religion," Skyeola whined and dropped his head back.

"I understand, but you still need to wear your mask. We cannot ever allow ourselves to get sloppy. You can be yourself around me, and around Citla—perhaps a little around Jarid and Hun—but you must continue to keep up appearances on the outside. Your father has eyes and ears throughout the kingdom."

Skyeola's long ears folded down. "So, I will never be free?"

"In a manner of speaking, freedom is an illusion."

Skyeola's shoulders slumped, causing his wings to slacken. "I apologise."

The Prince shook his head.

"You do not need to apologise. I understand your desire to shake off the identity your father is crafting for you." He laughed weakly. "I, myself, do not even like my own name."

Skyeola's ears perked up suddenly. His forked tongue rolled as he whispered, "Why do you not like it?"

The prince frowned. "It does not feel like it belongs to me. It feels like it belongs to someone else entirely."

"What…what is it?"

Skyeola's large red eyes looked up at him with such hopeful wonder that the prince could not resist the word that slipped out of his mouth, no matter how bitter it tasted. "*Deiniol.*"

Skyeola's neck feathers fluffed. He seemed to lift onto his foot-claws as though he was trying to float away. He whispered the name several times. "Deiniol. Deiniol. It is like stardust!"

The prince shook his head. "It belongs to someone else."

Skyeola moved to the window, seating himself on a pillow at the ledge. He playfully kicked his foot-claws back and forth as he watched a number of sky-carts leave the harbour. "Perhaps because it is in Ancient Pennadotian."

"Well, I am the Prince of Pennadot."

Skyeola laughed. "Yes. True. But." He held up a single claw. "From what I've read, the reason a Sovereign was given two names was so they could fracture their identity." He held up another claw.

"You can be both the Sovereign of Pennadot, the King of the People, and, also, just a man behind the mask."

"So, you mean...ordinary...?"

"As ordinary as someone who glitters can be."

The prince snatched up a glass of water and flicked some at the kitten.

Skyeola yelped, erupting into laughter as he hid behind a wing.

"Mercy, mercy!" Skyeola poked his head out tentatively.

The prince came to sit beside him on the window ledge. "It echoes in my head, reminding me that I cannot remember who I am. I feel empty whenever I recall the name."

Skyeola touched his chin thoughtfully. "How about 'Daniel', then?"

The prince looked up.

"Daniel?" He raised a hand to his lips in surprise.

How strange.

Why did it seem as though he had heard the sound before?

It almost—it almost seemed like he could hear someone— if he tilted his head slightly—

No—

It was gone.

Skyeola smiled up at him. "It's the direct translation of your Ancient Pennadotian name into Common Basic. You wanted something ordinary."

"I suppose I did." He ruffled Skyeola's hair fondly. "I like it. From now on, you can call me Daniel."

"Really?" Skyeola leapt up and jumped around. "I can call you by a name!"

The prince tilted back. He had not expected such a force of energetic glee. "Yes, of course—"

"I am so excited!"

Citla caught Skyeola before he had the chance to bounce onto the nearby bed. "As excited as you are, Skyeola, please get dressed and pack your books. The servants will be coming to take our gear to the sky-carts while we break our fast." Citla quickly bundled Skyeola's braids into a neat bun. Skyeola wriggled, full of energy until the Maiden released him and he bounced away to his small nest. The prince approached, watching in amusement as the kitten threw on a new robe. There was no indication of his tail anywhere.

It was impressive the lad was managing to hide the flamboyant display of feathers.

"I hate to imagine the usual state of his abode, if he was able to make that mess in a day," the prince commented.

Citla winced. "The maids tell horror stories of rats."

"Rats? I had heard it was untidy but, really...rats?"

"Yes. Rats. Apparently, he calls them his pets." She exaggerated a shiver.

The prince covered his mouth, holding back a laugh.

"It is not funny."

"No, it is very, very funny."

"Zilon should be ashamed."

"I can request to have him moved closer to our quarters if it would make you happy?"

"Zilon would never permit it."

"Hm." The prince sighed. "True."

She shook her head. "This Summer will be good for him, getting him away from that man."

The prince leant on a wall, folding his arms. His Maiden's pure, blackened hatred for the Steward of the Emerald Throne was something he had never managed to find an answer to, though perhaps it had something to do with the Uprising of the Province Lords ten sol-cycles prior. Without proof of the Steward's involvement, he could do little to move against the man, nor would he. Lord Zilon Mazaki had been the right-hand man of his Father—at least, that was what he had been told.

Despite the white, powdery makeup that Citla was now covering herself with, thickening her lips and blackening her eyes with charcoal, the prince noted the subtle shift in his Maiden's demeanour. It had gone from simmering hatred to peaceful watching of Skyeola's frantic rushing.

"What is troubling you, Maiden?" He almost reached for her hand, pausing before he breached the space between them.

Citla's black lips curled with the faintest smile as Skyeola scrambled around, stuffing his loose books into his bag.

"Nothing. Nothing is wrong, Your Highness. Sometimes he just reminds me of…" She shook her head. "Never mind."

He sighed. "Keep your secrets. It is not like I am going anywhere."

Citla frowned. "Your Highness—"

Skyeola suddenly poked his head over the top of the futon. "Have you seen my favourite pen? We absolutely cannot leave without it!"

"And then he reminds you that he is still very much a kitten…" Citla muttered.

Daniel laughed.

CHAPTER FIVE

The light of the Sun shines upon all;
In the morning, it is young,
In the betwixt, it is youth,
In the evening, it is old.
So, you see,
Under the Sun,
We are all one.

Sun-Saint Harilo Quin of the Summer Monastery

Borukoshu listened to the harmonic drizzle of the acidic rain as it pattered gently on the forcefield of the roof. The smog storm had gusted away overnight, but day-rise had yet to creep over the industrial under-levels of the Sunken Cities. Borukoshu played its fingers over the clear, cold exterior of a slim crystal prism.

It shimmered with colour spectra, revealing the imprinted song within the sliver of technology. The data it held was old, the technology to read the information even older still.

It noted its reflection in the smooth surface. It was not a Kimwyn Human who stared back at it. Sometimes it was caught unaware, drifting between runs it had lived.

It was a Zaprex again, merely a dying one, hollow and worn by the grip of time. Its thin chest deflated with a heavy intake of breath and it sank back into its chair, the anti-gravity of the furniture catching its weight. The prism slid into its lap and it indented its robe as though it weighed far more than its tiny size permitted.

Borukoshu closed its eyes, tracing random, tangential thoughts and pathways that sparked with decay in its cybernetic networks, yet it was drawn back to its reflection. A jab of electric pain jolted it as the recollection of a younger face emerged from the recesses of its memory banks. Its first cycle. Its first life.

Xavier Osiris.

So many runs it had been through, again and again, cycle after cycle, after its data had been scattered across Livila. No matter who, or what, it had lived as, something of its basic programming had always remained, staying true to the original Zaprex it had been created as.

Osiris. Pharaoh. Destroyer of Worlds.

And here it was again, a Zaprex once more, watching the fall of the civilization it had once ruled. Would the hatchling it was raising be the seed of another civilization, or the end of all life upon Livila?

There was only so much it could teach Semyueru. Even when the hatchling hibernated, feeding it songs to store in its memory banks for later reference seemed superficial when it knew that nothing could prepare the Fusion for the world beyond the Great Shields.

"Nothing ever goes as you plan it…"

Borukoshu muttered at the image in its mind. When last it had seen Hazanin in this life, its ancient bonding partner had been escaping the cities into the World Above. It was not the memory it wanted to recall, those frantic, terror filled moments when neither of them thought they would survive the wrath of the Assembly.

The Hazanin it preferred to remember lazed at a bar with a cigarette in one hand and an oil drink in the other, uncaring of the bodily damage either did. They had both been on pathways of self-deletion back then; Borukoshu's had been perhaps a little more immediate when it had jumped off the highest point in Cal'pash'coo.

If Hazanin had not been there that day—

Borukoshu smiled wearily.

That had been the Hazanin of Borukoshu. The one who saved.

When had it stopped being Borukoshu? When had all the lost, fragmented pieces of Osiris finally recollected within it to reform the program it had once been?

It flicked its gaze towards Semyueru's hibernation chamber. Ten sol-cycles. The death of the last of Osiris' scattered data packages, and the day Semyueru had hatched.

"And the day I felt your connection start to fade..." Borukoshu shifted its attention to the prism once more. It was barely bigger than the palm of its hand. Semyueru would need to find three more like it, and the device that allowed it to be read. It was an enormous task for the hatchling. Perhaps they were asking too much of it.

"It will not be doing it alone, Biri."

The voice tickled its ears, or an illusion of a voice. It closed its eyes, focusing on the sound through its receptors. Oily tears dared linger on its lashes, forcing it to wipe them aside.

"I will not be with it, so it will be alone, Hazanin...as alone as I am without you."

"Come now, do you genuinely believe I would forsake you or our offspring? You know me better than that."

"It will be the last of us, so, it will be alone."

"Where there is one, there is always another."

Borukoshu dared to open its eyes. Its vision blurred through its spectacles and it removed the holographic lenses. They would not be able to register the existence of the being that was currently sitting perched upon the edge of Semyueru's bed. Energy of the Secondary Realm pooled around the Zaprex in a filter, distorting the very fabric that shaped the Primary Realm. Borukoshu surged out of its seat in a fluid movement.

"Hazanin, get away from Semyueru."

Deep pain was evident in its luminous eyes.

"Just a bit longer; it is so precious—"

"You're distorting the Realms. Hazanin, your Program

is frozen. Don't force anything that may damage other components."

A sad smile was cast its way. "Forever the worrier."

There had always been something sadistic in the atmosphere around Hazanin, judgemental and brutal, constantly calculating with an aloof omnipotent view. Slowly, angular features shifted, and the wry smirk softened. The fierce red of its tainted pupils dimmed, and it floated away from the bedside of their hatchling. The robe draped around its slender frame was a pool of space, an illusion of fabric that swirled with galaxies, stars, and worlds. Liquid-like, it flowed over the floor to waver away into the air, momentarily forming pockets of stars. Slowly-turning metal cogs were fitted into the luscious material, creating belts, sleeves, and collar, as if trying to create some form to the inky concoction.

"Why are you here, Hazanin?" Borukoshu whispered.

Red eyes flickered with amusement beneath square-rimmed holo-spectacles.

"Nostalgia."

Borukoshu huffed. It walked, wincing at the pain the action caused, towards a bench. Reaching for a jug of glucose milk, it poured itself a mugful.

"I've known the day of my death from that moment I locked eyes with you on that bridge." It gripped the mug with crippled, arthritic fingers.

"Time had other purposes for you than you deleting yourself that day." Hazanin drifted up beside Borukoshu, coming to sit comfortably on the bench. "Do you wish you'd not met me, this run through?"

That was a ridiculous notion to even consider, the thought of never knowing its cycle companion. Its neural processing grew uncomfortably quiet.

"No," it levelled Hazanin with a glare. "No. I would have lived this run a thousand times over to see the product of our Bonding again, to see Semyueru alive and not in pain. Seeing my death gave me time to prepare for this day…" Borukoshu frowned in discomfort. It touched its forehead as pain flared between its eyes, causing a distortion to blur its optical lenses.

"*Anata wa hontōdesuka*, Hazanin?[4]" it asked. "Or are you only a memory from one of my runs that keeps sparking against my processor core?" It trailed off the words and stared upward, wistfully, through the windows of the ceiling to the glittering heights of the city's towers.

Hazanin reached out and gently wrapped a hand around its own, solid, firm and just as smooth as ever. "I am whatever you wish me to be, Biri. *Watashi wa anata no taiyōdesu. Eien ni.*[5]" Hands grasped its cheeks. The swirling galaxies encapsulated it in threads.

Borukoshu stiffened as Hazanin bent forward and pressed their foreheads together. The spark that had once flickered strongly within its Matrix Crystal flared, and it flinched at the sensation of invigorating energy spreading down its spine and through its thickened philepcon liquid to loosen its limbs. It released a sigh. It had always been so with Hazanin, one touch was enough to cause a release of its negative energy. For the first time in decades new philepcon liquid filled its systems. The pain in its rusted joints eased away as moisture glided over dried circuits, replenishing what was arid.

"So, tell me, was that real?" Hazanin whispered into its ear.

Its pocketed hand-device buzzed.

Borukoshu jerked around, staring in fright at the holographic screen across the room, floating above its crystal console, and the deep red of warning it flared.

"Sounds like your time has run out." Hazanin floated away, beginning to fade into a folding of pixels. "*Karera wa anata no tame ni kite imasu. Jikkō o kaishi shimasu.*[6]"

"Hazanin!" Borukoshu snapped. "You utter twit!"

It had to move, and it had to move fast. There was no more time. All its preparations had led to this moment.

---

4   *Are you real, Hazanin?*
5   *I am your Sun. Eternally.*
6   *They are coming for you. Start running.*

Borukoshu snatched up the prism, reattaching it to the lace of silver around its neck. Without hesitation it began the process of waking Semyueru from recharging, removing the glowing wires attached to its tiny frame, feeding it nutrition. Borukoshu glanced at the nearby holographic display. The hatchling's immune system had not yet stabilised. It breathed out uneasily as it removed the final cable plugged in to Semyueru's spinal cord and the protective green skin quickly reformed over the hatchling's metal hull. This was all the boosting the hatchling was going to receive. From this point on, it would have to manage its own Matrix Crystal and philepcon liquid levels.

"Semyueru, time to wake."

Semyueru's eyes slid open, a bright flare ran across the lenses, and a whirr of inner mechanisms quivered as the child stirred from hibernation and sat upright. It scrubbed at its eyes, giving a yawn, a long ago pre-loaded action no Zaprex programmer had managed to remove.

"Biri. It…it isn't…awakening time…is it…?"

"No. No. It is not. But we are going on an excursion, *hai*, an excursion."

"A…an…excursion!" Semyueru erupted with a squeal, throwing arms into the air.

"Are we…going to the…turbines again?"

Large eyes widened with hope as Borukoshu slid the hatchling's holographic glasses on.

"Sorry, no." Borukoshu shook its head. "Someplace you haven't been yet. So, up you get. Put on your warmest clothes, and don't forget your hat."

"*Hai! Hai! Yoshi!*" With a spark of electricity, Semyueru scrambled out of the bedsheets and dashed towards the wardrobe hidden in a wall, vanishing within, its squeals muffled.

Borukoshu took the stairs, pausing at the foreign sensation of working hip-joints no longer seizing and catching on rust. It touched a trembling hand to its forehead, drawing it away into a tight fist.

"Thank you…"

Its optical lenses refocused, scanning the room below, highlighting and categorising objects, dismissing everything unneeded and erasing their existence from its listings. Heaving on a weighted, protective overcoat Borukoshu felt the nano-bots activate with a rush as they encountered the song of its flowing Matrix Crystal.

It had been a long time since it had been in melodious sync with any Zaprex technology, and it fought back the oil leaking between the fuses of its optical lenses. A hiss bled into the air as it dragged its hand across a panel in the kitchen wall. The drawer opened with an azure glow, filling in the pattern of the Pennadotian Ten-Armed Sun. The smell was distinct, still, even after ten sol-cycles, the Pennadotian hip-bag stashed away had the scents of soil crushed under military boots, imbued with a heavy richness of campfires.

Hazanin had not known what to do that fateful day, a day the Time Master had not foreseen. An abnormality. Borukoshu glanced briefly towards the stairs. Semyueru. Borukoshu had escaped the Sunken Cities only to return to them with an egg to nurture—nurture and hide.

Borukoshu smiled, shaking its head as it pulled the hip-bag free. It had been a surreal experience, to have had the opportunity to meet one of its parallel runs, the young Starborn King of Pennadot, Delwyn. Borukoshu held the Pennadotian bag to its chest, hugging it as though it was the warmth of a Human.

"Protect our children, please," it whispered.

It did not take long. It had systematically prepared for this moment throughout the sol-cycles, collecting everything Semyueru would need for its future. Much of it was old technology, but Semyueru had hopefully had time enough to learn the songs and the neural-processing linkage. Healing equipment, several cases of backup philepcon liquid, and a hand-device that most Zaprexes had once been equipped with.

Its attention flickered to the slim, silver weapon hiding deep inside the drawer. Muscles bunched as it hesitated to reach for it. Borukoshu withdrew automatically, frowning at the warning signals flaring out across its optical lenses. "Well, that is an unexpected result of reassembling my software; the old restrictions are back."

It gritted its teeth, reaching for the firearm once more. Sparks scattered down its spine. Beneath the hull plating of its arm, philepcon liquid hissed, causing a rush of steam through the joint vents. It focused. It was not a Zaprex. It was a Human, unbound by ancient ethical restrictions, by rules that had twisted their civilization around and around.

It snatched up the weapon. It was so light. Easy to hold. Simple in its slim, smooth design—and yet—would Semyueru even know what it was?

A Zaprex did not need a weapon.

They were a weapon.

Camouflage. Speed. Metal. They were killing machines.

At least—

They had been—

Borukoshu shoved it roughly into the hip-bag. Releasing the pent-up breath it had been holding, its trembling fingers relaxed their grip on the firearm. It choked on air, stumbling slightly, grabbing for the nearby table as a crutch. No amount of energy returned to its Matrix Crystal would repair damaged components.

"Please..." it reached down, gripping at its knee. "Hold on a little longer."

"Biri! Biri! Biri! I am...I...am...ready!"

Semyueru skipped eagerly down the stairs. Borukoshu watched the ecstatic child, dressed in a blue frock that mushroomed around its slender legs due to its anti-gravity drive. More so than ever it envied that anti-gravity drive as its body struggled to reboot sections after forcing past the restrictions.

Semyueru twirled on its high-heeled, knee-length boots, their dark, stormy tone matching its choice of stylish overcoat and top-hat. Settling a hand on its hip, Borukoshu arched an eyebrow at the getup. Semyueru had always been extremely particular about clothing, so much so, it was left wondering if it was because the hatchling lacked an installed refraction crystal. It was sending Semyueru into the unknown, without the required tools a Zaprex needed to assimilate and hide. In all its wanderings throughout the Sunken Cities, it had been unable to uncover the technology for the hatchling. Would the simple glamour be enough?

"Would you like one of my canes to go with your coat?"

"Can I? Oh, please, Biri! Please!"

"Go on, you can choose your favourite."

Semyueru released a squeal of glee and dashed towards the door where the canes lined the wall. Borukoshu followed it, choosing a stick for itself. Semyueru held up its selection, grinning up at it with eyes as bright as the Pennadotian Sun. A cane spun from the old metal of some long-discarded ship, capped with amber that held a trapped crawling insect.

"Interesting choice."

Semyueru peered at the insect curiously. "I like…the…the…metaphor."

"Oh, really? What metaphor?"

"We're all…trapped in something."

They were, indeed, all trapped, perhaps more so like the insect in the amber than Semyueru could possibly comprehend. Borukoshu sighed. It had hoped it had given Semyueru an unbiased palette to begin upon, to build up its own database, to form its own opinions, so it would not be weighed down by the generations of failures behind it.

"Are we having breakfast, Biri?" Semyueru blinked, its holographic glasses shining as it spotted the usual hip-bag. Borukoshu clapped its hands sharply, causing Semyueru to snap its attention back to it.

"I bought this for you yesterday." It pulled out a colourful lollypop from its heavy coat and held it. Semyueru's eyes became enormous globes.

"Lollypop! Lollypop! Lollypop! I love lollypops!" The high-pitched shriek caused Borukoshu's ears to tweak rearward.

"Yes, yes, I am aware." Borukoshu smiled. "Now, eat it

slowly. Ah no, no, do not try to stuff the whole thing in your mouth. Just lick it. Oh, for goodness sake, *ko*. Come along." Borukoshu tapped Semyueru's head gently, leading it out the doorway.

Fleetingly it glanced back at the comforting confines of the little home it had made. Its thick iron walls, its cool insides against the smoggy heat and acidic storms, had been a fortress to protect not just Semyueru, but to protect itself from crumbling under fear.

"Come along, little one." It urged Semyueru down an alleyway.

The air was heavy with black plumes of smog rising from the power generators several levels below them. Every so often, beneath the rickety metal walkways they carefully manoeuvred through, bursts of sharp light ignited the darkness to reveal the twisted underbelly of the Sunken Cities. Only maintenance bots ventured that deep, and there were few of those machines still left functioning at full capacity—several it had repaired itself.

"Are...are...we going...go fix another...robot?" Semyueru balanced on a thin beam, its anti-gravity drive humming as it kept it level. In this unstable world of collapsing beams, rusted scrap walkways, and disintegrating stairs, the hatchling was far more equipped to handle falling than Borukoshu was.

"No, no, we are heading into the Quarantined Zone."

Semyueru frowned, its large eyes narrowed into tiny yellow slits. "Isn't that where *Atum-Ra*'s Matrix Crystal breached its containment field and got contaminated? I thought—"

"We shan't be staying long," Borukoshu reassured it.

Semyueru's head dropped to one side. "Isn't it dangerous?"

"It is."

"So, why?"

"Haven't you always wanted to visit *Atum-Ra*?"

Semyueru pouted. "*Hai.*"

"Then, today, we shall visit a piece of *Atum-Ra*, the birthplace of *Our People*."

With a nod of acceptance Semyueru twirled the cane it held and bounced on ahead, singing a melody that carried a lonely echo through the undercity.

"*Sora o tonde iru hoshi. Watashi o ie ni michibiku chīsana aoi wakusei.*[7]"

As heated wind rushed past, carrying the hatchling's voice, Borukoshu gripped its bowler hat fiercely against the torrent of the turbines. It was still some distance ahead, rising out from a swirling of steam and yellow gases, shimmering in the deep red glow of the burning power generators far below—the last, fallen remnants of *Atum-Ra*. A crumbled pyramid, hanging like a basket caught up in threads of countless spiderwebs made of metal. It had plunged from lofty heights during the Sinking of the Cities, and here it had remained, a monument of the Zaprex Empire's failures.

Like static splintering across its optical lenses, data-logs of its original run as Osiris flickered, revealing the true splendour of the ruins as a wavering echo. *Atum-Ra*—the centrepiece of the *Conurbation* that had led the Great Migration—and it had helmed the migration as Pharaoh.

"A long time ago…" it whispered.

Semyueru had run ahead, then paused to hang over the side of a boulevard and peer down into the swirling clouds below.

Borukoshu joined it, gripping its shoulder.

"Careful."

"The songs are dying down there."

"Yes. I know. The turbines are gradually failing."

"Can't we fix them?"

Borukoshu shook its head wearily. "Unfortunately, it would take more than you and me to fix Cal'pash'coo, Semyueru."

"But that is what Zaprexes do—we fix things!"

"We used to. Perhaps we shall again, someday."

It tweaked Semyueru's nose fondly.

"In your stories, Biri! We always fix things." Semyueru

---

7   *Stars flying in the sky. A little blue planet that leads me home.*

chased after it, floating around it in circles as it balanced across a beam. "We fixed Livila!"

"Did we?"

Semyueru pondered the rebuttal. "You...you said we built the Towers, and we fixed the half-planet because it was all shattered apart. We made a harmony to bring all the pieces together."

"We used the harmony that was already here, and we tried to bless the people of Livila with our protection. We gave them the gift of our technology." Borukoshu climbed carefully down onto *Atum-Ra*'s suspended platform. Semyueru clutched its cane to its chest as it stared up at the tilted pyramid. It had lost much of its lustre to grit and grime that clung to the once shiny hull, but Semyueru's eyes still glittered against the dull glow of the golden metal. Perhaps it could see what it had once been with the enthralment of its imagination.

"The Dawn Child rose up, bringing war and chaos..." Semyueru whispered. "They called it the Dragon, for it devoured all in its path."

Borukoshu leant on its cane. "Yes. It did."

"We...we...could not stop it." Semyueru's sharp movement caused its gown to bell out erratically.

Borukoshu breathed out. "That's right. There came the Thousand Sol-Cycle War. The Dragon whispered many things into the ears of those who would listen. It established Overlords, who brought ruin and destruction wherever they went."

"We could not stop it. Livila died." Semyueru halted beside a fallen obelisk, climbing its way atop the damaged beam; sections of it shimmered at its touch. There was still some life left within *Atum-Ra*. That much Borukoshu could hear in the soft thrum beneath its feet. The song was faint, but it still lingered, deep in a dying Matrix Crystal.

"It exploited our greatness weakness, and our Empire crumbled, just as this world had crumbled, and so it fell again without our songs."

Empty. Songless. What would the world outside the Great

Shields be like for Semyueru?

Would it echo with the same nothingness Borukoshu had encountered?

"No, Biri. That isn't how the…the…story…ends, silly!" Semyueru turned on it, pouting. "You always said that some Zaprexes remained and…and they…they came together to make a plan…they…they fused the Northern Lands together to…create…"

The hatchling sucked in a deep breath. "To create a physical spin. This forged a gravity-well to maintain the other lands. It kept the Data-Stream working. The Great Song could continue!"

Borukoshu waved a hand.

"Yes, but that physical spin will only last so long."

"The Time Master will fix it!"

"Ah. I see."

"It is a Dragon slayer!" Semyueru squealed.

"Well, not quite—"

"It squished the Dragon!"

"Goodness me, such violence." Throwing out its arms in mock-horror, Borukoshu shook its head as the hatchling stomped around, pretending to trample things under its boots. "I do not think 'squished' is quite the right word. A Fairy does not squish a Dragon."

Semyueru blew a rasp. "I know. I know. We are Masters of Illusion."

"So, what did the Time Master do?"

"It tricked the Dragon." Semyueru pointed its cane towards the entrance of *Atum-Ra*. "And locked up the scary beast in the Data-Stream, making it in…incor…bleh…I can't say it."

"Incorporeal: '*to be without form*'," Borukoshu offered.

"*Hai*! *Hai*! Yes. That."

"And what is the Data-Stream?" Borukoshu asked.

Semyueru gave a dramatic sweep of its arms. "The Data-Stream is what Zaprexes called the collective Realms that make up this universe's dimensions." The hatchling stared at it with a pout.

"You are correct."

Semyueru grinned, though slowly the grin faded, and its long ears drooped across its thin shoulders. "But why, Biri? Why trick the Dragon into the Data-Stream?"

Borukoshu turned its gaze to the crooked ruins of *Atum-Ra*. The once smooth sides of the pyramid warped and bent, old obelisks crunched by some immense force that had twisted them like clay.

"You shall have to seek your answers beyond."

"Beyond…beyond where, Biri?" Semyueru flittered around it.

Borukoshu's ears tweaked rearward as a low whine began to fill the lonely expanses. Semyueru cried out, curling into a tight ball. It had thought it would freeze in fear, just as its hatchling had, but the dying of the ancient turbines was a strangely solidifying song. For so long it had known it was coming, and now, finally, it vibrated through it not as a haunting part of its future, but a reality of its present.

It was out of time.

Borukoshu unbuckled the old hip-bag from around its waist and knelt, looping it around Semyueru's thin, trembling shoulders. "Take this." He urged it towards the opening of the pyramid. "Go inside and stay there. Do not come out; no matter what you hear, you must stay in there. You will be safe inside."

"But…but…Biri…the turbines…shut down…the Great Shields will fail. The…the cities will be crushed—"

"Get inside. Now!" Borukoshu dared to raise the frequency of its voice, and with a bolt of energy Semyueru vanished into a dark corridor in *Atum-Ra*'s side, leaving Borukoshu standing in the courtyard. Its gaze drew to the upper levels, through the swirls of dissipating smog. The Great Shields that had stood for centuries were dissolving. Distant alarms screamed from the depths below; with no Zaprexes, and no maintenance bots to respond to the warnings, they would wail like an ending

chorus. Water droplets splashed against its cheeks. It blinked, raising a hand to wipe them aside. Not acidic rain. It was beginning then. With the Great Shields' demise, the Black Sea would crush them all.

"Greetings, Xavier Osiris…"

Borukoshu closed its eyes, tightening its grip on its cane. The name of its first run, from the lips of an enemy, brought a flood of energy surging up its spine. It cocked its head, peering over the rim of its spectacles to face the hideous mutations behind it. Formed of vomiting toxins ripping the Primary Realm apart, enough that the courtyard pavement buckled and splintered, and pieced-together flesh and bones that had once belonged to a scattering of other creatures.

"Gentlemen, neither of you appear yourselves. I would barely recognise you."

A mouth of yellow teeth split as a face appeared amongst the slime. Red eyes focused down upon it, one larger than the other, taken from separate corpses. "It has been long, Osiris, longer for us than you."

Borukoshu glanced momentarily at the information displayed across its optical lenses. The songs of the two Ki'rayh before it were familiar. Bulut and Houa. Its first run had encountered them long ago. Circles. Always the world ran in circles. Even now, at the end of it all, a circle was being made. Judging from the warning signals blaring across its lenses, it was doubtful it had enough energy to take them both down—

It clicked its tongue in irritation.

"So, the Dragon sent you to find me. Took you long enough to escape that time dilation field. Was it painful? It looked painful."

The furthest Ki'rayh snarled.

Borukoshu grinned. "Ah. So it was. Good."

"We cannot allow your song to be restored." The Ki'rayh stepped forward on a long talon. "This world belongs to the Dragon. Your existence is not necessary."

"I see." Borukoshu tapped its cane on the pavement. "So,

I presume you have a way of stopping my reinstallation process then?"

Bulut sneered. "I shall grind you into dust."

Borukoshu drew its cane back, preparing a combative stance. "Then let me ask you this, Bulut, Houa. Which one of you wants to die first?"

Houa's dozen yellow eyes swivelled in an inky, open skull full of tarry liquid. Eight, spindly legs propelled the Ki'rayh forward as it screeched. Borukoshu fired its old anti-gravity drive, the sudden surge of energy ripping through its Matrix Crystal and cracking several branches, but the pulse was all it needed. Power tore out of its arm through the plating vents as it smashed its fist into Houa's chest.

The Ki'rayh slammed into an obelisk, causing the old column to crumble, and debris bulleted the courtyard. Borukoshu danced through the chunks, using several larger pieces to propel itself into the air. Bulut's tail whipped past. Borukoshu slashed its cane down like a blade, hewing Bulut's arm from the shoulder. Thick, acidic blood, as black as tar, smothered it as it drove itself into the Ki'rayh's chest. They tumbled over, untangling after the final roll.

It landed roughly, skidding across the pavement, sending an electric charge through its trembling legs as its knees screamed in protest. Bulut wiped its snout, flicking aside blood that burnt the ground with a hiss. Borukoshu brushed at its threadbare clothing and the slick, melted remains of its protective layer of green skin. Twizels and their corrosive existence. Every part of them seemed to rip and shred the very fabric of the Realms apart.

"You're torturing yourself, Bulut, trying to remain in this Realm." Borukoshu stepped back, raising both hands defensively once more.

"And just whose fault is that?" Bulut sneered.

"Yours." Borukoshu charged forward with a bolt of energy that split the air blue. Bulut crumpled against the force of its strike. Keeping its momentum going with a blast of energy through the vents in its back, Borukoshu spun around the Twizel's neck, slicing through the thick, stringy flesh with bladed nails. In a twirl of lightning, it tore Bulut's spine free, ripping it from the cage of shadows. Landing in a skid Borukoshu paused to watch as Bulut's eyes rolled backwards before its monstrous shape crumbled without a root connecting it to the Primary Realm. Gripping the still writhing bones it held, Borukoshu crushed it. It fell limp at its feet.

A screech of rage stung its ears. Borukoshu turned. The second Ki'rayh had managed to crawl free of the rubble that had pinned it. It dragged a hand over its eyes, wiping away acidic blood along with globs of its own skin.

This was such a bother.

Why could the Dragon not have simply come itself—

"Oh," Borukoshu droned. "Yes, of course. Silly me, a monster that huge and gluttonous wouldn't fit in anything ordinary."

"You will die, Osiris."

Borukoshu dodged a chain swung at it. Bricks splintered, bursting into scatterings of data as they dispersed. If the world around it was not already set for deletion it would have been furious at the disregard for the balance of the Realms. It dashed for the nearest fallen beam. Whips of shadows belted its hull, heating the metal. Warnings flashed over its optical lenses. Its hull was not going to last much longer, not with the lack of philepcon liquid being produced through its old and brittle Matrix Crystal.

It needed to go fast—faster—it was only going to get one shot.

"Biri!"

Its processing sped up. An injection of philepcon liquid burst through its systems, sending its body into overdrive as its lenses focused on Semyueru, completely out in the open. Houa's reaction was immediate. Another chain lashed out in the direction of the precious hatchling. Borukoshu slammed into Semyueru, rolling from the force. The heated metal chain scorched its way through its hull, ripping and tearing into organs and mechanics. Philepcon liquid streamed across the pavement as it struggled to halt its momentum. Borukoshu glared through a red, enraged tinge at Houa. The Ki'rayh had stepped back. The bones that shaped its beastly features had drawn blank in alarm. Borukoshu clutched at Semyueru's trembling body, lifting them both. It staggered, hissing at the philepcon liquid draining from its wound.

"Impossible," Houa's multitude of eyes narrowed. "A hatchling…"

Borukoshu took advantage the fiend's confusion, and raced for its discarded cane, snatching hold of it with its free hand. Steam released from vents down its back as it swung its arm, releasing the cane like a spear. It ripped a trail through the ground before gouging into the Ki'rayh, sending the creature slamming into the side of the Pyramid. Marble shattered on impact. Borukoshu dragged Semyueru deeper into the old corridors of the Pyramid. Its knees buckled. In a scraping of metal and flesh, it rolled, clutching Semyueru to its chest as they tumbled down a flight of stairs, landing with a heavy clank.

Philepcon liquid erupted from its mouth and it spluttered it onto the floor. The glow illumed the darkness. Several crystal consoles hummed to life as the liquid seeped into old, exposed crystal wires. Dragging itself across the floor, Borukoshu lifted a trembling hand, slapping it down on the closest terminal.

The room ignited in a brilliant shine, the light beginning in the centre, spreading out in an array of hexagon patterns, linking together to form a swirl of spinning galaxies. Its optical lenses fizzed, momentarily losing functionality.

"Biri?" Semyueru's little hands gripped its cheeks. "Biri?"

Flickering, tiny pixels reformed, though the edges of its lenses crackled in protest and warning, but the face of its precious, beautiful hatchling allowed a breath to seep into its ruined lungs.

It slid up against the nearest wall. Distorted holographic

murals shone with shapes and figures, starships and planets, creatures unknown, great wars between galaxies. A story of *Their People*, the *Journey* through the void between universes. How it wished Semyueru could have—

It flinched as Semyueru touched its gaping wounds. It fought to manage a reassuring smile even as the large, glowing eyes that stared at it began to fill with oily tears. It was so relieved it had taught the concept of death to the hatchling.

"Little One." Its arms whined as it lifted them, wires pulling from somewhere within its body as torn crystals failed to reignite to give energy to the appendages. "Listen…listen to me…you must keep running. Do not ever…ever let those fiends use you. Promise me…promise me that…"

"I…I do…Biri."

It unhooked the lance of the slim prism around its neck and pressed it into Semyueru's philepcon liquid stained hands. "You are the only Zaprex left untainted. Only you can begin the cycle…again…" Gripping the fabric of Semyueru's robe, Borukoshu narrowed its red eyes. "You must find the other… three pieces of this infor…information…ar…array…it will form…a…a Map."

"Map?"

"Yes, a Map. It will lead you—"

A rumble sounded from above, and a screech called down from the stairs in a long, wailing echo.

Borukoshu stared at the entrance. "The Towers. It will lead you to the Towers. The Machines that kept this world spinning. You must restore the Lands. Remember the circles."

"*Hai*. Biri."

Its chest ached and, though it knew it was the burning decay of its Matrix Crystal beginning to disintegrate, an illogical piece of its mind felt as though it was from the ripping sensation of knowing it was parting with its child once again.

Always—always they left.

Always they had been torn away.

Its lips parted in a weak warble. "Oh, Semyueru, I wish

we'd had more time, but soon, even our world...will...run out...of time."

"I don't understand, Biri."

"That...that is what you must...discover..." Biri smiled, brushing hair from Semyueru's damp cheeks. "Begin your journey...find...find new data...save...the world."

"But I'm not the Time Master!" Semyueru sobbed.

"No. You're our hatchling."

Confusion caused Semyueru's eyes to flicker. "What..."

It gave it no chance to process the new information. "Now go."

"Go?" Semyueru clutched at the prism.

"Go." Borukoshu weakly dragged itself upright as the sound of thunderous talons carried down the corridor.

"Sing the song of defragmentation."

Semyueru's eyes widened in fight. "But I can't sing that song; it's dangerous."

"Sing it!" Borukoshu screeched. "Sing me that song! Sing it! You need to run away. Only here will it work. The Data-Ways are not yet open. You must sing it!"

Houa's twisted shape burst through the tight entrance in a vomiting mass of shadows and bones. Alarms flared throughout the old central control room. Machines hummed to life at the melodious voice rising from Semyueru. Borukoshu charged forward, taking the brunt of the Ki'rayh's attack.

It was forced to its knees as it gripped a blade forged of bones. Rusted metal cracked. Its knee joint broke in a ripping of pain.

Before it had the chance to rearrange a processing pattern, Borukoshu found itself connecting with a wall, warping metal and stone with its impact. Through its fading senses it barely caught Semyueru's horrified cry, the outstretched hand reaching for Borukoshu as Houa leapt into the swirling defragmentation the hatchling's voice had conjured. Semyueru vanished in a scattering of pixels. The world plunged into darkness. Borukoshu's head dropped to one side with a clank. Life drained from it in a whine as it slid down the wall, collapsing in a pile of twisted metal and crackling, burnt flesh. It spluttered out philepcon liquid, the sensation of it dribbling down its chin drawing it weakly back into the reality of the dark surrounds.

Its laboured breaths filled the emptiness.

This was the end—

The end of this run—

It had always known—

Somewhere in the distance the rumblings of the collapsing cities echoed, creeping steadily closer. Thunder. Like the roar of a ship's engines igniting to journey to distant stars. If only it could reach out. Its arm strained, wires pulled, crystal veins shattered, and its brittle metal hull clanked to the floor as it stretched its hand to the dark ceiling.

Stars. It could see them. Swirling around it in a great melody it had once danced to. A hand folded into its. Hazanin emerged from the stars as though crafted from them. The ghostly Zaprex delicately floated beside Borukoshu, cradling its limp head.

"Hazanin..." Borukoshu choked out. "I failed...A... Twizel...got through..."

"You did not fail. That is just how this game is played."

"I...could not...protect our...hatchling."

"That's no longer your concern." Hazanin pressed a kiss to its forehead. "Our Dynasty has long ended. The cycle is beginning again; that is what truly matters."

"I missed you," Borukoshu whispered.

Hazanin's tainted red eyes flickered blue momentarily. "I told you that at the end of all things, I would be here. So, here I am."

The weight of its head became impossible to keep upright as its Matrix Crystal lost another section. It rested it against the shoulder of the positive Zaprex who held it tenderly, and stared, haunted, at the eerie, flickering holographic mural across the room of a near identical image of the ethereal Zaprex. The cycle may have begun again, but it would not be the same, and it hoped—it hoped—this time—

A groan shook the central control room and a crack bent the walls. Water burst in from the ceiling. Borukoshu's Matrix Crystal shattered.

CHAPTER SIX

Never trust a Human; they have too many faces,
And you may never know which one is facing you.

Kelib Saying

Zinkx breathed in deeply as a swell of wind picked up a dance of leaves around him. Pennadot's Summer Sun had yet to break the crest of the Ovin-tu Mountains, leaving the land washed in a peaceful morning lull. His chest felt no peace, just a tight aching clench of regret. It had always been the same, whenever the battlefield had forced his hand—forced a choice out of his grasp—the disgust would swell up.

He should have—

No, his Khwaja had given him an order.

He had followed it.

They would wait another three days in Hulbrath.

He would have to deal with the building hatred twisting within him.

The town of Hulbrath lay between the borders of the Pulza and Ivaht Cor Provinces. A border-crossing town. He groaned, dropping his head back. They would need to get travel papers. It was always such a bother dealing with local authorities.

"Can't be helped, I guess. Pennadot is a land of trade, travel, and pilgrims."

He would have to come up with some sort of excuse for a Human and to be travelling with a Kelib woman. In the soft breeze he caught Shanty's scent of wildflowers and honey; he scanned the emerald field for her, spotting her slowly wending her way up the hillside. Despite the weight of her near-unbreakable bones, she walked with the grace of a water-reed in the wind, though he could tell her wounded feet were still giving her grief.

The diabond followed her like an obedient puppy, her broad ears upright and excited at her freedom. Upon sighting him, she erupted into a run and he felt the surge of happiness burst like sparks down his back from the dreamathic link.

The diabond lunged at him, knocking him flat on the grass.

"Whoa, whoa, girl!" He rolled out from under her, using her saddle to hoist himself upright as Shanty joined them. Leaning on the diabond, Zinkx smiled in greeting.

"Feel better after a wash?" The nearby Morndra River, fed by the greater Lake Kartoth high up towards Mount Tyikr, had several creeks spilling out from its silver sheen.

"I do not believe I will ever be rid of the foul stench of the slavers that still follows me." She rubbed at the intricate tattoo visible across her shoulder.

"Time, perhaps, will make it less potent," he offered.

She could only sigh as she shrugged on the overcoat of the gown his Khwaja had provided for her. Still, she wore his armour vest amongst her assortment.

"If you would like some better-quality armour, we should be able to find some in Hulbrath."

She tossed her heavy netting of hair over her back. "I do not wear it for the reasons you do. I have been stripped of all that makes me a Kelib woman, now I wear Human clothes." She averted her eyes. "And walk with a Human man."

"Am I really that bad?"

"Your eyes are flat; your skin is strange, and you have hair all over you."

Zinkx rubbed at his bristled chin. "Apologies for the beard."

Shanty reached out for the diabond's mane. "You look like

the diabond."

"That is an honour; she is beautiful." Zinkx leant on his arms. "If I am to be your travelling companion, I do not wish you to be uncomfortable."

"When was it decided I would travel with you?" Shanty arched an eyebrow.

Zinkx smiled. "You're free to leave whenever you wish."

She laughed. "You would not last a day."

"You're as ruthless as my Khwaja."

Silence dropped between them like a stone. Zinkx scratched the back of his neck. Shanty picked at the red dress she had been given and finally heaved a dramatic sigh. "I would like a corset. I feel extremely…exposed without one."

"You're talking about some sort of binding?" He frowned. "But you are free now, you do not need to do—"

"It is tradition." Shanty huffed. "Do Humans not have such things? As I stand now, I bring shame to my Sisters and my Mor-Mor."

Zinkx leant his chin on his hand. "Fair enough point."

Her hands were clenched, her jaw raised slightly, enough for it to be a defiant, irritated gesture, but a sadness lingered in her eyes. She had lost something to the slavers that she was grappling to get back.

Maybe she never would. Zinkx frowned, glancing away. He certainly had never found what he had lost.

"What if I made you one. We can get some materials in town. It will give me something to do with my hands instead of sitting around worrying." Zinkx leapt onto the diabond's back, offering his hand to her.

She hesitated for a moment before she accepted his help to clamber into the diabond's saddle behind him. "I would appreciate it."

"Then that is what we'll do."

They started down the hillside towards Hulbrath.

"Also, if you think of some brilliant excuse for a Human man and a Kelib woman to be travelling together, do tell me."

Zinkx waved his hand flippantly. "We're going to need travel papers."

"Why not simply tell them the truth?"

"The truth?" Zinkx turned around in confusion to face her warm smile.

Shanty nodded. "That we are on a pilgrimage to the ancient Zaprex monuments across Pennadot. No one would question such an explanation. You are my Human protector; I am a Kelib shaman. Is this not the truth?"

Zinkx laughed. "Glad I asked. I was making that far too complicated in my head."

"You do not give yourself time to stop thinking, do you?"

Zinkx directed the diabond towards the shimmer of the Spider Road amongst the green meadows, its golden limestones beginning to pick up a shining tint of the rising Sun cresting the Ovin-tus.

"No. No I don't. My mind goes…it goes to places I do not wish it to when I pause too long."

"I will take note of that."

The gates of Hulbrath had long been opened for the morning trading. Already several caravans had lined up at the gatehouse. Zinkx groaned at the blue sky-sea and the itchiness of the Sun that had started tickling his skin. Emerging from the Forests of Pulza, spoiled by the magnificent shade, felt akin to bursting out into a firepit with Pennadot's Summer sunshine cooking his flesh.

"Patience is as the tree grows," Shanty commented behind him.

She had wild moments where her wry wit would break through the cage around her. It made him ponder the lives of Kelib women, cloistered away where few could ever see or hear them, existing only in the shadows.

"You won't be hearing much Kelib from here on out." Zinkx twisted in the saddle. "I'll be switching to Common Basic. Hulbrath is a trading town but, from what I was led to believe, Kelibs tend to stick to their Clan Lands, correct?"

She nodded against his back. "Kelibs beyond the Clan Lands are those who have the authority for trading with Humans, or have been excommunicated, like me. My Mor-Mor would tell me tales of such Sisters and Brothers."

Zinkx rubbed his chin. "So, this rich Spider-Road Merchant your Sister is with could be excommunicated then?"

She shook her head. "That would be unlikely. He would not have been allowed to buy my Sister if that were the case."

"Then a Kelib with authority to trade with Humans—"

"You are forgetting something," Shanty interjected.

Zinkx looked back to face her.

"He very likely is a half-breed."

"Of course…" Zinkx murmured. "Someone who knows how to blend into both cultures. Well, someone in Hulbrath might know a man with such a unique name, I am sure."

Shanty nudged her forehead against his back. "Thank you."

"Do you know much Common Basic?"

She shook her head. "Not much."

"Something we'll work on, then. Most Traders and Merchants will know some Kelib, but learning Common would be helpful for you."

"Humans have so many faces, and yet only one tongue?" Shanty asked.

Zinkx looked around the swell of carts heading down the road towards the rising brick walls of Hulbrath. "Actually, we have many tongues, but Common Basic is, as its name suggests, the one we all have in common, and thus allows all Humans to interact as one. Though, I am sure there are pockets across Pennadot that no longer speak Common. Pennadot is rather large."

"Many tongues for your many faces. Do your many faces have names?"

"Our many faces?" Zinkx touched his cheek thoughtfully. "I suppose, similar to how the Kelibs have the Nine Clans, Humans have separated themselves in a manner. I'm a Wynnila, also often referred to as a Muddie, due to the affiliation we have with all manner of agriculture. Wynnilas are the largest population of Humans across Pennadot, though we mostly congregate within the Wynnila Basin."

"Hence, its name, I presume?" Shanty quipped.

Zinkx chuckled. "I suppose so."

"Wynnila…" Shanty murmured. "That is simply a word for rock."

"Ah, yes…and no… Technically it means 'blessed rock', which is then in reference to a pink topaz, that gives us the divine protection of the Sun. All groups of Humans are named after gems." Zinkx gave his gem pouch a pat. "Take the Obilbs; they are named after obsidian. You'll find them clustered in Tempath up South where the mines are. They're revered as Master Traders when they do leave Tempath, honoured for their silver-tongued skills. The Soatrins are who you would be familiar with, as they inhabit the Western Provinces and the Forests." Zinkx gestured to the faces surrounding them.

"Sodalite?" Shanty offered.

"Correct."

Shanty was quiet for a while before she spoke. "What then of the quartz-Human, with the pink eyes."

"You've actually seen a Kimwyn?" Zinkx twisted in his seat, staring at her.

"At a slave market. They were selling one. Awfully expensive." Shanty frowned. "He was but a boy."

Zinkx turned away, fingering the diabond's reins. "They're rarer to find, I suppose. Folks call them cousins to Wynnilas. A Wynnila is a pink topaz, a Kimwyn is a white quartz, something like that. They get called Imperials because they tend to never leave the major cities, and if they do, it's for pilgrimages. If we were to meet one, they'd likely be a Sun Monk."

"And that Human?" Shanty pointed across the road. Zinkx followed her line of sight to a red-haired boy, bouncing a red ball. Spotting them and their staring, the boy halted his play and waved.

Zinkx waved back.

"That's a Retenna. Red-hair, fair skin, freckles, sometimes blond hair. They inhabit the east, towards Sin'musk'qu. He must be with a caravan to be this far west. Retenna means—"

"Firestone." Shanty interjected.

"That's one translation, but, yes, I suppose firestone is correct."

"You seem to know much of this land and her people..." Shanty's tone was wistful.

"I like to read. My home had a lot of books. Reading allowed my mind to think of other things."

"Reading is not living," Shanty offered.

"Ouch, that stung." Zinkx urged the diabond towards the gatehouse. "Fine. Well, how about we go live some of Pennadot."

"I would love to see the tales my Mor-Mor told."

Zinkx herded the diabond in the direction of Hulbrath's gates. They acted like a funnel, shepherding oncoming travellers through a single point. The gatehouse guards wore the colours and insignia of the province. They would all blend together eventually in his mind, the colours that made up the patchwork quilt of Pennadot's countless provinces.

"Stay on the diabond," Zinkx urged as he swung off upon approach to the gatehouse.

"Will they accept you at your word that we are pilgrims?"

Zinkx looked back with a wry smile. "There is a reason Messengers pass through Hulbrath."

It was the largest Human city nearest to the Pass of Osiris, the easiest entrance into Pennadot from Coltarian and the House of Flames. As far as he was aware, the Underground Messenger Network had long been established within Hulbrath.

There was an odd nervousness adding to the clamminess of his skin, though, a numbing of his fingers that wrapped around the diabond's reins. Countless campaigns he had managed across the Battlefields, and yet it was the clamber of everyday people and their voices that felt like a chokehold around his neck. Without his Khwaja an unsteadiness was seeping into him, as if one of the beams that had held the fragile, makeshift repairs of his psyche together had been tugged away.

He bunched tight his muscles and knocked back the straw hat he wore, allowing the gatehouse guard full view of his face. Zinkx greeted him with a cheerful smile.

"Good morning, sir. My companion and I are travelling pilgrims making our way through Pennadot to pay homage to the Monuments of Old. Unfortunately, we ran afoul upon the Spider-Road and our Travel Papers were lost. We need new ones assigned to us."

The gatehouse guard studied him for several moments, glancing up at a tense Shanty briefly, before returning his gaze squarely to Zinkx's eyes. Without a word, he motioned to the gatehouse door.

Zinkx inclined his head and passed the reins to the man. Waving up at Shanty he said, "I'll be back soon."

She held up a hand, as though she was about to speak, only to freeze as she glanced at the gatehouse guard, her body stiffening in the saddle. Zinkx slipped into the gatehouse's front room, passing several travellers.

"Through there, sir." Another guard pointed to a nearby door. Zinkx nodded his thanks and quickly ducked into the next room.

"Shut the door behind you." A voice called out. He followed the order and turned, facing the head wall-guard behind a desk. The man's hair was greying, his skin browned by the Pennadotian Sun, revealing how long he had spent on the walls of Hulbrath. He peered over a pair of spectacles, studying Zinkx with mild fascination.

"It's been a long time since one of your lot have passed by. Begun to think ye'd all died off."

Zinkx approached, inclining his head in greeting. "High Commander Zinkx Maz, of the Blood Armada."

His title felt like ash against his tongue. Did he still have his full military ranking, or had the High Elder stripped him of it the moment he had left the House of Flames? Zinkx's jaw tightened.

He had to go home.

He had to return with the Key, or everything his rank protected would be torn away.

"Don't imagine ye'd want that on yer papers, heh." The man smirked as he jotted down several notes.

"Perhaps not." Zinkx forced a smile. "Merely a humble protector, guarding a Kelib shaman on a pilgrimage to see the ancient sites."

"Hm." The head wall-guard nestled his chin in his hand. "Is that so?"

Digging around in his hip-bag Zinkx settled a small pouch on the table. "For your troubles."

The wall-guard sighed as he took the pouch, tipping out the contents into his palm. He shook his head at the gems. "You Messengers always do offer the best. All right, Zinkx. Have a steed? Wagon? Wares?"

"Only a diabond, fire elemental breed."

"And your female Kelib companion. Her name?"

"Basic or Kelib?"

"Basic will do."

"Shanty Shir-Hara."

"Clan?"

"She's been…what's the word?…Excommunicated."

"Doesn't matter. Still need her Clan."

"Eighth Clan."

The head wall-guard glanced up, concern etching deep the wrinkles of age around his brow. Zinkx shrugged. "You asked."

The man shook his head. "She'll need to keep her tattoos covered while here. It is always possible members of the Eighth Clan are visiting. Women of the Eighth do not get excommunicated; they are either sold or hung."

Zinkx sighed. "I do not understand their—"

"Ain't our place to understand, but if she wants her

freedom, that's her prerogative. It simply won't be easy."

"I'll let her know." Zinkx dragged a hand through his hair. "While on the topic. You wouldn't happen to know a Spider-Road Merchant by the name of Bkyri-kirk?"

The head wall-guard folded back in his chair. "What an *unlucky* name. I think I'd remember a Merchant with such a title. He one of your people?"

"No. My Kelib companion believes her Sister is with him."

"Ah. I see. I'll check my records for you."

"Thank you." Zinkx bowed.

"Return tomorrow; I'll have the documents written up for you and see if I can find anything on your Merchant. For now, here are your passes for your stay in Hulbrath." He held out two gold amulets. Zinkx accepted them with a nod.

"Thank you, Sun's Blessings."

"I hope you do not bring Osiris with you, Messenger." The head wall-guard crossed his arms on his desk. Zinkx glanced over his shoulder, lifting his eyebrows wearily as he gripped the doorframe. "As do I. I'll see you tomorrow."

Shanty was where he had left her, atop the diabond, her eyes fixed on the door he had exited. The tension seemed to roll off her as he drew closer, though her expression gradually shifted from relief to a stormy frustration.

He held out her amulet of passage. "This is for you. Don't take it off while we're in Hulbrath, or they'll arrest us."

"I did not appreciate being left alone."

Zinkx paused as their hands touched. He settled the amulet in her palm, letting his fingertips linger for a moment. "I apologise. I did not think."

Her lips pressed thin.

"The head guard also offers the following advice. He thinks you should cover your clan tattoos while you are here; since Hulbrath has dealings with the Eighth Clan they may have members visiting for trade. He's worried they'll notice you."

Shanty nodded. "He is wise to impart such knowledge."

Zinkx heaved himself back into the diabond's saddle. He

was not sure if it was wisdom, or simply that the old wall-guard had seen too many Kelib women of the Eighth Clan lose their short-lived freedom.

"He's also going to look into the merchant for us."

"Such kindness."

Zinkx laughed. "It is surprising what kindness jewels can get you."

She flicked his ear in annoyance.

Shanty's heart had not stopped racing since they had entered through the gates of Hulbrath. The chaos and terror of the slave pits in Crinn had been overwhelming and would haunt her nights for sol-cycles, but Hulbrath was a bright, dazzling flower bejewelled by the morning dew in comparison.

Fresh and vibrant, it flowed with sounds not steeped in misery and despair. The markets Zinkx lead them through rang with a symphony of voices, the clattering of carts, the banging from smitheries, and laughter. Somewhere, her ears picked up the distant playing of flutes.

Zinkx turned the diabond down another street. "Sounds like some bards are in town. Hulbrath gets a lot of travellers."

Her home in the Family Halls had always felt dark and cloistered away in the depths of the earth. Her Mor-Mor had told her often that they were seedlings, preparing to be born out into the Sunlight; someday she would become a sapling that would reach to the glorious sky-sea. Her fingers lingered over the scars marring her shoulders, the stinging of the poisonous ink burning in her flesh. She had grown, but her branches were weak, withered, torn by a storm. It did not seem right to feel the warmth of Sunlight on her cheeks, nor see the colours of a luscious flowerbed like the many hues of Human faces surrounding her.

Zinkx suddenly swung off the diabond, landing with a bounce to his step. He offered her his hand. A sign hung above a nearby door, leading into a brightly painted wooden building, sprawling out in a circle.

"The Dry Wood Inn?"

Zinkx aided her down from the saddle. "Resting spot for all Messengers passing through these parts. The Innkeepers, Marlin and Darlik Quincy, come from an old family sent out from the House of Flames a while back." Zinkx pointed to a symbol etched into the doorframe, a teardrop flame, pierced by an arrow. "If you see this etching, the place is a safe-haven. Say my name; you'll be looked after."

Shanty memorised the picture. "You're well known?"

He shrugged. "I suppose so." He did not seem enthused by the notion, but, then, sometimes he was difficult to read with the fake smile he wore on a face hiding overwhelming pain. The ball of irritation churning in her stomach bunched up even more. If only she had her herbal kit.

Her gaze drew back to the alluring noise of the market in the streets yonder.

Zinkx chuckled. "There will be time enough for that. I want to check in first, let the diabond rest. Make sure we have a base for Khwaja Denvy to return to."

Yes, the forest-god. She had promised him she would stay with the Human, and she would, at least until she found her Sisters. She sighed, heaving her pack off the diabond's saddle as Zinkx hitched the beast of burden to a nearby post. He knocked on the inn's door. A window was flung open above them and a head poked out.

"Ahoy!" a man called out. "Be down in a moment. Got a fresh room ready!"

Zinkx waved. He shoved through the door. Shanty followed. The corridor was lit warmly by windows and trickery of mirrors. It opened into an immense round tavern where, already, a small gathering of travellers had congregated around tables. There was no life left within the wooden floorboards beneath her feet, but, even so, the feeling of such worn and trampled timber eased her wounds. There were stories in the walls and floors. Zinkx had halted beside an altar, displaying an intricate Sun design woven from old rusted metal. He dipped his hands into a bowl of liquid gold, smearing his forehead before clapping several times and moving on. Shanty paused at the altar. Her presumption had been that Zinkx cared little of customs and cultures, but perhaps he was more aware than she had assumed. Zinkx reached for her wrist, stopping short of touching her when she flinched away.

"You don't have to. It's a Human custom."

"I don't understand?"

A woman entered through a nearby door. "It's a cleansing ritual. The liquid comes from the Sun Temples, blessed by the Sunstones. You'll find little altars like these at most inns and taverns throughout Pennadot."

Shanty set her bag down. "Then if I am to stay where Humans stay, I shall partake in your customs."

Zinkx shrugged. "Your choice."

She repeated his actions, staring curiously at the golden liquid drying quickly on her green skin. It had an illumed quality in the sunlight, shimmering a multitude of shades as she moved her hands to grab her pack.

"Shanty, this is Marlin." Zinkx gestured to the Human woman, with a Soatrin face, if she recalled correctly. "And her husband, Darlik." A man emerged from a flight of stairs, wearing as cheerful a smile as when she had first seen him from the window. A sparkle of merriment seemed to radiate from his flushed, sunburnt face as he saluted.

"Commander Zinkx Maz!"

Zinkx managed a meagre salute in reply.

"Heard you might be heading our way through the Underground Network. Then some slaves arrived at our doorstep saying a Messenger set them loose." Darlik offered a room key from a collection around his belt. "Had an inkling you wouldn't be far behind."

"How are the slaves?" Zinkx enquired.

"We patched them up, and they all went their separate ways, wanting to return to their home provinces. Apart from the boy. Near as we can tell, he has no home to go back to. He is a good lad. Bit quiet, but that is to be expected, I suppose."

Darlik sorted through his keys. "Would you like the connecting room, milady?"

He was talking to her. A Human man was addressing her directly. Shanty clutched a hand to her chest, frantically trying to open her mouth around the Common Basic. "No. I..."

Zinkx headed for the stairs. "It's fine, Darlik. She's with me."

"There is only one bed, sir."

"I'm fine on the floor. Let's unpack, Shanty, so you can hit the markets."

She bowed to Darlik and pursued Zinkx up the stairs. She wanted to grab a hold of his belt to slow him, for his pace was quick and airy, while she made the wooden stairs groan. Would he flutter away as the wisps of sunlight through the leaves? Even if she managed to reach out for him, could her hands even grasp something so elusive?

Her lips curled with the faintest of smiles. Would her Mor-Mor and Sisters even believe her if she told them of such a Human man who could tame lightning, and float like a leaf?

Zinkx roughly shoved open the door of their room. He flung his pack down on a nearby chair and headed for the window, throwing wide the shutters to bathe the small, wooden world with light.

"Well, at least it isn't a cage," he muttered.

No, but the way his shoulders refused to loosen, and his eyes darted to the two exits within the room, told her he thought of it as one.

"Feel free to rest up, do, I don't know...*womanly* things. I'm going to stable the diabond. I'll meet you downstairs."

"Womanly things?" Shanty snorted in amusement as the

door clipped shut.

She was alone. Shanty slumped down on the bed and stared through the open window to the sky-sea. Hulbrath's maze of buildings and scattering of towers coiled around each other in circles, until they summited at what she could only presume was the Sun Temple Marlin had spoken of. She gripped the window ledge, breathing in the scents carried by the breeze.

The scent of freedom.

Below her Zinkx was uncoupling the diabond, leading the beast of burden away to the stables. She leant on her elbows, watching the Messenger work. Despite the cheerful demeanour he forced out, something was boiling beneath his skin. She rubbed at her arms, recalling the heat that had overcome her the day of her escape. Not even the Sun that she could now feel so harshly on her green skin felt at all encompassing, enveloping, and smothering as the heat the Human man had emitted.

Shanty shoved away from the window ledge and began unwinding her hair. She may as well try to get the slimy, disgusting feeling of slaver scum off her again while she had the chance.

The only market Shanty had ever been to had been the slavers' market in Crinn. Not even when she had been amongst her own people had she been permitted out into such a hubbub. She gripped the sleeve of Zinkx's shirt tightly as he wove fluidly through the throng of colour, the swirl pushing and pulling like a magnificent river. Kelib women smiled behind stalls, singing out for her to see their wares. She would have delayed if Zinkx had halted, gone to them to ask if they had seen her Sisters, but the overwhelming fear of losing her only solid ground in which to root her tree in this new world kept her from releasing him. He seemed fixated on a destination and turned them down a street littered with signs for blacksmiths.

She hung close to him as he browsed, purchasing new armour to replace that which he had donated to her. Eventually, he lingered at a larger stall, his fingers brushing over shirts of intricately woven chainmail.

"You do good work," he commented to the blacksmith. "Not many still know the art of smelting Fey metal."

"It isn't easy. I'll give yeh that." The man looked up from fashioning a spear head.

Zinkx sorted through his hip-bags. "How much for these?" He handed over several misshapen wads of metal. The blacksmith took one, eyeing it thoughtfully. "Fey metal? You been snooping around the Monuments of Old."

"Let's say it's a skill I have."

"The protectors don't give you trouble?"

Zinkx gestured to his neck. "Still have my head, as you can see."

"I'll give you twenty sapphires for the lot."

Zinkx clicked his tongue. "You are not going to be getting items like these again for a while."

Shanty watched curiously as the blacksmith sighed and rubbed his chin. "Fine. Thirty-five."

"Forty." Zinkx started reaching for the metal ingots.

"Thirty-seven. I will not go any higher."

"I'll take twenty, if you throw in that leather." Zinkx indicated a nearby assortment. The blacksmith sat back in his chair, tapping the metal he held on the table thoughtfully for several paces, before grumblingly agreeing. Tying up the leather, Zinkx added it to his hip-bags and bounced the pouch of jewels in his hand as they walked back down the street.

"What was that?" Shanty looked back at the stall they had left. The blacksmith wore a smile, seemingly as pleased as Zinkx was.

"It's called bartering. I hate it." Zinkx pocketed the jewel pouch.

"Why?"

He rubbed the back of his neck. "Not sure, really…" Stretching his arms out he gestured to the markets surrounding them. "Shall we?"

"I…I don't even know…" Wait, she did know. She wanted a herbal kit, as well as brewing supplies, and sewing equipment. Zinkx's smile was wry as he offered his sleeve to her again. She hesitated. It was only the scent of dirt, of burial herbs and spices, and the recollection of the warmth that he radiated that allowed her to grab at his sleeve.

As Human as he appeared, she was sure he was more, the question remained simply—what?

Evening crept across Hulbrath in a slow yawn, gradually dropping the temperature as the blistering heat of the day escaped into the endless sky-sea. Shanty watched as children dashed through the streets, lighting lanterns hanging from walls and receiving jewels for their efforts. Zinkx walked beside her, counting out their remaining currency. Her fingers lingered over her new herbal kit attached to her hip-bags, along with the second-hand brewing and sewing equipment from an elderly Mor-Mor of the Fourth Clan who had been selling her old wares. Though well used, she felt they had a far deeper meaning than anything purchased new. Many sisters of many different trees she had asked, and none had known where she could find her Sisters. Their sad gazes burned her more so than her hidden tattoos. She was without roots, without foundation—so easily could she fall.

Marlin greeted them at the stables of the inn, dusting hay from her apron and hair. Shanty stepped back in surprise as a Human child she had not expected to see again bounced joyfully out from behind the innkeeper's wife. She did not know the child's name; though she had shared her own, the Humans had been unforthcoming in giving theirs, and she had struggled to understand the Common Basic of the adults in the wagon.

But the boy had gravitated towards her since the slave markets of Crinn. She had called him Zu'un'Alnokun, Boy-of-Summer, and now the name slipped out.

"Zu'un'Alnokun…"

The thick mop of untamed, dusty brown hair twirled about to face her. He flung up his arms. "Shan'ta'lee!"

Her legs were smothered in a hug.

Marlin covered her cheeks. "So that's where he got his name. We thought it a little odd; it sounded so Kelib."

Shanty blushed. "I apologise. I called him thus when we were bought by the same slaver."

Marlin grimaced at the mention of such a past. "Think naught on it now." She untangled Zu'un'Alnokun from Shanty's legs. "Go, Alnokun; the Messenger is here. Greet him as well."

"Yes, Mama." With a skip to his steps, Alnokun sped off down the pavement.

"What does it mean?" Marlin asked. "We only call him Alnokun; Zu'un'Alnokun is a bit of a mouthful…"

Marlin spoke simple Kelib, even simpler than Zinkx, but they were still at least able to converse in a butchered mixture of Common Basic and Kelib. Did all Pennadotians speak in such a way outside of the Forests of Pulza, or just the trading cities and towns?

"Together, it means boy-of-summer. *Alnokun*, itself, I suppose, is a way of saying born-of-sun or born-amongst-sunshine. If you desire a simple translation, you could simply say it means summer-born."

"How beautiful." Marlin hugged her hands to her bodice.

"We…I…purchased these for you." Shanty offered a basket of fresh vegetables to Marlin.

The innkeeper's wife took them, smiling gracefully as they continued down the road towards the inn. Zinkx had heaved Alnokun into the air and was throwing the child playfully up and down with ease.

"Will you keep the boy?" Shanty asked.

Marlin tugged back a loose strand of her black hair. "My husband and I have been wishing for a child. Perhaps this is the Sun providing that which we have longed for in a way we could not have fathomed."

"I am glad." Shanty glanced at the red-coloured sky-sea above them as it faded gradually into the blanket of dancing stars.

"Alnokun has spoken of you." Marlin took Shanty's hand. "He is convinced he is alive because you protected him."

"I am a Kelib woman. I will always protect children."

"Even Human children?"

Shanty frowned at the suggestion behind such a question. "Of course."

"Thank you." Marlin mounted the steps to the inn. "He is our Sun-kissed child."

Darlik settled the tray lined with their evening meal upon the small table within their room. "Apologies for it being a bit late. We've had a fair few guests this evening."

Zinkx stirred from the window, turning away from the night and the distant glow of the Forest of Pulza's eerie, reflective cup trees blanketing the horizon. Shanty remained seated at the bed, uncertain of her position between the two Human men.

"No apologies needed, Darlik." Zinkx waved absently, pulling out a chair and collapsing into it. "The hot meal is appreciated."

Darlik's eyes hesitantly flitted her way.

"It's fine, Darlik." Zinkx picked up a warm bread roll, breaking it open. "You can speak freely."

Was it because she was Kelib—

No. She had seen the innkeeper couple talk with their numerous Kelib customers. His eyes trailed over her shoulders, her neck, and it seemed that, perhaps, the head wall-guard had been right to caution her to cover her tattoos. Was she the first woman of the Eighth Clan Darlik had ever encountered?

Slowly she wrapped a blanket around herself.

"What's the news from the House, sir?"

It was momentary, but she caught the pain that involuntarily clenched Zinkx's muscles. He quickly regained control, sighing loudly to distract from his unease. He rubbed his nose, looking back out the window.

Shanty fiddled with her mortar and pestle, wishing the scents of blended ginseng and rosemary would chase away the forlorn and pained look he wore.

"Not much. It is the same endless war."

"Hope is fading…" Darlik whispered. "The Dragon is winning, then."

Zinkx managed a smile, returning to buttering his bread.

"I'm here to find hope."

"The Key?" The innkeeper queried. "But…it is purely a legend. My ancestors never found anything."

Zinkx's gaze hardened. "I need to find it and return. Lives depend on it." He gripped the butterknife. "I will rip the legend out of the fog of the past and make it real if I have to."

"All right. How long will you stay?" Darlik leant on the doorframe.

"My Khwaja…" Zinkx paused. He breathed out uneasily. "He was a few days behind us. We'll stay until he catches up."

Shanty caught the hesitation in Darlik as he looked to speak. His lips pursed, thinning into faint red lines, before he nodded. "You're both welcome as long as you need. Please. Rest."

Zinkx settled his knife against the table. "One moment, Darlik. Was Alnokun's leg broken when he arrived here?"

Darlik frowned. "No. He was not injured at all. Should Marlin be worried?"

Zinkx shook his head. "Its nothing."

"Goodnight then."

Shanty was sent a reassuring smile before the innkeeper ducked out, shutting the door with a gentle thud. Zinkx collapsed back in his chair, throwing the bun he held back onto the plate as though it disgusted him. He stood, heading for the window once more to gaze wistfully out at the forest yonder.

Shanty set her mortar aside and dusted off her dress. "You're not going to eat?"

"Oh, I will." He glanced over his shoulder. "Sorry. My mind is…"

She took the seat across from his. "I realise you're worried about your Master but staring out the window pitifully will not bring him here any sooner." He arched an eyebrow at her, and she waved at the hot bowl of soup on offer. "Your meal will grow cold. It would be a shame."

Zinkx chuckled. "Would be, wouldn't it?"

He joined her.

They ate, a companionable silence settling between them, with the melody of the outside streets drifting through the window calmly lulling the evening on into a deeper night as the world crawled to a slow trickle.

Shanty slept fitfully, the bed oddly too comfortable. After months in cages and the cold, hard ground of slaver cells, the mattress beneath her had the illusion of floating. Under the faint glow of a candlelight, Zinkx sat against the back wall, whittling away at the leather he had bought. If he slept at all, she was unaware, for by the time predawn leaked through the shutters to warm her cheeks, he was already pulling on his new armour and heavy boots.

A strange, twisting panic began to rise within her as he

made for the door. She could barely move, barely speak. He was leaving her. She would be alone—alone in this alien world—surely, he knew that he was all she had—

Shanty scrambled up in the bed.

Zinkx paused at the door. His blue eyes seemed to shimmer as they focused on her flushed, panicked face and Shanty could do nothing but stare. "Will you be fine here while I head back to the guardhouse for our papers, or would you prefer to come with me?"

Her chest swelled with gratitude that he had paused to ask. The anxiety dropped away like hip-bags slipping from around her waist. Her trembling hands unwound from the tangled sheets. "I…I would prefer to go…to go with you."

Zinkx nodded. "I'll wait outside."

"I won't be too long." Shanty quickly bustled to her feet.

"No rush," he replied. The door thudded shut behind him. Shanty gasped out, bending forward, holding a hand to her racing heart. Had she replaced one cage with another?

Throwing on the sky-sea-toned skirt she had fashioned the night prior, Shanty buttoned up Zinkx's old leather armour as the bodice, before wrapping herself in the large red overcoat the forest-god had created for her. She finally added a thick shawl, hiding any visible remains of her glowing tattoos and vicious scars. Slipping out of the room, Shanty thudded down the stairs, wincing at the creaks and groans of the old wood beneath her bare feet. Zinkx stood in the entrance of the inn, young Alnokun bouncing around his heels trying to catch a paper crane the Messenger had folded.

"Sun's Blessings, Shanty," Marlin greeted her. "Zinkx was explaining you'll both be heading to the guardhouse."

"Yes. We are." Shanty nodded.

"You wouldn't mind picking up an order at the bakehouse for two dozen rolls? I would usually send the kitchen hand, but he has not come in yet…" Her frown creased her forehead.

"Is something the matter, Marlin?" Zinkx had crouched in front of Alnokun, handing the boy the origami crane. His voice was jovial, inquisitive, but his free hand had come to settle on one of his blades resting comfortably at his side.

The innkeeper ruffled up her apron. "I sent Darlik to investigate. I am sure everything is fine."

Zinkx nodded, seeming to accept her dismissal. He shoved open the front door. "We'll be back with your bread, then. Be a good lad, Alnokun."

"Yes, sir!" Alnokun waved cheerfully from the porch. Shanty returned the gesture before quickening her pace to match Zinkx's. She caught his sleeve once more, using it as her lifeline as they again dived into the river that was the festive marketplace.

"Was it fine to leave? What if something is wrong?"

Zinkx shrugged. "Darlik and Marlin are Underground Messengers. They can handle themselves. Their family has held this Outpost for generations."

Her fingers tightened on his sleeve. The uncomfortable feeling growing in her chest had to be from the new world she had been flung into.

Surely the Human man she had rooted herself to knew what he spoke of.

The guardhouse at the gates of Hulbrath wherein they had entered was as busy as when they had arrived, but Zinkx pulled her through a different entrance. He waved to a nearby young wall-guard who let them pass with only a curious look her way. Zinkx rapped his knuckles on a door and a voice called out from within.

"Enter!"

Shoving open the door, Zinkx lead her inside an office. Shanty hid herself behind Zinkx at the sight of the Human man standing by a window. His hair was a strange, muted colour, not the shine of the Kimwyn boy she had seen in the slave markets but dulled with age.

He was the oldest Human she had ever seen.

"Commander Maz."

Zinkx inclined his head. "Zinkx is fine."

The head wall-guard relaxed. "Your travel papers." He gestured to the nearby table and the rolled-up leather scrolls sitting there.

Zinkx picked them up, unfurling one. Zinkx nodded in gratitude. "Thank you. I appreciate it." He dug around in his hip-bag, pulling out a small pouch, and setting it down on the table.

"You already paid me, Messenger."

"This is compensation."

"Are you bringing Osiris to this town?" The head wall-guard sighed.

Zinkx shook his head. "Osiris is always with us."

"Yes. Yes he is." The man shifted to a set of drawers and pulled out a scroll. He passed it over. "It is not much to go on, I'm afraid, but a Bkyri-kirk Kiv passes through Hulbrath every four seasons."

"Four seasons…" Shanty whispered.

Zinkx glanced back at her. "That's another four sol-cycles."

"If we do not have a Twin Winter, which the Sun Monks are predicting," the head wall-guard grumbled. He indicated a map on his wall. "I'd head to Ninnian or Iliaion. It is likely, as a merchant, this man does the Arrow Road from Alya to Xienia, Xienia to Crinn up South, or Uti down North. If he's heading for Crinn this season, he'd stop at Ninnian or Iliaion."

Shanty bowed. "Thank you so much."

The man waved absently. "I hope you find your roots again."

He turned to face the window again. Zinkx took it as a dismissal and repeated Shanty's bow before they slipped out of the room. Shanty quickly followed him as they exited the gatehouse. He stashed one of the scrolls in his own hip-bags before handing the other leather-bound papers to her.

"Your travel papers. Paramount for any Pilgrim of the Spider-Road. Please keep it on you at all times."

Shanty tentatively reached for the papers. This was her new life. This was the beginning, a new thread in her tapestry.

She clutched them to her chest, breathing out unsteadily. Gradually she opened her eyes, looking up. Zinkx's hand was outstretched, offering his sleeve once more. His weary smile drew her forward.

"Come on, let's get that bread order for Marlin."

Marlin and Darlik's kitchen hand had not been found. Not even when the evening rush of customers flooded the inn had he shown himself. Seeming to surprise even herself, Shanty had offered to aid Marlin in the kitchen. Zinkx would have avoided the common room entirely if the choice had been his, but Shanty's eyes had beset him with fragile trust. She feared being alone in the unfamiliar world beyond her Family Halls more than she feared his Humanness.

Enduring the intensity of the bustling common room, after the swelling mass of the markets, had an effect like the grinding of two stones into his temples. The pain bunched every muscle in his neck and shoulders.

Darlik had been waiting the tables, moving through them with all the ease of a street dancer. Zinkx idly sipped his honey-dew, watching as Alnokun carried a large, overburdened tray back into the kitchen behind the bar counter. The boy got a cheerful round of applause for his effort from the nearest table.

There was absolutely no sign of the child's once broken leg—had he seen it wrong?

"He's fitting in well," Zinkx commented as Darlik rested back wearily on the counter.

"He is. Thank you."

Zinkx waved absently. "I did what I could."

"Not many can do what you do."

Zinkx sighed. "You need to hear more Myths from the House. I'm really nothing special. The Healer in my Squad,

141

now I can tell you a great Myth about her."

Darlik laughed. "You know, I would love to hear some Myths from the House. If only our kitchen hand had not vanished…we would not be so rushed…"

Zinkx frowned, glancing through the doors into the kitchen. Shanty and Marlin hurried about, though the smiles they wore on hot, flushed cheeks seemed to indicate neither of them were particularly overwhelmed. He would have offered to help, but more than likely he would have been a bother.

"You checked out the kitchen hand's house, yes?" he asked.

"There was sign of a struggle…but…" Darlik picked up the meals Shanty placed on the counter, thanking her with a nod. "He was only a lad of eight and ten. It is possible he got caught up in something. Hulbrath is notorious for its black market…being close to Crinn and all."

He sounded as though he was on the verge of trying to convince himself with the story he was spinning.

Zinkx swirled the honeydew in his pint. "Perhaps."

"Marlin is upset. She liked the lad."

Smiling, Zinkx leant on his hand as he studied Darlik's fretful tapping. Marlin was not the one who was most upset, it was Darlik. He liked people, he got along with everyone, the entire common room had come alive the moment the innkeeper had walked in with a cheerful smile and welcoming good wishes.

"Marlin likes everyone." Zinkx raised his pint in cheer.

Darlik laughed. "True, that." He swept away into the evening crowd of patrons, bearing the meals to their tables. Zinkx propped his chin on his fisted hand, watching Shanty bustle about in the kitchen. That she had even offered showed she was comfortable with the two innkeepers, but her insistence that he remain nearby made him hyperaware of how deeply her trauma ran. Hesitantly, he rubbed at the scars unseen on his arms and shoulders. The thrumming noise of the room was like a crushing mountain thundering down upon him, ready to trap him under an avalanche, and the wall of bodies surrounding him did nothing but compress his chest with the sensation that he had no air to breathe.

Suddenly a plate was set in front of him. His pint of honeydew was refilled with a warm beverage and, as he looked up, Shanty's flushed face greeted him.

"I am not sure what Humans eat, so it may not suit your tastes."

Zinkx raised an eyebrow at the tenderly cooked meat and fire-roasted vegetables. "To be fair, Shanty, it looks like the nicest meal I've had in months."

He may as well have activated his gravity control with the way she seemed to float on her feet at the compliment.

Shanty finished wiping down the tables in the common room. The last of the inn's patrons had drifted back upstairs or left for their nearby homes. The Dry Wood Inn also appeared to be a hub for many of the townsfolk who worked in the lumber-mills. Darlik and Marlin had fostered a warm, welcoming environment for all.

"You've done enough, Shanty, dear," Marlin called out from behind the counter.

Shanty paused, realising she had begun to straighten the chairs. Zinkx turned sightly from the spot he had not left the entirety of the evening, a single chair at the bar. Shadows hung dreadfully under his crystal eyes, and, if anything, he looked thinner than a Human should have. At least he had eaten the whole meal she had provided, unlike the soup the night prior.

She bowed her head. "Thank you, Marlin."

"Oh, no, no!" Marlin waved. "Thank you! You were such a help. I don't know what I would have done if you hadn't stepped up."

Zinkx had already made his way to the door. Shanty pursued him, hearing him take the stairs. "Good night," she offered, hoping Zinkx's rudeness would not be noticed.

"Sun's Blessings," Marlin's voice carried through the walls. Shanty quickly followed Zinkx to their room, shutting the door behind her. He stood wearily by the window, like a hanging coat. Shanty shifted to her spot by the bed, pulling out her pack. Her fingers traced her brush. So, few possessions, and, yet, she finally owned things. This had to be a Human concept—or, at least—a concept that was taught outside the Family Halls. She had been owned; she had never owned anything herself.

"You could stay here, you know…" Zinkx startled her. "Marlin and Darlik, they're good people. They'd look after you. You could wait until your Sister came with the Merchant."

Zinkx's expression was difficult to discern in the dim candlelight, but a loneliness seemed to hang in the air around him like a fog.

"You do not wish for me to accompany you?"

He shifted uneasily. "I do not want to put you in danger."

Shanty returned to braiding her hair. The heavy stone in her stomach easing a little. He was uncomfortable, his shoulders hunched, his arms folded. There was little about him that was relaxed as he studied the world beyond the window. None of the Kelib men she had ever met had been so tightly wound, living with an aura of death. It could not simply be a Human thing—

Perhaps it was a burden carried by Messengers.

"Marlin and Darlik are good people," she replied. "But…" Shanty stared down at her bandaged feet. The drum beat of the great forests was faint, but it was still a constant noise that called to all Kelib, and it sang to her of vastness beyond the trees of her Mor-Mors. She would find no place here to settle her roots; her home was not behind these Human walls.

"But I want to see what is out there. I do not want another cage, and here… here would be another cage."

She caught Zinkx's nod. "Fair enough," he added.

He slumped down in a chair and reached for the leatherwork

he had been sculpting, taking out his tools to begin idly picking away at the intricate bodice he was slowly piecing together. Lighting another candle, Shanty joined him by the window. The forest-god had not yet come. Another evening had fallen across Hulbrath, and the Forests of Pulza were igniting in a shimmer as the magnificent cup trees reflected the last rays of the Sun.

Zinkx tapped the knife he held against the window ledge. "We wait one more day," he offered. "Then we have to leave."

There was an urgency she could not understand. Was it the foul creatures that had pursued them? The task the Messenger was undertaking, that was now wrapping itself around her, too, like a tangled thread?

Shanty sat herself on the small nook seat within the window alcove, bunching up the pillows placed there.

"Can you tell me what…what the Key is?"

Zinkx looked up from his leatherwork. It was the pain again, as though he had been struck fiercely and his muscles flinched from abuse. "Messengers aren't really sure. It is an old Myth we have, one of our oldest. Messengers love myths." He smiled wistfully at a fond recollection that soothed the ache. He set his leather tools aside and held out his hands, bunching one into a fist. "A long time ago, during the Forging Age, this world was whole. The Titans ruled this turbulent, chaotic world and slowly made it peaceful." Gradually his fisted hand uncurled. "Then came the Age of Crumbling. The world was shattered, torn, ripped apart. There was naught that the Titans could do as the Secondary Realm—their Realm—began to fade along with the world they had forged."

Shanty inched closer. "Then came the Seven Falling Stars," she whispered.

Zinkx pointed to her. "Ah, see, you do know this story."

She scoffed. "Of course. The Seven Falling Stars brought the Humans to Pennadot. All Kelibs know of such a tale. It is deep in our roots."

"They did not only bring the Humans." Zinkx retook his

tools. "They also brought the Zaprexes."

It was that word again. It still sounded foreign to her ears, and even more eccentric to speak with her tongue, for it was neither Basic nor Kelib. Zinkx resumed his fiddling, his attention returning to the intricate leatherwork. "With the arrival of the Zaprexes, so began the Dawn Age. They built the Towers, said to be great machines, that fused the world back together, and allowed the Secondary Realm to resonate again. Peace returned."

Shanty wrapped her arms around her legs, pulling them up to her chest and resting her chin on her knees. "Peace did not last."

"Does it ever?" Zinkx murmured. "The Thousand Sol-Cycle War spread across Livila. The Zaprexes were brought to ruin by the Dragon and his Overlords. Yet, their technology surrounds us…" He set his work aside once more, looking up to face her. "It slumbers. I am sure you felt it."

She gave a soft sigh as her toes curled in recollection of the lonely song that had seeped up through the old metal of the Zaprex Ruin they had camped within.

"Their Empire did not fall. It did not crumble. It simply… went to sleep… waiting… waiting for the day when a Key would unlock it all again and awaken that which slumbers."

Shanty hugged her legs more tightly. "But you don't know what it is."

"No. No Messenger does. Nor do I know what the Dragon is. All I know is that our world is dying, and somehow…" He sighed. "Well, it is worth living a life trying to save it."

"How noble." She leant back.

The smile he wore was wry and worn. He had not genuinely believed his own words. What drove him, then, if not a mere noble desire to defeat this allusive *Dragon*? He was grasping at something else entirely, something that agonised and shamed him. Peeling back the layers of his mask was going to take time, there was no telling how many tiers he had crafted to hide behind.

"I was not aware that Humans knew of the Tapestry. Its threads are in all of us, linking us as one." She spread both her arms. "Now that our paths have crossed, we have become two threads interwoven in its great loom."

"You mean the Secondary Realm?" he asked.

Shanty nodded.

"Of course we know. It is expressed in many cultures under many different names. I'm sure it's called different things even by different Humans across Pennadot. The Elementals call it Olympus, though we're fairly sure that word was given to them by the Zaprexes."

"The Elementals. My Mor-Mor said they had long passed. For even the Ovin-tu Mountains have grown silent and no longer dance." Shanty stared out the window, to the curtain of stars. The Ovin-tu Mountains were a faint, dark outline against the shimmering sky-sea.

"Some remain, but, like the rest of us, they're clinging to a crumbling world."

She had never thought of the world as though it were crumbling.

But, then, she had never thought of much else beyond the forests, and beyond surviving. Her hand lingered over her stomach, where the uncomfortable stone seemed to sit, having little to do with her monthly moon cycle. This weight called for freedom, but what if it were not her freedom it was seeking? What if, now, she could finally feel the weight borne by the Human man sitting across from her?

The weight of a dying world.

Zinkx stared at the door of their poky room. Dawn had barely broken. The Sun had not yet peaked over the highest tips of the Ovin-tu, but already the bustle of noise was beginning to rise from the markets as traders and stallholders began preparations.

In another hour, the horn would sound across the town, the gates would be opened for the long line of caravans most likely waiting to be received at the gatehouses.

None of that concerned him. It was a normal song that played across Pennadot every morning across countless cities and towns. Yet this morning he could not hear the distinct melody of Marlin and Darlik beginning their day. They were late—

Several hours late.

The inn was silent. Not even the floors and walls hummed as feet shifted over old dry wood, there was not a single guest stirring, no clattering in the kitchen, no thudding of doors or whispered apologies. Slowly his fingers curled around the hilt of his nearest blade and he eased to his feet. The bed creaked. He froze, stiffening in alert. Shanty sat up, wiping at her eyes.

"Zinkx, what is it?"

Was it so eerily still that even she had subconsciously been roused by the uneasiness?

"It's too quiet," he whispered. "Marlin and Darlik should've been up by now."

"They're not up?" She made to move, and he held out a hand, waving her back.

"Stay here." He picked up the twin of his blade, attaching it to his belt as he expanded his gravity bubble, making no noise on approach to the door. He edged it open. Darkness greeted him. None of the lanterns were lit. He glanced back at Shanty. "Please stay here," he insisted.

Zinkx crept down the passageway, checking several of the other bedroom doors, each locked, none showing any sign of stirring from within. He leapt in alarm as a muffled clattering sounded from below. Propelling himself forward by shoving off the nearest wall, Zinkx somersaulted off the small balcony, ignoring the stairs entirely, landing in the common room. A light swayed back and forth from inside the kitchen, beckoning him across the bar. Zinkx halted at the entrance, taking in the scene of carnage. Marlin lay in a tangled heap, her spine dislodged from her back, her blood a river around her. A clang of a knife hitting the floor snapped his attention to Darlik, pinned to a wall. The innkeeper's limp body slid down as a black tentacle withdrew from his torn torso. The rippling tentacle slurped into Alnokun's shoulder. The boy turned his head and Zinkx flinched at the deadened gaze that faced him.

"You're not supposed to be awake," the boy murmured.

Black liquid oozed from Alnokun's eyes, pooling at the boy's collarbone, seeping into the cotton shirt he wore. Zinkx cursed under his breath. Too many young Fledglings he had witnessed die in the same unimaginable pain, their tiny bodies incapable of holding the presence of a High-Class Twizel. Already, Alnokun's body was beginning to break down, his flesh hissing as it liquified.

"My plan is ruined." The Twizel stepped over the bodies of Marlin and Darlik. "I was going to play the innocent little child and come along with you."

"You think I would have been fooled by such a ploy."

"Perhaps not you, but the Kelib woman would have." The Twizel flapped Alnokun's hands in a puppetry motion. "All of this would have been blamed on the kitchen hand, the real murderer."

Zinkx stepped closer. "You are not as clever as you think yourself to be." He gestured to Alnokun's leg. "The boy's leg was broken when I freed him. I already felt something was wrong."

"Ah." The Twizel grimaced. "So that's what tipped Darlik off."

Zinkx glanced briefly towards the innkeeper. Why had he not asked for aid? All Messengers knew never to approach a Twizel without backup—

"Your Master is not coming." The boy sneered. "I had the personal pleasure of snapping his neck."

His grip tightened on his blade, before he let the comment roll off his shoulders like water. "Khwaja Denvy would not fall to the likes of you, Twizel."

Hissing laughter wheezed from Alnokun. The Twizel lazily picked up several fallen knives, twirling them far more skilfully than a child's fingers should have allowed. "You are a fool, Messenger."

Zinkx dodged. His cheek stung. The Twizel's tentacles propelled Alnokun through the air, spinning, the knives it held dancing in vicious synchrony. Zinkx blocked several strikes, rolling over the kitchen bench, upturning it and sending it flying at the Twizel. The fiend's tentacles hewed the wood apart, splintering it across the room. Zinkx ignited his birth elemental, latching onto the scattered metal bolts that had once held the bench together. The lightning surged down his arms, striking around Alnokun.

The Twizel's tentacles retracted. A screech ripped from Alnokun's mouth. Clarity filled the boy's eyes as he snapped his head up, gazing through the cavorting energy. "I ca...can't..."

Zinkx snatched a dagger from his belt, throwing it. It burrowed through Alnokun's neck, and the boy crumpled to the floor. Pulling his lightning back with a heave, Zinkx bit back the cry as the birth elemental gift rebounded, scorching his bare hands and jolting sharp pain through already abused muscles. He stepped over the scattered kitchen utensils and broken pottery, crouching beside the fallen boy. Black, acidic waste seeped from his mouth and eyes, draining away into the cracks of the kitchen flooring. Zinkx drew out his sizzling dagger, studying the corrosive damage before flinging it away.

"I am sorry, lad..."

He bowed his head. Damaging the backbone meant damaging the connection to Livila. There was no returning the child to the flow of the Secondary Realm. He could not journey to the Sun. Zinkx glanced briefly towards Marlin and Darlik. The Twizel had severed their spines with great ease. Three souls Osiris could not claim.

"Zi...Zinkx?" from the door Shanty's voice quavered.

Zinkx stood and wearily turned to face her. All colour had washed from her emerald cheeks, leaving her a pale jade.

How long had she been there? He squeezed his eyes shut as she brushed past him, falling to her knees beside Alnokun. He snatched at her shoulders, pulling her back before she could gather the boy into her arms.

"You can't, Shanty. He's been contaminated; his blood will burn you."

She sobbed, clutching at his hand on her shoulder.

"What...what happened...?"

"It was a Twizel. It had attempted to take a living host."

She shuffled away. "Those things that attacked us in the forest?"

Zinkx nodded. "They mostly take the dead as hosts, but some of the Higher Classes can take the living. It is usually rather difficult for them." Zinkx urged her to stand. Her gaze remained fixated on Alnokun, though his own kept being drawn to Marlin and Darlik. The awful, rising thought began to wind itself like a vine through his mind: if he had not come here, the couple would never have suffered such an ugly fate.

Or was this how their Tapestry had always been woven?

Shanty stumbled. He caught her, forgetting to alter his gravity and he landed on his knees with her, cursing at the pain. Shanty scrambled quickly to her feet, lifting him easily. "Sorry, I am so sorry!"

He winced as she fussed over his wounds. "I'm fine."

"You're bleeding."

Zinkx hesitantly glanced back at Alnokun. The boy's body was decomposing rapidly, and the smell was growing rancid. "I was Paladin Blessed it was not a Ki'rayh, otherwise this would have been an entirely different outcome."

She paused in rolling up the sleeve of his shirt to inspect his lightning burns.

"Alnokun would never have managed to resist a Ki'rayh, but he fought the control of the Twizel bravely. Enough for me to make a move."

Shanty clutched at his arm. "You killed him?"

Zinkx headed for the door, dragging her with him.

"We need to leave."

"Zinkx, you killed him—?"

"He was dead from the moment the Twizel consumed him." Guilt prickled him. Very few...only one he knew of... had managed to overcome a Twizel's control. Would Alnokun have...?

A loud thud sounded as Shanty collapsed against the nearest wall, holding her stomach. Zinkx breathed out unsteadily.

"Shanty." Zinkx reached for her hand. She did not pull away as he gripped her trembling fingers. "This is the world I inhabit. You do not have to follow me into it."

Her eyes refocused on him, her decision clarifying hard and fast. "But it is still our world; they are not two different things, therefore I will walk this road with you. At least for now, Human."

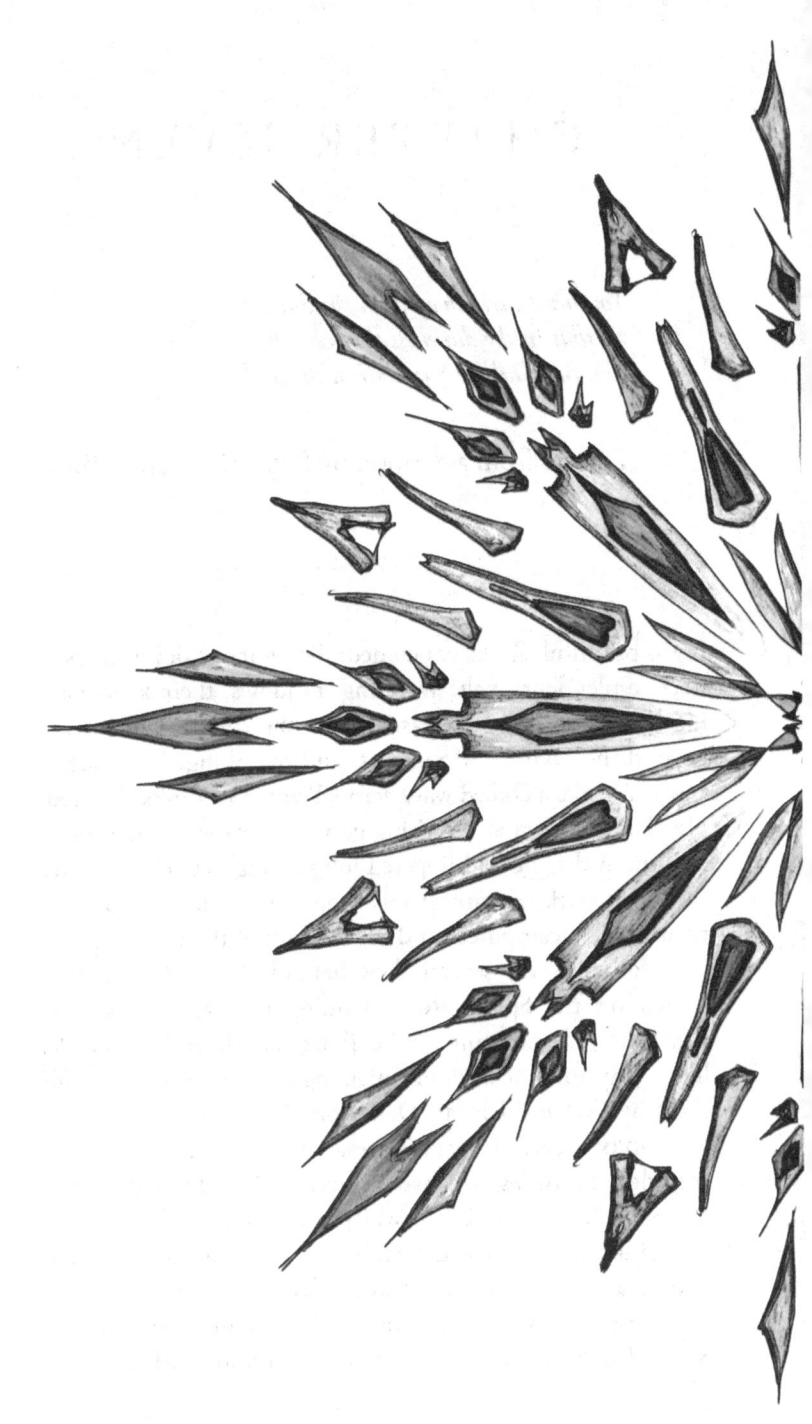

CHAPTER SEVEN

You must turn away from the Sun,
So that in the darkness that remains,
You can find the Sun within the soul.

Extract from a Sermon by Sun-Priest Julian Tulia

It was beautiful, Zinkx concluded: the sight of a dozen colossal trees resplendent in the wavering meadows, their solar-soaking leaves capturing the last rays of the sinking Sun. It fell beyond the Ovin-tu Mountains, and the plunge in temperature came like a chilled wave across Pennadot. Zinkx shivered. He glanced down at the rising gooseflesh over his bare arms, a warning that he had lingered long enough collecting water from the nearby stream. It was time to make his way back to their small encampment and the warmth of the crackling fire.

Hulbrath was several days behind them. Zinkx's gaze settled on the Spider Road winding its way through the meadows. The taunting of the Twizel had been inescapable, like a tiny splinter of doubt niggling its way deeper into his thoughts. What if Khwaja Denvy had fallen—

Zinkx squeezed shut his eyes. The old man had survived countless centuries. He had to accept that their paths had diverged. "He's fine," Zinkx whispered. "He's fine."

Zinkx leapt down the path towards their encampment within a small cove tucked away from the elements under the twisted roots of a protective tree, some distance from the Spider Road. The leaves of the tree were already curling tightly against the bitter night, casting around it a haloing shield of glittering spores. As rough as their camp was, he felt far more comfortable between the dirt and the sky-sea than within the walls of any inn. He was not certain Shanty felt the same. The past few days he had noticed the absence of her usual defiant shine and berating tartness.

Could he simply treat her as he had the female members of his Squad, or was that unsuitable for their situation? He paused. Was it though? His people had been raised from birth as child soldiers, born and bred only for war; they had become slaves to that very ideology that all freedom had been stolen from them.

At the core, was a Kelib woman of the Eighth Clan much different?

He groaned, rubbing an aching shoulder. "You're over thinking this...as usual..."

Zinkx batted through the spores.

"I got the water." He held up the stretched skin, expecting a querulous reply for his tardiness. Instead, the response to his grandiose entrance was a startled clambering as Shanty dropped a bowl, causing a scattering of herbs to spray across the ground. She hurriedly gathered her gown around herself, clicking and clacking in lengthy Kelib curses.

Zinkx made to turn on his heel. "I'll wait out—"

"Do not bother, Human. I've finished." Shanty combed a hand through her hair and waved him inside. Zinkx set the water-skin alongside the slumbering diabond.

Shanty suddenly dropped to sit with a heavy thud. She nursed her head in her hands, mumbling bitterly.

"You were not to know."

Zinkx frowned. "That you are a breeder?"

Her glare from beneath her hair was enough to make him wince.

"Khwaja Denvy already mentioned it." Zinkx raised his hands in truce. "And, while the term is not used at the House, most Kelib women who are breeders tend to become Fledgling

Fosterers within the Cultivation Guild. They raise all Messengers." He scratched his chin. "We have an eerily similar system to Kelibs, I think. It is forbidden for birthparents to raise their children," he said, his voice strained. It was forbidden for families to exist, but that did not mean they had not attempted to try in rebellion. "Your kind are an important part of Messenger society. I do not know much beyond that, though."

He caught the roll of her eyes.

"Yes, yes, I know, I am but a stupid Human man." He gave his chest a firm pat before approaching the fire to crouch down. He added another log to the coals, grimacing as the heat seared his hand.

"This is not something for you to concern yourself with," Shanty muttered.

"True. Perhaps not. But I do feel that, as your travelling companion, it would be remiss of me to not make sure you're… comfortable." He sat back on a raised root.

She smiled wearily, surprising him. "I can look after myself. Kelib women have been doing so for centuries. We have lived off the land, through the land, and across the land, and all I need the land will give me."

"The land certainly sounds very generous." He ducked a rock as it was tossed in his direction.

"Your mockery is not appreciated."

He puffed out his cheeks and blew a long rasp. "So, it's your moon-cycle." Zinkx clapped his hands onto his jittering knees. "I'll remember to give you space when the Twin Moons are at this position." He reached for his bag, tugged out his leather-bound journal and charcoal stick, flipped open to a blank page, and quickly jotted down a note.

"You're uncomfortable with this conversation," Shanty stated.

Zinkx peered up. "This isn't exactly the situation I was expecting myself to be in, but, in saying that, I had three women on my Squad and, when you live in the sort of conditions we did, their experiences became a part of our lives."

He idly tapped his charcoal stick on the paper. "They'd take a form of contraceptive developed several centuries ago. We don't even know much about it anymore. We don't...know much about..." He shook his head, clearing the thought that had muddled the conversation. "Anyway, I presume you were doing something similar?"

Shanty shook her head. "No. It was a poison. There are ways to halt moon-cycles without the damaging effects. I had no desire to bear children to such men." Shanty spat the words. "Therefore, I took the poison my Mor-Mor provided me before I was taken from the Family Hall."

Her shoulders bunched tight as she curled forward. "I never expected..."

Zinkx held out a hand. "No, no. Please. I know where this is going. Please, don't relive it aloud."

Her mouth pressed thin.

Zinkx reached for the bowl that had clattered to the ground when he had entered. "I gather you were trying to remake the poison?"

"Something similar, I think. I did not wish to be a problem."

"It's not. It's life. Besides, out here, who is going to care? And by no means do I want you to suffer because you think I'll be inconvenienced. I'm really not fussed about much these days." He rubbed his nose.

"Yes. I'm beginning to notice."

"I'm not saying nothing is important." He stood and wearily stretched his back, feeling muscles pull against old scars. "I've...become a bit...numb."

The way her eyes tracked his childhood limp told him she found his choice of words considerably humorous as her lips twitched with the faintest of smirks. His wounds, both new and old, were a constant irritation to her, much to his own amusement.

"If I no longer..." Shanty hugged herself. "When the poison wears off entirely, I shall begin producing sap again."

"Why not sell it?" Zinkx tossed the remark over his shoulder as he removed his shirt to reach the chainmail beneath. "There is no Kelib man standing between you and making a pouch-full of jewels, anymore."

"So very Human of you," she quipped. "Thinking of trade."

"Cannot help what I am." He hung his armour over a nearby branch.

"I suppose your idea has merit. There must be Kelibs beyond the Forests living in Human cities and towns who do not have access to Breeders. Perhaps this is why we fetch such a sum at the slave markets."

"Something to find out." He pulled his shirt on again, adding another layer against the encroaching cold daring to enter in between the thick branches of the camp tree.

He looked back at her as she faced the fire, her stare distant and forlorn.

"So, should I be checking my food? For poisons?" he jested, causing her to jerk her head in his direction.

Shanty laughed, the hurt momentarily vanishing from her face as she kicked her legs out playfully. "I think I'll keep you around a bit longer yet, Human. At least until I find my Sisters."

Zinkx pulled out his bedroll. "Glad to hear that. I rather like being alive."

No—he was lying—

Being alive was beginning to feel like a betrayal. If he could not find the Key, then he may as well have been dead to those who needed him. His hands clenched around the bedroll, dreading the pull of weariness. Marlin and Darlik had joined the multitude of those he had failed, their eyes forever watching him in his sleep.

She was uncomfortable. Herbs could only quell the discomfort so much. She bunched her hands into fists, pressing them against her stomach. It was simply due to the release of the poison, surely? Digging her bare feet deeper into the soil, Shanty sought the distant drum of the forest. Her Mor-Mor had given her something terrible, something that had poisoned her roots, dried up the life within her. Shanty stared through the slowly unfurling leaves of the camp-tree, allowing the Sun to leak down into their little comfortable cove. Perhaps Zinkx was right—out here, who would care? She was finally away from the Family Halls, the Breeding Farms, the slave pits. She owed no one and was owned by no one.

A small smile crept slowly over her lips as she sat up. Zinkx's bedroll was already packed and the Messenger was crouched by the fire, stirring a pot. He had a love of a hot brew, bitter to her taste, but he seemed to imbibe the black liquid at an alarming rate. They would need to find more of the little brown beans for him soon, otherwise she worried he would gripe something awful.

A warm mug was given to her as he hunkered down in a squat. She slowly accepted the unsweetened brew. "Thank you."

"Not sure if it will do anything, but my Medic always said anything warm helped her."

He gave her knee a gentle pat before standing, rubbing at a pain in his side. He was not much older than she, but it seemed as though he had lived lifetimes more. Every scar had to have a story. Shanty raised her fingers to her own cruel marks. There was no removing the intricate, glittering tattoos that branded a Kelib woman, but she had tried.

She sipped the beverage, watching as Zinkx quietly packed their small camp.

He kicked out the fire. "The Forests of Shalamic shouldn't be too far, about six weeks, maybe. That'll give me a few months to search, I hope."

"What about those…creatures?"

"The Twizels?" Zinkx nodded, and something like anguish crossed his face. "We'll need to keep away from the main road as best as we can. Twizels are hidden by the Sun but revealed in the shadows, unless we encounter the High Classes." He sighed, looking to the sky-sea through the canopy of the camp tree. "I had not expected such a Twizel presence in Pennadot. It is worrisome."

He turned away, fiddling with one of the packs, pulling something free. Shanty startled as he dropped it into her lap as he passed by her to pick up the empty mug. Her hands wrapped around the finished bodice. It was beautiful. She had never seen a more handsome piece of leather work. Not even her Sisters, nor her Mor-Mor back at the Family Hall, had a bodice so lovely. He had painstakingly worked in the blossoms of a cherry tree, the branches delicately interlaced with the bone bracing. Somewhere he had bought golden cord for the lacing, to contrast with the deep emerald of her skin, and the red of the gown she already wore.

"Zinkx…this is…"

He looked back from packing the diabond's saddle, his eyebrows raised in concern. "Is there something wrong?"

"No. I…I did not expect…it is very beautiful."

The Messenger continued with the bags. "Glad you like it."

She hefted onto her feet and removed his old, threadbare leather armour, replacing it with the bodice. Pulling the cords tight, Shanty tucked them away, before smoothing out the red dress the forest-god had given her. Shanty smiled as she spun on her heels. Now she was free. Her new life lay beyond the horizon, she need not ever dwell upon the darkness of yesterday.

"Shall we be off, then?"

His Human hand was offered to her from where he sat perched upon the diabond's saddle. The morning Sun accented the glow from his earthy skin as he smiled with all the warmth of Summer. A flute seemed to momentarily join the drum beat of the forest and she curled her toes into the soil before she stepped forward, accepting his hand. The weightlessness of his gravity manipulation swirled around her. Zinkx lifted her easily onto the diabond. He urged the beast of burden towards the Spider Road with a soft tug of the reins.

Shanty stirred.

Hot Sunlight burned her cheeks, indicating that the umbrella that had been shading her was no longer functioning. Blinking, she roused herself from sleep. Her eyes adapted to the brilliant glare from the golden Spider Road and corresponding fields of wavering meadows. She was still atop the diabond and the umbrella had slipped from its bracket to lean away from the Sun. With a grunt she moved to rearrange it and shade once again covered her. It had been a purchase of her own, with her own jewels, and Zinkx had laughed merrily as he had installed it upon the diabond's saddle late one evening. Her concern had been not so much for herself, but his Human skin burned red after hours in the Sun, and he was a deeper shade of earth now than he had been when they had met.

She had not understood what he had meant by six weeks, but, now, after the long, quiet days that had stretched on into chilly evenings around a campfire, she was finally beginning to understand the depths beyond the Forests of Pulza.

Pennadot was vast—

The world, then, had to be even more so. Her Sisters were out here, somewhere, in such vastness. Her heart fluttered in her chest and she clutched a hand to her breast, trying to calm the rush of excitement.

Zinkx suddenly jolted, grabbing at the saddle, catching himself before he toppled off. Shanty grappled for his arm, pulling him back onto his perch. He rubbed wearily at his eyes. Sweat had stuck his shoulder-length hair to scorched skin, making him look even more exhausted and wrung out.

Nightmares plagued his slumber, so he mulishly did not sleep until his body gave into the urge. He was allowing himself to wither, like a single tree foolishly alone in a meadow, fighting against the elements. She knew he could not continue in such a state, yet she could find no solution to it.

"We should rest," Shanty urged him.

"We're almost there." He yawned. "We'll be at a village inn soon enough—passed out of Ivaht Cor into Shalamic about two hours back."

"We did?" Shanty looked down the Spider Road. There were several lone travellers, and slow-moving caravans lumbering along some distance behind them. "I did not get my Travel Papers signed."

Zinkx rubbed at his shoulders. "Awh, I got them done. You looked too peaceful, sleeping and all that." He yawned again. "You know, I am rather looking forward to an inn…"

She smiled at his admission. "A hot bath would be wonderful."

"Hm. I suppose so."

Shanty hoisted herself up straighter in the saddle, trying to gain a better view of the surrounding province. The pastures seemed unchanged, the gradually darkening horizon still without clouds. There was nothing to show that they had ventured into new territory. Her heart sank slightly. From the tales she had heard at several of the Spider Road taverns where they had stayed, Shalamic was said to be a splendid sight of strange, unique landscapes.

Zinkx chuckled at her reaction. "Over this ridge, you'll see what all the fuss is about."

The hill rose ahead of them and the diabond plodded its way up the golden Spider Road. Zinkx eased the beast into a slower pace as they summited into a gust of wind. Shanty's mouth opened to the brilliance. Across a tremendous stretch of land, trees cascaded down folds of abused earth that had been sliced into cliffs. The surfaces of the forest's canopy were like the tufts of great clouds, bulbous and white, dense enough

to appear as though there were no glades. Everything from the ridge they stood upon and beyond seemed ashen, void of the bright, flamboyant hues of Pennadotian green and gold. Stolen, she thought—it was though the colours were stolen, leaving behind a pastel landscape, with the pastures an eerie purple hue.

"Zinkx…what…what happened?" She touched his shoulder.

"Well, as the stories go, a long time ago something transpired here that scarred the land and tainted it, turned it into something…different…"

It was as though a sky-god had run a knife over the crust of Livila in torture. Whatever had occurred had been vicious, a deep, terrible upheaval of the land; yet she could recall no stories from her Mor-Mor's tales passed down through the Tapestry of any such deed.

Zinkx urged the diabond into a canter down the Spider Road, heading towards the small town on the edge of a large lake, fed by several arms of a river. Glittering lights were a last sign of civilisation before the wilderness of the unnatural forest began.

Shanty squinted at the horizon. What she had at first presumed was a peak of an Ovin-tu caught a bright ray of the Sun and flared it across the land in a great blaze. "What is that?" She pointed at the hazy silver spiral sitting like a spear amongst the sea of trees.

"That, I believe, would be the Turret of Shalamic. An old Zaprex Ruin that is now inhabited by the Ruling Family of the province. Shalamic's major city, Iliaion, is built around it."

"Are we heading there?" Iliaion had been one of the places they had been told the Merchant and her Sister might be.

Zinkx shook his head. He rubbed the back of his neck, causing his long hair to flick sweat. Shanty pulled away and he muttered an apology.

"If there was any fairy life left in the Turret, no one would be able to inhabit it; the protectors would not allow it.

Therefore, I can only presume it is of no use to me."

Shanty frowned at the great spire. "Then where are we going?"

"There are a lot of Zaprex Ruins and machinery in the Forests of Shalamic; it's practically glowing with fairy life, or so Khwaja Denvy said."

"You hope to find the Key?"

He shrugged. "Hope being the operative word." Zinkx's sigh was one of defeat. "It'll be like finding a needle in a haystack."

"Needle in a haystack?"

Zinkx turned slightly. "Oh, is that a Human-only idiom? It means that something is difficult or impossible to find, like a sewing needle in a dry pile of grass."

"Ah, but at least someone who is seeking this sewing needle knows they seek a needle. You do not even know what it is you seek."

Zinkx laughed. "Hopefully, something I can carry."

She smiled at his optimism.

They arrived at the gates of Ninnian just before they closed for the evening, slipping in through with the last of the traders and caravans. A wall guard directed them towards the nearest of the inns. Though it was a town on the edge of such an eerie forest, Ninnian did not seem swallowed up by any sort of fear of the unknown; indeed, its walls were painted with the brightest of colours, and festive lanterns lit up the dark night. A distinct smell seemed to permeate through everything; even the walls of the inn they entered could not escape the overwhelming odour.

"Fish. Ninnian is a fishing town, being on a lake that is joined by several arms of the Cor River System," Zinkx commented over his shoulder as he partook in the cleansing ritual by the Sun altar.

"Fish?" Shanty frowned at the Human word.

"Never had fish before? It's superb with potato, fried in oil, and a *mountain* of salt."

She shook her head at his amusing love of food before repeating the cleansing ritual, listening to him enquire after a hot bath from the innkeeper. As the golden water dripped off her hands into the bowl, she stared at her reflection in the brass metalwork of the Sun sculpture. A hesitant part of her, strange and fearful, worried terribly that she was on an edge of a dream—

Forever poised to wake up and return to the nightmare.

Zinkx clapped shut the door to the small stable stall, locking the chain in place. He leant over, giving the diabond a fond rub under the chin. With Shanty indulging in her beloved hot bath he had decided to give the diabond a much needed and well-earned brush down, along with a good-sized bone purchased from the inn's kitchen.

The hound's tail wagged happily against the hay-covered floor. She urged closer, a low rumble emanating from her chest.

"I'm fine." Zinkx rubbed the bridge of his nose.

She nudged his hand and he blinked back the heat in the corners of his eyes.

"No, you're right, I'm not fine," Zinkx murmured as the diabond gently pressed her forehead to his. The comforting bubble of warmth from their slowly blossoming dreamathic bond drew away the ache of exhaustion. It was not as solid as Khwaja Denvy's overwhelming dreamathic presence, which had given him a constant unmoveable foundation, but it was peace, warmth, and friendship.

"Thank you," he whispered, lifting his head away, feeling as though he had slept at least several hours. An overwhelming realisation filled him; he was unbearably hungry.

The diabond nipped his hand, berating him with a tart glare.

"Yeah. Yeah. I know. I'll eat, I promise." He pushed away from the stable door.

"See you in the morning, darling." He ruffled her behind a long ear. Zinkx could not help whistling, thanks to the infectious sense of playfulness the diabond had transferred to him through their connection. He coiled the key before pocketing it and ducking out of the stables. The bitter air nipped at every bare spot of skin. He had no desire to linger longer, despite the alluring siren call of the magnificent stars overhead. He burrowed his hands deeper into his hip-bags and headed for the light of the lantern at the inn's back door, diving for the warmth inside. The low ceiling and smoky light from the candles created a grey, misty environment. Together with the rich odour of fish, the smell of pipe weed and ale had long seeped into the dark, mahogany walls. Wafting up from the common room the merry sound of good cheer from the locals and travellers tugged at his mood, but at least the diabond's dreamathic salve would ease the sting of his ruminations for an hour or so. How was his Squad? Surely they had been disbanded by now. How were the children? What of all the underground work the Medical Guild had undertaken, returning wounded Messengers to the battlefields with prosthetic limbs? Had the High Elder found out about more than just their radical attempts at raising children outside of the Cultivation Guild?

Zinkx pinched his nose, heading up the stairs.

Each inn and tavern they had stopped by along the Spider Road had its own uniqueness, its own flavour, showing just how vast a land Pennadot was. Yet they all still made him feel equally uneasy and hemmed in. Knocking lightly on the door to their room, Zinkx called out, "Shanty, are you decent?"

"You can enter, Human."

Relaxing, he scooted inside, relatching the door behind him.

"Good timing; your...fish...was just delivered."

Zinkx breathed a sigh of relief, giving his tight, unpleasantly empty stomach a pat. From where she sat on the bed,

Shanty scoffed with amusement as he eagerly took a seat at the table. She patted her hair dry, looking far better for her wash. A radiant flush of blood had returned to her cheeks. In the glow of the oil lanterns on the walls, her tattoos gleamed blue against her emerald skin, outlining her features in the small, dank room. In one of the earlier villages she had purchased herself an under-dress, a simple piece of white fabric to slip over herself, allowing the removal of all the heavier clothing come evening. It fell loosely around her shoulders, making him overly aware of her trust during the vulnerable night time hours between them.

Her smile grew brighter as she waved at an assortment of fabrics spread out across the bed.

"Do you like them?"

He picked up his eating utensils. "Ah, sure."

"I bought them for my new dress. I'll make some new shirts for you as well...yours are..."

"Tatty?"

"One word for them, I suppose."

He chuckled. "Come on; your meal is getting cold."

Shanty rifled around in her bags, tugging something free, before heading to the table and easing herself down to join him. She placed two objects before him. Zinkx raised an eyebrow at the sight of bejewelled, hand-carved Pennadotian hair-rolls, crafted out of pve'pt bones.

"Ah, what?"

Shanty picked one up, handing it to him. "It is for you."

He accepted it. The Pennadotian traditional headwear was highly prized, their carvings often engraved with blessings and spells to keep the owner safe from harm. Tentatively, Zinkx ran his fingers over the typography etched into the bone as Shanty made herself busy curling her own hair-roll through her mass of braids.

It bore a simple, but very telling, word in Kelib: protector. He smiled.

Tugging out the leather tie from his chaotic tangle of hair,

Zinkx wrapped the hair-roll up tightly into a somewhat neater bundle.

"Thank you."

Shanty hesitantly bent her head and he was sure the dim light was hiding her blush.

"So, this is fish?" She took up her eating utensils.

He grinned down at the plate in front of him, spearing a large potato. "Fish and fried potato. Genius."

CHAPTER EIGHT

When you call someone a fool,
You are naming the foolish thing in yourself
that you cannot see,
Because you are the real fool.

A Travelling Bard's words after being put in the
stocks for insulting a lord's daughter

Daniel narrowed his eyes against the harsh glare of the Sun.
His arrow soared across the meadow, its tail feathers leaving a
trail of cool vapor as it hissed through the air. It gave a faint
thud, hitting the target dead centre.

From the other end of the lawn, eerily tinted a pastel
purple, a cheer echoed from the small crowd sheltered from
the noonday Sun in a large marquee. A servant dashed out
to quickly retrieve the arrow. Daniel lowered the elegant bow,
sighing in disappointment. He had intended to miss, yet, as
usual, he had hit the centre with perfection. Not once had his
arrow skipped a single mark. It was irritating to be praised for
something he had never worked for.

A cool breeze twisted playfully around his bare legs as he
made his way back to his tent and he self-consciously tightened
the gold belts holding up his pale green kilt.

The trip to the Province of Shalamic had taken three
months, three months of princely duties at every stop along
the way, three months of forcing a caked-on smile, a cheeriness
to his voice, and laughter from his lips. Still, even now, so far
from the halls of the Palace, he was in a cage. They had come
so far enticed by a missive from a province lord, and, now,
frustratingly, they were being paraded around like the finest
silken garments the Lord of Shalamic had acquired.

Daniel glanced to the sky-sea, blue and clear, and mocking in its vastness. He was not sure how much longer he could be bothered playing a pleasant game of house.

"You did not miss, Your Highness. I thought you were trying." Skyeola joined him, smiling brilliantly.

Daniel set down his bow, giving the young kitten a playful ruffle of his raven hair. The traditional Pennadotian kilt Skye-ola wore was such a contrast to the kitten's usual Palace attire, revealing a slim torso coated in black fur and silver scales. He drew many stares, even from the nobles surrounding them, which perhaps should not have been a surprise. While the kitten's outlandish appearance had long ago become normality for Daniel, very few Pennadotians outside of the Eastern Regions would have ever laid eyes upon a Batitic.

"I did try." Daniel lazily rubbed the back of his neck. "I think I must be enchanted. I can never miss."

Skyeola shrugged his thin shoulders. The movement tugged the muscles around his hips that held fast to his wing junctions, rattling the magnificent appendages. "I checked you over myself. You are not enchanted in any way. Maybe it is a gift! Like my conducting is in my blood, so is your talent with a bow."

Daniel looked down at his hand, coiling the fingers into a fist. It was more than a talent with a bow. Talent, in of itself, still took an investment of time to foster.

Skyeola sidled up to him, whispering, "Lord Galvon's daughter looks as though she wants to speak to you."

Daniel massaged his brow. "I am sure she does."

"Does it get annoying?" Skyeola enquired innocently. "Having so many suitors?"

He laughed, tweaking one of Skyeola's fluffy ears. "Very much so."

Skyeola offered him a drink. The coolness of the water drew a sigh from him. So far, their week spent in the Province of Shalamic had been peaceful. They had time to go riding on the twisting roads that snaked through the strange forests, and the nightlife of the city of Iliaion was vibrant and festive. No doubt Jarid and Hun appreciated their allotted time to themselves. Though it felt like a subterfuge to distract them from their goal, truthfully he could find no reason to complain; a small part of him enjoyed the idling. Daniel shaded his eyes, staring out across the glade. The heat was doing well to keep them indoors, though, and it seemed only the early mornings and late evenings were fit to venture outside. He would take what he could—after all, the point of the Summer was to escape castle walls.

The Turret of Shalamic was inhabited by the Ruling Family of the province. He had never seen any splendour like it, not even in Palace Town. For sure, Zaprex monuments and ruins lay scattered all across Pennadot, but to approach them was foolhardy and called upon death. To dwell within an ancient, magnificent piece of history—he envied Lord Galvon. To have access to such a vast wealth of hidden knowledge…it was no wonder the man had become formidable. The singular, great turret stretched high into the sky-sea, gleaming like liquid crystal in the sunlight. At night, its tip would illuminate the surrounding city and forests as a beacon. Iliaion was like a skirt around the tower, built in layers down cliffs, falling into the tufts of white cloudy forests below.

What had such a vast, spiralling turret—that they could barely inhabit a fraction of—been built for? To reach the stars, perhaps. He sighed again, sipping his water.

"Your Highness, if I may have a moment…" A deep voice startled him. Skyeola had backed up to tuck himself away neatly behind him with all the behaviour of a frightened child, and Daniel turned rapidly. Lord Galvon stood far too close, with his daughter at his side. Daniel stepped back, placing the small drinks table between them. The tension in Skyeola's body relaxed slightly.

"Ah, Lord Galvon, yes, of course."

Perhaps finally they would get to the business of the promised Zaprex treasure.

Lord Hoinhine Galvon was a stocky man with curls of dark brown hair flowing over his shoulders and across a bare chest littered with golden jewellery. His family had risen to prominence within Shalamic some several generations prior, after a war with the neighbouring Ivaht Cor had killed the previous Ruling Family. Every so often it happened, a small skirmish between provinces that led to new Ruling Families, though Daniel was unaware of one having taken place in his own lifetime—at least, not since the Uprising of the Provinces.

He would have found Lord Galvon overly intimidating had it not been for their difference in height. He stood about a head taller than Galvon, though he was not entirely convinced that was due to the man being a Wynnila. Both Galvon and his daughter were true Muddies, skin, hair, and eyes all earth-tinted, looking like they were born of the soil of Pennadot, far more than he.

"I do not believe you've had the opportunity to meet my youngest daughter, Argrona."

Daniel forced a diplomatic smile as the girl stepped forward. So much for his hope for Zaprex treasures.

The girl bowed. "Your Highness. If I may be so bold: the rumours that you never miss a target are apparently true."

"A target is one thing." Daniel looked back at the archery range. "I often wonder how I would be if I were to truly take a life."

"A wise speculation, Your Highness." Lord Galvon nodded.

"Perhaps you would like to partake in a hunting game with my brothers?" Argrona piped up. "I am sure they would be most delighted to arrange one for you."

There was far too much hope shining in her hazel eyes. Daniel had to wonder what Lord Galvon had told her was going to happen over the course of the Summer.

"We shall see. Thank you, Lord Galvon, for the use of your range. I have greatly appreciated it." Daniel waved a hand in dismissal. The province lord bowed low, his daughter quickly following suit.

"You honour us with your presence in our province, Your Highness."

Daniel watched them both leave across the meadow, towards the marquee for the fellow lords and ladies of the Ruling Family. His adviser, Jarid Telvon, seemed to take that moment as a cue to leave the tent and march past Lord Galvon a little too fast, as if someone had lit a candle between his legs. Daniel paused in collecting his equipment as Jarid approached.

"What's wrong? Has Hun been thrown out of another tavern for drinking?"

"Your Highness." Jarid touched his shoulder, emphasising the importance of his next words, whispered in his native province tongue, "Do not leave Skyeola alone with Lord Galvon."

His adviser was gone before he could turn to query such a troublesome remark. Daniel squared his shoulders and gathered up his archery equipment. It seemed he could never escape the all-consuming game of Pennadotian politics. He noticed that Skyeola was lost in a dreamy daze, staring up at the Turret of Shalamic, his gaze full of childish wonder.

"Come along, Skyeola."

"Coming!" Skyeola jerked around. "I am coming!"

Daniel sighed as he slipped onto the couch beside a low table where Skyeola's books and scrolls were scattered, along with the small mountains of paper-cranes. He made space before setting down a pile of thin papers scribbled with hurried commentary in Jarid's handwriting. The notes described the flow of finances through the provinces of Pennadot, but the records were useless when dealing with the large quantities of funds that were funnelled into the royal state treasury over several sol-cycles. Every decade the province lords paid their tribute.

Even the volatile city of Tempath paid taxes. He highly doubted Tempath, for all its bluster, desired to cause civil unrest.

So—

Why, then, was the royal state treasury bleeding funds like
a punctured water skin?

He steepled his fingers, studying the reports Jarid had
provided. Each was on a particular province lord or lady, and
their corresponding Ruling Family. He had to hand it to his
adviser, the man was extremely talented in his research.

Daniel collapsed back in his seat.

They all had something in common. They had all been
involved in the Uprising of the Provinces a decade ago. That
was not a coincidence. He did not think so, and neither did
Jarid.

"Surely they are not *that* stupid," Daniel murmured. "Or
am I the stupid one?" He stared at the high ceiling. The Turret
of Shalamic had an eerie hollowness to it at times. Even the
Palace, in all its vastness, felt as though it constantly had air,
as though there was life being breathed. Shalamic was empty.
Lifeless. The metal walls, despite having Pennadotian wall
hangings, and the floors covered in vast rugs, provided a cold,
dead environment.

It almost seemed like he could hear the echo of his own
empty mind and the endless nothingness of his blank childhood. He knew there was a childhood there—somewhere—
almost in reach—but, like the Turret of Shalamic, it was no
longer accessible on the surface.

Daniel groaned. "I have no power. I am a prince who
cannot rule, will never be crowned King, it seems. It is no
wonder they think they can take everything out from under
me, when they already won ten sol-cycles ago."

Without the Steward's approval he could not take the
Emerald Throne as King, and Zilon insisted on the full co-op-
eration of the Ruling Families before giving that approval.

"Tell me I am worth something," he asked the seemingly
empty room.

"King is purely a title, or a role, if you will; you can be one without it." Citla emerged from the shadows, her black robe trailing around her ankles as she glided across the chamber to his side.

He snorted.

"Even if you were King, the province lords and ladies have lost all respect for the position, and all honour for what it brings to our land. It is doubtful they would behave any differently to how they do now."

"So...what do you suggest?" He gazed up at her and her steady, unwavering expression of solitude.

"I think you need to be prepared to woo Lord Galvon into a sense of ease."

He breathed in deeply. "Have we not already been doing so?"

She remained silent.

"I see. So it means probably going hunting with his obnoxiously annoying sons or spending time with his bedazzled daughter."

The smallest of smiles touched the corners of her mouth. He knew she was amused by his irritation and discomfort. "Sometimes, Your Highness, duty requires such difficult things of us."

He snorted at her sarcasm.

"Tell me, do you believe Galvon has some Zaprex treasure hidden away here?"

"It would be foolish of us to presume otherwise. Entertain him, Your Highness, and allow Jarid to lure him back to the Palace where we are strongest."

Daniel bent forward, picking up his quill.

"Galvon is not the mastermind behind this mess."

Citla inclined her head. "You will not catch a fox without a rabbit."

She drifted away, leaving him to his work. A tapping stirred him out of his foggy haze of numbers and calculations, returning him to the reality of his chamber; the familiar sound of Skyeola's foot-claws upon the marble flooring of the outside corridor.

The door slid open with a grinding of old mechanisms.

"Your Highness." Skyeola dashed in.

Daniel turned in his chair as Skyeola rushed towards him in excitement. The kitten carried his conduction equipment bundled in his arms. A silver goblet dangled from a chain around his wrist.

"Skyeola, slow down, or you will trip again."

"I did it! I did it! I have to show you!"

Daniel smiled. He leant forward and cupped his chin in his hand as he watched Skyeola dash about.

"Show me what, exactly?"

"It is incredible."

"Sounds like it."

Skyeola set the silver goblet down upon the floor and filled it with wine from a pouch.

"So, as you know, my people have the skill to summon and bind Elementals from the Secondary Realm. This is called Elemenancy, or in Common Basic, Elemental Binding."

Daniel nodded as though everything the young kitten was saying made complete sense. He had learnt it was the only prudent thing to do when Skyeola began one of his enthusiastic outbursts.

"Well…well…much of this ancient art has gone out of practice now amongst the Blood-Clans, due to loss of so many memories in the Sin'musk'qu Wars. Many of the Batitic Schools of Conductions were lost. It is extremely sad."

"Yes. It must be." Daniel empathised.

Skyeola breathed in deeply. "But I have discovered I have an attribute for Elemenancy!" He scribbled with chalk on the floor, drawing a rather wonky circle around the silver goblet.

Daniel frowned in thought, recalling to mind earlier babbling sessions. "Is this not some sort of forbidden magics… or…what not?"

"Phf!" Skyeola stuck out his forked tongue in amusement.

"I am not a Necromancer, Your Highness. Besides, for a conduction to truly be forbidden, as you say, a conductor must use their blood, or the blood of another, to act as the fusion. That is very dangerous. A fusion can be conducted with water, or another liquid, like wine or even hot metal, or even a solid if your conduction is in the Deconstruction School."

"I see." He, in fact, did not see. Skyeola had crossed into an area of the nonsensical. Though he tried to keep up with the kitten's studies so he would have something to discuss with him, it was difficult to grasp the details of the knowledge that Batitics had transferred through generations of linked memories.

"Well, then," Daniel flicked through the papers in front of him, "I do hope you do not blow a hole in the floor, again."

"I did that once in my entire learning experience," Skyeola squeaked in horror.

Daniel smirked at the embarrassment the mention of the accident provoked in the kitten.

"Ah, yes, but it was classic, Skyeola. A story worth being passed down to your children's children someday. You, the son of the greatest Sorcerer of this Age, blew a hole the size of the Southern Moon in the middle of my chamber." He shook his head, his eyes tearing up from the force of supressing laughter at the recollection. Without memories of his own childhood, any recollections he could clutch hold of were like treasures. Those moments, few and far between as they were, had become like towers grounding him to his very existence.

Skyeola was pouting as he knelt beside the circle he had drawn.

Daniel laughed, waving a hand in the air. "Oh, go on, Skyeola, lad! I am playing with you. I have every faith in you and your abilities. So, I gather, you are going to try and summon an Elemental?"

Skyeola's mood switched instantly. "Elementals are already here, everywhere, we simply cannot see them. They exist with-in the Secondary Realm and can only pass into the Primary

Realm if they are given an anchor to hold onto."

Daniel nodded. "Makes sense."

"I am going to make a momentary anchor with this goblet so you can see a Vapor Elemental. I noticed there are heaps of them living in Shalamic."

"Only a momentary pact?"

Skyeola laughed hesitatingly. "I am far from ready to form a Bond with an Elemental, Your Highness. It is a lot more involved than this little parlour trick."

"I bow to your knowledge."

Skyeola's neck feathers preened at the praise. "A Vapor Elemental is a particularly good element for armed combat between two opposing sorcerers. It can move through things, like a shield, or armour. If you were ever in trouble, I could call upon it and conduct it to protect you. So, this is still good practice."

"Conduct it to protect me, heh?" Daniel rubbed his forehead. "What about yourself?"

Skyeola's chin lifted, mimicking Citla in a manner that was quite amusing. "You know very well, Your Highness, that you are the future King. Without you the Land would wither and die. The King's life is the life of his Land. You must be protected above all else."

"Your father would not agree."

"Papa never agrees with me." Pulling out a rolled-up pack, Skyeola spread it across the floor. He uncovered several long sticks of different heights packed in the silver fabric. "Now, which conductor should I use?" He tapped a claw against his mouth, studying the line-up of sticks. Some were carved from wood, others from rare stones and metals. The intricate patterns across their smooth surfaces would gleam and shine when the magic in the kitten's blood sang, thus conducting the energy the Batitic could manipulate.

Several more moments passed, and Daniel laughed. "You do realise that in the middle of battle, Skyeola, you would not have the time to stand around looking for a wand—"

"Not a wand! A conductor!" Skyeola snapped. He jerked up and glared. "How many times do I have to say it, Your Highness. Con…duc…tor…!"

"Forgive my ignorance," Daniel corrected himself. "You would not have time to find the right conductor from your collection."

"Really, Daniel?" Skyeola finally plucked a silver and gold conductor from the selection. "Since when would you know anything about battle?"

Daniel paused. He gaped in surprise as he watched Skyeola station himself before the goblet. The air around Skyeola crackled as the energy of the realms gathered around him. The conductor and the chalk scrawls upon the floor began to glow an ebbing swell of bright purple, indicating that a connection between the Realms had been established.

"I suppose you are right." Daniel sighed off-handily and settled back in his seat to watch the show. He had never found himself in the middle of an actual battle, therefore he had never had the chance to learn the true art of fighting. He had his guards, and Citla, to protect him. He, himself, had never touched a sword, nor learnt a deadly strike of the hands.

His bow—perhaps—

But he had been honest with Lord Galvon and his daughter; he really did wonder if he could use his bow to kill anything living. Steward Zilon had been a constant in his life, drilling into him that he was a prince, a figurehead; his job was to rule his court and not seek battle and valour.

A strained peace existed between the Kelibs and Humans, but it was peace, nonetheless. Truthfully, though, he felt it was far more due to the Kelibs' inability to forge alliances between their own Clans. If even a few of the larger Clans joined forces with the purpose of wiping out the Humans—

Peace. It was a strange word. Little skirmishes between Ruling Families would crop up from time to time. Natural disasters caused terrible unrest. But there had been no true war since the Uprising ten sol-cycles ago. But he had no recollection of that, despite being told that he had been in the thick of it. His glare momentarily shifted to the papers across the nearby table. Something had happened that had caused the province lords to dare betray and kill the Starborn King and the Royal Family, leaving him alone. So alone.

Daniel winced at the sound of a crack. He swung his attention back to Skyeola, who danced elegantly on his foot-claws as he waved his conductor in fluid movements. A glow gathered at the tip of the stick and orange liquid dribbled to the floor and gathered around the goblet. The intense burning of the light shattered. The goblet tipped over, and a soft, fluttering mist formed, twisting and contorting into demented shapes. Daniel smiled as a sleek eel-like form slithered out of the mist. Two small, blue eyes peered out from a triangular head. The Elemental danced playfully through the air, before settling itself around Skyeola's outstretched arm in obedience. Its delicate fins rippled with mesmerising colours until, gradually, it faded back into the light of the air.

The room returned to its natural sunlit glow. Skyeola relaxed his arm. For a moment Daniel watched the dazed kitten; he swayed a little, as though about to faint, and Daniel made ready to catch him. Suddenly, Skyeola burst out a squeal.

"I did it! I did it! Daniel! Daniel! Did you see? I did it!" Skyeola threw his arms skyward, jumping about in glee.

Daniel laughed. "I saw. I saw. Well done."

Over Skyeola's shoulder he noted Jarid entering through the sliding door. Lean and lanky, with the fiery red hair and freckles of a Retenna, ears a little too large under his curls of hair, Jarid was an unremarkable man, all things considered. But his breed had one distinct difference that set them apart from any other Human: their eyes were storm-cloud grey with eerie white pupils. Retennas could see in the dark as clearly as any Batitic. The wives-tales told of Ancient Humans breeding with Batitics, thus leading to the Retennas' unnaturally gifted linguistic skills and night-vision. It was a widely disregarded myth, but Daniel had a vague inkling it had some truth to it.

Still, he could not deny that the eyes gave the young lord's otherwise slightly disjointed and not altogether handsome face a rather unsettling, other-realmish appearance.

"Jarid." Daniel waved to him. "See what Skyeola accomplished today?"

Skyeola squeaked in surprise and spun on his foot-claws. He blushed as Jarid laughed richly and reached out a hand to ruffle his hair. "You are a true gem, Skyeola. Congratulations on your summoning."

Daniel shifted uneasily as Jarid's strange eyes fell upon him. The young lord, though they were close in age, always gave him the feeling that he was a child who needed to be chided for not completing a chore. Jarid kept him in line. Without his ever-faithful presence, Daniel knew his ability as a prince would have been highly deficient. He could not rule his court without those who barred him from his freedom.

Jarid was both his protector and his jailer.

"Your Highness, I need those papers reviewed soon. Please." His voice was a soft, entreating command spoken in the smooth, rich accent of his province.

Daniel flicked back his hair. "I understand, Jarid. They will be finished by the morning."

The young lord bowed. "Thank you, my liege. Come, Skyeola, let us leave the Prince to his work. I would prefer you not to walk the halls alone."

Skyeola's brow crinkled in confusion. "I am fine, Jarid. I am not a kitten. You do not have to hold my claw and escort me everywhere."

Jarid crouched, aiding in gathering Skyeola's conduction equipment, and shared a momentary glance of amusement with Daniel.

"Yes, of course, but we are not in the Palace. This is a foreign province. You need to take care not to wander around unaccompanied. So, come along, I shall take you back to your chambers."

Skyeola sent Daniel a pleading look. He could only shake

his head. Skyeola begrudgingly allowed Jarid to lead him out, and the door slid shut behind them. Daniel returned to his papers, though his mind idled. "Citla, why is Jarid so concerned about Skyeola being alone? He has never acted in this manner before."

He could not see his Maiden, but he was well aware she was nearby, lurking in the dark. Even when he appeared to be alone, he never was. Her monotone voice came from behind him.

"I cannot speak on the matter, Your Highness."

His brow creased. "If I ordered you to, would you?"

"I cannot speak on the matter," she repeated.

"I see. A higher authority than I has silenced you."

"I apolo—"

"Do not apologise. Just, tell me, is it…serious? Should I worry?" He turned to catch the slightest shimmer of her cloaked form in the shadows, lingering there as though she owned the very darkness.

His Maiden, his shadow, his jailer.

"All will be fine, Your Highness."

Daniel frowned. Well, it sounded like he would start worrying, then.

Daniel had been working on affairs of state all evening, making him unapproachable; either Jarid or Citla would chase him away if he dared try to bother the Prince. Hun had gone to enjoy the Iliaion nightlife, probably to do scandalous things that made Citla purse her lips in a very irritated manner. Jarid, at least, had the decorum to not flaunt his ventures; likely he respected Citla's scathing glare more than Hun. Everything they did or said would reflect upon the Prince, after all.

With everyone so preoccupied, he was thought to be studying, yet Skyeola was certain that if he looked at another book on alchemy or conductions the contents of his skull would melt and drain out of his nose.

"That's the problem with a Batitic Memory," he mumbled.

He had read all the books he had brought with him several times already and memorised them on his first reading. Now it was simply a matter of the practical applications. What made it all worse was that Shalamic had nothing remotely resembling a Library. The nerve of a Ruling Family of Pennadot to not have a Library or a Record Room; it was disgusting and practically a crime, in his opinion.

Groaning as he lifted himself off his bed, Skyeola headed for the window. Shalamic's forests, with their luminous glow, had the same appearance as cumulus clouds, making it almost seem as though there were two sky-seas. They had not been permitted to venture into the tangled webs of the distinctly alien trees, only to ride their horses around the already cleared paths.

He wanted more.

He wanted to follow his impulses and dive right into the shimmering allure of the bioluminescent undergrowth.

Skyeola shoved away from the window sill, spinning on his foot-claws. He was inside a Monument of Old, a Zaprex ruin—surely, he could find something to do. His claw hovered over his conduction equipment. Jarid's very stern warning not to walk around unaccompanied echoed in his head like a gong. Then—then there was—*Lord Galvon*—Skyeola's fur hackled unconsciously at the thought of the vile man.

That man and his eyes, there was something about the way the province lord watched him that made his neck feathers fluff and his scales stiffen. Every Batitic sense within him registered the man as a predator—which was irrational: he was a mere Human. In battle a Batitic was the predator of a Human, so why, why did Lord Galvon seem so terrifying?

Skyeola shook his head, clearing his mind of the tumbling thoughts.

He was just going to poke around. After all, he had spent

his entire life exploring the Palace of Pennadot and no one had ever noticed him in the shadows there. The Turret of Shalamic was bound to be the same.

Gathering up his conduction equipment, Skyeola ducked quickly out of his chamber and slunk his way through the wide, yawning hallways of the great tower. Whatever it had once been to the fairy-race, the Humans who now inhabited it had done a masterful job of redecorating. Skyeola was personally extremely grateful for the vast rolls of rugs that seemed to run forever along the halls; his foot-claws had less of a chance of slipping on them, nor did they make the obvious clicking sound that usually alerted someone to his presence.

He loved that the ceiling climbed in arches formed of hexagon shapes, the strange patterns mimicked everywhere, in the tiniest of detailing, from the railings of the walkways, to the way the stairs fitted together in spirals.

Skyeola halted. A noise—was it—?

He frowned, glancing at the floor in confusion.

His ears tweaked rearward, though it was not a noise he could hear with them. It thrummed through his wings like a chiming of hundreds of bells. Skyeola spun, searching the lonely hallway. A song—a melody that echoed from deep within his ancestral memories, urging him somewhere, but where? He had to move—

"Hello?" Skyeola whispered. "Where are you?"

A light. He caught the shimmer beneath a wall-hanging and darted for it, heaving the great tapestry aside, sending dust bursting through the air. Blinking and coughing, Skyeola waved his arms, dispersing the sol-cycles worth of grime. Faintly twinkling on the wall, a pattern of tiny hexagons danced in an azure shine. His claw was reaching out as though he were in a daze, touching the middle of the circle of hexagons, and a doorway revealed itself, with a set of stairs glittering in semi-darkness. Skyeola clutched his claws to his chest, glancing around the empty hallway.

Should he go and find the prince, or Lady Citla?

Skyeola glanced back at the opening. His wings rattled with the intensity of the song calling up from the stairs.

No. He could not wait. He had to go. He had to find out what was seeking him.

With a deep breath he plunged down the stairs; they lit up beneath his foot-claws, welcoming him with chimes as he spun around and around in a dance until he burst out into a larger chamber. The song that had beckoned him was suddenly loud, suddenly in his ears, and surrounding him. Skyeola pinned himself against the nearest wall as a glow encompassed the floor, spinning the crystal gems encircling the hexagon platform. He felt it in his wings, the moment something triggered the enormous crystals, and they abruptly halted their movements. Light burst in the centre of the platform, forming tiny gemlike flakes in the air that gathered into a cluster.

"Oh, by the Twilight." Skyeola raised his claws to his cheeks as the radiance faded, leaving the limp, twisted body of a tiny, delicate fairy sprawled out upon the glass floor.

The lights died around him.

CHAPTER NINE

One is never alone.
There are far too many invisible
living organisms floating around
for anyone to ever be truly alone.

Zaprex Quote

Skyeola rubbed at his eyes as they slowly adjusted to the darkness. He resisted the urge to tug free his conductor and mutter a light spell. There was no telling what sort of reaction his conductions would have on the energy humming in the air.

Carefully he crept up the stairs to the platform and crawled to the limp, sprawled out body. It was so tiny. He had read descriptions of the fairy race in old documents, and, while depictions of them were found in murals throughout the Palace, he had always considered them exaggerations. Yet here one lay, as though torn out of a page of an ancient tome. His claws trembled as he reached out, rolling the delicate body over.

Flaccid arms clunked with weight, like Hun's armour. Skyeola jolted in surprise. That was not a noise he had ever equated with anything living. A faint azure glow began to seep into the joints of the fairy's limbs, running in hexagonal patterns down its arms and beneath the torn coat it wore. The shine intensified under the material, concentrating in the centre of the thin chest. To his ears, it sounded like chimes on the wind, soft at first, then quickening, to be joined by whirring and clicking. Damaged. The beat was off. Something inside the fairy was broken, or at least strained in some manner.

Its eyes suddenly opened.

Skyeola jerked back, covering his mouth in alarm at the squeak he released.

Nothing happened.

It did not move.

He crept closer again. The enormous eyes, yellow like flames, stared at nothing. He waved a claw over them several times.

"Well, what am I to do with...this...?" he muttered.

Could he sneak it back to his chamber? He could conduct up a basket perhaps, hide the little thing away and carry it under his wings. What if it needed medical care? He had read no books on Zaprex medicine—he doubted there was anything at all on such a subject left.

In his fretting, he barely noticed the eyes of the fairy narrow into the thinnest of pin holes to focus on him, until the sensation of being watched tickled his neck feathers. Skyeola tensed and slowly looked back at the fairy.

"I'm a friend." He held out a claw.

Nothing. A blank stare. It did not even blink.

It looked around the room, ignoring him entirely. Did it not see him? Or had it understood him after all? Skyeola clambered to his foot-claws as the Zaprex struggled to stand upright. It turned its globular eyes up at him and spoke in a burst of hurried, high-pitched, sing-song tongue.

"*Hayaku. Iku. Kite iru.*[8]"

"I do not understand you."

Its brow furrowed in irritation, yet, before it could speak again, the floor beneath them began to vibrate. The circle of enormous crystals surged back to life, igniting in a pulsating song. Skyeola snatched the fairy up and dashed towards the entrance. The Secondary Realm energy was pooling in the room again, being gathered and conducted in an eerily similar manner to that which a Batitic could deconstruct and reconstruct. He had only seen examples a few times of what was

---

8   *Quickly. Go. It is coming.*

being reconstructed in the centre of the platform, and usually from far away while he hid from his father.

"Is that…? That's a Twizel," Skyeola hissed, gripping the Zaprex to his chest. "Are you being chased?"

The fairy simply stared up at him. He wondered if it understood anything he said.

"We need to get you out of here," he decided. "Come on. Hopefully it will not realise you have help, so if we move fast I should be able to get you out of Iliaion." He rushed up the stairs in a flurry. "This way."

There was more information on Zaprexes in books and scrolls than there was on Twizels. What details he recalled about such monsters came either from his ancestral memories, or from the few Underground Messengers he had managed to release from his father's torture chambers. He knew Twizels had several levels of intelligence, based entirely on how much flesh they had consumed, be it dead or alive. Some could take living hosts, others only the dead. Shadows could reveal their true form, that was information every Underground Messenger had drilled into him. But if it was a High Class—a Ki'rayh—then none of that mattered; it would be old enough, and have a strong enough bond to the Primary Realm, to sustain itself within a host. He had to act now, while it was confused and disorientated.

There was no time to assess what type of Twizel they were dealing with here. They had to run. Skyeola bolted through the corridors of Shalamic, halting only when they came to a guarded exit. He hissed. That was right. On his own, he would never be allowed through the checkpoints out of the Turret and into the city. Perhaps, if it were daytime, he would have managed to slip out undetected, but his kittenhood worked against him at night. A guard would very much want to check with Maiden Citla or the Prince, or, worse, with Lord Telvon, as to why he was out of his chamber at such a late hour.

Grumbling, Skyeola retreated. "New plan. I have wings. We will have to fly out."

The Zaprex's eyes stared at him from beneath his robe where he had stuffed the little fairy. It fitted rather neatly into the folds, and, if they were not under threat by a Twizel, he had no doubt it would have snuggled up and fallen asleep. The noise—song—it emanated still sounded unwell to his ears.

"Maybe I should…go…find Daniel…" Skyeola shook his head. No. He could not get the Prince caught up in something involving a Twizel. A Twizel meant the Dragon. He could not allow the Prince to become entangled in the mess of his Blood-Clan's ancestral inheritance.

"It's fine." Skyeola opened the nearest window. "I can fly…I can fly. I can…fly." He latched his foot-claws onto the ledge, flinching from the sudden lashing of cold night air. His father had never actually permitted him to fly. Anywhere. He had—of course—broken that rule numerous times, and had flung himself out of several of the towers in the Palace. Not the highest peaks, but high enough that the fall would have killed him had his wings failed him. Really—those had all been experiments—merely experiments.

Skyeola gaped down at the city of Iliaion below. Far below. The shimmering, dancing lights snaked like rivers, weaving through the darkness. His claws dug into the window ledge. This was not one of the towers of the Palace. This was so much higher.

The little fairy shouted something at him.

"It's fine!" He called back. "I can fly. Hold on." Ignoring his racing heart, Skyeola lunged out. They dropped, like a rock, for several feet, until he felt the swirling updraft and unfurled his wings. Like a spring he twirled into the midnight sky-sea, releasing his tail in a brilliant burst of feathers. If only he had been allowed to do this in Palace-Town, the places, the things, he could have seen.

With a whirl, Skyeola surged forward, heading for the wrought iron walls surrounding Iliaion. He landed with a solid thud, skidding in the grass. He almost toppled over and only righted himself with a coil of his tail.

"Whoa, that was incredible." He curled his tail back beneath his robes, tucking it away and gradually folded his wings against the chilled air. He had foolishly not even thought to grab any sort of coat. Would the fairy be warm enough?

It wriggled out of his robe and landed on all fours, picking itself up with an irritated muttering.

"You should have a good head start on the Twizel." Skyeola knelt. "There is so much old Zaprex tech in Shalamic, I am sure you will find something useful to you here."

It looked at the forest ahead of them, like a boundary as intimidating as the walls that surrounded Iliaion.

The Zaprex held out its tiny hand to him, gesticulating vigorously. "*Anzende wa arimasen. Watashi to kite.*[9]"

He could not understand it, but he did not need to understand the words it spoke, the gestures and posture were universal. It wanted him to come with it. Every muscle twitched with desire. The Forests of Shalamic, glowing with incandescent allure, beckoned him with a magnetic song, but nothing was as strong as the will-o'-the-wisp eyes of the fairy floating delicately in front of him. They had a lure that dragged at his wings, pulling on the energy that fuelled his conductions. His foot-claws trembled with the intense, overwhelming need to follow it—where, exactly, he had no idea—but he just had to—

The allure faded.

Skyeola blinked.

Slowly its arm lowered.

Skyeola stepped back, shaking his head. It was not really asking him. He could never go with such an amazing creature. He would only taint it with his existence.

"I cannot, I am sorry. I…" He clutched a claw to his chest, looking back at the Turret of Shalamic. "I…cannot…"

It nodded and its hand wrapped around a slim, glass pendant around its neck. "*Arigato gozaimashita.*[10]"

In a flutter it was gone, somewhere into the forest.

---

9   *It is not safe. Come with me.*

10   *Thank you very much.*

Skyeola's shoulders dropped as his wings fell limply around his foot-claws. It was gone. Just gone. Why had it not stolen him away like the legends always said fairies would?

His fangs bit deep into his lip, drawing blood. In shame, he looked back at the walls of Iliaion and the great Turret reflecting the dancing starry sky-sea. "Now…comes the punishment."

Presenting himself to the guard station at the walls of the Turret of Shalamic seemed like the most sensible thing to do, since he had no desire to risk further exposure of his tail by leaping from a smaller building. A climb back up the Turret would be gruelling on barely-exercised wings. He could already feel the muscles aching and twitching from his little jaunt down.

He must have looked a sorry sight, dressed only in his night robe and a thin coat, fur all fluffed up. Five sets of wide eyes stared at him in mounting horror until the head-guard finally groaned loudly and tossed his hand of cards down on the table.

"Someone go and send word to Lord Telvon, the little kitten escaped…again…"

Another guard thumped out of the door and Skyeola pouted as a thick coat was flung over him and he was heaved up and plonked on a seat by the fire. "Ye're a real little sneak."

"I have perfected the art, yes." Skyeola flashed a grin.

"Be careful, sir." The head-guard crouched in front of him. "Some folk out there, they mean harm to little black kittens."

"I can look after myself."

He ducked as his hair was ruffled by a large hand. "Do not do that," he whispered, bunching his shoulders. His father did it. It was far too condescending an action, meant to remind him of his place in the world, below his father.

The head-guard pulled back. "Apologies, my lord."

Skyeola frowned at the head-guard. Such familiarity was confusing. He had never met this man, so why did he feel that they were acquainted. He closed his eyes. It had been a long evening. His wing junctions hurt.

The door opened, revealing the guard who had gone to fetch Jarid. Skyeola tensed. Jarid was going to be livid. He would probably confine him to his chamber for a few days and make him write an awful essay about the economics of Pennadot.

"Lord Galvon has offered to take little Lord Skyeola back to his chambers."

Every thought froze. Skyeola choked, covering his mouth. Lord Galvon? What was Lord Galvon doing—?

"I will take it from here." His head was touched. He wanted to jerk away, but he was frozen stiff in a terrible, unbearable fear that clenched his limbs.

Where did it come from?

Whose fear was this, which ancestor—or was it his own?

Siblings—

A sibling—

His eyes widened and he jerked his head up at Lord Galvon. "Do not touch me."

He stood and headed for the door.

The head-guard moved forward, showing sudden concern. "I'll come with yeh, sir."

"No, we will be fine." Lord Galvon nudged Skyeola out the door. Skyeola looked back at the head-guard, begging with his eyes. They could not leave him alone with this man.

They did. Lord Galvon swept him away with a large hand burning into his back. Skyeola focused intensely on the corridor ahead of them and the noise of his own foot-claws clipping upon the floor, anything other than the Human man steering him from behind. After several flights of stairs and long hallways, Skyeola dared to halt.

"This is not the way to my chamber."

Lord Galvon looked around innocently. "Oh, forgive me,

it is not. A simple mistake." He took hold of Skyeola's shoulder.

Skyeola wrenched out of his grip. "I said do not touch me." It was his voice, but the words echoed from his ancestral memories.

Lord Galvon's whisper in his ear sent a shiver through his fur. "You do not seem to comprehend the situation you are in, little Lord Skyeola. Your father has promised—"

"Lord Galvon, thank you for finding my young sorcerer," Daniel's voice called out. Skyeola twisted around, relief flooding through him at the sight of the prince striding towards them. The head-guard was with him, and, by his panting, seemed to have been running, and fast. Skyeola's chest clenched. That was impossible; there was no way the head-guard could have run the distance to the prince's chamber—

He did not care. He really did not care. The prince was here. He was safe.

"I will take him from here, Lord Galvon." Daniel's shimmering light filled the corridor in a sudden, enveloping warmth that caused Lord Galvon to flinch back. Skyeola made a mad dash for the safety of that light and every protection it offered. Like soap, it washed the touch of the province lord from his shoulder, and his erratic heartbeat began to ease allowing air back into his lungs.

Lord Galvon bowed. "Your Highness."

He had never seen Daniel's green eyes so fiercely cold, burning with the rage of the Sun behind them, as the prince tracked the province lord's departure. He heard the soft whisper: "Absolute scum."

It was so rare for the prince to express such emotion out loud.

Daniel took him by both shoulders and wrapped him protectively in his heavy nightrobe.

"Thank you, Almet." Skyeola peeked out of the robe just far enough to see the prince hand a gem to the head-guard. "I am extremely grateful."

"Your Highness." The guard inclined his head.

"Skyeola, say thank you to Almet. He has ruined his career as a guard here in Shalamic for you."

Skyeola lowered his head. "Th...thank you."

Almet gave his shoulder a firm pat. "Ain't nothing ta worry about, kitten."

"Seek out Hun of the Fifth Clan," Daniel, said. "He will find you a position in our company."

"Thank you, Your Highness." Almet bowed.

Skyeola squeaked as Daniel grabbed his arm and marched him down the corridor.

"Um, Your Highness?"

Daniel did not reply. Bunching up his wings, Skyeola quickened his pace to match the prince's. Had it been any other situation, he would have admired the blazing shine of his starblood refracting off the metal walls of the hallways, but it was frightening to see the prince with a face of stone. Was this another mask, or was this the real Daniel?

They came to the prince's chambers. Citla stood waiting for them. She flung a shawl around his shoulders, checking him over.

"Nothing happened?" she asked.

"I do not believe so." Daniel glanced down at him.

He was wedged between them both, their tall Kimwyn bodies like two shields. His own father had never fussed over him like this. The Harem Maidens and Butlers always did the fussing when he was caught out and about. He should have been used to it, but it always felt odd, to be cuddled and worried over.

Citla anxiously touched his forehead and he fluffed his neck features in irritation.

"I am fine."

"Fine?" Daniel rounded on him. "Then what, Sun Above, possessed you to sneak out in the middle of the night?"

Skyeola shied away. Those eyes were like furnaces. "I was...I just...I was doing some astrometry."

"You could have gotten frost bite, Skyeola." Citla pushed

him down onto the couch, and passed him a hot mug of steaming tea. Daniel nursed his head in his hands.

"Frost bite. That was the least of my worries." Daniel groaned. "What if someone had kidnapped him?"

Skyeola flinched. How he wished the fairy had stolen him away, but not even a fairy thought he was worth stealing.

"What if some slave trader had taken him," Daniel continued, "or, Sun Forbid, what if Lord Galvon had—"

"Your Highness, he is fine," Citla urged gently.

Daniel stood again in agitation. Skyeola watched with wide eyes. He had never seen the prince in such a state. This was not over him—surely?

Daniel pinched the bridge of his nose, breathing out steadily, before kneeling in front of him. He placed his much larger hands on Skyeola's knobbly knees and squeezed firmly.

"Have you any idea what could happen to you out there, in Iliaion, alone? You are a little kitten—someone, anyone, could have hurt you."

Skyeola sulkily slumped back. He puffed out his cheeks.

"I can look after myself."

"You are my responsibility." The prince reached up a hand, cupping his cheek. "I know you think that you are free of your father's influence here, but that does not give you permission to run about willy-nilly without consequences."

Skyeola drowned in the fluorescent green of the royal gaze.

"What about you?"

"I am insulted you think I do anything without first considering the consequences."

Skyeola snorted. There was even a light cough from Citla.

"I heard that, Maiden." Daniel tweaked Skyeola's nose.

Skyeola buried himself in the blanket, cocooning himself away in his wings. He could not tell them about the most beautiful thing he had ever seen, about the fairy, and the magic, and the song. About almost being stolen away.

He held out his claw. He could still feel it, the electric touch of the Zaprex's tiny hand. Those huge yellow eyes that had stared at him in wonder. The fairy had been real, and he had not run after it.

But—

Looking up, into Daniel's bright, shimmering eyes of green, Skyeola's stomach twisted into knots. That was why the fairy's eyes had been so awfully familiar, why staring into them had pulled at him so much.

They had the same glow.

Daniel had fairy eyes; he was sure of it.

CHAPTER TEN

"I'm telling you this now, Sibling,
A Twizel's smile is worse than its bite,
If you live long enough to see it smile, that is…"

Messenger High Commander Tal Telvon
Killed in Action During the Battle of Wharf Nine,
2305DC

It did not rain in the Pennadotian Summer. Zinkx wiped the water from his eyes. There was no other word for it, though, but rain. Overnight, the temperature within the immense Shalamic Forests dropped and the world froze, and then, as the Great Sun rose and heated the atmosphere once more, the frozen water melted into a steamy rain.

He was drenched. Drenched through to the bone, as Khwaja Denvy would have joked. At least back on the Plains of Blazing Fire he had worn a battle-suit, able to regulate his temperature with the old Zaprex technology. Without it, he was exposed and constantly at war with the elements. Always feeling either disgustingly hot or cold in this appalling polar weather.

He was exhausted. For several days he had been away from the camp he had established with Shanty in an old Messenger Hideout, checking the Zaprex Ruins nearby, and, while he had managed to uncover a fair amount of fey metal for trade, there had been nothing of military value he could summarise.

Zinkx sprinted down the path he had checked was free

from the dangerous carnivorous plant life that grew in the shadows of Shalamic's twisted and brightly coloured undergrowth. The diabond had made the journey into the forests easier than it would have been had they taken it on foot, her elemental shifting manipulating the forest around her. But there was still something eerie and dangerous about Shalamic's dense plant life. It had an awareness of its own, whispering and speaking to itself in melodies.

Shanty was convinced the forest would protect them, but he was not so sure. He had not yet sensed the presence of any Twizels, but it was the influence of the Dragon he feared, infecting even the susurration of the trees. Shanty, however, knew more of forests than he, and her insistence that she was safe even in such a foreign environment had given him leave to search for the Key.

Zinkx swept aside the overhanging vines concealing the network of caves, and ducked inside. He squinted at the change in light, a cool blue glow from the sparkling minerals coating the cave walls. He rubbed at his eyes. At least it was cooler down here, and protected from the not-rain outside.

"The forest seems full of unrest," he commented as he shook himself dry.

He threw the animal he had caught onto a wooden block by the fire. Hot coals already burned brightly in the darkness, keeping the belly of the deep cave a pleasant temperature, chasing away the mugginess.

"Pardon?" Shanty glanced up from beside the orange glow, prodding at the embers to ignite a deeper burn. Zinkx noted the flush of red across her green cheeks from the heat of the rising flames as she piled more dry wood into the pit that had been cut out of the stone. The mahogany gown she was sewing with the material she had bought was only half completed and was slung lazily over one shoulder. When finished, with his hand-crafted leather bodice added, he knew she would look like the wild shaman beauty of the woodlands she joked of being.

Zinkx gave a faint smile. "The forest's uneasiness is unsettling, that's all."

She reached for the skinned animal he had caught, studying it thoughtfully.

"A Human man thinking of the forest—what have I done?"

Zinkx shook his head. He stripped off his shirt, wrung it out, and hung it in front of the fire. Shanty had made him several new garments, each one embellished with fine embroidery. Suns and stars mixed with autumn coloured leaves. She was making him feel stately, like a prince, with such handsome wear.

"You're overthinking things again." Her comment startled him.

He stirred, realising he had stopped with a shirt over his head. Quickly he pulled it on, blinking rapidly, allowing his mind to catch up with the present. "Actually, I was…"

Shanty sighed heavily. "Sit down, before you fall down, Human."

He did so. Rifling around in his bag, Zinkx brought out a dented tin. A gift from his lieutenant, who shared his love of an old brew that had given considerable comfort in the Trenches. Kaitla would have come with him, and a tiny part of him wished he had, but the man needed to be with the family he had built, and not out here searching for something intangible.

Zinkx twisted open the lid, staring into a void. Another piece of home gone.

"*Melltithiwch yr Haul.*[11]" Zinkx tipped up the tin. "We're out of coffee." He collapsed forward with a groan. "What point is there in going on…"

"I put the last spoon on for you." Shanty gestured.

He looked up, spotting the pot over the coals. Zinkx breathed in sharply. "You are a Krrirren."

Shanty smiled. "Drink your brew, Human."

It calmed the jittering the of his knees a little, tasting home, smelling home.

---

11   *Curse the Sun.*

"I take it your search did not turn up anything?"

Zinkx shook his head. "No." He sighed into his coffee. "I may have to start circling out further, but...that will mean..."

"Do not worry about me." Shanty glanced up from stirring a second pot over the fire.

"You ask much," Zinkx muttered.

Shanty sipped a spoon. "I know." Seeming content with the taste, she poured out stew into separate bowls. She offered Zinkx the food. He set down his mug, taking both bowl and the accompanying flatbread with a smile of gratitude. A long, comfortable silence stretched out between them as the rain outside gradually began to ease.

"It's good," Zinkx commented finally. "You're an excellent cook."

"Thank you." She hid her happiness at the praise behind a shrug. "The forest around us is full of many different flavours; I managed to find some herbs for your tastes."

"An open scroll, am I?"

She frowned.

"It means someone is easy to judge or to comprehend their emotions."

"Then no. You are not. You would be a Great Oak with many rings one must burrow through before reaching the centre."

"So, I'm old and you are a tree-worm."

She laughed, delight showing at his comeback.

Zinkx scooped up stew with a chunk of bread. "Well, I appreciate the food. I feel like I was raised on tasteless ration bars. Couldn't carry many supplies in the Trenches." His mind drifted, the echo of cannon-fire, the clatter of rocks, eruptions of lava. It was a strain to pull his thoughts back to the present. "Decent food is a nice change."

"Was it so bad?" Shanty bit her lip, her question coming out as a strained whisper. "The Trenches?"

At the query, Zinkx finished his mouthful and blinked. He started reaching for his coffee, but Shanty was quick to replace it with another mug he had carved from wood, one long, sleepless night—a night he had lost to memories of war. She had to be aware of the cold fits he had and his inability to chase away his nightmares. He glanced at the contents of the mug, a mixture of one of her potions. The opportunities she had to simply poison him and run were countless and yet she fed him like he was a starving child. He gathered, in her eyes, he was very much lacking bodily nutrition. Maybe she was hoping one of her herb mixtures would cure his insomnia; it would be a Sun-sent blessing if it were so.

"The death…will always be bad, losing life is painful—" He swallowed a gulp of her warm, spicy herbal mixture. "But I had a good family, a strong family. My Squadron. You would have liked them." He smiled fondly in recollection. "That is the thing about adversity; it brings folk together and weaves tight strands of fates."

Shanty spooned more food into her bowl. "You speak as though we have no power to change our fate, Human. That is a lie preached by your Sun Monks." She touched the spoon to her lips thoughtfully. "You may walk to the edge of Livila itself if you so desire it, and no one shall stop you."

Zinkx pointed to her, giving a chuckle. "Is that why you were thrown into that cell where I found you? You believed you could change your fate?"

She smirked behind the spoon she held.

"I ate his keys, did I not?"

He laughed. "Fair enough point, Krrirren."

The tranquillity of the world surrounding Shanty was astounding, yet, in contrast, Zinkx spoke of war and pain, of bloody battles waged across a land scarred with molten rock, never-ending glaciers, and toxic fumes. Her mind had trouble comprehending the ghastly stories the Messenger told her while she felt so much at peace within the deep forest.

He had fashioned her a shawl out of cleaned, dried skins, to keep off the strange rains that occurred periodically throughout the day. She wrapped it neatly around her shoulders, loving how he had made sure it matched her mahogany dress and the bodice. He leapt lightly on his feet beside her as they wove their way back towards the Caves. Every so often she lost sight of him as he vanished into the shadows, flittering away like a leaf on the wind.

She wondered often if it was a trick of the light, how his skin sometimes had the eerie illusion of similar pictograms to her own tattoos, burning beneath the surface of his muddy tint, waiting to be released. As they neared the Caves the diabond bounded out to meet Zinkx with an enthusiastic show, yipping happily and bouncing around the Human as he bounced around her.

Shanty smiled, placing her basket of gathered herbs down, watching the amusing display between the two as Zinkx flung himself onto the diabond and the two rolled around.

He called it 'establishing a dreamathic bond'. She knew better. He loved the tactile touch of the fur so much like that of the forest-god, Khwaja Denvy. At first glance, Zinkx may have appeared a man of few words, bottling up emotions, his opinions repressed behind iron bars, lips thin and closed, yet when given leave and safety to speak, he had a sharp blade of a tongue and a laugh that mimicked that of the forest-god.

He wrote often in a leather-bound journal, and, not only did he write, he was a skilled artisan. It no longer surprised her, after seeing the images he could draw, that the intricate detailing on her bodice and shawl had come out so fine and wonderous.

"Zinkx...?"

From where he crouched gathering his packs, he looked back at her with a raised eyebrow. "Yes?"

"I was...thinking of going down to Iliaion while you did your loop. We did not learn of anything about the Merchant Bkyri-kirk or my sister at Ninnian; perhaps in Iliaion I shall."

He paused, his shoulders tensing. Shanty clutched at her bundled dress.

"I am going to be heading further out," he murmured.

"And how long will you be?"

Zinkx dropped his head back. "About three, maybe four, days."

She swept past him. "Precisely."

"I won't be able to...if you're in trouble...I can't..."

"I will be fine." She waved at his concern. "The Fifth Clan is scarce in this area and they're a very tolerant Clan."

The way his lips pressed thin told her he was extremely reluctant to believe hearsay.

"Take the diabond with you."

"I was planning to."

"And a blade." He held out the weapon to her and she stared at it.

"I do not—"

"I am very aware of your brute strength, but what if you come up against another Kelib? Please. Take it."

Nodding, she accepted the small token. He bundled up his supplies, strapping them around his hips. "Keep an eye out for Twizels."

"I know. Light hides them. Shadows reveal them," Shanty repeated the phrase. "I would have thought it would be the opposite. Light reveals, shadows hide."

Zinkx shrugged. "I am sure there is an explanation. But be careful."

"I want to make some enquiries about the Merchant."

"Fair enough." He smiled. "I shouldn't be more than four days. If you're not here when I get back, I'll tear Iliaion apart to find you."

Shanty followed him to the entrance of the caves. "That attached to me, are you?"

He threw a grin back over his shoulder. "More attached to your cooking."

Shanty shoved him.

"Sorry, I couldn't help myself." He sprang away from her with a twirl. Before she could blink, he vanished into the branches without a sound. The forest about her whispered with the lightest of lonely melodies, echoing the ancient, slumbering ruins that lay deep in its shadows. She hugged herself, staring at the space he had voided. The diabond nestled up to her side, resting her chin on her shoulder. Shanty ruffled a hand behind her ear.

"Come on, darling, I want to see this new city."

It took a full day of travel upon the diabond to reach Iliaion, and approaching the city's gate as evening fell seemed befitting, as the forest came alive with luminescent plant-life. With a two-night pass given to her at the guard house, Shanty led the diabond through the powerful, fortified walls. If the forests came to life at the falling of the Sun, then it seemed that Iliaion also mimicked the environment it dwelt within. The vast sprawling layers of buildings were lit with fine, glowing ivy and shimmering fungi that ignited the still bustling streets with a warm ambience. Shanty breathed in deeply the scent of crushed dirt, hot spices, and sizzling meats. Food stalls hustled with business, offering wonderous looking meals to be eaten on the go, and travellers seemed none the wiser that night had fallen beyond the walls.

She clutched the diabond's reins. "So, this is Humanity."

Her gaze turned upward, to the massive Turret of Shalam-ic that ruled the skyline of Iliaion. From afar it appeared as though a great spear had struck the earth and shattered all that surrounded it. Up close, the detailing of the spiral was breath-taking. It had twists and corners, despite its smooth appearance, and reflected the starlit sky-sea. Who had the fey been to have built such a structure? And what for? What hope did Zinkx have of finding his needle in such a haystack?

She shook her head, amused at his Human analogy.

She had her own illusive needles to find. Somewhere, in this bustling of life, surely someone had met her Sister.

Finding a suitable inn was less daunting than she had anticipated. She had expected to be hassled far more, and, yet, the Humans she pressed through seemed content to ignore her. An aching pool grew in her chest as a slave boy, a brand burned harshly into his pale, freckled skin, was sharply ordered to lead her to her room.

The disturbing reminders of Crinn seemed to taint her footsteps.

She requested an extra hot bath.

At first, she had been far too blinded by the overwhelming beauty and wonder of Iliaion. Come morning, and her venture into the markets in the blistering heat, the splendour of the previous evening had evaporated. She wanted to forget the shady glances and tolerant smiles, unsure if she was imagining them on the faces of the Kelibs behind the stalls she visited. Hearsay seemed true: the Fifth Clan was liberal, but her actions made her obviously not one of them even with her tattoos and scars covered. Humans seemed far more comfortable with the idea of exchanging goods with her. It was near thirst-like, the excitement she provoked in the eyes of the Human merchants, yet even that grew tiresome as the day wore on.

Shanty sipped on a cool tea brew as the diabond lapped at a communal trough. "My Sisters are like Autumn Leaves on the wind." She rubbed the hound's chin. "Here for a moment, gone the next."

She sighed, swirling her sweet tea. "I hope they are safe, dear." She leant on the diabond. "Do you think they are?"

The diabond's warm, red eyes studied her before she

returned to the trough. Shanty nodded. "Yes, you're right, I am sure they have found a place for their roots to grow deep."

She crunched up the small paper cup, casting it into the nearby bin. "Right. One more item." Shanty stood, dusting off her gown. "Then I think we shall head back early. I have decided I much prefer the lonely melodies of the strange forest to the rumble of Iliaion."

She had seen several of the Human merchants selling the little brown bean Zinkx had treasured from his home. It seemed a commodity of Humans, for none of the Kelib stalls offered it. If there were different varieties, she could not tell, and with a limited understanding of the language being spoken she could only manage simple transactions.

That she even succeeded in purchasing a sack from a trader was a minor miracle; the man took his time, muttering under his breath at her. She was sure he only handed it over due to the growling diabond at her side. Perhaps it was the presence of the diabond that had lulled her into an odd sense of security, that she had not needed to be as wary as she should have been. When the thief struck, snatching out her jewel pouch as she was tying the sack of brown beans onto the diabond's saddle, her reaction was slowed by the scattering of her purchases across the road. She tackled the Kelib man to the ground, retrieving her pouch from the thief. Shanty went for her concealed blade, only for her wrist to be grabbed with equal force.

She jerked her head, peering out under her tousled hair at the half-breed who held her.

"You have him, lady. My men can take it from here."

In fury, Shanty smacked the thief back against the ground and got to her knees as several guards, their attire bearing the Sun emblem, descended upon him. She ignored his wails and looked around at the brown beans that had scattered from the broken sack. Even with the jewels left in her pouch, she would not have enough to purchase more.

"They really do teach yeh Eighth Clan women how to fight, heh? Seems rather stupid, given your purpose."

Her nostrils flared at the intruding voice. Shanty turned, looking up at the half-breed. His too-Human eyes, like white-glass orbs in pale jade skin, studied her curiously. "Yeh'll wanna cover that tattoo up, lass."

Shanty struggled with her shawl, wrapping the thick stole around her shoulders again. She slapped the offered hand aside, glaring at the litter of little brown beans. Heat burned the edges of her eyes. Tears. Was she really—

Was she about to cry over spilt beans? Her fingers trembled as she gathered them into her dress, along with wads of dirt. It was no use. They were worthless now. Covered in the filth of the road. She could not give these to Zinkx.

Someone knelt beside her in the mud. Delicate. That was the first word that flitted through her mind. A delicate man, with delicate hands. Clarity struck her as light like that of captured rays caught by a diamond danced across the road. The stories, every Mor-Mor passed them down to every Sapling, the tales of Humans born of the stars.

He was kneeling beside her, in the mud and the filth, picking up the brown beans with such smooth, unblemished hands, glittering and shimmering under the holy light of the Sun. A breath escaped her. He was indescribably beautiful, draped in jewels that only enhanced his glow.

"Your Highness, honestly!" a Retenna man upon a nearby horse called out. "Could you try to not get yourself filthy?"

"It is just dirt, Jarid," the starborn responded. She barely understood the thick, rich accent that flowed from their lips. If not for time spent listening to Zinkx, she undoubtedly would never have managed.

Warm green eyes met her own. Green. Like the Pennadotian fields. Like the Leaves of the Krrirrens. Shanty quickly lowered her head enough to be respectful.

"I apologise. You have lost all you purchased. Allow me to buy you another bag."

"It was not the fault of Your Highness," she managed her dry tongue around the Basic.

"Whatever one of my subjects does reflects upon me, as their sovereign, and, therefore, I should repay their debts."

Her spinning head finally caught up with his moving lips. He was speaking fluent Kelib, far better even than Zinkx.

"I insist." He stood, brushing at his muddied attire as though it would make a difference to the stains.

Shanty breathed in deeply. To refuse seemed counterproductive. She had dearly wanted the brown beans for Zinkx—he was losing pieces of his home-tree and at least this she could provide him.

Slowly she inclined her head.

"Thank you."

His magnificent smile dazzled with all the brilliance of Sunlight upon the surface of a pond. "Come, then, walk with me. Where did you purchase the coffee from?"

"Coffee." Shanty tasted the word with a roll of her tongue. Zinkx had called the brown beans 'coffee' also. This must be the Human term for the dried seed. Rising to her feet, Shanty took the diabond's reins and gestured back down the market road. The prince stepped out as though the crowd meant nothing, and it did not to the Imperial, for the swelling of people dissolved around them as he walked with purpose and authority. She felt caught up in a gravitational pull, forced to walk beside him as though she was one of the Twin Moons.

Every so often a child broke the strange allure, entering the hallowed ground that seemed to surround him. He joyfully heaved each child sky-seaward, catching them skilfully, and jewels were passed out, along with sweets from his deep pockets. He smiled at her bafflement.

"You build a kingdom on the dreams of children."

"Whatever brought you to the markets?" Shanty briefly glanced at the stains on the royal's attire. While he was dressed for riding, a blemish on such handsome clothes seemed disgustingly wasteful even to her.

"Happenstance." The starborn laughed. "We were out for a stroll. Hun noticed the thief before he noticed you. So, really, it is my fault we did not apprehended him in time."

Hun—so that was the name of the half-breed.

"I still thank you."

The prince looked to the sky-sea. "Someone once told me that the world is made of circles, and we are all just circling in loops, sometimes meeting, sometimes not. It is always best to treat one another with kindness, so, when our circles reunite, kindness is returned."

He was either so naïve it was unbearable, or he actually held unblemished ideals in a sweet, caring heart wrapped in wool. Zinkx would have been laughing, saying something dripping in sarcasm, but she could only smile at the genuine gentleness.

The stall-owner she had bought the coffee from turned pale upon sighting the starborn beside her as she approached once more, asking for another sack of the brown beans. It was readied far more swiftly than her last purchase.

"Trying to stay awake?" the prince commented.

"Pardon?" Shanty accepted the bag from the man behind the stall.

With a smile, the starborn offered a jewel to the owner. "Skyeola would likely know more, since he is an alchemist, but coffee has a property in it that keeps one awake. Unless I am crunching papers for some disastrous reason, I am forbidden to drink it past the mid-Sun." He pointed to the sky-sea and the blessed Sun overhead.

Shanty frowned. "I was unaware of this."

"Well. I am led to believe that the coffea plant is a Human import." He tugged on a jewel dangling from the ornament hung through his hair. "Just a moment." The Imperial turned and called out, "Skyeola! Come over here, would you."

Out of the entourage that had followed along behind, a slim, black-furred being, with silver bangles wrapping his arms, and large foot-claws, rushed up to them. Sweet red eyes, like crimson flowers surrounded by velvet night, looked up at her innocently. She was momentarily struck by the thought that, despite her height, the child before her was several inches shorter than she was, making the Imperial Prince all the more impressively tall.

"Yes, Your Highness," he burst out with great enthusiasm.

"Skyeola, go with this Kelib Shaman. Escort her to her desired destination. Tell her what you know about coffee."

"Coffee?"

The starborn headed back to his horse and the beautiful Imperial woman standing nearby, dressed entirely in black. Her stark gaze had not left them for a moment. Even now, Shanty was sure every movement she made was being judged and assessed by the fierce stare.

"You are both herbalists. I am sure you have much in common. Almet, keep him safe."

A Soatrin guard stepped forward. "As you wish, Your Highness."

The child's whole body curled up. "Please. Your Highness. I am fine on my own."

"Ah, ah, ah." The prince waggled a finger, his smile luminous. "This is for your own protection."

Skyeola sighed, sending a defeated look towards the man named Almet as the prince and his entourage left. Shanty smiled at the guard as he approached the diabond, who rumbled a low growl of warning that the Human man ignored. "A beautiful beast."

He spoke Kelib—

At least. She was sure it was Kelib she was hearing. Perhaps it was not. How strange, that he seemed to have such a common Human face, that she felt compelled to ignore his appearance, to glance away, like he was naught but a flickering shadow.

"Yes. She is."

"Does she have a name?"

Before she could speak, young Skyeola bristled at the guard. "Do not be so rude, Almet."

"My apologies. Is there anything else we could aid you with while you are here?" a steady, comforting voice replied.

A gnawing grated at her stomach. She almost mentioned the Merchant and her Sister, but the diabond's lips curled back as she growled once again. Shanty blinked, shaking her head, turning away. "No. Coffee was my last purchase. I am heading to the gates."

Almet took the diabond's reins from her. "Then we shall escort you."

Little Skyeola's furry presence did not have quite as dramatic an effect as the starborn on the market crowds but moving through the streets was subjectively easier with him beside her, for he so obviously did not belong amongst the rabble.

"You are not afraid of me?"

"Should I be?"

He scratched his head awkwardly, causing his bangles to jingle delightfully. "Most folk, when they first see a Batitic, they are rather scared. Apparently we are somewhat terrifying."

"I have faced far more terrifying things than a fluffy ball." Her eyes tracked Almet, who strolled lazily in the shadows cast by the buildings, and, yet, why was it that her eyes fought to focus on the man?

"I am sorry if I have taken you from your duties," she offered by way of comfort to the child beside her.

Skyeola shook his head. "We really were simply out for a stroll. It can get stuffy being inside all the time." He bounced on his claws. "How about you? Where have you travelled from?"

"Nowhere interesting."

"Then you must be travelling too somewhere interesting?"

"I am a shaman on a pilgrimage to the Monuments of Old."

A rattling of wings sounded. "The Zaprexes! You are exploring ruins. Oh, how exciting. What are they like? Do they really have monstrous machines in them that kill you if you trespass? Have you ever seen a real Zaprex? Or...or..."

Shanty laughed. "It sounds as though you should join us."

"I wish I could." He sighed. "I really wish I could." Skyeola cast a longing stare to the sky-sea. There was more than pining in the child's gaze; there was pain, an intense desire to escape—so like her own. He needed to run away from something, or perhaps even someone.

What was his shackle? This strange, thin creature with fur so rich, and black as oil, a being she had never seen before, nor even heard of, and yet he spoke her tongue fluently.

"You know of herbs?" She offered a new point of conversation.

Skyeola made an uncomfortable shrugging motion that caused the enormous wings protruding from his hips to judder. The action itself made her wonder if he had picked up such an unnatural gesture from time spent amongst company not of his own kind.

"An alchemist must know herbs, and, in learning about the herbs, you become knowledgeable of their healing properties. There are crossovers in many professions. It becomes difficult to compartmentalise." He dropped his head to one side. "I presume, as a shaman, herbs are your profession."

"I would have thought so, but it would seem I am lacking in the understanding of Human plants."

Skyeola raised his brow. "The coffee?"

Shanty nodded. "My travelling companion is a Human man. He ran out of his favourite brew. I desired to find it for him, but I was unaware that it might have been adding to his ill sleep."

"How restless is he?"

"Very." Shanty frowned.

"Ah, I see," Skyeola mused. "Well, I doubt it is helping the insomnia. I can only suggest a similar thing I applied to the Prince. Forbid the consumption past the mid-Sun. That should give enough hours for the effects to wear off."

Shanty sighed. "He will be displeased."

Skyeola laughed. He dug through his hip-bag, pulling out a wad wrapped in beeswax paper, and passed it to her. "This is chocolate. Have you heard of it?"

Another Human food? Or was this, perhaps, something Batitic?

"It comes from the cocoa bean, which is a seed of a cacao tree. It is another thing Humans brought to Livila, or so the legends say, though the largest plantation is actually in Sin'musk'qu." He rolled his eyes. "I am sure the Sin'musk'qu Wars were really fought over chocolate. Historians just failed to mention it."

His laugh twittered charmingly. "Add this to some hot milk and stir it in. It becomes an extraordinarily rich treat."

"This must be expensive," Shanty murmured.

"It is." Skyeola nodded. "There are not many cacao trees. They are considered endangered."

"Then I cannot accept this."

The Batitic smiled, showing tiny white fangs. "From one herbalist to another, a gift. Besides, the prince gets a shipment every few months for his patronage in keeping the cacao trees safe. So I will not miss it."

She hugged the offering to her chest. "Sun's Blessings."

"May the Twilight Guide you." He bowed his head, stepping back as Almet passed over the diabond's reins. The two dissolved into the afternoon crowd swelling around the gatehouses.

Having her travel papers signed for departure and returning the amulet a day early caused no fuss; indeed, she glowed with a sense of accomplishment that her solo journey had not taken a turn for the worse.

As she took the road into the forest her thought was drawn to the beeswax-wrapped package the young Batitic had handed her. Chocolate. It sounded so decadent, something only a royal would have access to. Rifling around in her hip-bag, Shanty tugged free the package, giving it a curious sniff. The diabond butted her shoulder gently.

"I know, I know, but it could not hurt to try it."

The hound mewed.

"No. I have no idea if it is poisonous to beasts."

Peeling open the beeswax paper, Shanty halted as a piece of parchment fluttered to the ground. She crouched, picking it up and flipping it over. A quickly scrawled note was written in Kelib.

"Run, Messenger. My Guard is a Twizel. Run."

Her heart thundered in her chest. Snatching the reins of the diabond, Shanty clambered onto the saddle and urged the hound into a canter. How far could she get? How long did she have until it caught up—

How did the young Batitic know she was connected to a Messenger?

Almet had been assigned to him. When Hun had arrived at the entrance of his chamber with the guard several mornings prior, Skyeola had repressed his grimace, accepting the prince's command diligently. It was not so much for Daniel's sake, though, that he had bitten his lip and held his tongue to fight the frustration at having a shadow mark his movements. No—it was for the fairy.

He had hoped to provide the Zaprex more time to escape, but it seemed this was all the aid he was going to be able to offer. It was unlikely the Twizel that had consumed Almet knew of the Underground Messenger Network runes, and they had been so subtly added to the Kelib woman's leather shawl and bodice that even he would have missed them if not for his pictographic memory. These particular signs had not been in circulation for sol-cycles amongst the Pennadotian Underground Network. She either knew a Messenger who was of the upper echelons within the House, or was one herself.

The burning irritation that he had been unable to converse with her longer gnawed at him. When he was finally away from the overlording gaze of his father, he had to have a Twizel glaring at his back instead.

Skyeola sighed, reaching for a sheet of origami paper on the nearby table. One thousand stars he needed for the ritual, and he was almost there.

"How long have you known?" Almet's calm voice spoke from the shadows of his chamber. Skyeola threw another origami star into the large jar that contained the others he had made.

"Since you saved me from Lord Galvon. It was physically impossible for Almet to reach the prince as quickly as he did, even if he had run from the guard station. Therefore, you must be the Twizel that came through the Zaprex machine that night. A Ki'rayh, I presume. Possibly a lower dreamathic type due to your light skill in shifting perceptions. Does not quite work on me though, does it?"

There was a long pause. Skyeola reached for another origami sheet, beginning another paper star. Nine hundred and nine. Almost enough.

"Where is the Zaprex Hatchling?"

"I do not know."

Something cold was pressed against his neck. A long, thick talon. It had taken its true form. The chill in the air behind him tickled his back scales, causing them to tense. Skyeola smirked, curling his lips in a mocking laugh. "You cannot save me and then threaten me. I am the precious son of your Overlord. You have a choice; either go after your order, or stay and keep me safe from the harm you know I am in."

Gradually, the talon was removed. "Then I shall have to trust the Prince with your safety, Little Lord."

Skyeola flinched as a burst of air pulsed through his chamber, the window thrusting open. The Twizel's presence vanished in the swirl. Skyeola stared out for a while before returning to his origami, completing the final stars. Picking up the jar of tiny, multi-coloured paper stars, he wandered to the open window and settled the jar on the ledge. The Sunset had painted the sky-sea a deep purple with veins of fiery crimson and lashes of yellow. The winged shadow of the Twizel stained the perfect hues as it dived for the cloud-like surfaces of the forests.

Tapping out his conductor from his wrist holster, Skyeola gently began a rhythmic beat against the side of the jar, whispering the conduction before biting down on his lip with his fangs. The crackle of the energy release played over the delicate skin of his lips as the transference was made, the small amount of blood drawn fuelling the uplink.

He tipped the jar. The one thousand origami stars lifted into the velvet night, glowing like tiny lanterns. Skyeola rested on the window ledge, smiling as they wisped away in the gentle breeze.

"Be safe, my little friend, wherever you are..."

CHAPTER ELEVEN

They were the fairy-folk,
The little people,
Born of iron and ice.
With a simple song they tamed the restless earth.
If you hear their voices,
Still lingering in the shadows,
And if you see the bobbing lights through the mist,
I beseech you,
Don't follow the little will-o'-the-wisp,
Because the fairy-folk are no more.
We lost them
To the Dragon.
They are gone,
And the earth weeps.

Tale of the Fairies and the Dragon

A blue screen covered Semyueru's vision.

Clearly written across it in slim black letters read: '*System reboot*'.

Somewhere inside its body something clicked, like a switch, and its limbs began to regain sensation. Its Matrix Crystal was beginning to vibrate again.

The words vanished, but the blue screen remained. It flickered for a moment. New words were typed, letter by letter.

'*This program has suffered a serious error. Please restart and try again.*'

Semyueru heard itself sigh.

The system rebooted. Whirring fans and sparking wires gave off an uneasy whine of protest, but they at least started. The blue screen blurring its optical lenses flashed, gradually replaced by the visible world outside its mind. Tiny pixels shifted, filling out a world of terrifying flora. The light for its optical lenses to focus on was bioluminescent, bright, intense, and sharp—enough to make its shutters flicker in pain. Its antennae seemed offline, and without them it was impossible to sense anything beyond its own hull. Though it might have been for the best, considering the overwhelming life surrounding it. It may as well have plunged into a vat of swarming nano-bots, only this was worse—far worse. Nano-bots, at least, sang a similar song to its own Matrix Crystal.

This city of living skyscrapers, twisted, tangled, bursting out of the ground in great craters, had a beat entirely contrary to that of its own melody. It could not lie here any longer; it had spent too long trying to repair damage to its systems. Using the defragmentation machine while the Data-Ways were offline—had it caused this much harm to its hardware and software?

If only that fluffy alien, with the red eyes like little pieces of burning coals, had come with it. It would not be so alone.

Alone—

"Biri…" Semyueru choked out. "Biri."

Sparks shot out from its joints as it forced itself to sit upright, pain sending ripples through its delicate hull. "Biri?"

Nothing. No reply. Emptiness. The dull void evoked an immense and sudden sense of unbearable loneliness. The chorus of Zaprex minds that had always filled Cal'pash'coo was gone, and it was not simply due to its antennae being offline.

They were no more.

Cal'pash'coo had been crushed.

Deleted.

Biri—

Biri—

It packed up the thoughts, the emotions, the swirling chaos that threatened to send it into another shutdown and slammed them all into a folder, filing the folder deep, deep and deeper down into another folder, and another folder. It would access it all later. It would process this all—later.

Semyueru curled its fingers around the Map piece.

Biri had assigned it a task.

This was important.

It had to save the world.

Rifling around in the bag Biri had given it, Semyueru tugged out a hand-device. While its optical lenses could do a rudimentary scan of the area, without its antennae it was impaired. A hand-device would capture the songs of far more distant terminals, reading more crystal signals than its antennae could. Biri must have known it would need one.

Semyueru hugged the device tightly before giving it a gentle shake to activate it. The holograms came to life, filling Semyueru with deep sense of familiarity in this foreign environment.

There seemed to be an overwhelming abundance of its people's technology in the surrounding area; most of it, however, registered as being offline. Semyueru pouted at its hand-device, turning the hologram around idly. The nearest accessible terminal to its location was the logical destination.

Clambering weakly onto its feet, Semyueru peered up through the enormous leaves and bulging cups of fungi. It took a glance at its HUB and flinched at the warning signal flashing above its gravity-drive gauge; it was still overheated from its abuse the previous day. Yet, without the drive, making its way through the ghastly, huge world surrounding it was practically impossible.

"Everything is so big, and I am so small."

With a hiss of irritation, it began the gruelling task of climbing, feeling every injured limb whine with the exertion. It was still in danger, though—

That scary monster—

It had come through the defragmentation after Semyueru.

Semyueru had no way of knowing where the monster was, when it might be coming, nor to even track it. Its only safety seemed to be that it was so small, and the world was so big. Its fingers curled around the slim, cold Map piece dangling loose about its neck.

If it was so small, and the world was so very, very big, how ever was it expected to find three more pieces of an even tinier device? Semyueru pouted. "Could have given me the whole Map," it grumbled, slipping on the smooth cap of a mushroom. The slick, shiny slime that coated its surface stuck to Semyueru's coat, making it glow with the same eerie sheen as the flora engulfing it.

It took hours, and it could feel its energy reserves dropping rapidly. Its Matrix Crystal was going to force another shut-down, it was certain, and fighting that urge grew as exhausting as clambering through the forest.

The moment it staggered into the clearing, Semyueru almost lost the will to remain functioning, sliding to its knees, panting heavily as it stared up at a clear sky-sea swimming with schools of stars. Its lungs expanded, taking in the lush, freezing, and so very fresh air. It could breathe this air forever without having to replace its lungs. It was sweet. Its Matrix Crystal hummed with happiness. Philepcon liquid flowed easily through its limbs again.

Purple tinted grass surrounded it on all sides in a perfect circle, leading up to several limestone obelisks protruding from the earth, covered in layers of moss and fungi. It reached for its hand device, checking the location. This was one of the Zaprex sites, but a blinking orange symbol warned of possible contamination. Getting to its feet, Semyueru waded through the thick grass, scrambling up onto the mound to reach the glass terminals. Most were long shattered, but several remained. With the sleeve of its coat, it cleared the nearest of grime. The surface shimmered weakly, lighting Semyueru's face with a gentle glow.

It could work with this; there was still life left in this Way Station. Perhaps it just had to fiddle around with some of the wiring to get more flow through to the terminal. Crouching, Semyueru began to pull at the vines and flora choking the terminal, pausing only to wipe oily fluid from beneath its spectacles. As it did so, it noted the faint blinking on the edge of its HUB.

A proximity alarm.

A rush of philepcon liquid flooded its systems, overloading gears, soaking through its hull, sparking wires. It propelled itself violently to the side, missing the claw that erupted out from behind one of the obelisks. A dozen red eyes, situated in a skull formed of greyed bones knitted together by strings of rotted muscles, tracked it as it dived for another terminal to hide.

A monster.

It had found it.

The monster had come.

"Biri. Biri." Semyueru panted, clutching at its head. "Biri. Biri."

The ground thundered, bouncing, as the monster approached.

Something swung over them, landing atop one of the obelisks. Semyueru processed the new arrival instantly. A Human. Male.

The Human struck the monster in a scattering of electricity piloted from two blades, and the energy followed him like a pair of tails as he landed in a rolling skid only to spring upright and rip back across the mossy surface of the ruin.

Semyueru curled back against the terminal. It squealed as the male somersaulted over the terminal, missing a projectile aimed for him; it sliced through his arm and not his head. Semyueru scrambled away from the sudden bombardment of keratin being spat out from the fiend's gaping mouth.

A nearby pillar shattered, blocks hammering down onto the platform. Crystals exploded, issuing jets of philepcon liquid into the dark night. The monster shrieked as another barrage of lightning ripped through the air, following the bleeding philepcon liquid snaking across the moss. The monster erupted into flames.

Semyueru stared. It had only seen this once before, when

Biri had been trying to fix a damaged drone, and the contaminated Matrix Crystal had been unsalvageable. A single, accidental spark from a tool had set the entire workstation ablaze.

The Human knew—he knew the properties of philepcon liquid—and had purposely lured the fiend into a trap and ignited it. Still, that had not stopped the monster. Its talons tore into the topsoil that had long hidden the Zaprex Way Station, and its dozen eyes focused on Semyueru. It charged. The Human landed amongst the flames and hissing philepcon liquid and drove a blade into the creature's chest. They both rolled with the momentum before the male sprang up with a bounce and ripped the blade free of the bulbous torso.

The bones crafting its form began to rattle as the liquid sludge that held it together dissolved, filling the air with a foul taste. Semyueru covered its mouth in disgust. The Human male made a brief gesture with his hands, whispering something to the slain fiend, before turning away. He flicked philepcon liquid off his hands, muttering about the pain. Semyueru processed the conflicting data. The philepcon liquid should have damaged the Human, even if it was not contaminated. No Human would be able to withstand such an intake of philepcon liquid.

Did he have a shield? He must have a personal shield.

Slowly, Semyueru dared to focus its optical lenses on the quickly rotting corpse of the monster. Its shape was dissolving fast, and the smell was hideous as fluids leaked out everywhere.

Was it the one that had attacked Biri?

Semyueru scanned the disintegrating remains.

No—

It did not match.

A tightness grew against the hull plating of his chest. Another one was still out there.

"It was waiting for you…" the Human murmured. "Which means they know you're here." Bright organic eyes of crystal blue looked down at Semyueru, and mounting horror seemed to fill the cold, voided air between them. Semyueru held out a small hand, slowly pointing towards the dense forests. The Human reached carefully for Semyueru and fitted it neatly into the bag around his hips. Semyueru peered up at the Human who began to wrap his wounded arm with tape. Red blood. Iron blood.

He smelt like burnt-out circuit boards, an overclocked CPU, and the compressed heat of an ancient device sizzling without a cooling unit teetering on the edge of breaking point. It was so comforting, daring Semyueru to recall the sounds and tastes of Cal'pash'coo.

Finishing with his wound, the Human stood and pocketed the medical kit. His attention turned to the forest surrounding them, then back to the decaying remains of the monster.

"I don't think I'll be fast enough," the Human whispered.

Semyueru squeaked as the Human suddenly propelled forward, dancing through the high branches of the wooden skyscrapers as though he had a gravity-drive of his own. Semyueru could only burrow deeper into the bag that held it as their speed continued to increase with each overwhelming lunge and swing.

Shanty leapt from the diabond's saddle, leading the beast to the nearby brook. They had almost made it back to the Caves, but her heart was still in her throat. Until the moment she was through the thick vines and beside the comforting fire, the sense of exposure would surely remain.

She crouched by the brook's edge, sighing at the soft, silky water as it rippled through her fingers. Bringing a handful to her mouth, she sipped. The ride had been fast and desperate. The diabond was skilled in not only navigating the tangled forest, but in keeping an inexperienced rider in the saddle.

The diabond's ears perked up and she began to growl, backing away from the bank. Shanty dropped lower, following the example of the hound, and spotted what had caused her alarm.

It was Almet. He had found them. Did he know about the Caves? Shanty clutched at her chest. The diabond's muscles tensed as she crouched into an attack position. Shanty grappled for her paw.

"No! No. Return to the Caves. Now. Go. See if Zinkx has returned. Go!"

The diabond licked her face with a heated tongue before lunging away. Shanty froze as Almet's eyes focused on her location. A leering grin split its features, revealing how inhuman it was. How had she ever thought it was Human? There was so clearly a foul, rotting stench wafting from the fiend.

"There you are, Messenger. Are you alone?"

It stepped into the brook, playfully tapping its sword against stones. "Such a beautiful Kelib woman should not be alone."

Panic flooded her limbs. She moved. Where she would run to, she knew not, but she ran, and the laughter of the Twizel followed her.

She shrieked as something grabbed her wrist, dragging her down behind roots and boulders. The hand of a Wynnila woman smothered her mouth, and Shanty caught a glimpse of blue eyes in the darkness. They sank together into the crushed undergrowth, listening to the sound of slushing water as the Twizel waded through the stream, passing them by.

Shanty's erratic breathing eased, and slowly the woman shifted off her with a whispered apology. "Quickly," a hand was offered to her, "we need to move."

Something compelled her to take the hand, and they crawled out together.

"This way…" the woman urged.

Shanty followed. They soon re-joined the path she knew led to the cliffs that protected the inlet to the caves. This woman—she knew where the caves were. Shanty removed her hand. It was so surreptitious. Tiny dancing boxes seemed to flake off the Human woman's body as she moved, distorting the forest as she passed by.

"You're a Twizel." Shanty stepped away.

The woman smiled. "No, but the fact that you can see I am not of this Realm makes you quite the boon amongst your sisters."

Shanty's lips pressed together.

"I would not be able to interfere like this if you were unable to see me." The smirk the woman threw over her shoulder was unsettling. "I'm bending a few rules."

"Rules?"

"The transference of data from one Realm to another must be equalised." Behind eyes as blue as Zinkx's, an intense glow began to blaze. "And burning through stars to appear here is unethical."

Shanty's head spun. Stars. Burning through stars. What did she mean?

"Who are you?"

"The name they called me when I took this form was Gwenhwyfar, the Fairy Queen. However, if you desire my true designated code, I am Hazanin-Ra of the Zaprex Pantheon, Time Master of Livila." Shanty's hand was taken once more. It was far less solid, the small flaking boxes struggling to hold their shape. "It is a pleasure to meet you, Shan-ta-lee Shir-Hara of No-Clan. Come, please, I do not have much time. Which continues to be highly ironic," she joked to herself.

Together, they crept towards the crevasse between the upheaved cliffs walling in the inlet that protected the caves. Shanty faced it with dread. Normally, either Zinkx or the diabond would be with her whenever she navigated the tight confines of the stones. The Time Master urged her on with a hand on her back. "Go. I am here."

She climbed in, feeling through the darkness one step at a time. The caves were on the other side. She was almost safe. Gwenhwyfar followed behind her, emitting a gentle glow as the flakes continued to dissolve from her body.

"Why are you here?" Shanty asked.

"My Bonding Partner sent our offspring here, and it is extremely important that the Dragon never gets a hold of the Key."

Shanty sucked in a sharp breath. "The Key." She looked back. The Time Master's face was weary, aged beyond the young mask she wore, her shoulders bearing an immense weight. "It is a burden I wish it did not carry, but no other can."

"Is your offspring nearby?"

"Yes. Very near." Gwenhwyfar's smile was faint. "My children are precious to me. I cannot care for them, for I am dead."

Dead. Shanty wet her cracked lips. She was speaking to an echo.

"You must act in my place."

Shanty looked down as a slim crystal was placed in her hand. It felt warm, despite the cold, azure colour it radiated in the darkness. "Above the caves, there is a weapon; long has it fallen to disrepair. You will only have one shot. So aim true."

Shanty curled her fingers around the crystal. She shifted her attention back to the crevasse, the light beckoning her to break free and make the mad dash for the caves down the inlet.

"I know you're out there, Messenger," the Twizel's muffled voice came. She froze in fear. "I can smell you."

Gwenhwyfar urged her away from the opening.

Shanty jerked around.

That was not the hand of a woman on her back.

"Zinkx." The eyes were eerily similar, but no longer was the presence behind her corroding away. Zinkx was solid, real, and drenched in a thick layer of sweat. He leant one shoulder on the nearby rocks, regaining his ragged breath. She reached for him anxiously, seeing the medical tape strapping his arm.

"Are you hurt?"

He shook his head. "Just a scratch."

Shanty searched the darkness. The Time Master was gone.

"I got here too late anyway," he muttered. "It's a Ki'rayh."

Her skin chilled. That explained why it had held its form in the sunlight.

"Where is the diabond?"

"I sent her ahead to the Caves."

"Why?"

"I did not want her to be killed defending me."

"That's...never mind..." Zinkx pushed away from the rockface, wincing in pain. He uncoupled a sack from his hip-bags and passed a small bundle into her arms.

"When I engage the Ki'rayh, run back to the Caves. Run as fast as you can, and bunker down. Do not look back. Run."

"Zinkx..." She felt the heat of tears against her cheeks. Suddenly, this was all too overwhelming. His words were sharp and definite.

"Do not come back for me."

He was saying such a terrible thing. Such an awful, disgusting thing. Why? He pushed past her, drawing his blades. Her nose itched with the irritating scent of a growing storm that she now knew emanated from his birth elemental beginning to activate.

"Don't do this. We can fight it together!"

"Shanty, you have never fought a Twizel before."

Her mouth dried and she flinched at the memory of little Alnokun's distorted, rotting corpse on the kitchen floor. Zinkx had barely won that battle alone.

"You need me..." she whispered.

He did not deny it, but his gaze lingered on the sack she held. Shanty carefully pulled back the fabric. Her chest clenched beneath her bodice. A slumbering child was bundled up tightly. Scarcely any larger than a babe, its delicate, sweet features were ethereal.

"This child is far more important," Zinkx murmured.

Shanty bunched her shoulders, understanding dawning on her. "The child has the Key."

His smile was pained as he slipped into the light of the entrance. "Run, Krrirren, run."

CHAPTER TWELVE

You have to be willing to step into the shadows
to find the true source of the Sun-light.

Pennadotian Proverb

Zinkx steadied himself. Fighting a Ki'rayh alone was the epitome of foolishness for a Messenger, and he could already hear an echo of his lieutenant's voice berating him. But he had never been one to follow any rules. He twirled his blades, sending a flicker of lightning down his arms.

"Do you have a name, fiend?" he asked the restless forest.

"Houa."

A laugh nudged his awareness to his left. He frowned, ducking swiftly to the right, missing the blade. A Soatrin man stood with a lazy, bemused stance, as though it were looking upon a mere toy to be tossed about.

"Dreamathic attacks don't work, it would seem," Houa mused.

Zinkx arched an eyebrow. "That was pathetic, if that was what it was."

A sneer slipped over the Ki'rayh's features. "Where did the Kelib woman go?"

"What Kelib woman."

It clicked its tongue in irritation and raised a finger. "I am looking for something."

"What a coincidence; so am I."

The Twizel laughed again. "Oh, I do like you, Messenger. I think I shall fit well into your body."

Zinkx inched a foot back, lowering himself to steady his weight. "Try it."

The Twizel met him with a clash of shattering force, driving him back through the soil. Zinkx forced his gravity bubble forward into Houa and twisted it, sending the Human body spiralling into the air. Houa latched onto a branch. Several tails of braided bones, lashed together by tendons of shadows, burst free of its back. Zinkx dodged each one, the force of their strikes spraying up soil.

Vaulting from a tree trunk, Zinkx used the momentum to slam into Houa, and the body danced beneath his blades as lightning bolted across the forest. The host burned, charring into nothing but blackened skin that slowly dissolved in an acidic pool. Red eyes stared at him through the sludge, and gradually, a mouth swam out, opening to reveal a rancid set of uneven teeth. It sneered.

Zinkx rolled away from a talon. It ripped through a branch, and the deafening noise of the thunderous crash could not be muffled by the dense undergrowth.

Zinkx dropped, twisted, skidded, and sloshed through water. There was no break. No time to halt his movements and gain his bearings as the constant tongues of bones whiplashed past him. He was going to have to come up with something, and he was going to have to do it fast; there were limits to his endurance. Skidding behind a mound of boulders, Zinkx tugged out a roll of wire from his hip-bags.

"I am going to regret this." He twisted the metal around his wrists and hand. Houa's vaguely humanoid shape stood in the brook, its chest rising and falling in fatigued gasps. At least he was not the only one who was exhausted.

"I get the impression you haven't been in the Trenches," Zinkx called out.

"My skills are useful for far more than playing make-believe war with children."

Zinkx hugged one of his blades close, breathing in deeply, crouching low in the cool shadows. "The thing about children and their make-believe games: they feel very real."

He burst out. Thrashing tails lashed at him instantly. He blocked the first with a swing of his blade, the second he leapt on, propelling himself high. Houa stumbled back as Zinkx smashed his gravity bubble downwards. He gritted his teeth against the rising pain in his lungs and the taste of blood. It was over in a blink as a searing heat flooded through his side—one of the boned tail tips slashing into his skin. Houa roared as Zinkx drove his blade down harder, increasing the pressure. He cracked through the bone breastplate and slammed through the Ki'rayh's chest, releasing a flood of lightning the moment he did so. The water erupted with steam.

Zinkx staggered, landing in a heap, his legs giving way beneath him. He reached weakly for the wound through his armour, drawing away his hand, smeared in blood and liquid toxins.

Houa sloshed through the boiling water. Zinkx spat out the foulness of his own saliva as the poison burned his mouth.

"Will you…just die…"

The Ki'rayh bent over him, its jaws unhinging. Zinkx wearily closed his eyes. Through the eerie loss of sensation creeping over his limbs, he mapped the muscles to his hand, gradually curling the fingers into a fist, building all the force he could muster into the strike, fuelled with a crackle of lightning dancing around the metal string.

It hit nothing.

Houa stood some distance away, its red eyes pinning him with a haunting stare.

Zinkx coughed out blood.

"What? Not…going to…finish the job?"

The forest suddenly burst into flame.

Shanty scrambled up the cliff face above the Caves, struggling as rocks and moss pulled away, tumbling down to where the diabond paced below. Sweat drenched the nape of her neck from her fear of the chilling height. She dug her toes deeper into the loose surface, refusing to fall. The thunderous noise of the fight echoed through the protected inlet, with lightning bursting sky-seaward, causing her skin to dance.

Zinkx was going to die.

With trembling arms, she dragged herself over the edge of the cliff, rolling onto her bare feet. Her nails were torn, fingers bloodied, but she ignored the superficial pain. What would a Zaprex weapon look like? This was Zinkx's area of expertise. How could she possibly find a Monument of Old when she knew nothing about them.

"Songs…" she whispered.

The ruin she had slept in the first night she had met Zinkx and his Khwaja had emanated such a sad, lonely melody, distinct from the drum of the Forests of Pulza. Shanty sank her feet deep into the moss. The taint of the Twizel was terrifying. It had distorted their beautiful little inlet and ruptured the melody of the forest with a fierce clattering. She drove through it, seeking the sorrowful allure of the fairy race. Her feet moved, pursuing the chime of bells until she bumped into a small, grey obelisk coated in moss and vines. Peeling back the layers of plant-life, Shanty ran her fingers over the multitude of slots within the ancient stone. Which one was she supposed to slide the singing crystal into?

A tug called her attention and she turned to face the heavy-lidded, barely-open eyes of the tiny fey in the bag at her hip. Even while blinking in a groggy state, they glowed with all the intensity of the Sun. A little hand gradually reached out, pointing to a singular slot.

"That one?"

The fey nodded.

Shanty shoved the crystal in. The air around her burst

with flakes of light, the ground sweeping in a spiral of hexagon patterns, clearing the rocks, moss, and grime. She was left standing before a shimmering, transparent field expanding from the obelisk, dragging all Sunlight towards it.

She had one shot.

Her fingers trembled as she took hold of the small, pulsing hexagon controls on either side of her. They snapped against her palms and her eyes instantly focused through the chaos of the trees, pinning the Ki'rayh, tracking its movements.

"Zinkx. No." Shanty's heart raced at the horrifying sight of him pinned beneath the creature, and with the sudden rush of her blood, the weapon thrummed to life. The Ki'rayh suddenly looked up, as though it could see her through the density of the forest. It moved.

Shanty's hands clenched down, and the world went white. The force sent her flying backwards, feet over head, rolling several times until she landed roughly against the rocks. Coughing and choking, Shanty dragged herself upright. The weapon powered down, the light scattering and the crystal shattering into tiny shards. The air smelt rich with a thick, intense burn and, slowly, she stood on trembling legs.

The forest below had been scorched in a single spot, where the Twizel had been. Where Zinkx had lain. Her bloodied hands, imprinted with hexagon wounds, clasped her face as a swell of nausea overwhelmed her.

"Zinkx…"

Shanty tore across the clifftop. Her climb down was frantic, her footing slipping often, but her panic overrode all fear of the decent. Landing with a solid thud, Shanty rushed past the diabond, calling to the beast with a shout, and they ploughed into the forest together. The trail of destruction that the fight had littered throughout the inlet was ferocious, but it allowed her to track a path to Zinkx's location. Shanty staggered to a halt, flinching against the searing heat rising from the molten, boiling ground in a perfect hexagon. Zinkx lay on the scorched earth, his skin a soft, faint glow. Shanty paced the hexagon, glaring at the invisible wall she could not pass. The heat was near unbearable. How he was even alive was—

She looked to the diabond for help. "Can you reach him? Can you bring him to me?"

The diabond studied her for a moment before igniting in flame. Shanty backed away, holding out her hands, hiding from the inferno the beast of burden had become as the diabond stepped into the boiling zone to approach Zinkx's limp body. She crouched, wrapping her jaw around his shoulder, and dragged him back to the coolness of the moss and undergrowth.

Shanty fell to her knees beside him. Threads of light wisped off his skin as the glow faded in pictographic patterns, leaving behind the signs of his vicious wounds. She had never seen his lightning burns so horrific. Shanty hesitantly reached out a shaking hand. Blood was already soaking into the ground beneath him.

"Oh, Great Mothers…" she choked out.

Something viciously sharp had sliced through armour and skin. He sucked in a weakened, shuddery breath. A trembling hand limply brushed against her arm, smearing blood. His eyes had focused on her, though they lacked all the clarity and intensity she had come to appreciate.

"It's…poison…toxin…"

"Poison? Toxin?" Shanty felt hot tears run down her cheeks. "What type?"

"Don't cry," he murmured.

"Zinkx! Please. Zinkx!" Shanty held his cheeks. "What type of poison?"

His eyes fluttered. "Paralysis."

"No. No. No." Shanty looked around helplessly. "No. I refuse this. You're not dying on me, Human." She heaved him into her arms, ignoring how light and lifeless he seemed. "You are not leaving me alone."

He was aware of heaviness. Every breath he took felt as though he was breathing with a pile of rocks stacked on his chest. Zinkx groaned. A muffled noise from somewhere in the distance grew closer. Footsteps, Shanty's footsteps. Weighted. Solid. Strong. His sluggish eyelids flickered, and the starry roof of the cave came into focus. He was alive. Zinkx clenched his teeth and tried to sit upright, only to find the ceiling still mocking him.

Frowning he wiggled his toes, and his fingers. He had feeling in them, but, along with the sensation, came the illusion of wearing a full set of iron mech-gear. It had been a long time since he had felt so much weight pressing down upon his body.

"Don't push it, Human." Shanty slid down onto her knees beside him. "Even with your gravity skills, you still need your muscles, and they're recovering from that awful toxin."

"Twizel poison..." he murmured. "I should be dead. The antidote...I wasn't permitted to bring any..."

She tossed back her hair in a self-assured manner. "Well. I am glad to know there is an actual antidote. I used a combination of several different remedies I know that negate the effects of some of Pennadot's deadlier fauna."

"Only you, Krrirren."

Exhaustion and anxiety still creased lines around her mouth and brow. Her hands lightly brushed over his arms. He barely felt the touch through the tight wrappings she had applied.

"I...your burns, though...they were much worse..."

He tried a reassuring smile.

"Don't worry. At this point, there isn't much of my arms that isn't artificial skin."

She frowned, whispering several of his words to herself, muttering them in Kelib to reaffirm their translation.

"It grows back a lot quicker," he added for clarification.

"I don't understand."

He raised his brow. "Burns are a specialty at the House. They've developed a lot of ways to deal with them. That isn't to say they're no longer a problem, though. A few sol-cycles ago my arms were injected with a type of regenerating liquid designed from my own skin-cells. It only works on the burns through. It doesn't heal anything else. It's targeted healing, or something like that."

"How long does it take."

"Depends on the damage. How bad was it?"

Her lips pressed together. Not a good sign.

"Might take a while, then." Zinkx sighed. "Probably best to keep it—"

"I do not trust your strange, alien healing liquids." She huffed. "I will continue making the cooling creams."

"Can you sit me up."

"It is better that you lie down."

"Shanty. Please. This is really awkward."

"Fine." Shuffling around, she fitted several blankets against the wall and gently lifted him. Zinkx hissed in pain.

She anxiously held his shoulders. "Can you hold up your neck?"

He nodded weakly.

"Let me know if you start struggling."

She bounced onto her feet with little effort and headed back to her cooking station, crouching down to begin rolling out dough.

Zinkx slowly looked around the cave. The diabond lounged lazily at the entrance, tail flicking back and forth every so often to swish away a tiny creature. Shanty had swept the stone floor, and laid out several skins. From the ceiling, the rows of sticks she had asked him to tie up were now filled with countless herbs and drying fish, as well as an unfinished weaving. Overall, she had made their cave a rather comfortable living place.

"We're going to need a wagon…" he muttered.

He studied his bound arms. Weak. Heavy. For someone who did not have the medical background of a House Doctor, Shanty had performed incredibly well treating him. He was surprised he was even alive—

Zinkx's head snapped up. "Wait."

Shanty looked back from her cooking. "Zinkx?"

"The Ki'rayh. I don't…I don't remember killing it."

"What do you remember?"

"White light."

She rolled out another scone. "There is a Monument of Old right above us. I used it."

"You used a Zaprex weapon to kill the Ki'rayh?"

"I do not know if it died." She studied her hands. "It was very fast, and my reaction was slow."

"No. I'm still stuck on the whole notion that…you…used a Zaprex weapon." Zinkx rubbed at his tired eyes.

Her smile was tender. "Is it not Messenger code to fight Twizels together. Well. You distracted it, I shot it."

"Shanty, you…you can't go and use a Zaprex weapon. That's not possible."

"I had help." She pointed a finger over the fire-pit.

At his first assessment of the cave, Zinkx had missed it, entirely, and the shock caused his breath to halt sharply in his chest. How had he not seen it? It was sitting there, plain as anything, on a little rock that was covered in a nicely woven rug. It grinned a full set of sharp little teeth, before sipping on an oversized mug of Kelib milk.

The Zaprex.

It was tiny. It was very real. He had not been imagining stuffing it into his hip-bags.

"Ah…Shanty…"

She looked up from setting her scones over the fire-pit. "Yes?"

"It's *awake*."

"Oh. Yes. It woke up a few days ago."

"A few days ago!" How long had he been unconscious?

She smiled, returning to her task. "I have yet to find out its name. It does not seem to speak our language, but it does seem to understand what I say to some degree. It has been very worried about you. This is the first time I have managed to get it away from your side since it woke up. I think it knew you were going to come to today."

It had lowered the mug, a mug that was enormous in its tiny little hands, and wiped away the fresh line of milk from its upper lip.

"*Anata wa sutāmandesu ka?*[12]"

Zinkx squinted. "*O-namae wa nan desu ka?*[13]"

The Zaprex's chest expanded and its cheeks turned bright blue. It leapt off its perch, flying towards him. "*Runnau Semyueru to moushimasu! Douzo yoroshiku o-negai shimasu.*[14]"

"*Watashi wa Maz Zinkx desu. Douzo yoroshiku.*[15]"

The Zaprex twirled about in the air, seemingly delighted.

"You understand him?" Shanty asked from across the cave.

"Very little, I'm afraid. Though, now we have its name. We'll have to come up with something a bit easier on our tongues."

Shanty scoffed. "Yes. You can't even get around my name."

Zinkx flashed her a grin. "I'm lazy."

She rolled her eyes. "What part of that gabble of sounds was its name?"

Zinkx frowned in the Zaprex's direction.

"Sem…yu… something?"

"Well, then, Semu-*chan*, perhaps?"

The tiny fairy erupted into a fit of giggles that sent it looping about in the air.

"I think it likes it." Zinkx smiled.

"It might be that it finds your butchering of its native tongue amusing, Human. Great Krrirrens know it amuses me when you try to speak Kelib."

Zinkx rested his head back, closing his eyes as exhaustion dared to tempt him back into the arms of sleep again.

"This is not something I expected to find," he murmured.

"Well, look at it this way," Shanty threw him a smile. "You're several steps closer to finding the Key, now."

---

12 *Are you a Starman?*
13 *What is your name?*
14 *I call myself Runnau Semyueru. Please treat me kindly.*
15 *As for me, I'm Maz Zinkx. Please treat me kindly.*

CHAPTER THIREEN

It was a formal invitation to a hunt. Daniel sighed, and dropped his head back as he folded up the fragranced paper, lavished with the same scent Lord Galvon's daughter wore. He held up the note. "Skyeola, an incineration conduction, please."

With a whoop of enthusiasm, Skyeola leapt out of his chair, but before he could hold up his conductor, the invite was snatched out of Daniel's fingers.

Jarid's unmerciful glare could have singed any paper.

"Your Highness, I realise you have no desire to humour Lord Galvon or his daughter, but…"

Daniel peered up at Jarid and raised an eyebrow. "But…"

"But, for diplomatic purposes you do need to put in an effort here."

Nearby, Skyeola hid a small snorted laugh behind a claw. Jarid sent the kitten a disproving frown.

"Do not think I have forgotten how extremely rambunctious you have been on this trip, Skyeola."

"I have always been this way; you are only noticing now because you are actually bothering to pay attention to me."

"I take offence at that." Jarid scowled, his dark red

eyebrows compressing. That comment had hit an interesting nerve in his adviser, more than any of Daniel's quippy remarks ever had.

"I have always, and always will pay attention to you, Skyeola," Jarid added. "Even if you think otherwise."

Skyeola's wings swayed as he folded his arms. "I have always been this way."

Jarid sighed. "No. You have very much come out of your shell without the Lord Steward's shadow hovering over you."

At the mention of his father, Skyeola shrunk back as if struck.

Daniel frowned. "Jarid, that is enough."

"He still has not explained what happened to the guard Almet."

Skyeola lifted his chin. "He left."

"That is not an explanation, Skyeola," Jarid insisted.

"Yes, it is. He left." Skyeola retorted. "Maybe out a window."

"I said that is *enough*," Daniel raised his voice, before flopping back in his seat, refocusing the conversation. "Do I really have to go?"

Jarid massaged his brow. "Your Highness—"

"Do you fear something happening?" Citla interrupted.

Daniel stood, his chair scraping over the hard floor. He rubbed his aching shoulders, moving away from his desk to the nearby open window. Jarid had quietened at Citla's intervention. His Maiden emerged from the shadows, carrying herself smoothly over the floor as though she floated in her silken black and silver gown.

The deep and mutual respect between Jarid and Citla he could never understand. They had a past, and his mind was foggy, his memories little more than blurred and burned sheets of paper in a book he could not read.

"Your Highness?" Jarid pressed him anxiously. "If there is something troubling you…"

Daniel shook his head. "Lord Galvon was one of the

conspirators who headed up the Uprising, was he not?"

Jarid nodded stiffly.

"The Uprising that was responsible for the deaths of my entire family, and not only mine, but yours as well."

Jarid's jaw tightened. Mentioning his family always provoked a reaction from the rigid adviser. Daniel had no recollection of how they had died, but from Citla's stark refusal to tell him anything, he could only imagine the worse sort of deaths for those on the losing side of a revolution.

"Jarid, in his eyes we are still the enemy. They fought to abolish the old monocracy and to establish their own aristocracy rule."

"You could say that technically they succeeded," Skyeola muttered.

"Were the Ancient Starborns any better?" Daniel asked openly, spreading his hands.

"Yes. They were. I can understand why you look back at history from our current position and question our ancestors, but the Starborns and their paladins were great warriors, and they protected this land, and her people, nobly and righteously." Jarid placed both hands on the desk, leaning forward. His pale, freckled cheeks had flushed red.

Daniel shook his head. "No one is all noble and all righteous, Jarid."

"A kingdom such as that of the Starborns does not rule for so long if it's rotten," Jarid protested. "But, just like Batitic Conductions, Humans repeat a cycle of deconstruction and reconstruction. This happens time after time, and the Starborns remained a solid strength throughout both periods, even as Pennadot decayed around them."

His adviser seemed to have built up a particular impression of their ancestors, and Daniel had to wonder if it was idealism and flowery hope, or if it had any flavour of truth.

"It is understandable that, eventually, deconstruction would come for even the Starborns," Skyeola mused. "If you look at it from that perspective."

"See Lord Galvon not as an enemy," Jarid offered, "but as a means of reconstruction. It helps me. Sun knows, I want to kill the man whenever I go near him."

Citla glanced at him with the smallest of smirks. "You almost have. Several times."

"My anger is deep," Jarid muttered, touching the sabre at his side. "And it is that anger, Your Highness, that allows me to continue this façade."

"Lord Galvon is running us around in circles, Jarid." Daniel held out a hand. "We are still no closer to finding out about the Zaprex treasure he mentioned to lure us here than we were when we arrived. No. I do not like it."

"I do not think you are doing a good enough job at making him like you," Jarid objected. He turned away, waving the invitation. "I shall accept it on your behalf."

Daniel pouted. "Fine. But I shall blame all of you if something happens."

Skyeola squeaked. "Even me?"

"Even you."

"That is not fair. I am innocent."

"Then stop turning Lord Galvon's wine into water," Jarid called out from the corridor.

Skyeola sheepishly twisted his foot-claws as Citla tut-tutted in disproval, making a show of straightening his clothes.

Daniel smiled. Yes, indeed, being away from the shadow of Lord Mazaki had very much allowed their little sorcerer to flourish. A chill crept down his spine, and he glanced out the window, at the dense forests beyond Iliaion. If Skyeola was a tiny flower, finally able to bloom in the Sun, would he whither once more if they returned him to the shade?

Skyeola bounced around him anxiously beneath the noonday Sun. Daniel straightened his riding boots one more time. They had the irritating tendency to slip down his shins. "Skyeola, I will be fine."

"I want to come with you!"

"A hunt is no place for you."

"Lady Argrona is participating."

Daniel laughed. "I am quite sure she has actually learnt to hunt."

"I can hunt."

Nearby, Hun burst into laughter. Skyeola's ears flopped rearward. He pouted. Daniel stood, bending to press a kiss to Skyeola's forehead. "Help Jarid with his mountain of paperwork. He will greatly appreciate the company, and I know you two can get along when you talk...boring...academic... stuff..." The look he received from Skyeola was wide-eyed, innocent begging. The kitten would never have attempted such a childish tactic on anyone else.

"Please, Your Highness, please can I come?"

The worst part was it almost worked. Daniel tipped his head back. "You can co-ordinate with Jarid to meet up with us after the hunt. That way you may ride back with us. Does that sound fair?"

Skyeola relented with a defeated, dramatic sigh. "Fine."

Hun approached with the horses. He ruffled Skyeola's hair, causing the young Batitic to cringe. "Don't worry, the worst thing that could happen to him is a kiss from Lady Argrona."

Daniel paused as he was about to mount his horse. "Do not even jest about it, Hun."

"Yes." Citla swept up to them leading her black mare. "Do not even jest about it." Her fierce glare pinned Hun down. Daniel accepted his bow from her.

"Well, let us get this done, shall we?"

He had absolutely no desire to cosy up to Lord Galvon, his sons, or his overly perfumed daughter. The faster he dealt with this hunt, the sooner he could enjoy being away from their obnoxious presence.

He had once been told by Butler Malik, who managed the

Harem Family, the very firm and profound words that shepherded his life; "*A royal is compelled to do much which they do not wish to do, for the sake of the Land and the People.*"

If partaking in games with Ruling Families was part of that, he would have to simply accept his role, and hope Citla's mere presence would be enough to fend off Lady Argrona's attentions.

Lord Galvon's sons, Master Halbrak and Master Muhzun were both robust boys, taking after their father in many ways. Though Muhzun, the youngest of the three children, at five and ten, had none of the loud, forceful nature that was so prevalent in the Galvons. Thankfully, he was not required to ride up front with Lord Galvon, since he did not know the dangers of the terrain they traversed.

How he wished Skyeola could have come with them as they plunged deep into Shalamic's untamed forests. The trees, like great towers themselves, held up an endless canopy that from the Turret of Shalamic had looked like the tufts of clouds, but below it was a world of tangled giant ferns, twisted roots, and mountainous fungi. How they were to ever hunt anything in such a chaotic environment baffled him.

Lady Galvon drew back her horse, coming along beside him. That she ever endured Citla's unbearable, piercing stare was quite astounding. "There are many pve'pt in this area, we shall not be lacking for game."

With a swing, she dismounted. "Give your horse to your guards. Follow me."

Daniel sent Hun a beseeching look. He received a mocking smirk in return. "Follow the little lady, Your Highness."

"You are enjoying this."

Hun sniggered. "Getting you back for all those times you win at cards."

Perhaps he would have enjoyed the experience of hunting deep through the forest, feeling the strange density of the air in his lungs, and the oppressive force of the mighty flora bearing down upon him. Yet he could not find pleasure in it, not with the present company. If Skyeola had been with him, giving an excited commentary on every tiny detail it would have been an exciting adventure, but instead he was subjected to Lady Argrona's insistence that he drop the use of her title and simply call her by her name.

Ahead of their small party, Argrona's brother stopped and waved to them. Argrona's smile brightened. "We are Sun Bless-ed. A pve'pt! Come, Your Highness."

He stepped away from her before she touched him, but followed behind her, sending Citla an agonised glance.

The pve'pt was grazing moss on a large root. Its long delicate legs balanced perfectly upon the difficult heights that surrounded them. Daniel tightened his hand around his bow. It was an easy shot, at least for him.

"Nah, you cannot make that," Halbrak muttered.

Daniel slipped an arrow from his quiver.

The usual surge of wind twirled down his arm and fingers, making his heart race as he focused, feeling the moss and soil crunch beneath his riding boots as he moved with the dense airflow. He was the arrow; the arrow would pierce the target—

Only—

The target was a handsome, colourful creature, full of life. It had only happened several times before, when he concen-trated, and it felt like he was peeling back a film across his eyes that constantly blinded him. Floating above the pve'pt's crown of coloured horns was a delicate green halo.

Life. It was alive.

"What is wrong, Your Highness. You have a clear shot," Argrona urged.

"I do," Daniel murmured, slowly lowering his bow. "And yet I physically cannot bring myself to loose my arrow."

From nearby he heard a lively laugh. "You Imperials really are soft and tender after all. Wonder if your meat is as white as your skin."

"I was unaware you were so strapped for resources that you had started to eat Humans, Master Halbrak." Daniel glanced around, arching an eyebrow at the young man.

"Forgive my brother, Your Highness," Argrona said. "He has addled his mind with mushroom powder."

Citla held out her hands. "Your bow."

Daniel smiled at her. "You sure? Usually you use a—"

"Your bow."

Citla's bold and overly familiar manner towards him provoked a sharp, shocked inhalation from Argrona. Such tartness coming from Citla, though, was perfectly normal.

"Well, if you wish." He handed over his bow and a single arrow.

By now the pve'pt had moved further away. He knew such a distance would not bother him, but he had rarely seen Citla use a bow. Only mockingly to amuse Skyeola when the kitten was glum. He need not have been concerned. With all the flexibility of a reed, she pulled back, poised and balanced, before releasing the arrow. He cringed at the soft thud of the pve'pt's fall, and he turned away, his stomach tugging. He stared at the mossy soil, certain he could feel the song wisp away beneath him.

"Your Highness?" He jerked at a touch from Argrona. It had been sol-cycles since anyone outside of his entourage had touched him unannounced. He stepped away from her, resisting the urge to clutch at the area her hand had settled. It stung.

He forced a jovial tone. "I am fine."

Citla returned, her eyes daring Halbrak to make a comment, and, thankfully, he did not.

Citla called out, "Hun, the carcass."

Hun thumped past them. "Oh, right! Get me to do the heavy lifting," he grumbled under his breath as he bashed through the undergrowth.

Citla handed back his bow. "Not as graceful as you."

Daniel raised an eyebrow. "Is it possible to kill something gracefully?"

Her black lips perked up enough to hint at a smile. "Of course."

"I should not have asked."

Hun shouted out. "Can we return now? I do not want to get pve'pt blood all over my clothes. It will stink in the Sun."

They returned to the horses. Lord Galvon and his men were already there, also packing up the spoils of their own successful hunt. Daniel fought back the foul taste in his mouth as he walked past the large haul to his horse.

"How was your first foray into hunting, Your Highness?" Lord Galvon merrily enquired.

Halbrak scoffed. "His Highness could not shoot the pve'pt. He is soft."

Daniel shook his head at the hot-headed young man. "True. I suppose. An interesting excursion, though, to learn I have no taste for harming that which lives on my land." He fitted his bow to the strap on the saddle. Even now seeing the poor creature that Hun had lugged over his shoulder being flung over the back of Citla's black mare made his stomach dance.

"No." Galvon waved his son down. "I had heard of such a myth, from long ago, but I was unaware it had been passed onto you, Your Highness. You are truly your Father's son."

"I would hope so," Daniel muttered. He needed to get away from the smell of blood, and away from Lord Galvon. He gently nudged his Maiden's elbow, pointing towards the lone figure of Muhzun kneeling in the nearby undergrowth. Lord Galvon's youngest child looked as miserable as he did.

"I will just be over there, with the lad. I promise I will not leave your sight."

She nodded. Daniel tracked his way across to Muhzun, smiling when he realised the boy was grumbling over his riding boots.

"I see your boots are also ill-fitted." Daniel crouched beside him, re-lacing his own irritating pair.

"I do not often need them." Muhzun managed a shy, uncomfortable shrug. "I am not one for such a sport."

"Hm, seems neither am I."

Muhzun ducked his head. "Your bow is to protect, not to kill."

"Sometimes one must kill to protect."

"And you will be able to fire it when that time comes."

Daniel stood, hesitating as he noted the ring of mushrooms Muhzun was crouched within. He arched an eyebrow. Skyeola had often rattled on about Zaprexes and the technology they had left behind. He doubted there was a Pennadotian alive who did not know about legends of the fairy-kin and the dangers of entering the Monuments of Old that had belonged to them.

"You do realise what you are kneeling on, do you not?"

Muhzun looked up with a smile. "It is a fairy circle."

"You know, I am quite sure standing in one of those will get you spirited away." Daniel held out his hand to the lad. "Best not tempt fate."

Muhzun laughed. "Do not be silly, Your Highness. I am the one who is protected."

"Is that how it works? Interesting. I thought being in the fairy circle was the cause of misfortune. I shall have to consult Skyeola on this folklore."

"It would appear you shall soon have that chance, Your Highness." Muhzun gestured with a wave and Daniel turned, watching the arrival of several horses and guards bearing the insignia of Jarid's province.

Skyeola was amongst them, the little kitten bubbling with excitement. Daniel grinned.

"This has been good for him." He stepped forward, raising a hand, calling out, "Skyeola! Over here!"

"No! Your Highness, watch out!" Daniel turned back to Muhzun at his shriek of warning. He was certain it was happenstance, for the look of pure horror on Muhzun's face could not have been faked. His stomach lurched as the ground beneath him gave way and he dropped into darkness, plummeting.

Down.

Down.

Swallowed by the shaft that had no end, until it did, and

he slammed into solid floor, loose debris showering him.

There was no light. Nothing for his skin to refract off. He was a diamond in a pool of mud.

Weakly, Daniel heaved in a breath. His chest pulled tight and a slice of pain burned through his limbs. He froze, tears flooding his eyes.

Pain. He had never felt such pain.

He reached out with a trembling hand, groping in the darkness, and encountered the rod through his side.

CHAPTER FOURTEEN

You tell a child to not be seen and not to be heard,
But have you ever wondered how much they see and hear
while they are not being seen and not being heard?

Author Unknown

Skyeola leapt off his horse, ignoring Jarid's frantic calls for him to slow down. He shoved through the Shalamic guards who stood around doing nothing—nothing to get Daniel back—nothing—nothing—Daniel—Daniel—

His foot-claws tore through the mossy undergrowth as he ran towards the place where Daniel had been standing just moments before. He could see a shaft. Daniel had fallen. Down. Down. Somewhere he could not reach. He had to get to him. Daniel was all he had. Daniel was his Sun. Daniel was the only one who cared. He had to find him. Arms wrapped roughly around his waist, hauling him backwards, away from the pit. Skyeola let out a shriek as Hun dragged him away.

"Let me go! Hun! Let me go! I need to find him! Let me go!"

The half-breed's strength overwhelmed his fragile figure. He was hugged firmly even as he struggled.

"Calm down. Skyeola. Calm down."

"No!" He clawed at Hun's gauntlets. "Let me go!"

"Skyeola!" Jarid grabbed his cheeks. "It is a wlip-o-wlip nest. You cannot approach it."

All fight drained out of him and he hung limp in Hun's arms. A sob broke out of him. "No…"

Tenderly, Hun lowered him, and he slumped onto the forest floor, curling into a ball. Jarid threw a shawl over his trembling shoulders, rubbing his back in a circular motion. He vaguely heard him talking to Hun, but all his focus was on the pitiful sensation of disgust bunching up in his stomach. He had failed to protect the one thing in his life that was good. Skyeola cradled his claws together, staring at the tears that dripped onto them. It was as though the light had gone, and he was dreadfully and fitfully cold, his fur hackling as fear drove a sharp dagger through his chest.

This was his fault. The Prince was gone because of him. He had distracted him. If Daniel had not turned to wave—

Suddenly, Citla's hands folded around his. "*Ria. Ria,*" she soothed him. "Calm yourself. We must be strong now, for our Prince."

Skyeola bit down on his lip. "I will try, *mam lleuad*.[16]"

She caressed his cheeks and softly kissed his forehead. "*Fy arglwydd bach dewr.*[17]"

At Citla's urging, he stood, his knees weak. It was already dark beneath the dense canopy, and, with the encroaching nightfall, what meagre light they had was quickly fading, to be replaced by torches held by guards.

Skyeola frowned at the increasing gathering of Lord Galvon's men around them. He had felt trapped by them in the Turret, but this was worse. This seemed as though the province lord was making a statement to their small entourage. Hun and his men were surrounded.

A youth he had only seen from a distance broke through Lord Galvon's men, approaching Jarid timidly with a low bow. He had thought Lord Galvon's two sons were miniature versions of the grotesque man, but perhaps he had been hasty in his snap judgement for, while Muhzun had much of his father's shape, very little else of the elder Galvon remained in his honey locks and hazel eyes.

---

16 *Moon Mother*
17 *My brave little lord.*

"Master Muhzun." Jarid inclined his head.

"I was with the Prince when he fell."

Skyeola's ears perked up sharply. Was this a plot against the Prince? Surely Lord Galvon would never be so foolish—but, then, this was perfect—to lose him in what could only be seen as a complete accident.

"It was not your fault, Master Muhzun." Citla held out her hand to the young man. "No one could have predicted such a happenstance."

Skyeola's neck feathers settled.

"Maiden Citla is quite correct." Jarid nodded. "Right now, we must work on dealing with the aftermath. Does your Father have any ideas?"

Muhzun stepped back, gesturing towards the wlip-o-wlip nest. Skyeola gulped. They were vicious vines, carnivorous and venomous, one of Pennadot's most terrifying flora. He had never expected to find himself so near an infestation.

"My Father is preparing a keg of black-powder, imported from the Tempath Mines. He believes that by attaching some pig flesh to it we can lure the wlip-o-wlip out and make it drag the keg down into the nest before the keg is set to ignite. Then, once the wlip-o-wlip has burnt up, we can lower someone down to seek out His Highness."

Jarid cupped his chin. "I see—"

Skyeola heaved in a panicked breath. "What! No! What if he is trapped down there? You'll end up burning him alive."

Jarid looked at him. "Whatever do you mean? We need to burn out the wlip-o-wlip to reach him—"

"Do you not know anything about Zaprex Ruins!" Skyeola flung up his arms. "Due to them not being maintained anymore, a by-product builds up. It is highly toxic and highly flammable." Skyeola punctuated his statement by pointing a claw at a nearby tree. "Why do you think Shalamic looks the way it does? For centuries, the forests have been absorbing this surplus of pollutants and filtering it."

"How do you know this?" Citla asked.

"*Every* Batitic Alchemist would know. And at least one of my ancestors worked on the by-product during the Sin'musk'qu Wars…ah…you know…for…*reasons*…" He flinched at having the awful memory resurface.

She nodded. "So we cannot use fire."

Jarid clenched his fists. "Then how do we get down to him? Is there another shaft?"

Muhzun raised a hand weakly. "It…could be…possible to navigate through the tunnel system from the Turret. I…I can…take you myself." He hesitated. "If my Father agrees." The lad glanced anxiously towards the scene of Daniel's disappearance. "It is exceedingly difficult to traverse. Lord Skyeola is correct; the air is toxic. Many men have died."

Citla turned away. "If there is an open path, Master Muhzun, I shall find it."

Jarid motioned to the timid young man to follow him. "Let us go speak to Lord Galvon. We need to act quickly."

Muhzun nodded. "Of course."

Skyeola felt his wings flop. This was going to take too long. Daniel was down there, alone, dying, and he could not reach him. He clenched his jaw until it burned.

Hun's hands settled on his shoulders, squeezing fondly. "His Highness will be fine. You know our *seren*; he shines no matter where he falls."

Skyeola wiped away tears. "I know. I just…I just wish I had fallen with him."

"Come on." Hun guided him through the wall of guards, heading after Jarid, Citla, and Muhzun. He had no desire to approach Lord Galvon, or even look upon the man his ancestral memories seemed so disgusted by, but, for Daniel, he would force himself to be in that presence.

He could hear the commotion before they reached their destination, and Hun's small allotment of their Palace Guards made tense movements, the sort that readied them for battle. Skyeola's neck feathers hackled.

Lord Galvon stood beside his horse, looking as though

he had been disturbed in the process of mounting. Muhzun was nursing a bloodied cheek and Jarid had almost drawn his rapier.

It was Citla, though, who had thrust herself forcefully between the province lord and his youngest son.

"You will allow us to take the tunnels," she demanded.

"I will allow no such thing, Maiden." Lord Galvon lifted his chin. "It is far too dangerous, and to even suggest it is a mockery of my hospitality."

"Yet you seem to be suggesting we leave His Royal Highness down there." Citla's soft, monotone voice was filled with more venom than any wlip-o-wlip vine. Skyeola shivered against the hiss of her tongue.

"I have said nothing of the sort. My men shall find His Highness. Lord Jarid, please return to Iliaion. It is terribly unsafe for you and your men to be out in Shalamic."

Jarid's trembling hand unwound itself from around the hilt of his rapier. "You cannot honestly expect that of us. The Prince's wellbeing and safety—"

"Lies with you, when he is with you. But he is not with you." Lord Galvon shook his head. "He is currently lost, somewhere, amongst my forests. Therefore, his safety is now of my concern and you are a foreign province lord upon my soil."

Hun shifted quickly, stepping up, putting himself between the two lords. Lord Galvon smiled. "Well, one of you has some sense."

"You are a coward," Citla whispered. "At least kill him with your bare hands, like you killed our King."

Lord Galvon hoisted himself onto his horse, gaining height over Citla. "You are nothing but a Maiden. Without your Prince, your voice matters not in this discussion."

Skyeola hung back against the nearest palace guard for protection as Lord Galvon rode past, leaving their small entourage in the growing darkness. He hugged his claws to his chest as Jarid and Citla came together in a single, fluid step of unity.

"What do we do?" Citla choked out. "Jarid. I have never…I

have never broken my promise…"

Jarid dropped his head. "We can do nothing here. Let us return to Iliaion. The Tunnels still seem like an option."

"Jarid…" Hun anxiously waved a hand. "Please don't start a war."

"I will do my best not to," Jarid muttered. "No promises, though."

Sleep.

How was he expected to sleep? The very concept was offensive.

Skyeola stared at the ceiling far above him, and the faint glow of the hexagon patterns that were only visible come nightfall when the ancient Zaprex turret showed its beauty. None of it mattered now—

Skyeola rolled around, clutching fiercely at his bedsheets as his stomach churned. Had tempting them to Shalamic with promises of Zaprex treasure all been an elaborate plot by Lord Galvon to slay the Prince? Or was it simply the vile man seizing any opportunity he could? That was more likely. Lord Galvon did not seem astute enough to orchestrate such a web.

He snatched his conductor, tucked beneath his pillow, pointing it at the door as it slid open. A shadow shifted into the room and then halted.

"It is just me, Little Lord Skyeola," the voice of Muhzun whispered. "I apologise for the late hour."

"No, it is fine." Skyeola pulled back the bed covers. "What is it?"

"We need to slip into the Tunnels before my Father has them sealed off."

"Now?" Skyeola looked up at the youth.

Muhzun nodded. "Yes. Now."

Skyeola rushed to the wardrobe, pulling out his thickest

robes. Muhzun was dressed heavily, so it seemed wherever they were going would necessitate extra layers. If only he had armour of some kind. He would have to commission some—

Snatching up his equipment, he tucked away his conductors within their allocated holsters. "Right. Let us go."

Muhzun held out a pack. "It may take us a few days, so I have brought some supplies."

"A few days…" Did Daniel even have a few days?

Muhzun nodded. "As I said. It is not an easy path, but I believe my Father has no intention of allowing Lord Telvon or his men permission to search the Tunnels. He highly values what lies within and would never let another province lord explore them. We must do this ourselves if we are to find His Highness alive."

The weight of the silence between them said enough. Lord Galvon did have every intention of only finding a Prince who was dead.

Skyeola seized the pack, strapping it around his waist. "Then we should depart, immediately."

"Indeed." Muhzun headed for the door. "Follow me."

"Wait." Skyeola paused, rushing back to his table. He scrawled out a note, tucking it neatly between the pages of one of his books, before sliding shut his chamber door. He answered the unasked question. "For Maiden Citla. If I am missing for a few days, she will search my things."

"I considered asking her to join us, but, in the event that something occurs above ground, I felt it best she remains with Lord Telvon."

"You are worried your father may try something?"

Muhzun turned down a long corridor, anxiously searching the dim shadows cast by heavy wall-hangings and iron statues. His furrowed brow had drawn hard lines in his skin. "There are very few province lords or ladies with direct blood ties to the Starborn Line remaining. Lord Jarid Telvon is one of those few. To claim his head, take his lands, his people, his armies, well, I would not put it past my father. Lady Citla may very well need to protect him."

Skyeola frowned. He had never considered such genealogy when it came to the convoluted twists of the Ancient Starborns and their paladins, but, considering how different Humans were to Batitics, it had always been so hard for his mind to grapple with.

"I never thought about it that way…"

Muhzun glanced at him with a smile. "If the Prince dies, Lord Telvon would be one of the few who could stake a true claim to the Emerald Throne. But, here, he is simply another province lord on foreign soil. There is little he can do without the authority of the Prince or his own province's army behind him. And I highly doubt Lord Telvon is the sort who desires to go to war with a province so far away from his own."

Skyeola sighed. "No. He is not. He sees it as a sense of pride that his province has not had a skirmish with any of the surrounding provinces for centuries."

"I wish my father thought similarly."

"Shalamic seems very peaceful." Skyeola frowned.

"What you see upon the surface does not reflect what lies beneath." Muhzun shrugged. "There are other ways to wage war than with fists and iron."

"That is true…"

"There is a power in words that can so often be far more twisted than a knife in the back."

Skyeola arched an eyebrow. He had seen knives do some ghastly things, and words had little effect in stopping them. "I think it would depend on the situation, Master Muhzun."

"True." Muhzun paused at the top of another long flight of stairs. Skyeola stared down into the darkness, sighing heavily.

"The Zaprexes sure made a lot of stairs…"

"I doubt they actually used them," Muhzun grumbled. "Sometimes I get the feeling this entire place is one big impractical piece of art."

Skyeola's ears twitched. "Or what we are seeing… perhaps…is not its true form."

Muhzun pointed to him. "Even more interesting."

Skyeola grinned. It was nice to find someone who was as enthused by the wonders of the Zaprexes as he was.

They eventually reached the sub-levels, and Skyeola felt thankful that he had been raised in the far larger Palace of Pennadot; he had grown accustomed to the exhaustingly long walks that had always been necessary to reach any destination in the Palace and his wanderings had clearly had an impact on his fitness and stamina. The Turret of Shalamic was small in comparison. But, still, he was overwhelmed by what confronted him. He had already felt tiny against the expanse of the turret's twisting corridors, but, standing in front of a circular entrance, the metal door long sealed shut by some incredible force, made him seem barely more than a speck of dust. He twirled on his foot-claws. Muhzun and his little light had vanished, leaving him alone in the darkness and his night-vision picked up the eeriest signs of an ancient skirmish. His wings fluttered, muscles pulling tight.

"Little Lord Skyeola, over here." Muhzun's lantern flashed, almost blinding him. His protective second eyelids blinked quickly, allowing for the increase in light once more as he turned. Muhzun's head poked through a smaller entrance beside the larger one. Skyeola hurried to join him. Muhzun sealed the door firmly behind them with a loud clank. Skyeola's fur shivered at the sound. He was really doing this—

"Should you have locked that door?"

Muhzun picked up his lantern. "I am afraid so. Nothing works in this area anymore. Do you see how there is none of that glowing blue liquid?"

"Oh…" Skyeola turned around. So that was what was missing from the walls, the absence of the azure shine.

"Not entirely sure what it means, but I have come to a vague understanding that, without that liquid running through the walls, I have to manually open things by force. Most of the time I cannot, but some of the smaller doors I have managed to figure out a workaround." Muhzun tapped the nearby wall.

"Yes, but why close the door after us?"

"Because you never know what is ahead." Muhzun stepped out. "And I would not want it escaping."

Skyeola clutched his claws to his chest. Right—they were in the depths of a Zaprex Ruin. How could he have forgotten that? No one survived exploring the Monuments of Old. He had been so enthralled by the adventure he had forgotten the danger—and forgotten Daniel.

"I presume you have some sort of Batitic way of making light that does not involve flames? It will be dangerous to use the lantern from here on."

Skyeola nodded and dug into his alchemic kit. He pulled out several large gems, finding an appropriately coloured one. He pricked the soft flesh behind a claw with a fang and drew a rune on the gem before muttering a soft incantation.

The stone glowed brightly and he flung it high into the air above them, letting it radiate its light throughout the enormous tunnel they stood within. Muhzun turned around slowly in awe.

"Amazing."

"Just do not tell anyone." Skyeola rubbed his neck. "Blood conduction is sort of out-lawed."

"I do not understand…Why?"

"Well. Usually because blood conduction involves linking the song of the conductor with the subject or object of the conduct. For example, I have just linked that gem with my song, so as long as blood continues to flow through my heart, or I cancel the conduction, it will continue to shine."

Muhzun frowned.

"The drawback to that, I presume, is it is consuming your blood, right?"

Skyeola nodded. "Yes. I am the focus of the fusion in this conduction. I could have used you, but that would have been highly unethical. If I start to tire, it is an option."

Muhzun touched his chest. "I would be honoured."

"Do not so quickly offer a blood conductor your blood."

Skyeola grinned. "Many a Human has lost their life to a Batitic sorcerer for such a deal."

Muhzun snuffed out the lantern, and returned the grin.

"I feel quite sure I can trust you, Little Lord Skyeola."

Skyeola laughed. "All right, what is it you want, Master Muhzun?"

They clambered over fallen rocks, causing several to tumble around them. Muhzun offered a hand to Skyeola, smiling. "You have seen through my cunning plan." He jumped down into a mound of faintly glowing mushrooms, reaching for Skyeola, and hoisting him off the rocks and onto his foot-claws.

"No Human does something for free."

"Perhaps someday you shall meet one who does. But, you are right, I would like something. I would like to be free of my Father."

"I can sympathise. But, when born into the lives we inhabit, we are rather confined to the family we are born into."

"Not necessarily. If I knew I could join the ranks of the Prince's entourage, even as a simple Knight, I would gladly disown my Family Name."

Skyeola frowned. Such a thing was serious, to denounce a Family Name. It was a very Human thing, as far as he was aware—though, Kelibs had a similar tradition. Batitics could never escape their heritage. It was a privilege certain species had to be able to forget their history. He would never escape the shadow of his Father, nor the taint of the Mazaki Bloodline.

Smiling up at Muhzun, though, Skyeola managed a nod. "If it is within my power, I shall attempt to aid you in this quest of yours. As I said, I can sympathise."

"Then, let us find our Prince."

Skyeola lost all sense of time. Though he was sure they could not have been walking, climbing, and clambering any longer than a day, the illusion of timelessness was eerie, deep beneath the earth as they were, surrounded on all sides by magnificent Zaprex walls, broken and shattered from the vast root systems of the enormous trees of Shalamic. Crystals had

formed from shattered panels, and Muhzun strictly forbade
him to go near any of the tantalising glowing forms.

"You will die," he had stated.

They stopped for a meal. By now it was more than likely
Jarid, Citla, and Hun would have noticed his absence, and he
was loathe to think how concerned he would have made them.
He had not thought this through. The Prince was missing—
and now Skyeola had left with only a note tucked away on his
desk.

He had acted very rashly, and very irresponsibly, and he
was going to have to face the consequences of his actions when
he returned with the Prince.

Skyeola finished chewing his sweet roll. "How do you
know so much about the Tunnel System?" he asked Muhzun.

"I once explored these tunnels, when I was a bit younger,
with several of my friends."

Muhzun held up a hand-drawn map. "We were foolish,
and naive, and did not believe the stories of the fey."

Skyeola's mouth grew dry. He reached for his waterskin,
taking a sip as Muhzun chewed on a cheese roll.

"You did not encounter any protectors down here?"

Muhzun shook his head. "They have never been a problem
in Shalamic, for some reason. Seen the broken hulls of them
lying around, though; we've actually passed a few."

"We have?" Skyeola looked around.

Muhzun grinned. "I will point them out next time."

"Sorry. I just…"

"You seem like the sort who believes." Muhzun rubbed the
back of his neck. "Even me, who was born in a city build by the
sky-gods, it took death to open my eyes." He glanced back at
the faintly glowing crystals. "I believe in them all now."

Skyeola frowned, thinking back to the sealed door they
had left behind. What was it Muhzun did not want escaping?

A soft fizzing alerted him to his little rune stone light
dying away above them. The tug of the fading conduction
within him hurt, just enough to make him aware he had been

donating blood longer than he had intended to. With a sigh, he fished around for another gem, muttering the spell, and throwing the rock into the air. Their light returned.

Muhzun was frowning at him in concern.

"If you need a break…"

Skyeola waved a claw. "No, no. Really. I am fine. I would feel uncomfortable using your blood. I can handle small conductions such as this. It is when you start conducting with blood in large scale warfare and for mage battles…" Skyeola shook his head. "You can destroy not only yourself, but many other lives. Hence, *outlawed*."

"I can see why Batitics are so feared."

Skyeola laughed and began to collect his equipment.

"Do not worry. It takes generations of perfect breeding to produce a highly skilled sorcerer such as my father. I am a great disappointment to him."

"I would not be so sure." Muhzun shook his head.

They started their journey once more, the terrain growing ever more difficult until they were slushing through something like mud in texture. By now Muhzun had instructed he cover both his nose and mouth, though it did little against the countless spores that thickened the air they walked through.

"Are we any closer?" Skyeola stopped and leant against an open doorframe, one of the many entrances to different rooms, storage warehouses, and vast chambers. He could have spent a lifetime exploring in here.

"We are, actually." Muhzun studied his map.

Skyeola's long ears perked up and he looked down the never-ending tunnel.

Daniel. Daniel was close. He narrowed his eyes.

"What is it?" Muhzun began to wade through the mud.

"Is that a light?" Skyeola pointed up ahead. It was a strange glow. Like a sunrise that encompassed the tunnel, gradually increasing in strength. It was Daniel—it had to be Daniel!

Skyeola ran.

CHAPTER FIFTEEN

Pain consumes me.
I dwell within a furnace.
I cannot escape.
There is no end to the endurance of my own existence.

Unknown Starborn

Zinkx glared at the entrance of the Cave from where he sat. His leg jigged in a fit of irritation. Over the past few days, a sickening feeling had crept its way into his gut as he watched Semu play happily within the confines of their Cave.

In no conceivable way could he return to the House of Flames with a child—a Zaprex child—and hand it over to the High Elder, the Council, and the Cultivation Guild. Not when he, and his Squad, had fought for the protection and rights of their own children.

Zinkx dragged his bandaged hands through his hair as the heat of tears threatened the corners of his eyes. They needed him—his Squad had needed him to return with the Key to protect their families. The High Elder had given him only a sol-cycle and his deadline was approaching.

But a Zaprex child—

Perhaps it was possible—

Perhaps Semu could guide him to the Key. He breathed in deeply, pulling a hand slowly away from his tangled hair as tension eased in his shoulders. Hope was still within reach. He could still protect his Squad, and protect Semu. Once he had the Key, he could leave the fairy in the safe arms of Shanty.

He could not bring a child into a warzone, and Shanty had her Sisters to find.

"It will work out..." he whispered. "It will."

"Gifu!" Semu's high-pitched voice jerked him around and Zinkx grabbed for his blade. He clutched his chest as his heart pounded.

"Sun Above, don't do that, Semu."

The fairy was clasping at the gown Shanty had fashioned for it, a mahogany robe in a similar style to her own attire. From the way its ears were vibrating, something had alarmed it. Zinkx slowly rose, his legs weak. "What's wrong?"

"Come. Hurry." Semu pointed down the long cave, into the darkness. "Hurry."

Zinkx sighed. He glanced back at the Cave entrance. Shanty had ducked out with the diabond to hunt. She had been relentless in her insistence that he remain confined to the Caves, despite how worried he was over the Twizel's attack and the need to return to the House. Every day felt like torture. Arguing with Shanty, though, was a fruitless endeavour when he really had little strength to follow through with his actions.

"All right." Snatching up his hip-bags, he followed Semu. "We're not technically leaving the Caves, so she can't argue that point." He was certain the underground network was some sort of ancient exhaust system branching out from the Turret of Shalamic, reaching far into the forest.

Semu tugged urgently on the sleeve of his shirt. "Quick. Hurry. Come."

Their communication was rudimentary at best. While the fairy seemed to understand them, Zinkx had a feeling much of what they said was lost on a conceptual level. It heard the words but failed to grasp the emotional and physical connotations behind them. Though, it was learning and absorbing— and doing so at an alarmingly fast rate—observing them with its large, yellow eyes that stared with a near constant hunger

for more information. The innocence made his confusion to return to the House so much more confronting.

"*Why? Name? What?*" Those simple words followed Zinkx everywhere. That was a fish, it was called a stream, they ate fish because they needed nutrition.

An *endless* loop.

It, at least, had given him something to do while he recovered. Semu seemed unfazed, every so often chattering with excitement in its native tongue.

"Semu, if we go any further it will start to get dangerous." Zinkx halted, holding up a lantern. The cave walls had been replaced with the pure sheen of Zaprex metal, no longer mixed with stone, but cracked by enormous tree roots, bleeding in trickles of water and mud. Fungi, large and small, grew in dense pockets all throughout the twisting corridors.

"*Hai.* Dangerous. Hurt. It is hurt. Help. Help. Cry."

Zinkx touched his aching chest, breathing out uneasily. "Wait. So…something is down here? Hurt?"

"*Hai. Hai.* Crying." Semu waved his arms at the nearby wall. "We hear."

"You're hearing it through the walls?"

He glanced at the metal walls, broken by the twisted roots from the great mutated trees far above them. Countless Zaprex Ruins he had explored, and he was finally delving into one with a fairy at his side—was he to believe it could hear things through the very walls?

"*Hai.*"

"Okay." Zinkx conceded. He crouched, first pulling free a scarf, and tying it firmly around his nose and mouth to ward off the intensifying fumes of the toxins in the air. In these close confines, the fungi of Shalamic's forests were as deadly as any Twizel's poison.

Shanty was going to be extremely upset with him. He sighed.

He tugged out another lantern from his hip-bags and lit the oil, passing it to Semu. The Zaprex happily whizzed around with the light illuming its path in the muggy passageway. Zinkx squinted through the dim glow. He drew out one of his twin blades and sliced through the nearest fungus blocking them. Together they slowly made their way deeper into the dingy depths.

His boots were soon slushing in thick mud. Foul smelling. Stagnant. Even the air was denser. Semu paused and floated back to him, pointing to his lantern. "No more. Fire. Bad. Flammable."

"Oil?" Zinkx glanced down at his boots.

"Is it some sort of flammable liquid? Or is it a gas?"

Semu's large eyes blinked several times. "*Kah-Boom.*"

"Yes. Yes. I understand." He stuffed out the flames and hung the lanterns back on his belts. Feeling through his hip bags in the pale light of Semuyeru's glowing antennae and warm eyes, he found the last of his glowsticks. He snapped them both, passing one to Semu, who instantly held it up with a squeal. "*Gurōsutikku.*[18]"

Zinkx chuckled. "*Hai, gurōsutikku.*"

The smile he received was dazzling, almost causing him to forget the reason for their escapade. He shook his head, clearing it of the haze. "Where is the crying?"

"*Kochiradesu!*[19]"

He followed the Zaprex through the sludge, struggling with each step, and almost fell over the man lying in the foulness. Zinkx stepped back in alarm, holding his glowstick out in disbelief.

"What…is…?"

"Hurt! Hurt! Help! Help!" Semu twirled before pointing the glowstick it held down at the man. The faintest sheen twinkled off the man's skin. Zinkx frowned, crouching. He touched the man's chest. It rose in a wheezing breath.

"Semu, go back and get Shanty. I cannot move him in my condition. Go. Hurry."

---

18   *Glow stick*
19   *"This way" or "It's here"*

"*Hai. Hai.* Gibo! Gibo!"

Zinkx watched as the light of the Zaprex's bobbing antennae and faint glowstick faded. Without the tiny Zaprex's presence he suddenly felt the oppressive force of the walls around him. Never had he felt so afraid of being this deep within the earth, and the loss of that equilibrium he had always known threw him. Zinkx clenched his shoulders, focusing on the man in front of him.

He ran his light over the limp body, pausing in shock at the sight of a rod protruding from the man's side. His arms and hands were skinned, bleeding from numerous gashes. Zinkx glanced around. How long had he been down here, breathing in the thick toxins of the fungi? Stripping his shirt, Zinkx began to rip it into long shreds, wrapping them around the oozing wound. He held his glowstick in his mouth, working quickly. He searched the area. Where had the man come from?

Zinkx stood, holding up his meagre light. Above where the man lay was an opening in the roof of the tunnel. "You fell?" Zinkx stepped closer and looked upwards, making out a pinprick of light a very great distance away. "You fell down a shaft. Oh. No. No. How are you alive? Something had to have slowed your fall…"

Zinkx slushed through the mud, searching, picking through discarded debris, throwing aside bits and pieces until his muddy hands encountered the torn vines of the deadly wlip-o-wlip. He looked up again at the ceiling and cringed. If he had fallen through one of the many shafts the carnivorous plant used as a nest, it would have cushioned his fall, but the poison—

"D…Da…David…"

The voice was so soft, and so desperate, it forced him to turn around without any will of his own. He slumped down beside the man, reaching for his limp hand, and gripping it firmly.

"It's okay," he assured him. "I'm here."

Who was speaking? His lips were moving—but was he

saying the words?

"Zinkx!" Shanty's muffled cry drew his attention. Lights approached through the dense, rich darkness.

"Over here." Zinkx waved his glowstick.

Shanty and Semu headed in his direction. Shanty had stripped off her thick layers, leaving just her thin night-shirt. Semu must have mentioned the mud. She had even tugged on the sturdy pair of boots he had made her for times such as this.

"Oh, Sun above…" Shanty clutched her hands to the fabric tied over her mouth and nose. "It is a Human. What is he doing down here?"

"He fell through a Wlip-o-Wlip nest." Zinkx pointed to the ceiling. "It slowed his fall. But more than likely he has been poisoned. Not to mention the rod through his side."

"Bring the light closer." Shanty waved. Zinkx held it above her as she knelt, looking over the man's injuries. Her tongue started clicking in an anxious tick.

"Several of his wounds have already begun to fester."

"It must be the toxins. This place is rotten."

Shanty looked down the way they had come. "We need to get him out of here. I cannot even begin to work on him in this environment."

"How do we move him?" With difficulty in his current condition, Zinkx raised a boot, glued with the thick mud.

"You'll have to use gravity control." Shanty worried her bottom lip. "If I move him on my own, I will cause further damage."

Zinkx massaged his brow. He must have appeared indecisive, not exhausted, for Shanty's next words sent a panic through him he had not been prepared for.

"Zinkx. He's the Prince of Pennadot."

"What?" Zinkx jerked in her direction. She was a Kelib woman, from the slaver pits of Crinn. Her statement made no sense. "How do you know?"

"I met him, in Iliaion?"

"What?"

Semu circled around them both. "What! What! What!"

"Quiet now, Semu." Zinkx gently urged the fairy to settle. "You cannot be serious. Shanty, what is the Prince of Pennadot doing lying in the mud way down here?"

Shanty flung out her arms. "How should I know?"

"That was a hypothetical question!"

They stared at each other in the dimness. Suddenly, the prince coughed, bubbling blood from his mouth, which oozed down his chin.

"Great Krrirrens," Shanty cried out. "He's going to die. Zinkx! *Do* something!"

"Right. Right." Zinkx waved her down beside him. "Get your arms under him. Yes, like that. Pretend you are carrying a plank of wood. Now gently stand, slowly...*very* slowly."

He could feel the strain on his gravity manipulation skill, like a string being pulled down his spine, increasing a sharp headache that speared straight through his skull.

Soon Shanty was standing with a completely flat prince lying in her arms. Zinkx squeezed his eyes shut. This was going to be a long walk back to their Cave. He tugged out his blade, weakly holding it out to Semu, who stared at it momentarily before taking it in two tiny hands.

"We'll need the path cleared. Can you do that?"

"*Hai. Hai.* Save. Save. Fix. Fix." Semu floated on ahead, his antennae bobbing in the darkness.

Zinkx staggered slightly, catching himself on his knees. He stared down at the mud. His heart raced. He could hear it thundering in his ears and feel his pulse against his left eye.

"Zinkx..." Shanty's voice hesitantly whispered.

He clenched his fists and forced momentum through his muscles. He had survived the Trenches; a little abuse of his gravity control was nothing compared to days of exhaustion.

"I'll be fine. Come on."

Daniel could not grasp why he was not waking up in his comfortable, plush, extravagant bed. Beneath him was something far harder than his customary soft mattress. A woollen skin wrapped him like a cocoon, but it did not give him the comfort of his feather quilts and mountainous pillows.

He had never expected to miss them so much.

And yet he so desperately desired them now, when every inch of his body felt like it was on fire, and a scorching, unbearable pain speared itself through his side with each breath he dared to inhale.

There was no intense Sunlight that he loved to wake up to; what warmth he could feel on his skin was that of a fire. He could smell it in the air; the scent of burning wood joined with the rich flavour of zesty herbs and spices. Aside from the firelight, there were sparkles of flaking blue lights dancing above him, like the night sky-sea.

People were moving around him. One person was of heavy enough build to make him aware it was not Citla. His groggy mind picked up two distinct voices. They were speaking Common Basic.

"Gibo, is he a starman?"

"Well. Ah. Zinkx, a little help, please?"

A twangy accent replied. "I believe, by your definition, yes, he is a starman."

"*Ohhhhhhhhh.*"

"No, Semu, calm down." The man must have stood quickly, for something clattered on the floor.

"Can I touch him?"

"Probably not the greatest idea at the moment, *gaki*."

"He is shiny. His skin goes all sparkly in the light. He is radioactive, yes?"

"He is royalty, darling," Daniel heard the woman respond gently.

"But Gifu's skin doesn't go all sparkly and he is…roy..al.. tly..ly…"

The man sounded as though he choked on something.

"No. I am *not*."

"Now, let's not fuss about it," the woman intervened. "The prince is a normal person. All he has is starblood in him. So, treat him nicely."

"*Hai, hai!*"

Why did it sound like the woman pitied him—no—wait—had she called him *normal?* He felt light with relief. *Normal.* She had called him *normal.*

The conversation drifted away, or, perhaps, his mind drifted with the pain encapsulating his body. The woman began to sing, and he relaxed to her soft voice. Slowly, over a gentle period, he sensed an alertness returning and his sticky eyelids managed to peel themselves open.

"So, you're awake. You had me worried, Your Highness. I feared I might have lost you." Her voice was near his ear, and, now, he knew it sounded familiar.

"By the love of the Great Krrirrens, you are still with us."

Sharp clarity formed around his lips. "Coffee."

"Ah. So, you remember me."

"The *coffee* woman."

She laughed, and his forehead was sponged with a sweet-smelling towel. "My travelling companion has been grateful these past few weeks for that coffee. Keeping him cooped up in this cave while he recovered from his wounds would have been disastrous without something to tempt him with."

So, they were in a cave. Daniel squinted at the ceiling. The soft blue lights that appeared as stars were gemstones, glistening in the firelight. Weakly, he turned his head, facing the Kelib woman. Her skin was a deep emerald, infused with intricate azure tattoos he had not seen the last time they had met. The enormous mass of her ebony hair was bundled up in gold and bone hair pieces that captured her rustic beauty.

"I never introduced myself." She placed a hand upon her breast. "My name is Shan'ta'lee Shir-Hara, formally of the Eighth Clan. But you are welcome to call me Shanty."

"Th…thank you…for saving me…" he managed the words around his ash-dry mouth.

Something smooth and cool was touched to his lips. Daniel gulped it down with relish. Never had something so cold tasted so glorious to his hot body. The Kelib woman smiled as he gave a deep sigh of relief.

"While I have helped nurse you, I cannot claim full responsibility. Zinkx and Semu found you."

"Zinkx…" Daniel tested the name. "That does not sound Pennadotian."

"No. It's Batitic." The rich baritone accent filled the cave like smoke. "Why I have a Batitic name, I do not know. Perhaps I am from Tith. Or perhaps my family came from defectors of the Sin'musk'qu War…who *really* knows…"

Shanty clicked her tongue, sponging Daniel's forehead again. "Apologies, Your Highness, he gets moody and philosophical when he has not had his daily walk."

"I am not a diabond."

"Really? I was beginning to wonder. You sure look like one."

"I look rugged."

"No, you look filthy."

"The word you are looking for is handsome."

Shanty snorted.

Daniel slowly raised a hand, letting it slip out from the blankets that entombed him. "Where…where am I?" He had fallen down a shaft, there had been pain, and darkness—so much darkness—and he had been alone.

"The Northern Moon," the man quipped.

"Zinkx," Shanty chided him.

"Fine. Fine. We're in a network of caves beneath the Forests of Shalamic. They're rather difficult to find if you do not know their location."

Citla was not with him. Of that much he was very aware. "I need…I need to…go."

The man—Zinkx—whom he still could not see, laughed.

Shanty grabbed his shoulder when he tried to sit up.

"You are not in any condition to go anywhere, Your Highness."

And he knew it. As soon as he had begun to lift himself out of the bedcovers, the pain had raged through his muscles, and his side throbbed. He whimpered, biting his lip. So this was what being wounded felt like—what a new experience.

"What happened...?"

"Zinkx, I think it best you come over here," Shanty urged.

The man moved from somewhere within the cave. Daniel frowned. His feet were heavy, and the moment the man crouched beside him, he realised why. Exhaustion. He was a Wynnila man, and while they may have been a similar age in sol-cycles, scars had damaged skin, and weariness had drawn lines and creases. He dragged a trembling hand through messy black hair, and heaved out a long sigh.

"You fell through a Wlip-o-Wlip nest, and, though it did save your life, their venom is not something to bark at."

He had fallen. Muhzun's expression of horror—the fairy-circle—the pain that had ripped through him. Daniel clenched his hands beneath the covers.

"Shanty is rather good with toxins, though, but it will take you at least a week or two to get your strength back. Besides that, you pierced your side with a rod of metal." Blue eyes focused on him. "My medic skills are patchy at best, but I do have some. I am fairly sure I was able to clean you up inside... but...I don't recommend moving for a while, until the chance of rupturing something goes down."

Daniel stared at the man, at the seriousness in his expression.

"I...did I...almost die...?"

"Ah." Zinkx scratched the back of his neck. "Hm. Nahh. It was not that bad. Put it this way: I've survived much worse. You'll be fine, *baka*." His shoulder was given a firm pat. Odd. He did not feel repulsed by the touch of a stranger—why?

"Zinkx! Do not insult the Sovereign of our Land!"

The man looked down at him with a wry smirk. "She is the sovereign of this cave."

He very much believed that.

It felt surreal having the Prince of Pennadot, their Sovereign, sleeping nearby. Adding to that, a precious Zaprex child in a macramé hammock Shanty had fashioned above their own bed-rolls. He was not well enough to protect a child and a Sovereign from danger. He could barely keep his eyes open, but sleep held very little rest as the darkness danced with tormenting colours from a battlefield. Zinkx rubbed at his eyes, studying the slumbering Starborn, finding it hypnotising the way the firelight glinted off the man's diamond skin.

"I think he's in danger." Zinkx looked up at Shanty as she settled herself down beside him, passing over a plate of stew and scones.

She arched an eyebrow at him. "Really, whatever gave you that idea? The giant wound in his side, or the fact that he, our Sovereign, ended up down a wlip-o-wlip nest?"

"You're upset at me," Zinkx muttered.

"You should not have gone off on your own whilst wounded. I had no idea where you were."

"Semu seemed to indicate that it was urgent, and it was." He pointed his spoon at the prince.

Shanty sighed. "Zinkx. We need to start working together."

"I was under the impression this arrangement was temporary. You're certainly not going to want to return to the House with me." He studied the bowl of stew. Despite how wonderful her cooking was, he could barely stomach eating.

"I do not recall you asking my opinion on the matter."

Zinkx looked up with a frown. "I assumed."

"Hm." She slapped her ladle against her thigh. "You assumed. Again. See, this is the reason we need to discuss things, together. You cannot just go off and make haphazard assumptions on your own."

He scrunched his tired eyes.

"You've found a Zaprex, Zinkx. Isn't that a good thing? Is this not a step forward? I thought you would be happier."

Zinkx stood, walking away, dragging his hands through his hair. "One step forward is nowhere near the final destination, Shanty. And...and...there's a child involved now...At the end of it all, I cannot take a child back to the House. Children aren't safe at the House. Children aren't sacred. So what do you think they'd do to a Zaprex child?"

She seemed to hesitate, but slowly the words were drawn out of her. "You could come with me?" She set her bowl aside. "We could find the Merchant and my Sister. Semu would be safe."

Slowly he glanced back, studying her in the flickering fire light. How he craved to hold onto her words, to wish for their truth, their security. If only he could—

Safe. How the word mocked him. Nothing and no one could be safe from the encroaching consumption of the Dragon. If he did not return to the House of Flames with the Key then that danger would only grow—

Zinkx rested his head on the cave wall. Cold, unfeeling stone. Ever since the battle with the Ki'rayh the boiling heat that had always simmered beneath the surface of his skin had been so much more difficult to supress. He rubbed wearily at his eyes. "I can't abandon my people, Shanty. I must return with the Key. They need me...they need me to return with the Key..."

Shanty stood, approaching him, resting her hands on his shoulders. "Do you remember when you took me back to your camp, after we escaped the slavers, and Khwaja Denvy explained a code of the Messengers?"

Zinkx frowned.

"He said that Messengers do that which is directly in front of them. Isn't that the way of your people? Your path will open up for you if you do what is before you, and, right now, Semu is the child you can protect, right in front of you. Protect Semu, here and now, and you will find your path, Messenger."

Zinkx sighed, slumping forward. "I've been searching and hoping for so long, and those waiting for me, trusting in me, I really...I don't know." He dragged out the words, hating how his mouth felt dry and hot as if he was back in the Trenches and gagging on toxins.

She tugged him to the fire-pit. "Getting yourself worked up over it now will not help. It is not like you are well enough to act."

She shoved his bowl back into his hands.

"Eat. Get strong. Eat."

"Is that all you think it takes—?"

"Eat!"

When next he woke, Daniel was highly aware that the man was the only one present with him in the cave. He sat beside him, whittling away at a piece of wood. Daniel's skin felt on fire beneath the weighted skins and he shifted jerkily, startling the man from his reverie.

"What's wrong?"

"Too heavy. My skin...it's..."

The man pulled the covers off, folded them, and set them aside. Daniel breathed. He raised a hand to his sweaty forehead. He drew his arm back in alarm, staring at the bandages. Wet and bloodied, they covered his hands and arms. He hesitated to glance at his legs. They, too, were bandaged. A flood of uncontainable tears rolled down his cheeks. Citla was going to be so upset. She had spent a lifetime trying to keep him safe and he had ruined her work in a single outing.

His shoulder was lightly touched. "Here, try to sit up and drink this. It will help with the pain."

It was difficult to get upright, and, by the time he had done so, his head was feeling light and airy, but he was grateful for the new position despite the burning pain in his side. The man held a cup to his lips and he sipped at the rich liquid therein.

Daniel leant back against the wall behind him. "Thank... thank you..." He searched his memory. It had been a Batitic name... "Zinkx."

Zinkx pulled over a small bag. "We need to change your bandages."

Looking down at his arms, Daniel swallowed. He was not sure if he could stomach looking at the wounds beneath the bloodied linen.

Instead, he gazed around him at the cave. It was homely and well kept. The stone floor was covered in several animal skins, and the walls layered with intricately woven wall hangings. It had been lived in, and loved, for probably many months. The fire in the firepit was a low burn of coals; therein a small pot hung, gently boiling.

"Where...where is the Kelib?"

"Shanty? She's gone hunting. We need food." Zinkx glanced at the vine-covered entrance.

"You cannot hunt?"

"I can." Zinkx sorted through the medical kit, pulling out new bandages, setting them aside. "But saving your royal *totu* set my own recovery back."

Daniel frowned at the man's trembling hands as they worked on cutting and unravelling the bandages around his arm. A strong scent of turmeric and honey reached his nose as Zinkx opened a little clay jar, mixing it gently with a spoon.

"And while Shanty is extremely skilled with her medicinal herbs, they are not really the same as an antidote," he grumbled. "Seems I cannot spring back to my feet."

He began to spread the herbal mixture over the wounds. Daniel jerked his arm aside in alarm, seeing the vicious, jagged slices that marred his once unblemished skin.

"Will you just sit still, Deiniol!"

"How...do you know...my identifier?" Panic seized Daniel.

Zinkx froze. The spoon he held dropped. "I..."

"How do you know that name?" If he could have, Daniel would have scrambled away. No random stranger in the wilds of Shalamic could possibly know his Name. As if sensing he was about to try to flee, Zinkx gripped his shoulder tightly.

"I don't know." Blue eyes focused fiercely on him, drawing all his attention like a lantern in the night. "Listen. I don't know how I know something like that. It just slipped out."

"You expect me to believe that!" Daniel spluttered. "You could be an agent of Lord Galvon, or ...or worse...Steward Zilon—"

"I'm a Messenger."

Daniel stopped his meagre struggling. He stared blankly into the blue eyes, raw, emotional, and honest. "A Messenger..." he whispered. A Messenger was a legend—a myth—a story—

Anyone could claim to be a Messenger.

Zinkx nodded. "A Messenger." He sat back on his knees, releasing Daniel's shoulder slowly. "I didn't want to tell you, to get you involved in our web, but...I swear..." Zinkx breathed out uncomfortably, rubbing his temples. "Sometimes, I just know things. I know a lot of things, to be honest. I could probably speak to you in fluent Ancient Pennadotian if you'd prefer that to Common Basic."

"*Na, mae hynny'n iawn, ond diolch.*[20]"

"*Dim ond cynnig*[21]." Zinkx shrugged.

Daniel stared at him. "*Pwy wyt ti?*[22]"

The gaze he received was eerily like that which he had often seen reflected in the mirror, distant, confused, and lonely. "*Weithiau, wn I ddim.*[23]"

---

20 *No, that's fine, but thanks*
21 *Just an offer.*
22 *Who are you?*
23 *Sometimes, I don't know.*

"*Nid wyf ychwaith yn I,*[24]" Daniel whispered.

He forced a smile, forced his tense muscles to relax. It would be no use to get this man, who knew his Name, offside. Zinkx returned to the herbal mixture and bandages, working carefully and deftly. It was obvious the man had dealt with many wounds, countless times over. He did not know if he found it comforting or alarming. Upon finishing, Zinkx packed away the medical kit, and headed for the pot over the firepit.

"Want coffee?"

Daniel's brow lifted. "Am I allowed coffee?"

"Shanty isn't here."

"That is how it works, is it?"

Zinkx smirked. "Naturally."

"Sure. Coffee."

Zinkx passed him a hand-carved mug, and sat down beside him, wrapping himself in one of the blankets, hugging his own drink with a happy hum. Daniel squeezed his own hands around the warmth.

"Oh. Before I forget." Zinkx shuffled around, setting his mug aside. He reached for a hanging bag, pulling it down, rifling through the contents. "Would you like a souvenir."

A metal rod was flung into Daniel's lap.

Daniel picked it up. It was heavier than he expected such a thin rod to be.

Zinkx sipped on his coffee. "It's Fey metal. Rotten luck you landed on it. I think it's one of the bolts that held up the door to the shaft you fell through."

Daniel winced. So, this was the cause of the searing pain in his side. A souvenir, indeed.

"Find a blacksmith who works with Fey metal. They are rare, but you should be able to engage one. Melt it down, make an amulet, or a ring, something like that. Make something nice with it. I highly recommend the effort, considering that you can afford the jewels."

---

24   *Neither do I.*

Daniel frowned. *Jewels*. Was he being ransomed? Surely Lord Galvon would not ask for finances from Jarid. Yet, was it possible he was he being hidden here until that ransom was paid?

"So, it can be melted?" Daniel turned the metal slowly in his hands.

Zinkx nodded. "Takes a particular process. You'll find the blacksmiths who can do it all have a family history that'll be traced back to Sin'musk'qu, or they have some affiliation to the Twilight Nation."

"It is Batitic skill, then?"

Zinkx held out his mug, tipping it slightly forward in a positive gesture.

Was he supposed to take this as a threat towards Skyeola? Did this man know about him—and how precious the little Batitic was to him?

"Interesting." Daniel tried to appear unfazed, taking a gulp of his own drink. His hands settled in his lap and his shoulders dipped.

Skyeola—poor little Skyeola—what sort of panic would the kitten be in?

He looked at Zinkx again. There could not have been much difference in age between them, and yet he felt like he was looking upon someone who had lived sol-cycles beyond his own lacklustre experiences. A *Messenger*. If he dared entertain that thought, the possibility, then he was sitting across from a myth—a figure told about in stories by bards—warriors who fought an ancient war against an ancient foe. Glancing at the man sitting beside him, casually sipping his coffee, he felt the eeriest sensation that he was in the presence of the mythical figures Skyeola often gushed about from old tomes the kitten had dragged out of the Palace Library.

"Oie, don't pick at your bandages," Zinkx barked.

Daniel snapped to attention, realising he had been fidgeting. "Oh. Ah...sorry. Ah. So..."

Zinkx arched an eyebrow.

"What are you doing in Shalamic?" Daniel asked.

Shaking his head, Zinkx sighed, leant forward, and gestured to the entrance with a nod. "Suppose it wouldn't hurt to tell you. It has been rather difficult to keep it hidden."

The vines covering the cave entrance parted like a waterfall divided by a boulder, as Shanty and an enormous white diabond pushed through. Shanty threw down several skinned hares as the diabond lumbered away to a large rock. It spat out chunks of boiling lava and rolled lazily into the burning pile. Zinkx waved a hand at the beast. "That's disgusting. Don't roll in your spit."

The diabond yawned, wagging its tail, defying the man entirely. Zinkx spread his hands, looking to Shanty beseechingly. "What is this? A revolution?"

"We stayed out a bit too long. The temperature dropped rather rapidly." Shanty picked up the pot over the fire, giving it a sniff. She sighed, shaking her head as she set it aside. "What did I say about the coffee, Zinkx?"

"That I could drink as much as I wanted." Zinkx flopped back dramatically.

Daniel took a long draught from his own mug. "Somehow I highly doubt that."

"Shut up, *brenin*[25]," Zinkx mumbled.

Shanty approached them. She crouched down in front of Daniel and he smiled as she checked his temperature before moving to his bandages. "I am glad to see you sitting up, Your Highness. Perhaps you shall manage a small meal this evening."

"I hope so. I am actually rather hungry."

"That is a good sign." Shanty stepped over his legs, giving Zinkx a gentle nudge with her foot. "Could you go and check on Semu—"

"It's fine." Zinkx sat up. "He knows."

Shanty paused. "Knows?" Shanty's anxious gaze fell upon Daniel. "Knows about…"

"I am not sure if I believe you are Messengers." Daniel held

---

25   *King, monarch, sovereign*

up a hand. He watched as Shanty's shoulders tensed tight.

"He wants to know why we are here in Shalamic. I figure showing him will be enough to help him understand that we're not a band of nefarious folk."

"If you are sure." Shanty worriedly fiddled with her dress.

Zinkx heaved himself to his feet to stand beside her. "Semu, you can come out," he called.

A giggle echoed through the cave. Like a twinkling of dozens of bells, it grew closer, until it surrounded them on all sides. Daniel searched around for the source, only for it to appear immediately in front of him in a blink.

"Hello, Starman!"

Daniel dropped the empty mug he held. "Great Sun!"

If he had thought Zinkx was torn out of the pages of an old manuscript, then the maniacally grinning little imp that twirled and pranced in the air was a pure manifestation of fantasy.

"Believe me now?" Zinkx smiled.

CHAPTER SIXTEEN

If you keep to the Spider Road,
The Sun shall cast your shadow.
If you leave the Spider Road,
The Sun cannot see you,
And neither will anyone else.

Spider Road Shrine Inscription

Muhzun pulled him back. "It is not the Prince."

Skyeola scrambled in the slick sludge. Muhzun was right. The glow ahead of them, like a tantalising source of hope, was a furnace of despair.

The heat was already intense against his fur, and, if it was this hot, this far away—

"Run. Muhzun! Run! Run now!"

Run where? They would never outrun it. They were days away from the entrance.

His sharp eyes spotted an opening as they rushed past it. Skyeola swung around, grabbing Muhzun as he moved, yanking the larger Human through with him.

He swirled his conductor, merging their bloods together, and dragged the metal and earth forth from around them, forging a plug in the doorway. They were plunged into a terrible darkness as the world roared and shook. Skyeola stumbled on his foot-claws, falling backwards, landing roughly on top of Muhzun, who grappled for his arm. The roaring felt like it lasted a lifetime, but it could not have been more than several minutes until silence settled.

Muhzun's panicked breathing was all he could hear. Skyeola struggled in the darkness, wincing as his wings twisted and pulled in odd directions.

"We need a light," Muhzun groaned.

Skyeola frowned. Light. "Wait. You cannot see?" Skyeola whispered.

"No. Nothing at all."

Skyeola refocused. Something nearby was giving off enough light for his night-vision to distinguish vague shapes and outlines. He looked up slowly, and sucked in a sharp, horrified breath.

"Do...not...move..." Skyeola breathed.

"Why?" Muhzun's whole body tensed.

"Because there is a protector right behind you, and it is very much awake."

Light now rippled through the chamber, mimicking the reflection upon the surface of a pond, radiating from the protector as its hulk lifted. Groaning metal ground painfully, causing Skyeola's ears to flinch rearward. It studied them with a single mechanical eye, pure crystal blue, the lens focusing slowly on him.

He could do nothing. No conduction came to mind, nothing from his ancestral memories surfaced. Only fear. The protector's enormous metal head slunk away, its sole blue eye gradually widening as it withdrew back into the darkness of the large chamber they had tumbled into. Skyeola clutched his stomach as he vomited, releasing the terror of the moment in an uncontrollable reaction. Not even witnessing his father torturing Messengers to death had made him feel this terrified. He glared down at the result of his terror in shame, breathing rapidly.

"It...did not attack us...why?" Muhzun murmured. "They always attack. Every myth, every legend, they always... they always attack. You never get out alive."

Skyeola hushed Muhzun with a claw. He gathered up the sliver of courage left within and called out.

"*Tasukete. Tasukete.*"

The protector halted its long strides. Its elongated neck turned, causing old, rusted metal to twist and bend as it refocused its blue mechanical eye on his kneeling form. Skyeola breathed in sharply, wrapping his tongue around the word once more.

"*Tasukete.*" He placed both claws on his chest. "*Tasukete.*"

Was he saying it right? Or perhaps it did not understand. He was making a presumption that protectors were infused with the language of the fairies. Slowly it turned. Muhzun grabbed his arm. "What are you doing?"

"We need its help. There is no way we will be able to return to the Turret now with the tunnels boiling rivers of death."

Muhzun slumped back. He scrambled away as the protector slid down on sparking, mangled legs to crouch in front of Skyeola. Skyeola reached out, withdrawing sharply as a static shock sparked through the twisted and bent metal of the protector's long-ago damaged head. He steadied himself with a long breath and settled his claw gently down upon the rusted hull. Warm. It was warm. And it hummed with a gentle, thrumming song of bells that ignited his wings in a rush of energy.

"Thank you…"

As though mounting a beast of burden, he climbed his way onto the protector's back. There was worn padding in an allocated groove, nestled in behind the long neck, indicating that his presumption was correct: at some point it had been rideable. Skyeola looked down at Muhzun, who had pressed himself up against the nearby wall in terror.

"You want me to get on it?" Muhzun choked out.

Skyeola nodded from his perch on the provided seating. He gave the padding behind him a pat. "Here, see, you sit on this, just like a horse."

"It is not a horse. It is…it is…a monster…"

"No. It is a *protector*. Come on. We need to hurry. Master Muhzun!" Skyeola held out his claw. Muhzun's eyes snapped up to his. "Think about what just happened. That fire…"

"My father…" Muhzun clutched his hands to his chest.

"Yes. Your father. We must get back. This is the only way. Get on. Please."

"Are you sure it will not kill us?"

Skyeola seized Muhzun's trembling hand, aiding him in clambering up onto the perch behind him. "I am afraid I cannot promise you that."

The protector lumbered onto all six of its legs, stumbling a little under their weight. A higher pitched hum echoed through the chamber, building from deep within the ancient machine, and the azure glow emanating from its chest deepened, creeping out through its limbs like ink blots across a page.

Suddenly it lunged. Skyeola yelped and Muhzun grabbed him tightly as they lurched forward into the darkness. That was all they saw, for the longest time—a solid wall of blackness and the warm glow of the protector surrounding them, until gradually the heat began to creep closer. Skyeola frowned as he clutched the metal shell of the protector beneath him, trying to time his own movements with its long paces to ease the stiffness of his legs against the hardened hull. Hun had once told him of a Kelib dish he loved, one that involved boiling frogs—boiling frogs alive. It was fun, apparently, to slowly kill an animal. He had been disgusted. He thought it far too similar to the drums of boiling oil his father used for killing Messengers. Once skin was stripped from muscle, boiled down to bone, and the oil mixed around, and around, it all started to look like a stew in a great big pot.

He had lost all appetite for meat.

He licked his dry lips. His fur was beginning to curl from the heat, his sweat evaporating too fast to dampen the thick mat across his skin.

They were the frogs, slowly boiling in the Kelib pot.

A sudden rush of cool air blasted upwards, from vents within the protector's hull. Behind him, Muhzun groaned in relief.

There was no halting. No breaks. They shared what little water they had remaining as the protector continued its a steady pace. The exit they reached was not the one they had entered through; it opened out into the forest of Shalamic. Skyeola stared out at the long blast radius that had erupted from the entrance of the tunnel and sliced through the forest like a blacksmith's hot tool. It went on for miles. Smoke still rose from several smouldering fires.

He slid off the protector's back. It had stilled the moment it crouched low. His claw rested on its head. No longer was a song humming from within it.

"It…it is dead." Skyeola stepped away.

"They are not alive." Muhzun urged him back with a hand. Skyeola pulled away.

"It used up all its power protecting us from the heat. It died for us! We should be dead."

"I know."

"The Prince…" Skyeola clutched at his chest. "The Prince."

"Lord Skyeola…please…"

"Your father!" Skyeola turned on his foot-claws. "We need to get back to Iliaion!"

They both faced the forest ahead of them. "We are not far from the Spider-Road." Muhzun peered at his map.

"Then let us go." Skyeola stomped off. He could feel it— his patience—hanging by a mere thread.

Skyeola stormed his way through the Turret, Muhzun close behind him. Getting back into Iliaion had snapped the last few strands of his patience. The seething hatred he felt due to the mockery of the guards burnt a hole through his chest. There was a level of contempt he could tolerate, but even that wore him down.

"Lord Skyeola! Look…" Muhzun grabbed his arm,

dragging him around, directing his attention to the scene outside the window. Skyeola staggered to a halt. It was as though a sky-god itself had dragged a flaming sword through the Forests of Shalamic several times over, leaving vicious burns across the horizon.

"Oh, by the Twilight." Skyeola's knees buckled. He grabbed hold of the window ledge. It had not been an isolated fire; it had consumed the entire network. A chain reaction—

Daniel was dead.

"Where would your father be?"

"We really should go and see Lord Telvon—"

Skyeola twisted, glaring up at Muhzun, who stepped back, nodding quickly. "This way…"

Skyeola blinked rapidly. Curling his claws to his chest, he followed Muhzun. He was acting irrationally, but he could not stop himself. The wick was lit. He was following a burning urge deep within him to act.

If Daniel was dead—

Daniel—

His Sun—his…friend—Daniel—

Muhzun had paused at a large set of double doors. The guards barely had time to move before Skyeola barrelled past them, slamming the doors open with a wave of his conductor. Lord Galvon sat upon a chair towards the far end of the chamber, several of his advisers surrounding him.

Skyeola marched his way down the hall.

"You absolutely disgusting, filth ridden corpse!" Skyeola shrieked. "I should kill you where you sit." He pointed his conductor directly at Lord Galvon, ignoring every guard in the chamber as they drew their weapons.

Lord Galvon raised his hands, smiling innocently. "Now, now, calm yourselves. You both appear to have been through an ordeal."

"An ordeal, Father?" Muhzun gestured to the panoramic windows and the glow of distant fires against the gradual sunset. "We were down in the tunnels. We barely survived."

A momentary look of shock passed across the province lord's face, so briefly. He had not expected their adventure and it threw him.

Lord Galvon's eyes focused on Muhzun. "It was you. You left a door open."

"No. I did not," Muhzun insisted. "You think you know what is down there, Father, but there so much more than just the protector."

Lord Galvon's hands clenched, turning white. "You know nothing, boy."

Muhzun flung out an arm. "I know enough that your actions could have led to the very destruction of Iliaion."

"Watch your tongue—"

"Oh, I see," Skyeola interjected. "So you did set it off. Did you expect the chain reaction?"

"What? No, do not be ridiculous." Lord Galvon tugged on his tunic. "I would never harm my own province in such a manner. Something must have transpired. Perhaps the Prince himself—"

Skyeola drew himself up, thrusting his conductor against the man's chin. "If the Prince is dead, I will personally rip your throat out. And you do not want to see a Batitic do that! These fangs are not for show."

Lord Galvon managed a meagre smile. "Little Lord Skyeola, threatening a province lord—"

"You are a maggot. A slimy, filthy maggot that feasts on the dead flesh of a failing, dying system."

Skyeola stepped back, throwing open his wings, filling the chamber with a swirl of wind as he gathered the large, leathery appendages behind him in a trail. Muhzun raised his chin to his father and stoutly turned to follow.

"Muhzun! Get back here," Lord Galvon bellowed. "Muhzun!"

The young man spat on the floor. "Take back my name. I do not want it. Your son died in the tunnels." Muhzun left, and Skyeola threw a smirk back at the stunned lord.

Galvon's glare settled on him.

"You are very much your father's child."

From the entrance, Skyeola twirled his conductor.

"If I were my father, I would have had you flayed alive. I would then use your skin, your muscles, your bones, your blood, for every manner of twisted experiments my little mind could ever concoct. Be very...awfully glad...I am *not* my father."

CHAPTER SEVENTEEN

To live is to be brave.

Note left in Front Line Messenger's Journal

Shanty crouched by the trap she had laid out the evening prior. It was impossible for her to hunt in the manner Zinkx did, with speed and agility so akin to the lightning he wielded. He struck like a bolt, taking down his prey. Her way took patience and time. With the addition of the Prince to feed, it only increased the need for the basics. Carefully she removed the hare she had caught, whispering a soft prayer of gratitude to the Krrirren as she reset the trap.

"Well, dear, I believe this shall be enough for this evening's meal." Shanty rose, turning in the direction of the waiting diabond. She halted.

The apparition had returned.

The forest had stilled around them, eerie, without a breath of wind, captured like a singular, crystallised moment.

"It's you…" Shanty whispered. The woman who had aided her in escaping and defeating the Ki'rayh. She was tenderly brushing her translucent hands through the diabond's fur, causing fiery flakes to shimmer into the air.

The woman smiled, tipping her head to one side. "I am glad to see you are well, Shan'ta'lee." The woman slowly walked around the diabond, dissolving into flakes, reappearing at the other side of the hound in an entirely different form. Shanty dropped the hare in surprise.

A Zaprex. Semu had awed her with an overwhelming desire to protect and nurture, as though something within her was altered to see the fairy as her own offspring. This Zaprex made her legs weaken. It took all her strength to fight against the urge to bend her knee.

It was cloaked in a magnificent robe of night sky-sea, stars dancing throughout the inky black material that twirled between rusted metal cogs. Beneath the grey tint of its green skin, a deep, burning red glow emanated from cracks and joins in plates of metal. A fiery red. *Dangerous.*

She should have been running from this dangerous being, so why did she feel so safe in its presence?

"Hazanin Mi Runnaue." The tiny Zaprex bowed. "Time Master of Livila."

"Runnaue." Shanty whispered, looking back in the direction of the caves. "Semu…"

Hazanin inclined its head.

She twisted back. "It really is your child?"

"What an interesting assumption."

"I did not—"

"Yes. It is. I am its Positive Parent." Hazanin raised a slim hand. "Zaprexes are usually either Negative or Positive in orientation. However, in the case of a catastrophic scenario, a Zaprex Dynasty will produce a Fusion. A Dynasty Starter."

Shanty sat back on a nearby root with a thud.

"As a Kelib, I am certain sure you can comprehend the sheer importance of my child's existence."

"A Krrirren Seed." Shanty clutched at her skirt. Her people had not had such a blessing in centuries, but to learn that the Zaprexes had a similar concept was overwhelming.

"In a manner of speaking, yes."

Shanty's head snapped up. "Why are you here, telling me this?"

"Because you have a mother's heart." Hazanin's sharp, red

gaze softened. "And I cannot be with my childre—child—child. I cannot be with my child. The road it will walk…" Hazanin paused, looking somewhere off into the distance. Shanty frowned, turning, seeing nothing in the trees.

"My time is up." Hazanin shifted uneasily, stepping towards her. "Tell your Human companion this:

"What he seeks is found in simple tunes and great symphonies.
It brings conformity and regulation to that which has no unity.
Where there is an absence of direction, it knows the way.
All doors that are sealed shall be opened this day.
When the engine lies lifeless, it shall spark the burn.
And so the world shall once more begin to turn."

The Zaprex bowed its head. "Be safe, dear one."

Shanty blinked. She was suddenly standing in the low light of nightfall, and the crisp air caught her off-guard, causing her to violently slap the skin of her bare shoulders. Had it not been midday a moment ago? She jerked in confusion. Time—time had shifted—

"Time Master." Her lips parted, misting the cold air as she glanced at the diabond. "Come, let's get back. Zinkx will be worried."

The pain had been difficult to manage, and spending much of his time anxiously staring at the opening of the cave wondering if Galvon or Zilon would appear to deal the final blow only seemed to increase the throbbing. Daniel sighed. His strength was returning, but healing had been slow, as predicted.

Zinkx had finished sweeping out the cave, something the man did every afternoon. He was now proceeding to run through a series of what looked like overly-exhausting exercises. The man was a complete enigma, which what made him all the more terrifying.

Daniel steeled himself. It would take all his diplomatic skill to handle this situation. And he would have to make his captors believe he felt calm and relaxed in their presence. "I thought you were injured," he called out.

"I am." Zinkx dropped to the floor. "And it's aggravating my old war wounds." He rubbed at his left leg. "Metal shrapnel that was never removed… not to mention that the bone in my leg is held together with bolts."

Daniel clenched his shoulders at the thought of living with such a permanent debility.

"If I don't keep up my strength, endurance, and flexibility then I will weaken and take longer to recover. You should try it."

Daniel pulled a disgusted face. "Ah. *No*. That looks about as appealing as rolling in a pool of mud."

The sweaty man thudded down beside him, taking a long drink with a trembling hand. "You are never going to be able to wield a sword, or pull a bow properly, Your Highness."

Daniel scoffed as though affronted by the notion. "I am extremely skilled with a bow."

"Yes. Because you cheat."

"I do *not* cheat."

Zinkx arched an eyebrow and snorted. "And my lightning comes out of my *totu*."

"Now that is just rude." Daniel huffed.

Something rolled in the sheets beside Zinkx. He raised a hand, lifting the heavy skins to reveal the tiny Zaprex, sleepily stirring. "Good nap?"

"It was adequate. I need sustenance." The Zaprex yawned.

"Shanty will be back soon." Zinkx gently stroked a hand through frizzy curls of thick black hair.

"But I need sustenance now."

Zinkx rubbed the back of his neck.

"I thought sleep recharged you."

"It was adequate. It was not flawless. Systems are still damaged."

Daniel sighed. "We are just three wounded souls, heh."

"It would appear so." Clambering to his feet, Zinkx headed for a nearby jar. The Zaprex trotted after him, humming in delight as Zinkx poured thick, creamy liquid into a large mug. He handed it to the fairy. "Only one mugful."

"Only one mugful," the Zaprex repeated and happily carted the drink away to its little seat, floating up to sit on a pillow on a rock. Zinkx shook his head, returning to his spot beside Daniel.

He picked up his latest carving with trembling hands and began to work. Daniel settled back, smiling at the man's skills.

"So, what is…its name?"

Zinkx arched an eyebrow.

"The Zaprex. I presume it has a name."

"Semyueru. Semu-*chan*." Zinkx shrugged.

"Semyueru…" Daniel murmured the name. "I believe the Common Basic translation would be Samuel. The Kelib translation would be Sham'uel." Daniel paused. "Wait. Is it a girl?"

Zinkx shrugged. "I don't think their race is like Humans and Kelibs, Your Highness. They are rather unique."

"Fair enough point."

The Zaprex tilted its head to one side. It wiped thick cream from its lips with a long sleeve. "What would you designate me?"

"Designate you?" Daniel queried.

"It means *name*. What would you name it?" Zinkx offered from where he whittled away at a piece of wood.

"Do you not already have a name?"

The Zaprex shook its head. "I am remade. Reformatted. New place. New designation."

"I don't think it likes remembering who it is, or where it came from." Zinkx paused his carving. "And the name Semyueru, or Semu, even, prompts that recollection."

Daniel nodded. "Well, that is understandable. Have you thought of anything?"

"Hm?" Zinkx shrugged. "*Gaki*."

The Zaprex giggled.

Daniel rolled his eyes. He rested back with a weary sigh. The Zaprex sat so happily perched on the little rock by the fire, dressed in a torn blue and black robe, with a little overcoat that once would have been ostentatious. Everything about the child was extraordinary, otherworldly, and alien—

"Sam," he whispered suddenly. "I would call you Sam."

Wide, bright eyes focused on him with a smile of brilliance.

"Sam." Zinkx chuckled. "I like it. Simple. Effective."

"*Hai*!" The Zaprex bounced up and twirled about. "Sam! Sam!"

"I think it likes it." Daniel smiled.

Zinkx turned back to his carving. The Messenger had made a set of beautiful wooden diabonds, one for each of the elements the beasts were forged from. He was currently on the final beast of burden, the fire-type, and seemed to be putting considerably more effort into this one.

"What are you going to do with them?" Daniel asked as he studied the one of lightning that Zinkx had finished painting the night prior. It was intricately done, despite the man having few tools to work with.

"Sell them." Zinkx shrugged. "Shanty is very interested in trade now that she is a free Kelib woman, and she is convinced that if I keep my hands busy doing…things…my mind will have less of a chance to wander into the Trenches."

Daniel smiled. "I presume you will sell most of what you have gathered here?"

Zinkx nodded. "The jewels will then allow us to keep travelling. The cycle will continue."

"Where will you go?"

The Messenger was quiet, focused for a long time on painting the little wooden figure in his trembling hand. Daniel waited. Over the past few days, he had learnt the man had such bouts of lengthy silence, sometimes becoming lost entirely in the place he referred to as the Trenches. It would take time for him to climb his way back out.

Zinkx's vision refocused and he looked up, somewhat startled. "Sorry, what did you say?"

"I asked where you will go?"

"Oh." Zinkx leant forward, searching for another pot amongst his small collection of coloured paints. "Of that I am not yet sure. My orders are to return to the House of Flames immediately upon finding the Key." He sighed. "But I have not yet uncovered the elusive object. Perhaps with an actual Zaprex by my side, I shall fare better…"

Zinkx's gaze grew distant once more. "My time is waning, and I know…I know that, even if I have not found the Key before I am due to return to the House, I cannot take Sam with me. I'll be unable to protect it there. It is a child…and children are not considered sacred at the House. They are simply another commodity to use in the waging of war."

War. The word echoed in Daniel's empty memories. There had been war once, a war he could not recall, but it had shaped the political landscape he was now forced to dance within. Why—why could he not remember any of it? Not even the faces of his parents…

Zinkx was still speaking and he made himself refocus on the Messenger.

"You need to start thinking about how we'll return you to your people."

His people. Daniel frowned. He looked back to the cave entrance, the gnawing anxiety rising once more. He would not have put it past the Steward to fabricate this elaborate plot; perhaps even meeting Shanty in Iliaion had been a part of it. He was not out of the wlip-o-wlip nest yet. Under the blankets, he shifted his legs. It hurt to move—but he could move.

"Yes. Of course." Daniel plastered on a warm smile. "I am sure we will think of something."

Zinkx continued with his model. "Good. I imagine they're worried about you."

Zinkx sipped the herbal mixture Shanty had shoved into his hands to replace his nightly coffee. It was not as satisfying as the hot, thick, earthy taste that brought him so much comfort, but she had worked hard to find something to settle his nerves.

Though it did not seem it was *his* nerves that needed settling. Since returning from her hunt, Shanty seemed unnaturally quiet, lost in thought, drifting about with a lightness to her feet.

Zinkx held out a hand, counting the fingers. He frowned. "Shanty, did anything happen while you were out hunting?"

She tensed. "How did you know?"

He arched an eyebrow. "I'm starting to get a feel for your moods."

"Oh, really." She stood, dusting off her dress. "And what is my current mood telling you, oh-wise-man?"

"That something happened."

Shanty sighed heavily. She glanced at the slumbering prince, and at the tiny hammock she wrapped Sam in every night. It hung above their bedrolls, and he knew it was how a Kelib woman would treat her own babe.

"What do you know of Forest Gods?"

"In reference to Kelib culture, not much. But, if you're speaking in broader terms of the Ancient Ones, then probably a little more, considering Khwaja Denvy is an Ancient One."

"Ancient One." Shanty sat herself down beside him. "Explain this to me."

"Hm. Well…" Zinkx scrubbed a hand through his hair. "Let me see…"

He reached for his carving kit, pulling out several figurines, setting them out in front of them. "From what Khwaja Denvy told me, there are many different types of Ancient Ones. There were those who were once built for the purpose of sustaining particular systems in our world." He held up a statue of a snake. "Such as the Cor River System." He set it down. "And then there are those who have gradually been formed through the process of dreamathic convergence."

Shanty shook her head. "I do not understand."

Zinkx tapped his chin, tipping his head to one side as he played with the wooden snake. "Think of dreamathic convergence as...many people telling stories, legends, and myths, and those converge upon a place, or an object, and form a manifestation of that legend."

He indicated another carving, this time of a white stag, and placed it in front of her. "Your Forest Gods, I believe, would be in this category."

He rifled around in his kit once more, finding an uncarved piece of wood. "However, your great Krrirren Trees are over here, with the Cor River."

"Why?"

"They are system-gods. They are vital to the function of the world. Removing them would remove the forests themselves."

Shanty nodded along with his words.

She picked up the stag. "So, then, where would the Time Master sit amongst this?"

Zinkx had lifted his mug to his lips, only to choke on his mouthful at her question. She looked at him in confusion, quickly reaching out to pat his back as he recovered.

"Where...where did you hear...?"

Her brow bunched together. "I met it...today...out in the forest."

Zinkx stared. "Wait. No. Let me...let me process this. You're saying you encountered the *Time Master*?"

She nodded. "It was not the first time. I believe it helped me escape the Ki'rayh." She tugged on her hair. "It may have also...provided the means of using the Monument of Old."

"It *interfered*?"

"And," she added, "it seems that it can take on several forms."

"The legends mention that." Zinkx sipped from his mug,

trying to stall the trembling of his hands.

"Is it strange that I have not heard of the Time Master?" Shanty asked.

"Hm. Given that you were raised in a very secluded environment, no. Nor is it likely that every Pennadotian Human would know of it either."

"Yes, but the Forests should know of all legends, and, therefore, we Kelibs should also know of them."

"If it concerns you," Zinkx said, "ask some Kelib women as we travel. See what you can find out."

She smiled. "So, the Time Master? Who…what…is it?"

"The Time Master is a system-god." Zinkx gestured to the snake and wood. "Although, not on the same level as the Cor River, the Ovin-tu, or even your Krrirren Trees. Khwaja Denvy called them the Architecture Systems. The Time Master is, as its name suggests, *Time*, itself." He tucked a knee under his chin. "And what is a world without our perception of time? The Time Master is a Core System."

Shanty frowned at the thought.

"It's difficult to comprehend, isn't it? You could imagine a world without forests, or rocks, or rivers…but what would we be if we did not have Time. Would trees grow, would rivers flow, would children be born? The cycle of life…would it cease to exist entirely?"

Shanty managed an unsteady breath.

"Semyueru is its child."

Zinkx glanced at the hammock. He felt the weight on his shoulders increase.

Shanty played with the stag. "Semu…Sam is also something called a Dynasty Starter, a Fusion Zaprex. I think this means it is capable of restarting the Zaprex race." She paused, and said, as though to herself, "He…it is very precious."

The weight became an intense pressure, more oppressive than gravity itself. Zinkx closed his eyes. He had already been torn in his decision to return to the House of Flames, but, now, with such information offered—almost as if to confirm his bias—there was no way he could return with the Zaprex child. Would he be forced to leave Shanty and Sam behind?

He groaned into his hands. To abandon his people for his overwhelmingly strong ideals—was this why the High Elder had sent him off on a fool's errand, never expecting him to find and return with the Key?

He looked up suddenly, staring at the fire. Wait. What if—

No—

Surely not—

Surely the Zaprex race would not have staked everything on…

Zinkx sucked in a deep breath.

"What is it?"

"I just had the most terrifying thought." Zinkx turned to her. "What if *Sam* is the Key."

Shanty frowned, and her hand touched his arm. "The Time Master asked me to relay a message to you."

Zinkx moved closer, drawn by the softness of her voice as she began to speak again. Whether it was the weight of the words she spoke, or the crackling of the nearby fire, or even perhaps Shanty, herself, but something within their small cave felt heavier in that moment.

"*'What he seeks is found in simple tunes and great symphonies.*
It brings conformity and regulation to that which has no unity.
Where there is an absence of direction, it knows the way.
All doors that are sealed shall be opened this day.
When the engine lies lifeless, it shall spark the burn.
And so the world shall once more begin to turn.'"

Her glassy eyes blinked rapidly as she came out of the fleeting trance. Zinkx bent forward, steepling his hands. "I have no idea what that means."

"I am sure the Time Master would not have sent its child all the way here without a reason."

He reached for her hand, clasping it. "I know it sent me you."

Her expression was soft. "Drink your brew, Human."

Zinkx sprang up the cliff with an activation of gravity-control, landing neatly in the moss. It felt so good to be in equilibrium with Livila's spin once again. He turned to view Shalamic's forest encapsulating their little inlet, its great white canopy creating the illusion of rolling clouds, with rock peaks jutting out, like the one he stood upon. Up here, high above the world, was a sense that nothing was wrong, that all his problems were miniscule. The temporary serenity was broken by the barely audible sound of Shanty calling his name. He peered down, catching sight of her waving from the entrance of their cave.

He glanced across at Sam, who sat by the Monument of Old Shanty had used against the Ki'rayh. "Sam, promise to stay right there. I'll be back in a minute."

The fairy nodded without turning. "Not moving."

Zinkx vaulted over the edge of the cliff, halting his decent gradually, and finishing his landing with a twirl. Shanty arched an eyebrow at him. "Show off."

Zinkx grinned. "Happy to be on my feet again."

Her glare softened. "Yes. It is good. I am off to check my traps. I shan't be too long. Daniel is resting. Where is Sam?"

Zinkx pointed up the cliff. "It wanted to look at the Zaprex Ruin up there."

"You left it *alone*?"

"It's fine. It is far too interested in the Monument to wander off."

"That isn't…" Shanty began. "Never mind. Make sure to look in on Daniel."

"You left him *alone*?" Zinkx mimicked her tone.

Shanty kicked out at him. He skipped away with a laugh.

"He'll be fine," she said. "He's the Prince of Pennadot. The embodiment of the Sun. Not even the Mistress Wlip-o-Wlip could slay him."

"Yes, but he is actually in danger. Someone is out to kill him."

"He's sleeping. Please poke your head in later to see if he is still resting."

Zinkx saluted. "Will do."

Shanty heaved herself into the diabond's saddle, an action she had become adept at now. Zinkx stepped aside as the two bounded down the small path into the forest. He chuckled. Shanty had made herself comfortable, turning their little cave into a lovely home. He was almost loathe to consider leaving it. With a bounce, he climbed his way back up the cliff, springing free of the forest's canopy once more to greet the Sun and sky-sea.

Why could they not simply stay here, in this place—the three of them—together?

He landed neatly beside Sam, barely disturbing the soil. Sam looked up with a curious tilt of its head and Zinkx crouched.

"What are you thinking?"

Sam sighed. "It has no song left."

"Hm. So you think Shanty used up all its power?" Zinkx mused.

Sam rubbed at the junction of an antenna before reaching out to gather up broken pieces of crystal lying at the base of the obelisk.

"Maybe. I think the crystal she used bypassed the permissions gateway. To use Zaprex technology, someone would need to be a Zaprex or be a starman. That is what…what…" Sam blinked rapidly.

Zinkx gave its head a gentle pat. "I understand."

Walking around the obelisk, Zinkx sighed. "Think we could drag the prince up here to see if he could make it work?"

"The song is gone. Not even my Map makes it work. It is dead." Sam stroked the side of the machine sorrowfully, releasing sad notes in a soft melody.

What he seeks is found in simple tunes and great symphonies.

Zinkx frowned at the echo of Shanty's voice in his mind.

"Shame," he muttered. He paused, looking back at Sam. "What Map?"

The fairy's large, yellow eyes stared up at him from beneath its glittering spectacles, full of innocent confusion. "You do not know?"

"I don't know what?"

"About my Map? About saving the world?"

It brings conformity and regulation to that which has no unity.

For several moments, as the gentle wind twirled past them, Zinkx felt his panic rising. Had he missed a conversation? Had Sam said something and he had not listened? Was this something Sam had told Shanty and he had yet to be informed of? Zinkx breathed out, rubbing his forehead, steadying himself. He smiled as he crouched.

"I'm sorry, Sam, I don't know anything about your Map, or about saving the world."

Sam gasped in horror. "But I thought…I thought because you knew about philepcon liquid, and were fighting the evil monsters, and you speak Zaprex, that you knew!"

"I know such things because I am a Messenger." Zinkx lowered his voice to try and calm the child. "Sam, it's okay—"

"It is not okay! *Baka*! Biri said I need to find my Map pieces and save the world! This is my function!" Sam stood up and stomped away. Zinkx watched it go, rather amused by the fairy's tantrum. Every so often it would pause, look back to glare at him, before continuing to stomp away.

Zinkx sat down, leaning back on the obelisk. "Sam. Come and explain to me your function. Help me understand so we can save the world."

With a whirl, Sam was at his side, sparks of energy crackling through its limbs. "*Hai. Hai.* Save the world!"

"Right. We've established that's on the agenda. What's this about a Map?"

Riffling around beneath its gown, Sam pulled out a necklace, revealing a slim crystal prism on the end. It held it out and

Zinkx took it in his palm. There was nothing unusual about it; though it refracted rainbows in the Sunshine across the moss, it looked like every other information crystal he had seen lying around the House of Flames.

Where there is an absence of direction, it knows the way.

"Is this the Key?" he murmured. Was something as innocuous as a mere information crystal what he had been searching for all along? He glanced at Sam. Did this mean he could leave Sam safely in Pennadot with Shanty?

The focal lenses of Sam's eyes had narrowed into pinpricks. "No, it is a *Map*, not a *Key*."

"I think this is a translation issue."

"No. It is not a *Key*, Gifu." Sam shook its head. "Keys open doors, or turn on engines, but, first, I must find the doors and engines with the Map."

All doors that are sealed shall be opened this day.

When the engine lies lifeless, it shall spark the burn.

Sam pointed to the crystal. "It is one part of an array. I need three more. Together they will reveal the location of the Towers."

"The Towers?" Zinkx whispered. "No. That's not possible."

"Why not?" Sam frowned.

"They have been long lost to time." Even Khwaja Denvy, who had been alive during the Thousand Sol-cycle War, had been unable to locate the Towers. The very notion that they still existed and could be revived was unfathomable—

Zinkx's gaze settled on Sam.

Not so long ago, he would have thought that seeing a living fairy was impossible, and, yet, here one was.

And so the world shall once more begin to turn.

"That is why I have a Map! To find that which is unfound. So that I can open the doors and turn on the engines. And save the world." Sam snatched the crystal back. "*Baka.*"

"*Gaki.*"

Sam beamed, showing his thin, sharp teeth.

Zinkx dropped his head back, staring at the blue sky-sea.

So that I *can open the doors and turn on the engines. And save the world.* The Key, itself, was standing right in front of him. It had never been an object, or a great weapon to end the Dragon. The weight on his shoulders seemed lighter. The rope that had been tightening around his neck had loosened. Would his Squad forgive him for protecting the Key on a journey to save the world? Did this release him from his bond to return to the House of Flames?

He rubbed at his eyes and wearily looked down at the smiling, sweet face of the tiny fairy. A creature so small, attempting to save a world so huge. "You're not going to be able to do this alone."

Sam frowned. "Silly, Gifu. That is why Biri sent me here, to you, a starman."

"I'm not a starman, Sam."

Sam blew a rasp. "Yes, you are."

"No, I'm not—"

"Yes, you are!"

"No, I'm not—"

"Zinkx!"

Shanty's shout was snatched by the wind, but he caught the alarm in the cry, and bounced up with a spring of gravity-control. Grabbing hold of Sam, Zinkx leapt over the edge of the cliff, sailing down, landing with a roll at the cave entrance. Shanty's body vibrated with anxiety.

"What's wrong?"

"Daniel's gone!" Shanty thrust the vines aside.

Zinkx followed. Their home was empty. The bed the prince had been in was vacated. Zinkx felt it. Cold. The royal had been gone for a while, then.

"Did you check the water-hole?"

"I did." Shanty gestured down the cave. "I also checked the lavatory. He's not there. A bag of provisions is gone, though. So is one of your blades."

"He took one of my *blades*?" Zinkx hissed. "The idiot. As if he could use the thing."

"*Baka. Baka. Baka.*" Sam flew around.

Zinkx grabbed his hip-bags, bow, and quiver, and stormed out. He glared at the mammoth trees surrounding them, feeling a weight of dread stack heavily on his shoulders. "We need to find him. He could not have gone far. But bring some supplies, in case we're out for the night."

The temperature had already begun to plummet with the dipping of the Sun below the Ovin-tu Mountains, and the only light was the gradual increase of the bio-luminescent fungi and flora. Shanty pulled herself into the diabond's saddle.

"What was he thinking?"

"He's scared." Zinkx settled Sam into a pouch around his waist. "He doesn't trust us. I should have expected this."

"But he's been fine."

"He's wearing a mask, Shanty. He's exceptionally good at faking a smile."

The diabond led them to the inlet and Zinkx cursed as they made their way through the crack in the cliff walls. "I had hoped he'd have stayed in the cove. He's moving faster than expected."

"Zinkx. He is not well enough for this."

"Good. He will tire out." To think they were chasing after the Prince of Pennadot in the depths of the Forests of Shalam-ic. He would never have believed he would be in a situation like this when he had left the House of Flames. Zinkx bit back a shiver, dusting ice off his coat. The temperature was dropping rapidly, even beneath the thick canopy. The diabond shoul-dered up to him, radiating warmth, and he gratefully ran a hand through her mane.

"Picking up a scent, darling?"

Her chest rumbled low in reply.

"You lead the way, then. Chase him down."

"The Prince is not a hunting toy," Shanty yelped as the diabond charged forward. Zinkx leapt after them, keeping pace through the dense undergrowth.

"It amuses me how fond you are of a Human Sovereign."

She flowed expertly with the diabond's movements, a huge change from her initial stiffness when she had first ridden the beast. A trust had been established between them, despite her lack of dreamathic skills. Zinkx smiled as Shanty easily ducked a low fern that he leapt over.

"Respect is a gift freely given. He could not choose his fate. He is more imprisoned than I in many ways."

"That isn't respect, love. You're pitying him." Feeling a dreamathic tug from the diabond, Zinkx suddenly swept over her, grabbing a vine, twisting around a tree to land directly in front of Daniel. "And we found you."

The prince was in a pitiful state, kneeling in the moss, trembling with pain as he gripped his side. Zinkx could smell the blood; it tickled his nose. "You've reopened your wound, you idiot."

Shanty leapt off the diabond, rushing to the prince's side. Daniel drew the blade he had taken, holding it out with a feverish glare. Shanty backed away. Zinkx touched her shoulder in reassurance. Despite how impressive it was that Daniel managed to stagger to his feet, wielding the blade, there was very little intent in the prince. He was broken, confused, and more than likely in unbearable pain.

"Your Highness," Zinkx said soothingly, "please lower the weapon."

"No." Daniel stepped back a pace. "No. I will not. You will let me go."

"We cannot do that. If we let you walk away now, you will die, and Pennadot needs its King."

Daniel pointed the blade again. "Let me go. I...I want to go..."

"Where? Where do you want to go, Your Highness?" Shanty asked. "We can take you."

Daniel rubbed at his reddened eyes. "I...I do not...know."

Zinkx inched closer. Daniel thrust out the blade. Zinkx raised his hands and sighed.

"Do you really, really think you can use that against me?"

He gestured to the blade Daniel held. The prince glanced down at it and Zinkx struck, lashing out a foot, knocking Daniel off his feet, immobilising the hand that gripped the blade. He twisted the wrist, hearing Daniel yelp as he released the weapon.

Zinkx pinned him with a knee. "You would have faired better with the bow, Your Highness. I would have been concerned if you had taken that. Learn to hold a blade properly before you accidentally kill someone with one."

"Zinkx! That's enough. He is still wounded."

Zinkx heaved the prince up, setting him down on a nearby root. Daniel curled into his knees, hiding away the threatening tears. Zinkx tucked his blade into his belt as Shanty moved to comfort the royal.

"You are not well enough for this, Your Highness."

"I just...I just..."

"You don't know who to trust." Zinkx sighed.

Daniel nodded weakly.

Crouching down, Zinkx settled his hands on Daniel's trembling knees. "So, I know your Identifier. Would it make you feel better if you knew mine?"

Daniel's glowing green eyes seemed completely natural here in Shalamic's illumed forest. "You would trust me?"

Zinkx smiled, looking up at Shanty. "You're the Prince of Pennadot. Apparently that makes you trustworthy."

"What is it, then?"

"I cannot tell it to you, but you can see it."

Daniel frowned.

"You're a wind elementalist. You're one of the few who are blessed to have an elemental residing within you. A Simoon." Zinkx pointed at Daniel's chest. "It's why your arrows never miss. The Simoon is your bow. But a wind elementalist is also known for another skill, other than their marksmanship." Zinkx gestured at a point over his own head. "Ever seen odd little symbols, or baubles, above creatures or people, that you've never been able to explain?"

Daniel pulled back. "I do. Yes."

"That's your Simoon Sight. You've been tapping into it naturally. This is a very advantageous skill for a Royal. I suggest you try to improve it as much as you can."

"Why?"

"Relax your shoulders." Zinkx tapped the prince lightly. "Close your eyes. Focus on the sound of the wind in the branches, the rhythm of your breath. If you need to, pretend you've got a bow in your hand."

Daniel's fingers twitched. His erratic breathing had settled. Pleased at having calmed him, Zinkx carefully removed his hands from the royal's knees. "Open your eyes. You should be able to see information above my head. That is my Identifier."

Daniel opened his eyes, the green clarified and sharpened to an intensity that was hard to believe was real. Zinkx heard Shanty's sharp intake of breath behind him. It was little wonder an awakened starborn was coveted for their eyes alone if these gems were the result.

"Oh." Daniel pulled back. "Sun Above."

Zinkx smiled. "I suppose that worked."

Daniel's brow furrowed. "No. Yours looks wrong. It's nothing like those I have seen before."

"I have been told that." Zinkx shrugged. "Never mind. Can you see my name, now?"

Daniel leant forward. "I can—"

Zinkx clapped a hand over Daniel's mouth. "No. Don't say it out loud. Weird things tend to happen."

He stood, offering a hand. "Right. So, now we all know each other. Do you feel better? Can we get back to the warmth of our cave?"

Sam's head poked out from its carrier. "I am not cold."

"Good for you." Zinkx ruffled Sam's hair.

Shanty threw a blanket around Daniel's shoulders. "Help me lift him onto the diabond."

Zinkx shifted forward and paused in midstride, looking slowly down at the ground beneath his boot. Something had altered. It was subtle, but it had sent a twinge up his spine. The forest floor rippled again, the colours displacing in small flakes before settling and the sharp pain in the nape of his neck made him slap down hard on the area.

"Zinkx?" Shanty reached for him anxiously.

He stared at her with a frown.

"Something is wrong," he murmured.

Sam suddenly buried long, iron nails into his skin. "Gifu! *Kah-boom! Kah-boom!*"

Zinkx twisted. The noise roared through the forest, the shockwave sending them stumbling. Heat. He felt heat.

"Shanty! Run!" Zinkx grabbed her wrist and heaved, pulling her over a root. The ground rumbled, throwing them both off their feet. Zinkx bounced as his gravity-control caught him, and Shanty landed in his sphere. He caught her around the waist, rolling, dragging her upright. "Move!" he shouted over the roar. "Daniel! Run! Now!" He snatched the prince by the back of his shirt and hauled him forward. "Run!"

The heat was following them. He could feel it scorching the hairs on his arms. It was a sensation he had felt countless times out on the Plains of Blazing Fire. They were never going to outrun whatever was coming. Zinkx skidded beneath a twisted fern, tumbling his way down a crevasse. Shanty stopped beside him, Daniel and the diabond some distance away. Taking Shanty's wrist, Zinkx pulled her behind him as he leapt for Daniel. The radiation was blistering, the roaring drowning out Sam's screams. Zinkx yanked out a shimmering, velvety material from his kit and flung it over them all as the blast struck.

It thundered past in a rage.

Silence. All that remained was a deafening silence he had only before experienced on the battlefield. The prince moved to shift the protective film aside and Zinkx stayed his hand.

"Don't. You and the diabond are only ones able to survive out there, and that's dependent on how much oxygen is left in the zone. We have to wait for a reset."

"A what?"

"One of the nearby Monuments of Old will eventually reset this zone. It's what they do. When that happens, it will be safe to remove the shield. Won't be until morning though, most likely."

The prince's eyes shimmered in the meagre light from Sam's antennae. "Can someone explain to me what just happened?"

"*Kah-boom*," Sam murmured.

Zinkx glanced down at the fairy.

"Yes. Kah-boom."

"That does not explain anything," Daniel said.

Shanty pulled a waterskin from the diabond's saddle, passing it around. "It's hot under here, Zinkx."

"Because the outside temperature…" Zinkx reached for Sam's spectacles, plucking them off its nose. Sam squeaked before bursting into giggles as Zinkx put them on his own face with a smirk. "According to Sam's data it flashed at about one thousand five hundred degrees Celsius. But it is dropping. The ground is around eight hundred now."

"I have no idea what you're talking about," Shanty said.

Sam rolled around laughing. "It got hot."

"Yes. It got hot." Zinkx tapped Sam's glasses. "Nice that your lenses instantly link up with my House tech, Sam."

"Is this Messenger gear?" Daniel reached up to feel the smooth underside of the sheet they lay beneath.

Zinkx nodded. "In case of an eruption. Always need to keep a nano-shield on hand."

"That is what that was?" Daniel asked. "An eruption? But there are no volcanoes in Shalamic."

Zinkx shook his head. "No, Your Highness. I do believe that someone was playing with fire in the Tunnels. More than likely someone who wanted you very dead."

"But…no…" Shanty suddenly moved. "Our home! Zinkx! Our home! Our cave!"

Zinkx grabbed at her, pulling her away from the edge of the fabric adhering to the ground. He hissed out in pain as her elbow sank into his ribs. "Shanty. Stop. Shanty! You cannot go outside—"

"But my home!"

"I know."

"Zinkx! It was…it…everything…please…please don't…don't tell me it's all gone!" She clung to his chest.

"I'm sorry," he whispered.

"No." Shanty burrowed into the curve of his shoulder.

"I had finally…made my roots." She began to sob.

Zinkx carefully wrapped his arms around her, giving a long sigh. Gone was everything they had built together, and it had been lost so quickly, and so easily.

CHAPTER EIGHTEEN

Let your little flame burn, Young Conductor,
So you may become a burning maelstrom,
And scorch out your own path,
Away from the choking smoke of the past.

Batitic Saying

Muhzun was dead.

Skyeola stared at the mutilated body in a daze. Flayed. Messy. Amateurish. The hands that had done it had been rushed, inexperienced, scared. Was it odd for him to think he had seen worse in the dungeons beneath the Palace? Why was his mind bringing up the violated and tortured forms of Messengers being ripped apart by pulley ropes and blades, of unrecognisable corpses lying by his trembling foot-claws? That sense of helplessness dropped deep in his stomach as screams echoed in his ears. He was always only an observer, never—never—never could he stop—

Oh. Blood. He glanced down at the floor. The rug he stood on was seeped with blood and it squelched when he moved.

"Skyeola…" Citla's voice was distant.

"Skyeola…"

He barely felt her hand on his shoulder. She was trying to pull him away from a cliff edge, away from tumbling down, down, into a thick smog that wanted to wrap around his foot-claws and drag him into the depths of a pit of boiling lava.

Skyeola wrenched back as shrieks pierced his skull, the cries of ancestors, all warning him to never fall. He grabbed for Citla's hand, stepping away from Muhzun's bed, his eyes wide with fright.

"He is dead," he choked out.

"I am so sorry, Skyeola." Citla hugged him.

"Lord Galvon did this…"

Jarid crouched beside him. "Skyeola, you cannot throw that accusation around. We are on very, very uneven ground without the Prince—"

"But he did it!"

Jarid grasped his claws, holding them tightly. "I know—"

"He died because of me! Because I confronted Lord Galvon. Jarid, this is my fault!"

Jarid sighed, bowing his head. "Listen, I am not going to shield you. It could well be that if you had not said what you said to Galvon that, perhaps, Muhzun would be alive, but Muhzun was also responsible for his own actions yesterday. He denounced his position without consulting me. I was given no chance to even establish protection for him, or to send him away."

Jarid stood. Skyeola stared at the blood that had soaked his robe. Jarid did not seem to notice as he turned to several of their accompanying Palace guards, ordering them down into the city to engage an undertaker. Citla, with the aid of a guard, threw a sheet over Muhzun's body.

"Skyeola, what exactly did you say to Galvon?" Jarid asked.

Skyeola's ears drooped across his shoulders, his wings hanging limp. "I…I said…I said I would flay him alive."

"That doesn't sound like yeh at all," Hun muttered.

"No. I sounded like my Father." Skyeola clenched his jaw.

"Skyeola. We have had this discussion before. You are not Steward Zilon." Jarid's voice was harsh and sharp against his ears, making him wince. Skyeola nodded stiffly, wishing he believed the words that were forcefully shoved into his head time after time.

"What do you make of this, Citla?" Jarid ignored the blood he stepped through. Skyeola flinched with each movement he made. How did Jarid do it? How was he so strong and unaffected by everything that swirled around them?

"It was not done by a professional. It was performed by one who knew naught of the skill of death."

Her gaze flickered his way and Skyeola quickly looked at the floor.

"Was he alive when they did this?"

"No." She shook her head. "As I said, an amateur."

"I'd say it's more of a threat," Hun said. Skyeola looked up at the guard, who arched an eyebrow at him. "Yeh said you were going to flay him? Well." Hun gestured to the bed. "There is your answer, little lord. Yeh better be ready to get your hands bloody, now, because Galvon is willing to kill his own flesh."

"Hun, that is uncalled for," Jarid admonished him.

"Simply stating facts." Hun shrugged. "The little lord can't hide behind the shadow of his father forever. You all know he will eventually have to face the consequences of being what he is."

Skyeola turned away before his tears became too obvious. He rushed out the door, ignoring Jarid's calls to him.

He knew what he was—a Mazaki—and Muhzun may have been able to denounce his name, but no Batitic could never erase their heritage. He would forever carry the burden of his ancestry.

Jarid slid down the wall, barely managing to undo the first few buttons of his tight robe before the will to keep himself upright simply left him. It had been an appalling few weeks. If the Prince was even alive it was going to be a miracle of happenstance. He had lost all faith in anything else—

Why had he not brought more of his own men? He had known he was entering the territory of an enemy province lord—ah, right…because he had not wanted to cause any more political tension. Yet, now he was trapped. Unable to move. He was a useless monk on the chessboard.

Why did every step he took seem to lead him towards the treacherous path of war, when he had devoted his life to preventing it? Perhaps, once, under the banners of his forebears, his province had been a mighty powerhouse that had held the coveted seat of the paladins for generations. Yet now they were a miniscule dot on the map.

He managed a shaky breath. Surviving the death of the prince would take something other than mere military strength. He needed leverage.

The door to his chamber slid open, light streamed in, and a shadow glided through. Citla never wore perfume. It would have been foolish for an assassin to wear the overwhelming fragrances the ladies of court scented themselves with. However, he had always imagined she carried the freshest hint of citrus, and it would forever bring back memories of David. David had always, always smelt of healing citrus.

He dragged his hands through his hair.

"Any news?" he murmured, voice hoarse.

She shook her head, placing a tray on the nearby table. "Our men lowered someone down into the cleared shaft, but the heat is still too intense to get anywhere deep enough."

Jarid clawed fingers through his curls. "Sun…"

Skyeola had been correct after all.

"He is alive."

She would never stop saying those words. No matter how deep the despair went, her resolve would never change. Jarid breathed out unsteadily. "I wish I had your conviction."

"You do. You simply show it differently."

"Did you check on Skyeola?"

"I did." She poured out tea. His favourite blend of chamomile with a dribble of honey. She knelt in front of him, setting the cup aside as she reached for his buttons. "You really should take up Butler Malik's offer."

Butler Malik—the elusive man who never aged—who

should have protected his parents, who should have protected the King and Queen—and *David*.

How could he ever trust the man again after the Uprising?

"I am fine."

She deftly and swiftly unbuttoned his robe, allowing his tight chest room to breathe, and the ache eased.

"One of my Brothers would be happy to look after you."

"I am fine."

She sighed, offering him the teacup. "Jarid. You need help."

He sipped his tea.

"Do not mock me, Citla. Say what you really mean."

He must seem pathetic, sitting on the floor of his chamber, a ruffled, collapsed, exhausted mess. No one saw him like this—only Citla. They had a history, a history he could cling to like a lifeline. It was the only thing that kept his head above the raging maelstrom that so often threatened to drag him under the swell of overwhelming depression.

"You need protection."

He stared up at her, stunned at the way her black painted lips pinched with distaste at her words. He could not blame her. After all, he had made her admit aloud that the prince may not return. A pathetic paladin he may have been, but he was all that was left.

"I trust no one."

Citla sighed. She turned away, heading for his wardrobe. "I will speak with Butler Malik again."

"Citla, your father was barely managing to protect Daniel. Part of the reason we came here was to try and find a solution to that problem, and look where it led us."

Her shoulders tensed. "He does his best."

"His best got my parents killed."

"It was a war, Jarid! Palace-Town was burning!" Citla turned, her fists bunching into her gown. "The King ordered him to save the city."

Jarid scoffed, turning away to sip his tea. A long silence stretched on.

"We do not have to return to Palace-Town, you know," he murmured. "We could take this opportunity to make a break for my province—"

"You know why we cannot do that. Zilon would immediately muster the province lords and ladies against us for insurrection against the Emerald Throne."

"Not if we have a hostage."

She looked at him in disbelief mixed with disgust, an expression he had not seen in a long time.

So skilled was she at masking her expressions behind the thick makeup she wore that, when they did bleed through, they were raw and honest.

"Jarid," she choked out. "No."

"Do not tell me you have not thought of it. Returning Skyeola to that monster makes us monsters, too. We would be saving him—"

"Do not try to justify your idea," Citla snarled. "You do not get to *use* Skyeola. He is not a tool in your war games, Jarid."

Jarid snorted, taking another sip of tea. "I'm hardly the first. A tool is all he has ever been."

"You are letting your fear rule you."

"Of course I am," he snapped. "I am in an enemy province, my liege is dead, and I am next. Citla, I am terrified."

"Then let someone protect you."

"I trust no one."

"You trust me." Citla fished out his nightrobe.

He bowed his head, sighing heavily.

"And I am telling you," she continued, "you need someone with you. You are drowning, Jarid. I know you will never let another woman near you, so…one of my Brothers."

He cringed back, raising a hand, as if expecting a strike. His tea spilt. "Sorry." Citla's hands wrapped around his wrists, carefully lowering them. "I did not mean to bring the trauma to the surface."

"You speak as though all will be well. As though we will

find the Prince and merrily return to Palace-Town. I can barely think past tomorrow." He threw the teacup across the room. "My mind is consumed by that poor boy's last moments and the torture of his death. What if it is Skyeola next, or...me..." He stared down at his shaking hands. There was no blood upon them, but he recalled it, the blood that had once stained them, and his clothes, his shoes. Everything. Blood. Nothing but blood. Like his cursed red hair.

He had been helpless then, and he was helpless now.

Always, he was nothing but helpless.

"What use am I, if I cannot even protect His Highness?" Jarid curled up tightly. "I am a mockery of the paladins."

She pulled him close and wrapped her thin but strong arms around him. She was nothing like his mother, but he could imagine, just for a moment, that the powerful Warhammer-wielding blacksmith of the Icali-pi Province cradled him again.

Tears leaked down his cheeks and he crawled, sobbing into her lap, releasing the emotions bottled up over the long days.

Citla tightened her hold, rocking gently.

"I am so sorry," she whispered.

Gradually, his tears faded, leaving only the rawness of the open wound left in his soul. Time had done nothing to heal it.

He doubted it ever would. Slowly he rolled back around, staring at the faint outline of the Maiden in the candlelight. How he missed the innocence of the childhood they had shared.

"You lost everyone, too. That cursed day that was night."

Citla's lips pressed together. "The difference was, Jarid, I was prepared for it. You were not."

His laugh was weak, and he knew it was dreadful sounding as it broke from his chest. "No one is ever prepared to see what I saw."

CHAPTER NINETEEN

We have wandered so far…
Our feet ache, our chests burn, our heads throb.
Please—
Will you house us?
Will you feed us?
Or will you turn us back to the shadow of the Sun?

The Sorrow of a Refugee – Written by Bard Luko

They stood on the only patch of greenery amongst a sea of burnt out land. Zinkx knelt, reaching across the threshold, cracking a shard of black glass which he held up to the Sunlight.

"Reminds me of home," he murmured.

Shanty hugged his arm. "It's awful. The forest…the poor trees…"

He folded a hand around hers, squeezing tightly. "Shalamic is resilient. She'll regrow."

"Is it safe to walk on?" the prince hesitantly asked.

"Ah. No. Not with the glass. You and Shanty had best get on the diabond." Zinkx motioned to the beast of burden.

"Gifu! Your nano-shield is dying!" Sam wailed, holding out the shimmering fabric which fell apart in its tiny hands, flecks of it disintegrating into the wind.

Zinkx crouched beside the Zaprex. The shield had been one of the final remnants of the House; now all that he carried was his lava-forged boots and blades. "It's fine, Sam. It happens. They're only built for one use. We've never managed

334

to get them working more than once since they're all only copies of the original."

Sam hugged the dissolving sheet to its cheek. "Poor little nano-bots. Thank you for saving us."

Gathering Sam up, Zinkx settled it into its little carry bag. Shanty had already aided the prince into the saddle behind her.

"Are you sure it's safe?" Shanty asked.

"I'm pretty sure," Zinkx reassured her.

"It is safe," Sam piped up. "I scanned."

Zinkx smiled wearily. "Well, then, if Sam says its safe…" He leapt out, landing on a rock. The diabond followed and they gradually made their way across the barren, charred land towards the forest. It looked as though a hot knife had sliced its way through the tangled trees of Shalamic, carving into the fluffy tufts like they were cheese.

"You…you do not think Iliaion is gone, do you?" Daniel choked out.

Shanty wrapped a hand around his. "Do not think that. I am sure it is fine."

"But you said the Tunnels, and…they run…directly to the Turret."

Zinkx nodded. "They do, but I have explored a similar system to this one, and, unless someone left a door open somewhere, it is unlikely the Turret would be affected." Zinkx picked up a stick, drawing several circles and lines in the dust, until a starlike pattern was formed. He pointed to the centre circle. "This is the Turret. The Tunnels snake throughout these zones in here with these major structures acting as their support base. You can see them from afar—they're the cliffs. The fire would have likely escaped in several directions through these points." He gestured to the tips of the star-pattern. "Though it is also possible the fire affected only a section of the Tunnels."

Casting the stick aside, Zinkx considered their filthy state. The diabond's white fur was coated in a thick layer of soot.

"We should find the nearest river shrine." Zinkx scratched his chin. "We must give an offering to the river-god in thanks for our lives, and then we need to cleanse."

Sam held up a glowing hand-device. "That way! There is one that way!"

As they set out, Zinkx arched an eyebrow at Daniel on the diabond. The royal gripped his wounded side and winced in pain with every movement.

"If you dare wander off again, I will tie you to the diabond."

The sullen look he received was enough to tell him the prince had learnt some sort of lesson. "I will not," was all Daniel said in response.

It took them a solid day to reach the river-shrine and, by then, the blessed Sunlight was gone once more, leaving them in the mystic allure of Shalamic's illumed flora. Daniel was barely conscious, and Shanty had not seen Zinkx's concern so heightened since they had found the prince. She left him to work on the reopened wound. Her attention turned to taking stock of all that remained, and it was not much, only the emergency supplies they always kept in the diabond's saddle bags. Her chest constricted tightly.

"Gibo, I'm hungry and tired." Sam tugged on her sleeve.

"Help me with a fire and we'll warm you up some brew."

Sam settled quickly after its meal. Shanty looked around the small clearing wherein the statue of the river-god dwelt, her skin tingling at the eerie sensation beneath her. The ground felt charged and heated, as though a gentle harp played through the soil. She breathed in deeply, closing her eyes as the drum beat of the great forest and the flow of the harp swept around her.

Zinkx slumped solidly down beside her with a heavy, exhausted sigh. Her peace disturbed, Shanty tilted her head towards him. He rubbed at his eyes and yawned. Sleep had not been well accomplished in the tight confines beneath the protective shield he had flung over them the night prior, and her heart had been torn to shreds at the loss of their cave. They were both tired.

"Is the Prince...?"

Zinkx scratched the back of his neck. "I am grateful we made it to the river-shrine. With all the ambient power around here, he'll be able to absorb it and heal faster. A perk of being the Prince of Pennadot."

"You looked worried."

"He got speared through the gut. It's a serious wound. Guess I did not drill that through his head. I did not want to scare him."

"He was scared, though," Shanty whispered.

"Yes. Apparently so."

The ache was raw. Their cave was gone. She had begun to see the little inlet, tucked away in the depths of the alien forests, as their home. She had made it comfortable and liveable. It had been joyful to sweep through the vines to see Zinkx whittling away at his newest piece of deadwood, breathing life into that which had none.

"I'm sorry, love." Zinkx threw another branch onto the fire. Shanty watched the flames take hold of the wood and she cringed, looking away. Her little home, gone up in flames, when she had finally allowed herself to twist her roots down.

"We would've had to have left eventually—"

"It would have been my choice." She wiped away tears. "This was not my choice."

Zinkx nodded. He stirred the coffee pot. She shook her head, amused that of all the things he kept in his hip-bags his coffee was one of them. "You're used to it, aren't you? Being uprooted."

"Much of my time was spent on the Front Lines. You don't stay in one place on the Front Lines. You learn to pack everything you love down to a few things, and take those things with you."

"Like coffee."

Zinkx smiled behind his mug. "Like coffee."

She brushed aside her tears. "But, still, everything I had built up…"

He reached out and carefully wrapped an arm around her shoulder. "We'll build it up again. Like a forest regrows, so shall we."

"What have I done? You're using Kelib sayings."

Zinkx chuckled, before slowly setting his mug aside. His gaze grew distant. "I found out something about Sam before all the chaos started."

"And?"

"Sam is the Key."

Shanty breathed in deeply. "All right, so I suppose we're going to need to figure out what we're going to do now." She hesitantly met his gaze.

"In regard to that, I also discovered that Sam has a Map, or a piece of a Map, and it needs to find the next three pieces to save the world."

Shanty hunched forward. Sam lay smothered in a pile of blankets nearby. The soft sounds of whirring and clicking it made when sleeping was now entirely normal to her ears.

"He is a child, Zinkx—"

"'He'?" Zinkx asked.

"I cannot keep calling Sam an '*it*', like he's a thing. He's a child," Shanty repeated. "He, surely, cannot save the world."

"Not alone. No." Zinkx dragged a hand through his hair. "I hope they forgive me." He looked to the night sky-sea through the breaks in the canopy. "But this has become so much bigger than our war to defend the Northlands."

"The whole world, Human? That is…"

Zinkx arched a brow. "Cannot even picture it, right? I don't even know what the whole world looks like, do you?"

"No." Her world had only ever been the Forests of Pulza, then the compound of her husbands, the slave pits of Crinn. Her world had been stolen from her, and she had only begun to rediscover that there was a world beyond prison bars.

They both turned to study Sam as he slept. Shanty breathed in deeply. "I suppose we're going to find out," she whispered.

"Yes. I suppose we are."

Sam squealed as he splashed through the shallows of the river. The tiny, naked fairy danced and looped about, spraying water into the air, causing the droplets to appear like diamonds in the shimmer of Sunlight breaking the canopy. Zinkx crouched back on his heels, setting his damp shirt aside, reaching for his trousers to wash them. It felt marvellous to be clean again. There came a point where skin was so tight and gritty from grime that it was uncomfortable.

Sam dive-bombed from the top of the river-god statue. Zinkx ducked the splash. He threw his clothes into a basket, and pulled out Sam's gown. He sighed as he held it up, taking in the state of ruin it was in. Considering the way the little imp tore around without a care, he was amazed it was even still in one piece.

"Ah, well, Shanty will be thrilled to make another one in a new style," he muttered. "Maybe she'll design it in honour of the river-god here."

Shanty was beginning to turn around on her snooty disbelief in river-spirits, something he could not wrap his head around—why would she be so opposed to the concept?

"Must be a tree thing..." he commented as he flung a small jewel into the bowl the statue held.

"Thank you," he murmured as he clapped his hands.

"Can you throw one in for me?" the Prince piped up from his nearby seat amongst several tree roots. "As a thank you for the river-spirit's healing and protection."

Zinkx halted from his washing. "And here I thought that

amongst the aristocracy the traditions of the land had been lost."

"I am aware one must always make an offering to a river," the Prince responded.

"And what do you offer the Spider-Road?" Zinkx asked.

"The soles of your boots, the straps of your sandals."

Zinkx laughed. "You surprise me with how well versed you are in the mythology of your land, Your Highness. I suppose it is because you are able to spend so much time simply reading and learning your land's history and traditions."

"No, not at all. I have good people in my entourage who keep me informed—as much as they are able. I really have not had a lot of time myself thanks to the political intrigues at court that I rather think are designed to keep me too busy to be a threat."

Zinkx frowned. "You'd be surprised the things you can learn from myths and history lessons. We are the stories of our past. Perhaps the answer to your problem lies in one of them."

He heard the prince scoff and glanced across at the man.

"In the past?" There was a dark, depressive aura hanging heavily over the Prince.

This was the real man behind the sunshine mask that had been plastered on before. They had broken it away, and, now, they were talking to *Deiniol.*

"Perhaps, for people who remember their past," the prince added. "I find no satisfaction in looking backwards."

Zinkx studied him a while longer. "Any thoughts as to what you want to do about your current dilemma, at least?"

"You cannot return me to Iliaion."

That much had always been a given, and it was useful that the Prince was aware of the situation he was entangled in. "Figuring it out, are you?"

"I have been cognisant of the dangers to my life for a long time, and, though I think falling down the shaft was an accident, what transpired with the cave system seems far too convenient."

"It does a bit."

"I would like Lord Galvon to think I am dead. Having the upper-hand on him and his insurgents would be beneficial."

Zinkx leant wearily on his knees, peering up at the Prince through his damp hair. "Pennadot is a big place. Trying to rule it without the aid of the paladins will be extremely difficult."

"You do not think it is possible?"

"I didn't say that. I'm simply elucidating that your ancestors had technologies gifted to them from the Zaprexes that I am sure made ruling such a vast land a lot easier. You need to keep that under consideration." Zinkx turned back to washing.

Daniel sighed. "If Mazaki gets his fangs any deeper into Pennadot, there may not be a land for me to rule. Though he is the only reason the province lords and ladies obey any rule of order. I am afraid I do not command much respect. That's what I was supposed to be doing here: Galvon promised access to Zaprex technology that would have changed everything. But it appears it will no longer be a straightforward matter of forming an alliance with him. I cannot see a way that is both honourable and safe to find out what exactly it is that he has."

"When up against a stronger opponent, do not be afraid to use whatever tactics you can, even if they seem underhanded," Zinkx said.

"You are telling me to abandon my morals?"

"There is no moral arbiter in war, Your Highness. Simply two sides who believe they have a true and righteous justification to the ruin they cause." Zinkx looked away. "It is entirely up to the individual to keep their own feet on the ground."

"I do not believe you quite understand the position I am in," Daniel objected. "I cannot behave as an individual. What I think, actions I take, affect a collective."

"It is up to you, Your Highness, to separate the two individual songs within you and act accordingly. You say we are a collective, and, yes, this may be true, but we each have a singular song that makes up the melody that fuels our world. We are nothing without our individual experiences." Zinkx tapped his head. "We're the stories."

Daniel pressed back on the tree he sat against. "You sound eerily like someone I know."

Zinkx cracked a grin. "So, who'd be best to approach in your entourage about your miraculous survival?"

"Oh," Daniel spread his hands, the action heavy, betraying how weak he had grown. "That would be Citla, my Maiden. But...there is a problem."

"What would that be?"

"You mentioned metal shrapnel lodged within your body. And something about metal holding one of your legs together?"

"My left leg, yes. Metal bolts hold the bones together."

Shanty waded through the shallows, approaching them with a basket on her hip that contained the numerous layers of her own dress. Her hair was free of its constraints, wet from washing, and trailed along behind her in the water. She jerked to a halt at his words, waves tossing about around her ankles.

"Your leg is held together by *what*?"

Zinkx breathed in deeply, throwing Sam's gown into his washed pile. "Shanty, it's fine."

"You said your leg is held together with metal. How is this fine?" Her tone lifted an octave and he knew she was not going to easily forget his comment.

"I'm confused, what do my old war wounds have to do with meeting this Maiden?" Zinkx asked, turning back to Daniel.

"She is a Mahvash Assassin of the Harem Family. She can manipulate metal. And she does not like to ask questions first. If she senses even a hint of deceit, she will kill you from a distance. You will not even see it coming."

"Ah. Well, I do rather like being alive." Zinkx rubbed his neck. "Anyone else you can trust?"

He studied the Prince. The sincere look he received was too honest, and far too raw to be mocking. Zinkx shook his head, feeling almost sorry for the Kimwyn man who sat on the throne of Pennadot. Nothing about him was hardened; he was a raw egg, waiting to be cracked and bled.

That, perhaps, was the problem—the province lords and ladies who surrounded the poor royal all saw the same thing, and saw how easy the young Prince would be to break. But was that all another facet of the prism of personalities the prince had constructed to protect himself? Surely, somewhere, within the multifaceted prism, was a man capable of commanding the authority of the throne.

Daniel sighed.

"It is not so much a matter of trust, as it is a matter of them believing. Jarid is burdened….and Hun… I truly do not know."

"What of the little winged kitten?" Shanty asked from where she crouched by the stream, beginning her own scrubbing. She held up a hair-roll to Zinkx and he stepped around her, gathering up her long locks to begin braiding them.

"Winged kitten?" Daniel frowned. "Oh, you mean Skyeola?"

"Skyeola! Skyeola!" Sam burst out. "*Hai*! *Hai*! I like Skyeola. He helped me. I like Skyeola."

Three sets of eyes settled on the Zaprex.

"You have met Skyeola?" Daniel asked.

Sam skipped over the bubbling water, barely touching the surface. He twirled about, throwing a grin over his shoulder as his long ears tweaked rearward.

"Oh, yes. He saved me from the monster when I arrived here. I was sad that he could not come with me. I wanted him to be my friend! My very best friend forever!"

"Monster?" Daniel looked around hesitantly. "What monster?"

"The Twizel," Zinkx said, then turned to Sam. "He saved you from the Twizel you mean?"

"*Hai*, Gifu."

"So, he knows about Twizels."

"He is the one who told me his guard was a Twizel, when I went to Iliaion." Shanty held up her wet gown, frowning at the stains.

The prince was looking even more confused with each passing moment, much to Zinkx's amusement. He finished Shanty's braid. "I'll head off, then." He gathered up his basket.

"Wait, what?" Daniel spluttered out.

"This Skyeola sounds like he knows what is going on. I'll inform him where we'll be dropping you off. I am sure he can handle things on the other end."

"I do not think you understand: Skyeola is just a kitten. He…he is the son of Zilon Mazaki."

Zinkx hesitated. Well. That clarified things. How the kitten had read the Messenger code he had etched into the design of Shanty's bodice, and known about Twizels, and even about protecting a Zaprex. The son of the Overlord. He looked back at the prince, before settling his eyes on Sam, playing happily in the stream.

Zinkx smiled. "Oh, I do believe I understand very well, Your Highness. Write me up a note of instructions for the lad. I'll be back to pick it up. Shanty, do I still have some spare clothes, or do I have to wait for these to dry?"

"You could always run through the forest naked."

Zinkx threw a wet shirt at her. "That's a no, then."

CHAPTER TWENTY

Be mindful of the woman who does not weep.
She who shows no emotion
Is more emotional than she who does.

Human Proverb

Skyeola stared at the hexagon-patterned ceiling, watching the gentle flow of the strange azure liquid seep through the crystal vines. His chest clenched as the recollection of the protector's final moments crept back into his mind, the draining out of that glow, the fluid drying in horrible cracking sounds until the large, metal body became like a lonely statue, never to move again.

A relic.

He looked at his trembling claws. He had never thought he would miss his bed in the palace so much, but, suddenly, a hungry craving for the familiarity of his messy, unkempt chamber called to him.

He wanted the safety of the cage that had always held him. Muhzun had not understood—he had been foolish to try and escape—

So foolish.

Skyeola squeezed his eyes shut, ignoring the burning of the tears. It snuck up on him, the sense that someone was watching him. A smell, new to his chamber, first caught his attention, causing his head to turn. The scent of burial herbs, used by the Sun Monks, and coffee—

Dark and rich, with just a hint of bitterness, the aroma lingered on the tip of his forked tongue to twirl through his twitching nose.

Skyeola leapt up, snatching for his conductor beneath his pillow, and pointing it at the intruder. A man sat cross-legged in a chair by the open window, the gentle breeze playing through midnight-tinted hair.

Skyeola glanced at the door. He had not heard it open. "How did you…?"

"I climbed." The roughened accent made his ears twitch.

Skyeola scoffed. "Impossible."

The man's lips twitched with a smile. "Gravity manipulation, laddie."

Gravity manipulation? But that would mean this man had skills that were forbidden to be taught in Pennadot. "Are you from Sin'musk'qu?" Skyeola whispered.

"Interesting that you presume that." The man leant forward. "I hear the Humans over there have a flourishing territory under the rulership of the Batitics. They're even allowed to practice using their birth elemental gifts."

Skyeola narrowed his eyes. "So, you are not from the Okazu Territory."

The man held out a letter. "I was told to tell you that this is from *Deiniol.*" He heavily emphasised the name, adding to its weight. Skyeola slipped out of his bed, carefully leaning forward, accepting the note. He unfolded it, reading the script therein. It was the Prince's handwriting, and his flowery words, and it did not seem to be written under duress. Skyeola slowly looked up at the man as he tucked the letter away beneath his pillow.

"Who are you?"

"High Commander Zinkx Maz of the Blood Armada."

Skyeola sucked in a sharp breath.

The man nodded. "I had a feeling my full title would mean something to you. I presume you have heard of me."

Skyeola withdrew his trembling conductor. "Only… only

in passing… sir… Underground Messengers often speak of you, sir, but I never expected to ever meet you, sir."

"Please, no 'sirs', laddie."

"But you are—"

"Only a man, like you are only lad. We are all players in this world."

Players. Skyeola shook his head. He was not a player. He was a piece that was mockingly tossed around at the whim of the Twilight, stripped of his autonomy.

"Is he safe?" Skyeola shuffled to the edge of his bed. He should have felt more of a cathartic relief, seeing the Prince's handwriting, but maybe it was the exhaustion, or maybe he was emotionally dulled—

"He is safe. Well, as safe as he can be." Zinkx shrugged. "As for his health…he was wounded rather badly, but he is on the mend. Though his recovery will be slow, please be aware of that."

Skyeola relaxed his tense wings. The man chuckled at him. Skyeola frowned, glancing down at the claws he clutched together. It seemed he was more anxious than he realised.

"I see my words are like sweets to you."

"I have been worried! I even went into the tunnels to try and find him!"

Zinkx raised his brow. "The fire?"

"Oh, Twilight, no! That was not us. Lord Galvon is a maggot." Skyeola let out a hiss.

"Hm. The Prince was certain he was behind it. Hence the reason he does not wish to return to Iliaion. He feels it best to meet up with you outside of Shalamic, beyond Galvon's reach."

Skyeola nodded slowly. "I see."

"As per his letter, we shall be leaving in two days, and heading for the town of Cor Coeden in the Vivian Region. You already know my travelling companion, Shanty. She will set up a small market stall. Come find the Prince there."

Zinkx leapt onto the window ledge. Skyeola dashed to him, looking up into the sparkling azure eyes, surprisingly so much like those of the protector.

"I believe you also met a little fairy, yes?"

"I did! Yes!" Skyeola burst out.

Zinkx crouched. "Thank you for protecting him."

"Oh. No. Well. It was…" Skyeola shuffled uneasily on his foot-claws.

"You are walking on a knife edge." Zinkx held out a hand, placing it on his chest, and Skyeola closed his eyes as the touch sent a warmth through his body. "Be careful. It cannot be easy for you, knowing who your Father is."

When he looked up, the Messenger was gone, the window was vacant, and the glow of the Northern Moon cast an eerie shadow through the gently tossing curtains. Skyeola collapsed to the floor, strength draining from his weak limbs.

Zinkx Maz, High Commander of the Blood Armada—a Messenger.

Skyeola rolled into a ball.

"Why…why didn't you…take me…away…" he sobbed. "Messengers…are supposed to…steal children. I want. I wanted to be saved. Please. Come back. Please. Please. Save me."

Skyeola pulled on his robe. His claws refused to stop trembling as he fiddled with the buttons and the sash. He had not slept. His cheeks felt puffy, his eyes itchy from tears, and his fur sticky and unkempt. He frowned at his state reflected in the nearby mirror. He looked sickly.

Sucking in a deep breath, Skyeola turned sharply from his chamber. He swept out into the long corridor, heading in the direction of Lord Galvon's Castle Hall. Hun was waiting outside, with several of their Palace guards, and, upon spotting him, the half-breed moved to intercept.

"Hey, hey, Little Lord, you should not go in right now."

"Move, Hun," Skyeola snapped.

"Yeh know I can't—"

Skyeola shoved past the guard. "I said move."

He slammed the doors open with a conduction, the thunderous roar shaking the floor, walls, and panoramic windows. Every eye within the Hall focused on him as he stood at the entrance, his glare pinning Lord Galvon to his ostentatious chair.

"We are leaving." Skyeola stepped to one side, indicating he desired for Jarid and Citla to join him. "Lord Telvon, Maiden Citla, please prepare for departure."

It took barely a beat for Jarid to obey. He bowed to Lord Galvon. "Thank you for your hospitality, Lord Hoinhine Galvon." Jarid held out a hand for Citla and she glided to his side in one smooth step. Galvon surged to his feet.

"You cannot leave!" he spluttered out.

Jarid halted mid-stride, slowly turning. "Did you just dare to tell me I cannot leave? Lord Galvon, if you do not rescind that, I will send word to my province, and my allies—"

"The Prince has not yet been found."

"I believe it is very clear what has transpired," Jarid barked back. "And, therefore, I must return to Steward Mazaki and inform him of this devastating blow to our Kingdom."

"I must say, you seem to all be taking this…remarkably… well…" Lord Galvon frowned. "Accepting the Prince's—"

Skyeola surged forward. "Accepting it? Accepting it? Do I look like I am accepting anything? No. I am going back to my Father, and I am going to tell him to hang your entire family for treason." He spun on his foot-claws and stormed out. If he remained in the hall a moment longer, the conductor in his claw would have snapped under the amount of unchanneled energy he was forcing into it. Already, he could feel his skin burning from the heat.

They took the corridor in silence, walking for several flights until they reached their private chambers. Skyeola closed his eyes, giving a pained sigh.

"When you want to be petty little brat, you really put on a show," Hun piped up.

Skyeola threw him a glare. He hated releasing his emotions in such a manner, he detested throwing his father's weight around, and, most of all, he loathed being perceived as a 'brat'. He was still a kitten, and no one listened to kittens. He had to scream, shout, hiss, and spit to get any attention in a Court.

He could not do it often, otherwise it would lose its power.

His father always thought it amusing. Skyeola clenched his jaw. He was in half a mind to ask his father to deal with Lord Galvon, but he would never…he would never stoop so low—would he?

"You had better have a very good reason for this, Skyeola." Jarid crossed his arms.

Without a word, Skyeola passed over the note as they walked. The young province lord read it quickly. His tongue clicked several times before he handed it back, though Citla stole it out of Skyeola's claw, giving him no chance to snatch it back.

"Prepare our wagons, Hun," Jarid said. "I want to be gone by midday. I cannot stand the thought of staying another moment in Galvon's presence." He lowered his voice to barely a whisper, "And it appears it may be safe for us to return to Palace Town after all."

Hun nodded. "On it."

Skyeola growled as he watched Citla reading the note, her black painted lips pressing tightly together.

"Skyeola, who gave this to you. How do you know—?"

"Please." Skyeola bowed his head. "Please just trust me. Do not make me tell you. I cannot."

The agony he felt must have been written on his tired features, for Citla backed down, nodding, accepting his words. "I do trust you," she whispered.

"Thank you."

CHAPTER TWENTY-ONE

When you start a journey,
Remember to pack well—
You have no idea where the Sun will lead you.

Spider Road Wayside Inn Inscription

Several rivers ran through Shalamic, the main one being the Midori River that divided Iliaion. All other smaller rivers, streams, and brooks were fed by the Midori. It had seemed sensible to send Shanty ahead to a shrine along the Midori's banks while Zinkx slipped into Iliaion to seek out Skyeola.

Shanty had given him strict instructions, though, to buy several rolls of various fabrics. Zinkx could only hope he had purchased the correct sorts. When he had presented them to her the night prior, her brow had pinched tight and she had swept away without a word.

Zinkx held up the bags of provisions he had prepared. It was not much, but it was at least something to be offered to a fellow Messenger should they pass through the area. The safe house that had been the Caves was gone, but the lingering tradition to leave behind supplies at an Outpost remained. So often the tradition was the factor between life and death for the hunted.

After all—

Khwaja Denvy—

Zinkx breathed out uneasily as his fingers curled into the heavy fabric of the bags before he crouched, setting them down beside the statue of the lone naga with its bowl lifted to the unseen sky-sea. He picked up a loose stone and tucked a note beneath it.

"Stay safe, Khwaja…"

He stood, laying a hand on the naga's shoulder briefly before turning away, heading back through the enormous fern leaves to their small camp. Sam was traumatising Daniel, pouncing over the prince as he chased a make-believe butterfly.

Shanty had made the Sovereign an entirely new outfit. She had put considerable effort into it, embroidering the deep blue fabrics of the long jacket with stunning designs reminiscent of the night sky-sea. In the fire, she had lost all that she had built up to sell, but that which she had managed to make along the way to Cor Coeden was going to fetch a high price for its quality.

She appeared around the diabond, dumping a large sack in his arms. He panicked at its weight, barely activating his gravity control in time to catch it.

"Shanty! Careful. Warn me, please, before you throw things at me. I cannot carry as much as you. Sun Almighty, what did you pack in this? *Rocks*?"

She pursed her lips. "I want a wagon."

Zinkx jerked his head towards Daniel. The prince spread his hands innocently. "It was just a suggestion."

"You may as well be asking for the Northern Moon," he grumbled as he tied the sack to the diabond's saddle.

Daniel laughed.

"You try being a poor pilgrim, heh," Zinkx snapped back.

"Do not think I would quite suit the lifestyle." Daniel flashed a wry grin.

Zinkx rolled his eyes. He flipped over another strap on the saddle, tightening it. "It starts with a wagon, then it will be a whole portable house. Before we know it, we'll have cows, and chickens—"

Sam burst out between the diabond's legs, skidding in the undergrowth, squealing as he waved his cane above his head.

"Whoa, whoa, whoa." Zinkx dodged several of the random

swings. "What are you up to?"

"I am pretending."

Zinkx lifted a leg as Sam hurtled past, attacking a nearby fungus.

"Yes, I can see that."

"I am pretending to defeat monsters!"

"Good job." Zinkx stepped around the fairy. "Keep that up. Go and attack the monster over there." He turned Sam around, sending him in the direction of the prince. "Give his *totu* a few good whacks."

"Hey, hey!" Daniel snatched up a stick in defence. "I am not a monster."

"We are pretending!" Sam shouted.

Daniel yelped as he tried to defend himself from his seat by the tree. Zinkx chuckled, finishing with the diabond's saddle. He rubbed her muzzle and scratched her chin. "Sorry for the heavy load, love."

She butted his shoulder.

"Oh, I know you can take it." He glanced towards Shanty. Her gaze was distant, lost in the forest's tangle of undergrowth. Her longing made his own chest ache, and he forcefully shoved away the memories of his squad.

His choice had been made.

He had to move forward.

Zinkx reached for her shoulder and she stirred at his touch.

"There is an old Human saying: 'Home is where the heart is.'" He held a hand to his chest.

Shanty frowned, touching her chest in return. "What an odd saying."

"It means that we are home wherever that which we love and cherish is. So, perhaps, Lady Tree, you need to wrap your roots around something that moves."

She grinned, perking up. "Like a wagon?"

Zinkx deflated mockingly. "Oh, come on!"

She laughed, sweeping past him, snatching up the diabond's reins. "You fell right into that one, Human."

The destruction had been devastating.

Sitting upon the diabond's back, Daniel stared around at the blackened scar torn through the forest of Shalamic. Corpses of the great trees hung, branches detached, twisted, bent, no longer their magnificent flourish of life. It was naught but an expanse of barren, ash-covered land that stretched on for miles, the charred earth sucking in the heat of the high Sun. It was difficult to believe they had been amongst the carnage, huddled together beneath ancient technology. Covering his eyes with a hand, Daniel squinted, staring across the vast forest beyond the black line.

The firestorm had lasted barely a few minutes, but it had done its damage. Shalamic would take time to heal from such deep wounds. He touched a hand to his side, feeling the heat of his own injury. It seemed almost ironic—

A royal was connected to the land, after all, if one was harmed, so was the other.

He spotted Zinkx and Sam picking their way back through the soot. Dirty—again. Shanty was not going to be amused at all by the sight of them. Sam's high-pitched voice carried far in the eerie silence. No birds, no insects. Everything had fled the destruction. As they reached him on the edge, where the forest began again, he laughed at them both, covered nearly head to toe in black ash.

"Find what you were seeking?" Daniel enquired.

Zinkx shook his head. "The Monument of Old was buried under too much debris to bother trying to uncover it."

"But, Gifu, I need to make my Map work," Sam wailed.

Zinkx held up a hand to calm him. "We will find a working Zaprex Way Station, Sam. You need to be patient."

"The World is dying!"

"It will survive long enough."

Sam pouted and floated up to his basket, collapsing into it

in a stroppy mope.

"Where did Shanty go?" Zinkx glanced around.

Daniel pointed to the nearby trees. "She needed a ladies' break."

Zinkx clicked his tongue irritably. "She should have taken the diabond."

"Her argument was that the diabond had to stay with me. Prince and all that, you know."

Zinkx snorted. Daniel slid down from the saddle, wincing as he landed. The ride had been long...well, it had felt long for him, and the movement of a diabond was remarkably different to that of a horse. His legs had turned to water and he gripped the diabond's saddle for support.

"I wish I had such a wonderful beast," he said.

"I am surprised you don't," Zinkx responded in between splashing water on his face from the waterskin. "I heard they are the royal beast of burden. The loyal hound, the diabond. A Starborn Sovereign was always seated upon a diabond, or so the stories go."

"You and your stories."

Zinkx flicked back his damp hair. "We are but an accumulation of our history, and our history is made up of stories."

Daniel was not sure, yet, if he liked the way the Messenger saw the past. It had always been a vague, foggy blur to him, one he refused to try wandering through. Was it at all possible that he did not need his own past known to him, but could draw on the foundations laid by others? The notion was an interesting one.

Shanty pushed her way through several large leaves, re-emerging from the forest. Her heavy skirt was hooked in the belt of her dress, freeing up her bare feet. She took one look at both Zinkx and Sam and flung up her arms in despair.

"What did you do, Human? Roll around in the soot?"

"Maybe a bit." Zinkx pinched finger and thumb together.

She huffed. "You are washing your own clothes."

"I always wash my own clothes."

"No, you do not!"

"I thought I was clear about wandering off alone." Zinkx pointed to the diabond.

Shanty arched an eyebrow and began tapping a foot. "Do not be a hypocrite."

Daniel breathed in deeply, feeling the ache it caused in his wound. He had noticed this happened often, their verbal sparring matches. He had an inkling they both enjoyed the back and forth.

Zinkx held out his hands.

"I want you to be aware of the dangers—"

A whip of black tar lashed around Zinkx's legs and yanked. Shanty shrieked, snatching for him, coming up short as he was dragged through the dense forest foliage. He vanished.

Daniel stared at the space, his breath frozen.

"What…just…"

A sudden eruption of lightning exploded through the trees, shattering several branches that collapsed around them. Shanty shoved Daniel out of the way, her far stronger form taking the full brunt of a large limb. He watched as Zinkx somersaulted through the air, landing in a skid across the dusty ash.

A creature of vomiting black liquid surged out between the trees, foliage decaying and dissolving around it. Its numerous eyes settled on Sam, who had frozen stiff in his basket. Zinkx and Shanty moved simultaneously. Daniel scrambled away as Shanty snatched up a fallen log, swinging it viciously at the monster. Zinkx grabbed Sam and rolled away as the log splintered on impact several inches from them. The monster reared backwards. Zinkx bundled Sam into Shanty's arms. "Keep him safe."

She did not hesitate. Hugging Sam against her chest, Shanty dived into the undergrowth. Daniel curled up as the beast of burden leapt over him, spraying lava. The globs halted, suspended around Zinkx in a protective halo as the man drew his blades, lightning cracking the air.

"Daniel! Follow Shanty!"

He had to force himself, for the terror of what roared out of the splintered trees pinned him the ground. He had never seen anything so hideous. It seemed to suck in all sunlight, and dissolved the surrounding forest with a toxic miasma releasing from vents of twisted bones fused together by threads of rotting flesh.

He lost sight of Zinkx as he plunged after Shanty.

What was it—?

His chest burned.

Why had it appeared—?

He clutched at his wounded side.

Zinkx—

He had left—

He had just left—

Daniel stumbled. He landed roughly, his hands digging into the mossy ground. Tears soaked into the spongy surface and he stared down at the vanishing droplets. He was crying. This felt so—familiar—like an echo—

His fingers dragged through the moss and he snapped his head back in the direction he had come from, glaring fiercely through the foliage. The air was ripping against his clothes. Wind. It surged with the intensity of his racing heart.

Bow. Bow. Bow. He did not have a bow. He did not have a bow.

Why did he not have a bow? No—

Something sparked in the back of his mind.

He did not need a bow. What was he thinking? This was ridiculous! David would have been so ashamed of him—running like this. Again. He was always running.

"Daniel!" Shanty's shout startled him. She dropped down beside him. "Are you hurt? We need to find a place for you to hide with Sam, so I can go and help Zinkx—"

"Get me a stick!" He grasped her arm. "I need a stick, a long stick."

Her brow furrowed. "Can you do something?"

"I...I do not..." He shook his head. "Yes. I think so." He

staggered to his feet, searching the undergrowth.

Shanty shoved a long, dry branch into his trembling hand. Her usually soft features hardened as she grabbed his wrist and pulled him back in the direction they had come. They leapt over roots, batting aside the fungi and leaves.

Sam gave a sudden high-pitched cry of warning.

"Watch out!"

He ducked as a boulder sailed past them, slamming into several fungi, causing them to erupt in a spray of spores. The foul creature he had seen, with its many arms like pulsating muscular whips, like those of the venomous jellyfish that stalked the waterways of Pennadot, ignored the very existence of the forest around it.

They were minute specks to its focus—

Zinkx. The man danced with all the skills Daniel expected of a Butler in the court, missing every rock and tree limb tossed in his direction. He used the diabond that followed him as launching point, propelling himself through the air, lashing at the fiend whenever an opening was possible.

Zinkx tore up the ground like an earthquake as he landed. Daniel flinched as the nearby trees seemed to splutter, their shapes rearranging in awkward blocks. Lightning crackled, burning through the grass.

"Stay behind me!" Daniel glanced back. Shanty had shrunk against a tree, hugging Sam tightly to her chest. The monster's roar shook the high canopy as the beast sent a branch hurtling towards Zinkx. The Messenger hewed it apart, running up the falling debris, lashing out another rope of lightning, skidding around the creature and dragging his blades through its middle. Black, tarry blood spewed forth. The ground hissed and bubbled in protest.

In retribution, it smashed into Zinkx with one of its twirling arms. Zinkx flew past Daniel, landing in a roll. Zinkx clawed his way upright, panting heavily, shaking blood from his eyes. Bright green eyes, as stark and burning as Daniel's own, locked with his. Daniel held up his stick. Zinkx breathed in and nodded. He grabbed a fistful of dirt before running and bouncing into the air.

Daniel swung the stick out, holding it as keenly as any bow. Wind surged around his feet and a rush of heat pooled along his spine. The action was automatic, as though he had done it countless times, his body knowing the dance before his mind did. He pulled his arm back, aiming the invisible arrow of swirling wind. As Zinkx scattered a rain of dust and lightning, he fired. The monster's head vanished. Zinkx landed roughly upon its body as it crumbled. His twin blades ripped its chest apart in a shower of guts.

Zinkx staggered. The diabond caught him and he snatched hold of her saddle, sagging. Daniel sighed in relief. It was over—

"Daniel! The backlash!" Zinkx shouted.

He barely heard it. His arm. It was bleeding. His lovely jacket that Shanty had made was torn to shreds and skin hung off muscle. He held in the urge to vomit. If he had considered the monster grotesque, this was worse.

Shanty was suddenly at his side, steadying him as he shook.

"Zinkx!" she cried. "Zinkx, grab something to stem the bleeding. He'll lose his arm if we don't act fast."

Once again he was being fussed over. He could feel himself drawing back into a blanket of icy cold darkness, like the light within him was being snuffed out.

"Did...did we kill it?" Daniel murmured.

Zinkx was relentless in the strapping of his arm and the pain was scorching, keeping him from the cold bitterness. Those green eyes smiled at him, fierce, sun-filled eyes, as royal as his own, smiling with gratitude.

"Very much so."

The flames of their small fire spat and hissed as Zinkx added another piece of wood. There was much to be collected. Many trees had suffered, not only in the firestorm, but in the Twizel's rampage. Shanty could still feel the echoing pain of the forest through the soil she had buried her bare feet in. But it did nothing to distract her from the spinning thoughts in her head.

She studied her raw hands. She had acted without a thought. Her limbs had moved with the drums of the forest to snatch up the fallen branch, to swing it, to save not only Sam, but a Human man.

Zinkx.

In her heart, she knew the monster would have killed him, killed her, and taken their precious little fairy. So she had acted. She did not want to lose them.

Shanty clenched her jaw.

"Keep doing that, love, and you're going to crack a tooth."

Shanty glanced up. Zinkx was crouched by the fire, waiting for his pot of coffee to boil. It was an image that she had long become fond of, the man by the fire, and the smell of his bitter brew. It was familiar and comforting. Zinkx. Warmth. Coffee.

She smiled, resting her chin on her palm.

"I could not let you die," she whispered. "I want...I want to save the world with you."

He turned back to stirring the pot, but his shoulders had tightened. "You honour me."

"You should not have to do this alone. No. You don't have to. I will walk to the edge of Livila with you, if we have to."

He looked back, wearing a wry smile. "How very far we shall walk."

Shanty held out her hands. "We need that wagon."

Zinkx rolled his eyes. "Do I look like I am made of jewels, Krrirren?" He poured out his coffee and slumped down beside her. "Oh, I ache everywhere."

"Don't complain. The prince almost died...again..."

"He's racked up a considerable toll to owe us," Zinkx mumbled into his mug.

Shanty poked his ribs. "He is the Sovereign. He does not owe us anything. And he saved your life."

"I am surprised he even turned around to help, considering how scared he is."

Shanty dropped her head against his shoulder. "His eyes… they were like yours. Something…woke inside him."

"Hm." Zinkx sipped his coffee, glancing at the sleeping royal. "Well, whatever it is, I hope it stays awake. Something tells me he's going to need all the backbone he can muster."

She sighed. "Did we save his life, or did we set him on a terrible path of pain?"

"That is the question," Zinkx murmured.

Zinkx had vanished with Sam straight after the breaking of fast. The two of them, together, were a recipe for mischief and mayhem.

Shanty placed another pack down beside the diabond. Zinkx had not felt comfortable unpacking much of their meagre supplies after the unexpected attack. His hyper-vigilance had returned tenfold.

"Shanty, could I have a drink of water?" The prince's voice was soft.

She quickly snatched up a waterskin and headed to where the royal was seated in the curve of a tree root. She had not thought it possible for a Kimwyn to look paler, but the prince's skin was like paper-thin wax, void of its beautiful shine. Too much blood-loss. He had barely recovered from his previous wounds, and now this.

She was not sure how much more this fragile body could take. He sipped the water and she wiped the excess from his chin.

"Bit of a mess…" he murmured.

Shanty took his good hand, holding it to her cheek.

"You may have scars now, Your Highness, but with those scars comes a story of survival."

His smile was weak as he drifted into a feverish sleep. "You…sound…like my mother."

Shanty lowered his hand and gently wrapped the blanket more tightly around him.

"Keep watch," she commented to the diabond as she followed Zinkx and Sam's tracks through the forest. She was led to the scene of the battle. The two stood amongst the ruin, beside the foul carcass of the Twizel. She kept her distance from the tainted ground, twisting her hands against her scalp in disgust.

It was naught but bones, and a few pieces of rotted flesh, but the mutated shape remained. It was obvious that the Twizel had been an amalgamation of several different creatures it had consumed, along with both Humans and Kelibs.

"What's wrong?" she called out.

"I asked Sam to do a scan." Zinkx stepped back. "It is not the same one that attacked us back at the Caves."

Shanty's hands grabbed at her skirts, bunching them tightly. "It isn't?" Did this mean she had succeeded in killing the Ki'rayh with the Zaprex weapon?

Sam shook his head vigorously. "No. That one attacked me before. I know it. I made sure to keep a biological marker of it in my system. This one is not it."

"What does this mean?" Shanty asked.

Zinkx headed back to her, Sam floating along beside him.

"The Dragon may be aware the Key has been found. It is likely we shall be hunted. We really need to return the Prince to his entourage as soon as possible. It is dangerous for him to remain with us if Twizels are on our back."

"He is not well," Shanty said. "I fear if we move him…"

Zinkx rubbed the back of his neck. "He lost a lot of blood."

Sam looked from Zinkx to Shanty and back again. He scowled in frustration. "*Rikai dekitara inoni.*[26]"

Zinkx gave Sam's head a gentle pat. "The prince has been damaged, and the damage is getting worse."

---

26 *I wish I could understand.*

Sam's antennae buzzed. "I can fix him. Zaprexes fix things. I can fix him."

Shanty looked up at Zinkx and he shrugged. "Anything is worth a go at the moment."

She had to agree. If something was going to work, perhaps it would be fairy magic.

Back at the camp Sam rifled around in his small bag, pulling out bits and bobs, nothing that looked familiar to her, until he tugged out a chain filled with shimmering crystals. The Zaprex muttered to himself as he sorted through them, eventually tugging one from the chain.

Sam held out the faintly glowing crystal to Shanty. "Crush it, feed to him. It should stimulate blood production."

Shanty frowned at the crystal. "I do not understand…it is a rock."

"No. It is not a rock. It is a software chip. You need to install it. Therefore, he must consume it somehow. Crush it, so he can ingest it."

Shanty arched an eyebrow at Zinkx. His expression was blank.

He shrugged. "Fairy magic."

She groaned, taking the crystal. "Not everything will be solved by fairy magic."

Sam sucked in a gasp of horror. "I will save the world!"

She could only hope it would be as simple as crushing a rock.

It was strange, but Daniel was vaguely aware of the time that had passed since he had last opened his eyes. It was longer than a single nightfall.

"See. I fixed him," Sam's high-pitched voice squeaked out nearby.

He was being pulled along behind the diabond on a bed

of woven leaves and tightly strapped-together logs. A parasol protected him from the harsh, low Summer Sun.

"Good evening, Your Highness." Zinkx smiled down at him. The man was walking along beside the bed, Sam perched on his shoulder. "Feeling any better?"

Daniel breathed in. There was no pain. For the first time in what felt like an eternity, he did not feel pain when breathing. "I...I am..."

"See! I fixed him." Sam cheered.

Zinkx shrugged. "Fairy magic."

Daniel tenderly touched his bandaged arm. "How bad is it?"

"Oh. I won't lie. It was rather bad. You had Shanty very worried. We actually thought you were going to die...again..." Zinkx gestured to Sam. "You can thank Sam."

Sam grinned, his yellow eyes sparkling with all the intensity of small stars. "Fixed you." His little chest puffed out. "I'll fix the world."

Daniel smiled. "Thank you, Sam."

Sam cocked his head to one side, his demeanour shifting, like a mask slipping away. "I do not like death. It took Biri away." Floating off Zinkx's shoulder, Sam headed for Shanty on the diabond, and vanished into her lap.

Zinkx's stretched his arms out in front of him. "Death takes. Then what gives, I wonder."

"Time," Daniel offered.

"Time? You think?"

"Given enough time, you can hope for anything. You always need just a little more time."

Zinkx raised a brow. "I suppose so."

Daniel struggled upright. "Where are we?"

"We figured it was easier to follow the straight path carved by the firestorm, that way we could drag your sorry *totu* behind us. You have been asleep for two days. We've almost reached the edge of Shalamic's Forest."

"Two days..." Daniel groaned.

Zinkx shrugged. "You did not miss much."

"That monster…"

"Don't worry. Your arrow struck true. The Twizel is dead."

Twizel. The word was strangely familiar, but he was not sure where from. Daniel frowned. "Is this a Messenger thing?"

"It is. They are foul creatures born of great suffering, twisted into serving the Dragon. When we return you to your people, do your best to forget about it all."

Daniel pressed his lips together. That was going to be difficult. He felt as though his eyes had been opened after sol-cycles of walking around with them shut. The world was not the shade of grey he had always seen it as. It was richer, wilder, and full of fairy magic. How could he ever forget the Messenger, the Kelib shaman, and the electric fairy?

"You are asking the impossible."

"And, yet, I ask it." Zinkx smiled. "Forget about me, Your Highness. I am no one important."

CHAPTER TWENTY-TWO

Remember this little Messenger:
It takes a team to kill a Twizel,
So always fight with friends by your side.

Messenger Saying

His breathing laboured. Hot. Dragging like knives through his lungs. Denvy staggered his way across the boundary into the water shrine. There was no obvious, noticeable border, but the restorative energy coagulating in the area wrapped around him. Warm as a blanket. His wounded foot-paw caught on a stone. Denvy yelped at the sharp stabbing that flared through the soft under-pad.

His heavy body, weighed down like a sack of iron ingots, collapsed without warning. Denvy steadied himself on weakened arms beside the old naga statue and slumped into a pile. He felt like a dirty heap of hay, his fur a tangled, matted mess. Blood had caked with mud. Sticks and leaves were caught in the knots. There was no time for grooming while in constant flight.

The relentless pursuit had been arduous, even on an immortal such as himself, with no time to allow his wounds to heal, or for a respite to revive through the Secondary Realm. He was being gradually worn down, day after day, and he knew he was on the losing side. It was only a matter of time before his health level dropped too low to sustain any functionality.

Then—

They would strike.

Denvy tilted his head to one side, grumbling, "Now would be a superb time to come and offer some council, Hazanin-*sama*."

Denvy sighed. He rubbed at his eyes. The statue above him was old and worn, covered in moss and vines, but the face of Midori looked down with a kindly smile. Denvy raised a paw, laying it on the emerald scales of the naga's tail. "Thank you, Midori. Apologies for my rather uncouth state."

His gaze was drawn to the small pile of supplies tucked away beneath the statue. Denvy frowned. Odd. An offering, perhaps? Surely travellers in Shalamic no longer ventured this far into the forests to reach the shrine—surely there was a larger shrine in Iliaion? Denvy slowly eased himself upright, taking in his surrounds. There were signs of a camp. A small fire-pit. A woodpile set aside. Someone had taken time to clean the tiles around the shrine leading into the shallows of the water.

His chest inflated with a sharp breath and he reached for the supplies. Lovingly made blankets spilled forth, along with several jugs of water and jerky. Denvy closed his eyes in relief. He settled himself down in the curve of Midori's tail, tucking the blankets around himself. Finally, a moment to pause.

He was completely unaware of when he fell asleep; being pulled into a dreamless ocean of darkness was unsettling. He always dreamed. His mind was crafted to roam the space between realms, forever plotting courses through the Data-Ways.

But the darkness had been infinite and consuming, leaving him with a restless sensation as he stared at the twisting branches far above. He felt rested, and yet disturbed by the void that had been his own mind.

Denvy dragged a paw through his mane. "You are tired, old man," he muttered.

Struggling upright, he glanced at the firepit and the

gathered woodpile that had been left behind by the previous traveller. A fire would do his creaky old hearts good. He shuffled about, sweeping the blankets aside. A rock dislodged from the nearby pile of supplies, causing a sheet of paper to flutter down. Denvy snatched at it reflexively. His name was written clearly upon the parchment, in Zinkx's neat, cursive script.

"Wait…" Denvy slumped back and looked up at Midori. "Zinkx was here?"

His hearts raced as he flipped the note open, feeling as though he was drinking the ink from the pages.

Zinkx had found the Key. No. That was trivial—

He was only days behind Zinkx.

Did he dare hope—?

Denvy surged to his foot-paws. If he could just muster up the strength, he could run. Surely he could catch up with his young ward? Yes—he could—he could do this—

Snatching up the pack, he stuffed the supplies swiftly into them and threw it over his shoulder. He rushed to the boundary line of the shrine, thumping against a barrier. He slapped his paws on the invisible wall.

"Midori! Midori, let me out!" Denvy turned sharply, shouting back at the statue. "I need to go."

The river behind the statue swelled, causing the reeds to dance.

"Midori. Please." Denvy pushed at the barrier.

He bowed, pressing his head against the ethereal wall. "Please."

You will suffer a thousand deaths if you go.

Denvy looked back at the shimmering figure of a young man standing in the shallows of the river. The Sunlight refracted through his watery form, crafted by the smallest of fluttering flakes swirling together.

"Please. Midori. Let me go. I need to go."

The river-god's head bowed. *Stop torturing yourself, Uncle.*

The barrier faded, along with the warm presence within the shrine. Denvy shivered, touching a paw to his chest. He was alone again. He clenched his teeth. Zinkx was not far. Squaring his shoulders, he surged forth into the forest.

It was the burnt-out husk of a Twizel that confirmed to him that he was only days behind his young ward. The air still felt charged with elemental forces, enough that his fur kept spiking. Denvy frowned, turning on his foot-paws.

"Not just lightning..." he mused aloud. "There was a Simoon here."

Had Zinkx met up with an Underground Messenger? Rubbing a paw through his mane, Denvy turned away from the carcass.

He barely sensed it amongst all the elemental energy distorting the forest—the disturbance that ripped through the Primary Realm like a blade. He was not fast enough. Not against the Ki'rayh that struck from above. All he could do was defend, raising his water-sword, swirling a shield of ice. It shattered. But the impact was lessened as he hit the ground, sending up a shower of debris.

Denvy groaned. Through the cloud of spores released from disturbed fungus, the mutated shape of the Ki'rayh shifted, collapsing back into the form of a man. He did not know the man's face—that had changed—but he knew the signature of the Ki'rayh's unchanged data.

Houa leant over him, sneering. "Denvy Maz, Dream Master of the Northlands, it has been a long time."

Denvy growled low. "Not long enough."

Houa struck savagely, and Denvy folded instantly into darkness.

CHAPTER TWENTY-THREE

You have come to a point–
Two roads:
One leads to a mountain,
Another to a seemingly clear path…
Which do you take?

Sun Temple Proverb

Cor Coeden had all the vibrancy of a happy little Human trading town. Despite how Zinkx loathed the overloading of noise, how it forced him to rapidly compartmentalise everything surrounding him, there was something sweet about the colourful town. Its stone walls were high, with towers that overlooked the shimmering meadows beyond the large bend in the Cor River around which the town was built. He and Sam stood upon the civilian outlook on the east-facing tower. Shanty had fashioned a heavy coat for Sam, covering most of his foreignness, through the child was constantly picking at it in irritation. She had tried to mimic the hexagon designs she had seen amongst the Zaprex Ruins in her stitching and embroidery, adding embellishments to otherwise plain fabrics. They had only been in Cor Coeden for a few days and already she had sold half her stock of robes. She was greatly enjoying herself.

The reason for their climb was visible in the hazy distance. A Zaprex Way Station. Sam turned his large, illumed eyes to Zinkx, peering out from under the hood he wore. "I need to go there."

Zinkx rubbed his chin. "I could probably get us there in an hour or so. But are you sure the protectors won't attack? I can manage one on my own, but any more than that and I'd need a whole Squad."

Sam gave an overly dramatic sigh.

Zinkx had to wonder who the Zaprex mimicked that from: him or Shanty. It was most likely him. He did sigh more than Shanty. It was eerie having his own mannerisms displayed back to him.

"Gifu. What am I?"

Zinkx arched an eyebrow. "Well. They might not recognise you."

Sam seemed to consider this, for a soft, muffled buzzing emanated from beneath his coat. Slowly, he lifted a hand, clutching at the hidden Map. "Nevertheless, I must go."

"Right, then." Zinkx plucked him off the wall and settled him on his shoulders. "Let's go tell Shanty we'll be gone for a while."

"And say goodbye to the *baka*-Prince."

"Yes, but don't say '*baka*' to him. We only call him that in private."

Sam giggled, clapping Zinkx's head playfully. Zinkx jogged down the winding stairs, passing several wall-guards, waving to them in greeting as he went. He and Shanty had likely become the talk of the town upon their arrival. A Human man, a Kelib woman, and a child they covered up from head to toe. To anyone looking at them, they might pass as one of the rare Human-Kelib couples with a half-breed child.

He doubted Shanty had noticed it yet, but it seemed Daniel had. The Prince was insistent on the idea of the wagon. If the outside world saw them one way, sometimes the easiest option was to go along with it.

They approached Shanty's stall in the market. She would not have gotten a permit for it were it not for Daniel's skill in negotiation. No—it had not so much been a negotiation as it had been a set of instructions. The town official had been overwhelmed by the presence of the Prince.

Daniel currently sat in the shade, nursing his wounded

arm, watching the flow of the market with curiosity.

"We're going to head off, Shanty. Sam needs to explore a Zaprex ruin nearby."

Shanty turned quickly. Rifling around in a pack, she pulled out a prepared meal and a waterskin. "Be back before nightfall."

Zinkx saluted. "Can you pass me my hat?"

Shanty flung it at him, and he caught it, attaching it to his belt.

"You're leaving?" Daniel asked. "What if...something happens? We could get robbed."

Zinkx pointed to the diabond lounging behind Shanty. "No one would dare. Not with a fire diabond behind the stall. You'll be fine."

Daniel frowned. "There aren't many Kelibs here."

"Which is why it is pretty safe." Zinkx bent forward to whisper to Shanty, "Probably best not to show your tattoos, still."

Shanty rolled her eyes. "I am not a fool." She made a shooing motion. "Now, go. You are scaring away my customers with your scruffiness. At least Daniel brings them in with his handsome allure."

Daniel grinned. "Hear that? I am handsome."

Zinkx threw a grin over his shoulder. "*Hwyl fawr, Eich Uchelder.*[27]"

Once they reached the meadows, he permitted Sam to remove the hood that contained his long ears and antennae. Sam rolled around in the air, wailing as he clutched at the junctures where his antennae sprouted from his head. "It hurts!"

"I know. I know," Zinkx soothed him. "But you'll have to put up with it while we're in public."

"But it hurts!"

"Sometimes we have to do things that hurt." Zinkx held out the carry bag he had fashioned. "Come on, let's go."

Sam squeezed into the carrier and Zinkx strapped it over

---

27 *Goodbye, Your Highness*

his shoulders. He stretched his arms up, loosening his muscles, expanding his gravity bubble.

Running across green fields, with a blue sky-sea, was vastly different to running the Plains of Blazing Fire. The stark contrast, even between the colours that surrounded him and those that haunted his memories, was alarming. The world of his past was painted in flames and charcoal black, and now he was enveloped in warm hues of sunshine and green. Was he the lucky one? Had he abandoned his Squad, his people, for good? Would they understand his decision to do that which was directly in front of him?

The thoughts tumbled and tossed as the ran, the Monument of Old growing larger, taking on a denser shape. He scattered a herd of sheep as he mounted a small hill, bouncing to a stop on the crest to face the great monolith of a bygone era. He had thought it an illusion of the air that bled through his gravity bubble, but, upon pausing and dissolving the sphere surrounding him, the noise chiming across the moors grew only louder. It was not intrusive, nor irritating, but it was sorrowful and filled his chest with a deep ache. A melody of the wind through the curving crystal spires of the Monument of Old, singing out through the meadows in an unending tune.

Zinkx breathed out uneasily.

"Any idea what the monument was for?"

Sam leant over his shoulder, holding out his hand-device, revealing several highlighted pictograms. He pointed to one. "This means that the Way Station is active. It is sending out a signal to something." He indicated the other pictogram. "This means that the signal is being received." He shifted his finger to the final image. "And this means that the Way Station is uploading and downloading to the Data-Stream."

Zinkx nodded along. "Right, but that does not tell me what it is for?"

Sam sat back in his carrier. "It's creating a projection field, but I do not know why, nor do I know what it is uploading or downloading."

"Guess we'll have to head inside to find out." Zinkx picked up the pace once more, with Sam directing him to the entrance. Zinkx had been inside numerous Zaprex ruins. They were scattered across Coltarian, but those were in varying states of decay due to the volatile nature of the Plains of Blazing Fire. Even many within Pennadot had suffered under the ruthlessness of the forests, or the war that had beset their world long ago. The twisting spirals that emerged from the meadow like great crystals, glittering in the Sun, tugged at his chest. He ached—everything in him ached—for the return of songs he did not even know.

Sam climbed out of the carrier, floating towards the clear surface. Nothing denoted an entrance, as it often was with Zaprex constructions. Zinkx crouched, plucking a blade of grass. He folded it, pressing it to his lips to begin a soft tune. Sam turned to him sharply in surprise, ears tweaking rearwards.

From the ground, a warm azure glow crept up, forming several streams in the crystal, until a doorway was formed. Zinkx let the final note die away. Sam drifted back, his large eyes wide in disbelief.

"How did you...do that...?"

Zinkx ruffled the fairy's hair fondly.

"Khwaja Denvy taught me. I'm becoming a bit of an expert at getting into these things."

"It was amazing! I didn't know songs could be made that way."

Zinkx chuckled. "Thank you."

The dark interior lit up as Sam entered, and Zinkx had the impression of a beehive with honeycomb hexagons running along the walls in vectors, the lights leading them on down the passageways. His muscles maintained their tension, anticipating protectors descending on them at any moment. He had encountered numerous varieties of the machines, some as large as boulders, others as small as bugs. Zinkx twitched, forcing away the memory of the tiny bug-like protectors and the cruel manner of the deaths he had witnessed them execute when

Messengers breaching Zaprex ruins had run foul of them. There was a reason the notion of a curse existed, and, even now, he could feel the oppressive weight of centuries of fear and awe. Sam had no comprehension of what he was to the peoples of the world he had landed in, and that churned Zinkx's stomach. How could he possibly protect the child of a race who had built such splendours and then fallen so far?

Sam squealed in delight, twirling in the air as they entered a vast chamber. "The Central Control Room!"

Zinkx stepped in after the fairy. His skin tingled with a rush. He might be the first Human to walk through these crystal halls for centuries. The thought was thrilling.

Water flowed within the pillars that vanished into the ceiling above them, until Zinkx took a step backwards, gaining a new angle of the refracting light gleaming through the mammoth windows. The ceiling was water.

"Wow." He laughed. "Rather like the House of Flames, only, *not* lava."

He halted abruptly, tension violently swinging him around as he drew his blade. It was motionless, like a suit of armour standing vacant beside a pillar—a humanoid protector. Zinkx tightened his gloved hand around the hilt of his sword. Through gold-plated metal, formed into a curved helmet, azure robotic eyes narrowed, focusing on him. It was aware of his presence. If he moved—

Sam happily skipped past, turned, and threw out his arms in a gesture of confusion.

"Gifu, what are you doing?"

"It's staring at me."

"So?"

"It will attack if I move."

Sam flailed his hands about. "Don't be silly. It isn't sensing a threat with me here."

Zinkx hesitated. "Are you sure?"

Sam zoomed right up into Zinkx's face, his bright yellow eyes nearly blinding him.

"I am sure." Sam grabbed Zinkx's arm, and dragged him away from the protector, towards several glass terminals. Zinkx could feel it, though, the protector watching them like an ever-present custodian waiting for him to make a single wrong move on this hallowed ground. As with the technology of the other chambers, upon Sam's approach the terminals hummed to life with a soft tune. Sam's delighted giggle caused a surge in the lights as he removed his pendant from around his neck. Zinkx brought one of the several floating chairs across, easing down into it as the fairy held out the triangular crystal prism.

It still filled him with awe; the thought that, in Sam's tiny hands, a fragment of a miniscule Map could lead them to The Towers. The Towers—was it possible? Could they be real? For centuries, legends and stories had been woven about the machines that had stitched their broken world back together, and fixed the Secondary Realm until it resonated with a pure melody that fuelled all life on Livila.

The Dawn Age.

Peace.

But it had not lasted. Could peace come again? If the foundations of their world could be saved, perhaps then they could muster up the strength to protect themselves from the Dragon. A new Dawn Age.

He glanced down at Sam as the child fiddled happily with the controls in front of him, making tunes with the gentle touches of his little hands on each of the crystals. What if the term 'Key' was more literal than they thought?

"Is...that...what this is?" he whispered. "Are you not a weapon...but our beacon of hope?"

Sam poked him suddenly in the arm. Zinkx startled. He focused his attention on the fairy, who had tilted his head to one side.

Sam blew a rasp. "You're weird."

Zinkx clapped his hands together. "What do we need to do to find your Map pieces? I gather that is why we're here."

Sam waved his hand-device in the air. "This isn't powerful

enough on its own to link up to the Data-Stream, but here I can do that directly. I can download all I need!" Sliding the prism into a slot in the nearest terminal, Sam began running his slender fingers across the glossy surface. Several holographic displays flickered to life around them.

"*Ano*. It says we are here…in hex *Dôl y Dawnswyr* of the desktop grid, and this Turret is called *Gwynt Trist*."

"The Dancers' Meadow and Sad Wind," Zinkx translated. Had the Zaprexes built the Turret knowing that when the wind blew the melody would sound so filled with sorrow? Was there a reason behind such a song? Had some ancient Zaprex carved their Monument to sing a tune of remembrance for someone, or even something? Zinkx closed his eyes briefly. How the questions made him hunger for answers. The urge to dig for knowledge was deep. Dig—dig where, and how?

He dragged a hand wearily through his hair, laughing at himself for his foolishness.

Sam tugged on the sleeve of his shirt and Zinkx glanced down at the child. "It says we need to go here. The next Map piece is in hex: *Dyfnder Adenydd wedi'i Rhwygo*.[28]"

Zinkx stared at the image floating in front of him. For several minutes, he had absolutely no idea what it was he was staring at. Gradually, the glowing blobs began to take shape as he traced them back and forth, allowing the silhouettes to form. His lips parted with a soft pop.

"Oh. I see."

He had never come across a landscape depicted in such a manner; not even the cartographers at the House of Flames drew such strange maps.

He reached out a finger again. "I think it refers to terrains. The higher the area the brighter the colour. How fascinating."

Zinkx tugged his leather journal out of his hip bag, and found a folded-up piece of parchment he had tucked in there. He spread it out, looking from the crudely drawn map of Pennadot to the version in the hologram. "Yes!" He pulled free

---

28   *Shredded Wings Depth*

another sheet of parchment, unfolding it, adding it to the map of Pennadot. Sam peered down at the papers with a confused tilt to his head.

"This is Sin'musk'qu, Pennadot's sister land." Zinkx tapped the added page. "Your next Map piece appears to be located somewhere in Sin'musk'qu." He made a large circle with his finger at the hologram. "See those mountains? They are the Twin Mountains where the Pass of Sin'musk'qu lies. Your information crystal seems to be indicating we must travel through here."

"Is it far?" Sam blinked innocently.

"Ah. Yes. It is a bit."

Sam frowned. His antennae drooped. "Oh. Sorry."

"No. No. It's fine." Zinkx folded up the parchments, slipping them back into his journal. "If you must go to Sin'musk'qu, then we shall go to Sin'musk'qu."

"Is it a *bad* place?"

Zinkx shrugged. "I don't really know. It is the homeland of the Batitics. They are one of the beastial races. It is hard to judge them on stories alone."

"But Skyeola was friendly."

Zinkx smiled. "Yes. He was."

"Then won't we be fine?"

Zinkx sighed. "We really need to work on who you trust..." Zinkx pointed to the hologram again. "You arrived here in Pennadot via a form of Zaprex transportation. Could we use that?"

"Defragmentation."

Zinkx pursed his lips at the word. "Yes. That."

Sam shook his head, turning his attention back to the terminals in front of them. "There are only a few functional defragmentation machines in Pennadot, and none of them are nearby, either to us, or our destination. The Data-Ways have been closed. Those that are working are likely connected to major HUBs."

Zinkx did not know what a HUB was, but it sounded like

something important, central, and congested with people and traffic. It rang unappealingly in his mind, like—

"Palace-Town?" he murmured.

Sam fiddled with a few buttons before shaking his head, pointing to a red point on hologram. "It is *kinshi no*[29]. Palace-Town has been removed from the Data-Ways."

"That seems awfully inconvenient."

"Oh. It was on purpose." Sam jutted his finger at a symbol near the red shape Zinkx presumed was the pictogram for Palace-Town. "See? That means someone forcefully unlinked Palace-Town from the desktop grid. *Hijō ni utagawashī.*[30]"

Zinkx blew back his hair. "*Maa*[31]. We've got our destination."

Sam snatched his Map piece out from the slot, reattaching it to its chain. He hung it around his neck and stuffed it down into his coat, giving it a firm pat. Twirling in the air, Sam headed for the entrance, singing sweetly, causing the crystal pillars to radiate to the notes of his voice.

"*Chīsana aoi wakusei, watashinoie, watashinoie.*
Kore made no tokoro chīsana aoi wakusei.
Chīsana aoi wakusei, watashi wa
anata to anata ni modotte kimasu.
Watashi o mattekudasai,
One shinguru Star no chīsana aoi wakusei."[32]

Zinkx followed, pausing by the stationary protector.

He had never expected to find his feelings resonating with the lonely guardians of the ancient ruins.

"I promise…" He reached out a hand, placing it flat on the chest of the machine, where he knew the core lay beneath the golden metal. "I promise I will protect your most precious

---

29   *Forbidden*

30   *Very suspicious*

31   *Well.*

32   *Little blue planet, my house, my house. So far a little blue planet.*
              Little blue planet, I'll be back with you.
              Wait for me, the little blue planet of One Single Star.

artefact, and go where you cannot go, walk where you cannot walk, and protect that which you cannot protect."

His hand slid away.

Zinkx trailed the echo of Sam's song, leaving behind the lone watcher.

CHAPTER TWENTY-FOUR

There is nothing more wonderful
for a man than to come home
To a wife, his children,
and the warmth of the fire lit by the Sun.
Then, for sure, he should truly know he is blessed.

Pennadotian Proverb

Skyeola was in half a mind to just barge his way through the gates of Cor Coeden, wanting to make his displeasure, his frustration, his pure and utter annoyance at everything and everyone extremely obvious. Of course, Citla's disproving frown stayed his venting and he stood beside Hun, glaring daggers into the customs official as the man lazily signed and stamped their travel papers.

Finally, his pendant for travel in the Vivian Region was offered to him and he snatched it rudely from the wall-guard who held it out. Before either Citla or Jarid could chide him, Skyeola stomped off. It felt so good. Oh, Blessings of the Twilight, the gravel beneath his foot-claws crunched and crunched as he marched into Cor Coeden. They had intended to arrive two days ago, but, no, they had been stopped at the border between Shalamic and Vivian by Lord Galvon's men. Miscommunication, the guards had said when word finally came from Iliaion to allow them to leave Shalamic.

"Miscommunication, my tail," Skyeola grumbled.

"Skyeola! Wait one minute! Do not wander off alone." Jarid's sharp voice froze his momentum.

Skyeola hunkered down, wrapping his wings around himself in a cocoon as he glowered at their small company.

"You are all being so slow," he called out. "We need to find His Highness."

Citla approached him. She smoothed down his unkempt hair.

"I know you are anxious, Skyeola, but it is no excuse for forgetting decorum."

Jarid joined them. He still had an awful, pinched look on his face that he had been wearing for days now. Skyeola was sure the wind had changed at some point and Jarid was now stuck looking like he had eaten a sour grape. "I presume you know this Kelib woman His Highness is with?"

Skyeola nodded.

"Good." Jarid motioned to Hun and their Palace guards. "Follow along behind with the horses."

Hun saluted. "Will do."

Jarid gestured again and Skyeola flew forward as though released from a bond. He felt a sharp tug on his belt and glanced back. Citla was several metres behind him, but his belt was tight around his waist. She was using her birth elemental gift to grip the metal studs. He pouted at her. Her hold loosened, but he accepted her wishes, keeping no more than a few metres ahead of both Humans.

The market bustled with trade, but he barely noticed the bodies he pushed through, his focus on the stalls and those behind them. Humans. All Humans. Was this why the Messenger had chosen Cor Coeden? Because it was a primarily Human town?

With so many Humans surrounding him, Skyeola thought it would be the Kelib woman he would see first; she was, after all, an oddity in such a Human marketplace.

He had forgotten that Daniel was just as unordinary, and just as much an oddity. He drew people to him like a moth hungering for light. There was something tantalising about Daniel. How had he ever forgotten that?

Skyeola slowed his pace. He had never expected a sight like this. The Prince of Pennadot in mundane clothing, his starlit skin sooty and grey-tinged, hiding some of the glow that it usually radiated. Yet none of that had any effect on his natural allure. Children crowded around the Prince's feet, jumping for something he was passing around.

Chocolate. Skyeola laughed. The chocolate he had offered the Kelib woman upon her departure at the Iliaion gates. He broke away from Citla and Jarid, heading towards the Prince's turned back. The children spotted him, eyes widening in awe, some bursting into giggles as several attempted to make a beeline for his wings only to be snatched up by their elder siblings.

Skyeola held out a claw as Daniel turned to face the commotion.

"May I have a piece?"

He had never seen such relief, wrapped up in an overwhelming look of affection. His chest felt tight, and his eyes hot.

"Oh, Skyeola." The sound of his name broke him, and he threw himself into the Prince's embrace, folding up against him. He was real. He was alive. Warm, like the Sunlight on his black fur. An arm wrapped around his back, hugging him gently. Daniel smelt—different—something had changed.

Skyeola's nose crinkled at the new, burnt scent layered over his once-citrus tang.

"Careful, Skyeola, I am a little tender."

He released the Prince in horror. "Sorry!"

Daniel cupped his cheek. Vibrant green eyes smothered him. There was a raw deepness to them that had not been there before. "I knew you would come for me."

"Of course!" Skyeola gushed.

"He has barely paused to breathe," Citla's monotone voice added. Skyeola stepped back quickly as she approached. Daniel's smile slipped away into a pained look of shame as her hands reached for the arm tucked in a sling. She stopped short of touching him as he leant away from her. He had never done that before—he had never tried to avoid Citla's touch.

"How seriously are you hurt?" she asked.

"It was…he was gravely injured. He will need rest." The Kelib woman came forward and held a parchment out to Citla. "I had my partner write out a list of His Highness's wounds, and how we treated those injuries. My partner suggests you find a certified Human Healer, preferably one from a Sun Temple, to look at the wound in his side, and those of his right arm. Much of what the Mistress Wlip-o-Wlip did has healed well enough."

"Is there an issue?" Citla's brow creased.

The Kelib woman shook her head. "No. He has been healing very well. However, things can change quickly when dealing with such injuries."

"I see." Citla folded the parchment up, tucking it into her bodice. "Thank you."

Skyeola finally stepped closer, throwing out a claw. "Do you remember me?"

The Kelib woman smiled. "I do. We were never properly introduced, you and I. I am Shan'ta'lee Shir-Hara. But, please, call me Shanty."

"Little Lord Skyeola Mazaki." Skyeola bowed low. "Thank you so much for saving His Highness."

"Thank *you* for your warning." Shanty reached for his claw and Skyeola's neck feathers fluffed at her tender touch. She stepped away, gracing Daniel with a small curtsy. The Prince laughed, shaking his head. He brushed past Citla, heading for the horses. Skyeola watched in confusion as Daniel tore through several of their packs until he seemed to find what he was looking for. Jarid hand covered his face in horror and Skyeola had to hold back his laughter as Daniel returned to Shanty's small stall.

He smacked the green pouch down on the table, shoving it towards Shanty.

"For your wagon."

CHAPTER TWENTY-FOUR

"Your Highness. I couldn't." Shanty pushed the pouch back.

Daniel shoved it across again. "No. I insist. You *need* a wagon."

"Zinkx would not be pleased."

"Oh, and who made Zinkx sovereign of *your* camp? Last I noticed, that was you." He arched an eyebrow.

Shanty smiled, tucking loose hair behind an ear. "True. But this is too much."

"It is not enough, to be frank. Shanty, you lost your home because of me. Please."

Her lips narrowed. "That was not your fault. Please do not feel responsible for it."

"Shanty. You have no idea how grateful I am. Take it."

The Kelib woman sighed.

Daniel playfully pushed the sack closer to her. "Just think… wagon…ohhhhh, the things you could do with a *wagon*."

"Oh, fine!" Shanty snatched the sack up.

"And something else…" Daniel slipped off a pendant. Skyeola sucked in a sharp breath. It was his royal Sun Pendant. Even Citla's usually stoic mask was slipping, showing alarm on her powdered white cheeks. Daniel held the necklace out.

"Please, could you give this to Zinkx. I know he would never accept it from me."

Shanty took it, cradling it in her hands. "No. He wouldn't…"

"If you ever find yourselves in Palace-Town, show that at the Gates. You will receive aid."

Shanty tucked the pendant away. "That is very kind of you."

"Yes." Citla's gaze narrowed on Shanty. "It is."

Ignoring his Maiden, Daniel embraced the Kelib woman. "Thank you. Please tell Zinkx, too."

"I will." Shanty stepped back. "Have a safe journey." She sent a smile Skyeola's way. He was being included in her parting. She remembered him. She had not thought ill of him for being with a Twizel. A little knot in his stomach unwound itself. Daniel's left hand settled on his shoulder and they walked back towards the readied horses, Citla following along behind.

"What was that?" Jarid sidled up to them. "*Who* was that?"

Uncertain whether Jarid was addressing Daniel or himself, Skyeola ignored the irate man, which only seemed to further irritate him.

"You gave her half our funds!" Jarid flung out a hand.

"They need a wagon," Daniel responded over his shoulder as he mounted his horse.

"Your Highness—"

"Jarid, enough." Daniel glare fixed on the province lord, the usually jovial smile gone, replaced with something Skyeola had never seen in their Prince. It was a terrifyingly hardened expression. "They saved my life."

Jarid's jaw tightened.

"Now, I was told there is a lovely little inn on the outskirts of this town by some hot springs, and I would just love a bath."

"You need one," Citla said.

Daniel laughed, his jovial mask returning. "I know. I had quite an adventure."

"So did the little lord." Hun pointed to Skyeola as he cantered past. Daniel's gaze settled on him and Skyeola glanced down at his claws, twisted around his reins.

"It was nothing. Really."

"Somehow, I highly doubt it, knowing your tendency for mischief." Daniel sent him a tender smile, but it was colder than it had once been.

They left the stone walls of Cor Coeden as simply as they had entered. Now it felt like all they were doing was leaving, departing, and heading—

Skyeola shook his head, trying to stop his mind from the horrible train of thought.

Citla had halted her horse, which caused him to draw his own to a gentle pause. He looked back the way they had come. The Spider Road shimmered her pure golden shine against the green meadows, snaking through the low, tossing hills. He would miss this when they returned—

He froze the thought again, refusing to accept it.

Daniel was staring at something. A Monument of Old. Several long spires climbed high into the hazy sky-sea, twisting together in a beautiful dance, but it was lost to the distant horizon. It was a man, on the crest of a nearby hill, a conical straw-hat hiding his face from the harsh summer Sun, and a child riding on his shoulders whom the Prince appeared to be waving to. The child was waving back vigorously. They vanished over the hilltop in the direction of Cor Coeden and Daniel sat back in his saddle, his shoulders deflating slightly.

"And, so, our circles separate," he whispered.

"That was them, was it not? The Messenger and the Fairy?" Skyeola asked.

Daniel leant his head towards him. Once more, his smile was sad and cold. Where had the Sun that had been the Prince gone?

"It has been rather an eventful Summer. Let us go home," the prince said.

No. No. No. Home. A slimy, disgusting, foul word: home.

Skyeola clutched at the reins as his stomach twisted with the dozens of knots that had formed, growing as the Summer progressed, gradually forming each day with the knowledge that he would have to return—

Return to his father—

To his cage—

Home.

There was no denying it.

He was going home.

Skyeola bit his bottom lip. He should have gone with the fairy. He should have run away. No. He stared at the Prince's back.

He had made his choice. He would stay with the Prince.

He would protect the Prince.

Even if it cost him everything.

CHAPTER TWENTY-FIVE

What else is a Messenger to do but:
Fight for the weak,
Guard the lonely souls,
Protect the meek,
And build Hope for the children,
Of a future unseen.

Messenger Song
(Sung in the Trenches of the Front-Line)

Shanty tucked the pouch of jewels Daniel had given them into the bags nestled beside the diabond. With such a large number of gems having been handed over in such a public display, she felt the eyes of several curious folk on her. The Prince's entourage had made a spectacle in the market, and she was sure the identity of the man who had been behind her stall, and kicking a ball with the children from time to time, was being spread through the city like tongues of wildfire.

"Hopefully Zinkx will be back soon." She ruffled the diabond's mane fondly. "For now, you and I will do our best."

The diabond rumbled a puff of smoke in reply. Shanty gathered up her skirt as she stood, smoothing it back out. It had been confronting to face the Prince's entourage, and she had tried not to quake. The memory of the penetrating glare of the Kimwyn woman, dressed entirely in mourning black, with a face powdered with white minerals and charcoal thickly rimming her eyes and mouth, still seemed to burn like poison in her mind. Her very presence suggested death. And not a sickly, slow death, but swift, brutal, and cruel. Shanty shivered, hugging her shawl around her neck.

Surely, with such a protector lurking in his shadow, the Prince would be safe, would he not? Her lips pressed together.

Skyeola—a bell of a name—a bell chiming through lonely, empty fields. He had clung to the Prince as though in terror. It tugged at her gut even now. Something was dreadfully wrong with the little kitten. She should have spoken up. It was too late now. Their threads had been unravelled apart.

Shanty clicked her tongue, repositioning several of her remaining cloaks across the table. They were not up to the quality she preferred them to be, considering she had fashioned them rather quickly while on the move, but the compliments she was receiving seemed genuine enough. It appeared there were not many Kelib artisans in these parts.

She startled as a red-haired boy suddenly popped his head up over the edge of the table.

"Oh. Hello." Shanty smiled. "I'm so sorry, I don't have any more chocolate."

The boy shook his head. He pointed to one of Zinkx's wooden carvings.

"Can I buy it?" He gestured to the snake sculpture, fashioned after that of the Midori River.

Shanty picked it up. Zinkx had painted the carving in different shades of blue to mimic the waterways of Pennadot. She had already sold several. It seemed the towns-folk of Cor Coeden were rather taken with something that symbolised the river that flowed through their town.

"It's two quartz." Shanty held it out.

The boy dug about in a little pouch, pulling out the two quartz and dropping them into her palm. Shanty handed him the little statue.

"Thank you." The boy beamed. "I have always loved the legends about the river-gods. I think it so sad Pennadotians have mostly forgotten about them."

Shanty pocketed the gems. "I think more Pennadotians remember the myths and legends of our land than you realise."

"What about me?" the boy whispered, his shoulders hunching forward.

Shanty frowned at the oddity of the question. Behind her,

the diabond begun to growl low.

"Do you think…do you think they remember me? Was I not The First? Am I not the most important of all?" The boy's head snapped up. Shanty stumbled backwards, landing roughly against the diabond at the horrifying sight of deadened, black pits that had swallowed up the boy's eyes. A void. Everything around her crumbled away, piece by piece, until she was surrounded by naught but an endless emptiness, and even she was—empty.

The boy's leer spread, his mouth growing wide, revealing a hot, boiling depth. Shanty cried out. Her arms were grabbed, an intense pressure forced her down, and she snapped back to reality, sensing the heaviness of Zinkx's gravity control as his hands held onto her wrists.

"Shanty," his voice echoed. "Shanty. You're fine. Shanty."

She choked out a sob, sliding down the diabond, landing in a heap. A small crowd of her fellow market vendors had gathered, and she hid her face in her knees, listening to Zinkx send everyone away. Sam's tiny hands settled on her back, giving her gentle, little pats, in the same manner she often did when Zinkx collapsed into a Trench memory. Zinkx knelt beside her, holding out a waterskin.

"Drink something. Sam and I will pack up the stall."

"Zinkx, I—"

"It's fine. You can tell me later, at the inn."

It was not until after Sam was fed, bundled up, and settled into the hammock she tied above her bed, that Shanty finally found a moment to pause. She sank slowly onto the bed. It was difficult to even think back to the face of that boy with the red hair. It distorted in her memory, flickering and blurring, before she felt the sensation of plunging into an endless, devouring darkness and heat. As if her feet—her roots—had been grabbed and she had been dragged down, down, deep into the very depths of the unknown earth.

Shanty clutched at her chest, unable to stop shaking.

The door to their small room opened and Zinkx pushed through, carrying a tray from the kitchens. He slid it down on the nearby table.

"I asked for something light, so they made us soup."

His gaze settled on her trembling hands. Zinkx dragged a chair to the bed and reached for her hands. She breathed out in relief at the firmness of the touch grounding her in normality. It seemed to always slip her mind how strong his grip was, how worn his warrior hands were. She threaded her fingers through his, feeling the rough, scarred skin.

"I shouldn't have left. I'm sorry," he said.

"No." Shanty shook her head. "I...I was enjoying myself at the market. I...I...He was so...I felt like, for a moment, that I had been swallowed up by something hot, and cruel, it wanted nothing more than to devour and leave...leave us... with nothing..." She described the monstrous boy, or as much as she could remember clearly of his features.

Zinkx was silent. Shanty's breathing quickened. Why was he not saying anything? She jerked her head up, facing him. His eyes, usually so crystal blue, shone royal green.

"Zinkx?"

He stirred, the green glow fading.

"It sounds like you were describing a confrontation with the Dragon. One of the forms it takes is a child, I believe. I've read some old Messenger Journals about such...happenings..."

Her stomach twisted with a sickening disgust. "How...? But..."

Zinkx kept rubbing her hands, soothingly.

"Well. It stands to reason, if you saw the Time Master, you can see the Dragon."

But the Dragon—it was a beast only whispered about, something spoken of in dark corners, a story of an era long ago. Messengers fought the Dragon—

Messengers—

Her thread had well and truly become entangled with that of a Messenger.

She had told Zinkx she would accept this.

Shanty gulped back the rising fear.

She had to accept this. She could not—no—she would not—falter.

"Shanty." Zinkx shuffled closer. "Shanty…you can walk—"

She wrenched her hands away, gasping in horror.

"No! How dare you! I said I would stay with you. So, I will!"

Zinkx flinched away from her hand.

Shanty covered her mouth. "Sorry. I am sorry."

He did not have his gravity bubble around him. If she had hit him, even lightly… Maybe he was right—she *should* leave.

She curled up. "I should go."

Silence. A long, aching stretch of silence.

"I would…prefer…you to stay."

Shanty peered through her hair. Zinkx had clasped his hands tightly on his knees, his knuckles white from the effort, and his stark blue eyes were averted, though he tried to face her.

She lifted her chin. "Then, I will."

Zinkx sniffed a weak laugh, the tension in his body draining away. "All right."

He still had not activated his gravity bubble. She frowned at his casual recklessness so close to her. He pinched the bridge of his nose. "It seems you may have an ability to see into the different Realms."

She worried her lip. "Is this…bad?"

Zinkx waved flippantly. "No. Not really. It isn't unheard of. Dreamathics can do it."

"So, I am dreamathic?"

"Ah. No." Zinkx scratched his chin. "I'm not getting that from you at all." Zinkx tugged out a necklace, holding out one of the unusual gems attached to it. "This is a nexus gem. It increases a dreamathic…area…I suppose. I'm only very mildly dreamathic, enough to make a connection with the diabond. I've always had to wear one of these to manage communications in the Trenches. I don't sense a dreamathic ability from you." He tucked the stone away. "That's not to say you aren't. Like I said, I barely qualify, so you could be a Dream Master and I might not even notice. But considering Khwaja Denvy's dreamathic touch felt like an earthquake…well…"

Shanty sighed.

Zinkx squeezed her hands once more. "Come on, the soup is getting cold." He collected his chair, setting it down by the table and slouching into it. Shanty joined him. She had little appetite after feeling as though she had been devoured herself but, aware that the future ahead of them was unpredictable, a meal was always vital.

Besides, she could not waste the jewels she had earned. This was part of being a free Kelib woman, enjoying the profits of her own toil.

"Did you uncover anything at the Monument of Old?" Shanty broke away a chunk of bread, dipping it into the rich pumpkin soup.

Zinkx nodded. "We're heading to Sin'musk'qu."

She halted with a spoon half raised to her mouth and slowly let it fall. "Zinkx…that's…"

She wanted to say half-a-world away but, considering where he had come from—a land she had only heard of in stories—Sin'musk'qu was perhaps more of a reality to her than he—or Sam—had ever been.

"I know. Oh. I know. It's a long way." He collapsed back in his chair; it creaked under the force of his weight. He was still not using his gravity bubble. "We might need that wagon after all."

She forced her smile to hide. "What's in Sin'musk'qu?"

"The next piece of Sam's Map to save the world."

"That simple, is it?"

Zinkx chuckled. "With a fairy involved, somehow, I highly doubt it."

"And, then, after that?"

Zinkx shrugged. "Who knows."

"So we shall not be heading to the House of Flames?"

He sighed, looking through the nearby window, his gaze growing as distant as the stars. "Perhaps, someday, my road will take me back, but, for now, I shall do what is before me, as all Messengers do. I shall walk forward and not look back." There was no difference between his eyes and the stars in the night sky-sea as he turned to face her once more. "What about you? Your Sisters and the Merchant?"

Shanty set her spoon down. "The thread of my tapestry has joined another's. Perhaps, someday, it will reweave with the tapestry of my Sisters, but, for now, I shall spin my own wool."

Zinkx dropped his head back, chuckling. "I'll take that as an affirmative."

She kicked him ever so gently under the table, enough to make him wince.

"I have chosen my path. I shall walk it, Human."

"Oh, walk it, will you?" Zinkx grumbled, rubbing his ankle.

"Last I saw, Lady Tree did not do much walking. It was all me, the Muddie."

Shanty huffed. She stood, heading for their packs, pulling free the green pouch the Prince had given her. She dumped it on the table and thumped back down on her seat. Zinkx recoiled as he took a glance inside the pouch.

"From the Prince. For the wagon," she announced happily.

The look she received was worth every jewel in the pouch. Her Human slumped in the chair, pretending to melt like slick butter in the Sun.

"Fine, Krrirren, fine...you get your wagon," he huffed.

Victory was hers.

Shanty passed the Sun Pendant to him. "Daniel wanted you to have this. I believe it is of some importance."

Zinkx snorted, but there was no hiding his fond smile as he held up the golden trinket. "He was such a lark."

Shanty had a small fortune in the pouch the Prince had given her—them—no—*her*. If she were not so insistent on buying a Sun-Forsaken *wagon*, they could have lived off the jewels for the entirety of their journey. Still, it was all worth it, really, watching her and Sam prance around the wagon yard in excitement. They were acting like two bees in a field of luscious flowers, buzzing about everywhere, filled to the brim with joy.

Their pilgrimage was going to be a long one and they may as well do it properly and be prepared. Besides, it would make Shanty happy. Zinkx studied the wagon builder standing beside him. The grey-haired Wynnila appeared amused as Shanty bustled about, calling out, gesturing to a wagon that had caught her eye.

"We don't see many of your sort in these parts," the man commented as they began to wander towards Shanty and Sam.

Zinkx raised his brow. "It's not a problem, is it?"

"Oh, no, no." The builder shook his head. "It's simply unusual. Kelibs are rare enough, but a mixed-couple is practically a myth. Your child…?"

Zinkx could feel the question that was not asked. He had sensed it in every stare from the townsfolk who glanced Sam's way. Was the child deformed? Was that why they were covering him so heavily? He had no desire to add to the rumours and misgivings tossed about when it came to the children of a Kelib and Human.

"Sham'uel, come over here, please," Zinkx called out.

Sam spun about, causing his enormous robe to billow around. He happily skipped across the cobblestones and leapt—Zinkx caught him, settling him on his hip. He pulled back the heavy hood, revealing the innocent little face and large, blue eyes. The wagon-builder breathed in deeply, startled.

Zinkx did not blame him.

It had astonished both him and Shanty the first time Sam

had glamoured them, presenting a tiny, half-breed toddler in place of the fairy they knew. The illusion lasted only minutes, but it was long enough for a camouflage, enough to fool an enemy. Apparently, all Zaprexes had the skill, and it could be upgraded with the right equipment.

Zinkx had felt a deep, burning need for that equipment the moment Sam had mentioned it. The boon it would give them when confronting Twizels with Sam in tow, and the peace of mind upon their travels, would be incredible. Yet, for now, this quick, rudimentary projection-filter—as Sam had called it—would suffice.

Sam abruptly shoved the hood back over his head and wriggled down from Zinkx's arms, running back to Shanty.

Zinkx dragged a hand through his hair. "We prefer to keep him covered up. My wife fears slavers."

"Ah. Yes. I have heard they snatch up half-breed children." The wagon-builder tugged on his grey bread. They joined Shanty, who was crouching beside a large wheel, testing it with her strength. Zinkx tapped his foot on the stones.

"Careful, love. Don't break it before we buy it."

"What do you think?" She looked up with hopeful eyes.

Zinkx made an effort, studying the wagon she had chosen. It had a homey construction, the roof curved in the manner of a Sun Temple, and several little windows, with accompanying shutters built in. Opening the door, he peered around inside. The interior was basic, but he could work on that. It could be made into something—he could already feel an itch forming, an itch to do something with his hands.

He stepped back, glancing at the builder. "Would a diabond have any issue pulling this?"

The man shook his head. "Built entirely for a beast of burden."

"What about off-road?"

"You can swap out the wheels for when you desire such travel."

"So, I have to buy another set of wheels." Zinkx scratched

the back of his neck.

"Zinkx!" Shanty clutched at her dress.

"Shanty, I will need to make some alterations, and we have to paint it. Can you let me calculate—"

Sam grabbed him around the ankles. "Please! Gifu! Please! I want a moving house!"

Zinkx stared down at Sam. The fairy's eyes had magnified beneath his holographic spectacles, and he wobbled his little lips in a dramatic pout.

"I can see this is a calculated assault from both of you," Zinkx muttered.

"I believe you may have lost this battle, sir," the wagon-builder offered.

Zinkx shook his head. "Oh, let's not act like it was ever my decision. Shanty, please do hand the man his gems."

Allowing Shanty to barter down the price of the wagon meant he did not have to do it, which was fine by Zinkx. The less he had to negotiate anything, the happier he would be. Upon returning to the inn, Shanty placed the pouch down beside him.

"The rest is yours for working on the wagon." She twirled about, hands on her hips. "Right! Now, let's pack!"

Zinkx groaned into his hands. "At least we don't have cows and chickens."

The enthusiasm that Shanty radiated had not faded, even upon leaving through the gates of Cor Coeden. She had sat up in the front of the wagon with him, humming a cheerful tune as the diabond lugged them along the Spider-Road. The Sun had already been low when they left, and, by evening, pulling off into a nearby field to set camp, Shanty was still brimming with happiness.

"You are far too happy about this whole thing," Zinkx muttered as he thumped down on the wooden seat inside the wagon. First thing Shanty needed to do was make pillows, lots of pillows.

She opened the nearest window, sitting down beside it with her feet propped up, and rested her chin on her knees as she gazed out across the meadows. "It's...well...I feel as though I had been trapped inside a slavers' wagon for so long. I saw it only as a tool of oppression. I never thought..."

She breathed in deeply, facing him. Tears shone like jewels as they caught on her lashes. "I never thought of one as a means to freedom."

He was struck by this, overwhelmed enough that his chest pulled tight with the breath he could not exhale. This—this had been her line of thinking—this was why she had been so enthralled and captivated by the desire to have a wagon? *Freedom.*

He bubbled out a sudden laugh, dragging his hands through his hair as he bent forward. He could be so blind sometimes.

"Zinkx?" She reached for him in concern.

He stood, grabbing her hand, pulling her to her feet with a tug of gravity control. Zinkx climbed his way onto the roof and helped her up after him.

A sweet, high-pitched voice welcomed them. Sam sat, merrily singing as he fiddled with one of his mechanical toys, his voice harmonising with the sorrowful, aching song of the wind through the crystal towers of the Monument of Old in the distance. Shanty tucked her billowing hair behind her pointed ears.

"We've got a long way to go." Zinkx sat on the edge of the roof. Shanty nestled herself down beside him and Sam squeezed between them, snuggling up on their joint lap. They faced the Sunset across the meadows, the light glistening on the golden Spider-Road. A lone wagon trundled down the path, pulled by two pve'pts.

"But...but we'll be okay...won't we?" Sam's glowing eyes looked up. Zinkx brushed a hand between his antennae.

"Sure, we will. If we stay together, everything will be fine."

Sam nodded stoutly, fears averted.

Zinkx shared a smile with Shanty, entwining his hand gradually through hers.

Yes—everything would be fine.

EPILOGUE

Stories are told in many ways,
Across many forms,
Throughout many worlds.
Even you—your life is a story.
What your story tells, well, that is entirely up to you.

Hazanin Mi Runnaue – Time Master

The wagon rattled. Denvy's ears flicked in irritation at the constant noise. His chest inflated with the stagnant air and he breathed out heavily through mucus-encrusted air-gills. Slowly, his sluggish consciousness became alert, dragging his awareness back to the confines of the murky timber prison incarcerating him and the orphaned children. His cubs, as he had come to call them with fondness.

Time was a blur without Sunlight; he had no record of how long he had been confined since his capture. Food and water was passed to them through a single slit in the wood.

Raising a paw, Denvy clasped the heavy iron yoke clamped securely around his neck. The enchantments etched into the metal tore at his mind like blades, and burned with a heat he had long forgotten existed. Such a cursed instrument; created for the sole purpose of sealing and binding his dreamathic abilities—to jam his programming. He was at the mercy of the Twizels that were hauling them from someplace to somewhere.

He was mildly grateful, though; the fiends of the Dragon had no affection for the lesser-primaries who lived and breathed, and the torture of being fed only enough to remain alive was sarcastically caring in comparison to what he had witnessed in the Trenches.

At times, his cubs would cry from the pain of hunger and thirst, their agony a hammer to his chest, for he could do naught but offer words of comfort. They sought his warmth, the allure of his voice in the darkness, his larger presence a strength in the small, foul world they now inhabited. Tucked under his arm was a little Kelib girl. She shifted her position, releasing a whine of pain. The shackle around her neck rattled as the chain played over the wooden floor, and she slowly sat up. Denvy watched her scrub a hand through her lice-infested hair.

He gazed laboriously through the gloom at the other children beginning to stir, woken by the sound of their movement on the road. Jarvis was a Wynnila Human, the eldest at ten-and-two; where once, perhaps, a wild lad, full of vigour and bold youthfulness would have been, now a shell lay suppressed by the days of long captivity and the harrowing terror of whatever had transpired to bring him to the wagon.

Still, there was a glint of defiance within his ebony eyes, intense like the coming of a storm. He had rage, and it was festering.

The youngest of the prisoners was five, the tiny Kelib girl whose name was far too difficult to pronounce, even in Common Basic, thus she had been called *Ki'b,* by the exultant and flamboyant Clive, who was the only child amongst the six who seemed not to have fallen into a sodden depression. At nine, Clive still enjoyed some immaturity, yet his constant grin was clearly a mask, barely keeping at bay the fears that clawed at him.

Denvy sighed, rubbing at his brow, feeling the ache of the yoke hounding at his raw dreamathic mind. The vehement nightmares of the children disturbed his sleep, weakening him further with each violent, infectious dream. Slowly, like a poison, their nightmares were manifesting in him as a sickness.

"Khwaja Denvy, sir?"

They had begun addressing him as Messengers would, picking up the language from the stories he had to tell of his adventures with Zinkx. He had painted his young ward as a marvellous and heroic figure. The idea of there being a warrior beyond their captivity seemed to inspire a vague hope within all their heavy hearts—even his own.

"Khwaja?"

Blinking aside murk, Denvy peered through the gloom at the young girl calling to him, huddled in the furthest corner of the rattling wagon. Petunia, or Penny as she preferred, was the eldest of the girls, a dark-skinned Obilb from Tempath. With chewed fingernails, she scratched at the metal collar fitted around her neck, making worse the infection eating her raw skin.

"Yes, little *aiv'a*?" Denvy jostled into a seated position with a grunt. "What is on your mind?"

"Are we going to die?"

The question had been asked on numerous occasions. With families gone, the possibility of death was welcomed. According to Clive, their group had started with more than six, therefore they understood that, likely, others of them would also pass.

He chuckled wearily, feeling the rumble of his deep purr vibrate their wooden prison.

"No, cub. Not today," he assured her.

Penny hesitated, before managing a weak smile.

The easiest way to distract the children from their situation was another tale. He cleared his throat and they all shuffled attentively into upright positions.

"Listen, my cubs," he spread his large paws. "Once, long ago, our world was a very different place, so different that you would not have recognised a map if you were given one to look upon." He dropped his head back against the side of the wagon, recalling from the recesses of his memories the vague shadows of bygone times. "Pennadot was the jewel in a crown, a land that connected other lands to each other. Great sky-ships filled the sky-sea. Magnificent floating Cities roamed the Lands and oceans between." Denvy raised his head, gazing at the ceiling of their confinement. The tiny cracks in the wooden panels bled the faintest shafts of light, enough for him to envision the glittering silver sails that had once cut through the air and surrounded the golden Sun-disks of the drifting cities.

Ki'b gasped in excitement. "The cities—they really flew? In the sky-sea?"

Denvy grinned. "Oh, yes." He patted her head tenderly. "They flew."

"Tell us more, Khwaja Denvy." Jarvis propped his knobbly knees under his chin, rattling the chain around his neck. "Please!"

"You really want to know?"

Though their faces were stained with dirt, none of them had lost the spark of wonder and hope as they happily begged. Denvy smiled. The Dragon might have stolen them away from their families, but he had not won over their hearts and minds.

Denvy tugged on his beard. "All right, cubs. I'll tell you the story of the Towers." He breathed out deeply. "What do you know of the Zaprexes?"

"The fairies!" Clive's chain tinkled as the Retenna boy scrambled around into a better position in the straw. "My Papa was a bard, and he used to tell me they would steal you away if you followed their pretty lights!"

"Nicely said, Clive." Denvy nodded in approval. "There is some truth to that legend, but that is another tale altogether."

Clive looked extremely proud, grinning from ear to ear at the praise.

"The Zaprexes were a great race from across the stars." Denvy reached up a paw to the ceiling. "Beautiful, yet so delicate. But also strong and very fierce. They travelled through the endless pathways between worlds, and found Livila, our broken home. They said, 'We shall fix this world!' And, so, the Zaprexes settled here, and their vast Empire thrived. They gave Livila all sorts of fairy magic that allowed for travel and trade

411

between the four factions, the Southlands, the Highlands, Midlands, and Northlands. This magic and knowledge they gave to the combined races freely. For thousands of sol-cycles, their Empire reigned, and they protected our world. Without them, Livila would have crumbled into an abyss long, long ago."

"Then what happened, Khwaja Denvy?" another of the children piped up.

He sighed. "The Zaprexes uncovered something about our world that would eventually lead to our destruction."

"What was it?" Jarvis frowned. "The Dragon," he answered his own question.

Denvy nodded. "Oh, aye, the Dragon. They stirred the nest of a deeply slumbering beast clinging to the heart of Livila. I am sure, had they known it lay there…"

He paused for a moment.

"No. No. I correct myself. They would have tried, still. Zaprexes always fix what is broken."

He reached for the yoke tight against his neck and breathed out an uneasy breath, trying to refocus. Ki'b gently brushed the fur on his arm and he smiled tenderly down at the cub.

"The Dragon was devouring our world, piece by piece, eating away at the Secondary Realm as Livila slowly stopped moving."

"But we need the Secondary Realm," Ki'b whispered. "It is the Tapestry that holds all life, life that was, life that is, life that will be."

Denvy nodded. "That is true. Which is why the Zaprexes built us the Towers."

"Do they stop the Dragon?" Jarvis asked.

"Do they kill the Dragon!" Clive burst out.

Denvy arched an eyebrow at Clive. "The Towers were built to amplify the song of the Secondary Realm. I do not know if they will ever work again, not now, not without the Zaprexes."

"Is this meant to be a happy story?" Penny sighed. "The way I see it, we're all going to die."

Denvy raised his brow. "It may appear so, right now. However, just because we cannot see any fairies, does not mean they do not exist. They are master illusionists. They may very well be living amongst us, still…"

"Then, they can save us!" Clive threw himself upright, his chain yanking hard.

"Perhaps so, but they may have to remain hidden. For the Dragon cannot work fairy magic without fairies, and he is right now trapped in a space between Realms. If he finds a way out, he will try to take the Lands himself…and we shall all be his prisoners for eternity."

"Khwaja! This is not a happy story!" Ki'b punched him in the arm. He winced.

"Sorry." He laughed. "But it is, really. We have a hope. There is the Key."

"The Key?" Jarvis frowned. "To what?"

"Well, good question. I do not know. But the stories say the Zaprexes left behind a Key. I am rather hopeful my ward has found it."

"Well, if he hasn't, we're all dead! The whole world is dead!" Clive threw his arms high and flopped back into the straw with a dramatic thump. "Finally, dead!"

Denvy shook his head at the amusing boy. "We are still alive, lad, and where there is life, there is also hope. A Messenger fights to the last breath, and so shall we."

Dearest Readers,

An explanation is in order, I believe –

I was ten when I created the characters of Zinkx, Zilon and Shanty.

I wrote a little story about a stable boy finding an escaped slave girl in the woods, and the two of them went on an adventure to save a prince from an evil lord called Zilon. It had dragons, magical swords, and dark, scary dungeons. It was quite fantastical for a little girl's attempt at an epic fantasy.

Over each rewrite – with each iteration – the world expanded, bursting with characters, histories, and vast tales. Outside of my imagination, my personal world began to crumble around me, piece by piece, and this is when the true plot of my series began to take shape. As my own life fell apart, so did the world I had created – I had no control over what was happening to me – but my characters could save their *world*.

I first truly wrote the *official* version of KEY when I was fifteen. This version I - with my parents help - self-published in 2013. I was extremely proud of that work, and everything that came after it. I met wonderful people, like Elle – the incredible woman who has been editing my novel's since then. She has taught me more about grammar than school ever did – she gave me the confidence to believe in my skills despite my dyslexia. I am incredibly grateful for her continued support along this journey, even when I decided to rewrite the two books we'd already worked so hard on.

I adventured out to conventions, meeting all you lovely readers – which was my favourite part about this whole experience to be honest. Your support has meant the world to me. I cannot thank you all enough for sticking by me as I have stumbled along this path.

We'll get there. We will.

Deciding to rewrite my series was an enormous decision – but it was one I came to after much consideration of the self-publishing industry as a whole – and my own personal view of where I stood within that industry. I had to do something before I drowned in despair. This was the decision I made – to go back to the beginning

– to recapture why I loved writing, why began this journey – why I build worlds, and why my characters have stayed with me for over twenty years.

And you know what, I found that happiness again.

I found that love of writing and creativity, and it just – keeps burning – and I am so excited to go forward.

My world may be crumbling.

But my characters have a chance to put *theirs* back together.

And I'm going to write that tale, and maybe, in doing so, they'll save me too.

So, thank you for joining me.

I hope you enjoyed Book One.

I'd like to thank Elle – once again, for providing the most amazing editorial help, and for being so understanding of the world I've been building, and patient with my inability to know the difference between were and where, amongst many other amusing errors. ^_^

To Jorge Jacinto, for doing a beautiful front cover, despite being so very, very busy. Thank you.

And to the family of the Hub Café, who continue to welcome me with smiles, providing croissants and diet coke. I'm pretty sure I've just become a part of the furniture now. I am grateful for such a safe, kind place to write. Cheers.

Finally – to my family – my parents – my sister, cousin, aunt and uncle – my grandparents –

You have all gifted me with feathers from your own wings, in the hopes that someday my broken wings will take me from this dark labyrinth towards the sun. I cannot even begin to express the gratitude I have for your love.

With all my heart, *Thank You,*
Kylie Margaret Leane

Kylie Leane is the author and illustrator of *The Dynasty of Earth and Stars* and its expanded universe.

She lives in a little cottage, with her pet cats, Charcoal and Winter, and enjoys spending time in her garden, going for long walks, watching anime, playing a good game, and curling up by the fire in winter.

You can contact Kylie by email at:
authorkylieleane@gmail.com

Or find her online on her website:
kylieleane.com

She is always happy to talk ^_^